William C. Ward

Sir John Vanbrugh

Volume 1

William C. Ward

Sir John Vanbrugh
Volume 1

ISBN/EAN: 9783337399979

Printed in Europe, USA, Canada, Australia, Japan

Cover: Foto ©Andreas Hilbeck / pixelio.de

More available books at **www.hansebooks.com**

SIR JOHN VANBRUGH

EDITED BY

W. C. WARD

IN TWO VOLUMES

VOLUME I.

LONDON

LAWRENCE & BULLEN

16 HENRIETTA STREET, COVENT GARDEN, W.C.

1893

London :
Henderson & Spalding, Limited,
Marylebone Lane, W.

CONTENTS OF VOL. I.

INTRODUCTION.

I.

WHAT authentic intelligence we possess of the birth and parentage of Sir John Vanbrugh is derived mainly from three sources: the first, an account furnished by himself, in 1714, to the Earl of Suffolk and Bindon, Deputy Earl Marshal, on the occasion of his claiming the right to bear the arms of his family; the second, the scanty information collected by his colleague in the College of Arms, Peter Le Neve;* the third, certain parish registers in London and Chester. Of the last two sources of information, unexplored by previous biographers of the dramatist, I have made considerable use in the following pages. The first, already familiar to students of Vanbrugh, supplied Mark Noble with the particulars published in his *History of the College of Arms*, London, 1804.

From Vanbrugh's own account it appears that he was of Flemish extraction, and "that before the persecution of the Flemish by the Duke of Alva, Governor of the Spanish Netherlands, his family lived near Ghent, in Flanders; that Giles Vanbrug, quitting his native country for the enjoyment of the reformed religion, retired to England, and having been bred a merchant, settled as such in London, in the parish of St.

---

*See Le Neve's *Pedigrees of the Knights made by King Charles II.*, &c. Harleian Society's Publications, 1873. Le Neve was created Norroy King of Arms in 1704, in which year Vanbrugh was made Clarenceux.

b

Stephen, Walbrook, where he continued until his death in 1646, and having purchased a vault in the church, was buried in it."*

The Vanbrugh family seems to have been both ancient and honourable. "John Baptist Gramay in his Antiquitys of West Flanders, in his discourse of the City of Ipres, Chapter 2d, says that the prætorship of that town was possest by severall eminent knights, amongst whom he names John Van Brugghe in the year 1383."† Le Neve states explicitly what Noble implies, that Giles Vanbrugh fled from Flanders during Alva's persecution; that is, between 1567 and 1573. It is difficult to reconcile this statement with the fact that a son was born to him some sixty years later. We may suppose, on the one hand, that he was carried into England when a mere infant; or, on the other, that the actual date of his emigration was much later than that assigned. The latter conjecture seems to be supported by Le Neve's assertion, that Giles Vanbrugh was "made denison by King James 1st by letters patent."

Whatever, then, may have been the date of his migration, Giles Vanbrugh resided in the parish of St. Stephen, Walbrook, and followed the occupation of a merchant. In 1628 he was churchwarden of St. Stephen's: "Gillis Van Brugg Churtwarden," he writes himself in the parish register. In September of the same year was born his eldest son, William. A second son was born in April, 1631, who was baptized by his father's name, Giles, and who became the father of John Vanbrugh, the dramatist.‡

---

*History of the College of Arms, p. 355. The family vault of the Vanbrughs was under the north aisle of St. Stephen's: no vestige of it now remains. Giles Vanbrugh was there buried, according to the entry in the parish register, on the 21st of June, 1646.

† Le Neve.

‡ I have copied the following entries from the register of St. Stephen's:— "1628. 25 September. was Baptized Willem the sonn of Gillis Van Brug and Mary his wyff."——"Gyles the sonn of Gyles Vanbrugh marchaunt &

Of Giles Vanbrugh the elder I find no farther record. Giles the younger married, not later than the winter of 1659-60, Elizabeth, fifth and youngest daughter and co-heiress of Sir Dudley Carleton. Dorothy Carleton, the second daughter of Sir Dudley, was already the wife of William Vanbrugh, who had, it appears, succeeded to his father's business in Walbrook.* The name and arms of this William Vanbrugh are engraved in the frontispiece to Thomas Fuller's *Pisgah-Sight of Palestine* (1650), together with the names and arms of the other Mæcenases, whose " benevolent hands " had contributed to the safe delivery of that work to the public. The inscription in Fuller is " Gulielmo Van Brugs † Mercatori." The arms— " Gules, on a fess, Or, three barulets, vert, a Lyon issuant arg. Crest, demy Lyon arg. issuant from a bridge composed of three arches reversed Or "‡—were subsequently (in 1714) claimed and borne by Sir John Vanbrugh as those of his family.

The family into which the sons of the Walbrook merchant married was of some note in the diplomatic circle. Their father-in-law was nephew to a more famous Sir Dudley Carleton, who had filled with distinction, under Charles I., the

---

Margarett his wyfe was Baptyzed the 27th apryll 1631." The discrepancy in the wife's name I cannot account for: possibly Giles Vanbrugh was twice married.

* In Burke's *Landed Gentry*, Le Neve, and elsewhere, Dorothy Carleton is mentioned as the wife of William Vanbrugh. On the other hand, the register of St. Stephen's contains two entries (of January 1, 1657-8, and July 6, 1659) recording the baptisms respectively of William and Dudley, sons of " William Vanbrugg merchant and Mary his wife." The fourth daughter of Sir Dudley Carleton was named Mary. The name of Dorothy occurs in the Vanbrugh family, the brothers, William and Giles, each having a daughter of that name.

† The name was very variously spelt. We find Van Brug, Vanbrug, Vanbrugg, Vanbrugh, Vanburgh, Vanbrough, Vamburg, Vanbrook, Vanbroge, &c. Sir John himself, in such autographs as I have seen, spelt his name " Vanbrugh."

‡ Le Neve.

posts of Ambassador to Holland, and principal Secretary of State. His faithful services, and advocacy of the King's cause in Parliament, were rewarded by Charles with a peerage. In May, 1626, Sir Dudley was created Baron Carleton of Imbercourt, near Esher, in Surrey; and in July, 1628, Viscount Dorchester. But he did not live to assist his master in the time of his greatest need. He died in February, 1632, and if we may credit Cowley, among whose juvenile compositions may be found an elegy on his death,—

" The Muses lost a Patron by his Fate,
Vertue a Husband, and a Prop the State."

Dorchester left but a small estate, of the value of not more than £700 a year; and the heir, a posthumous child, dying an infant, the manor and residence of Imbercourt, which, together with the title, had been bestowed upon the deceased statesman, became the property of his nephew, the Sir Dudley Carleton whose daughters, Dorothy and Elizabeth, were married to William and Giles Vanbrugh. This Carleton, also, figured in public life. He acted as substitute for his uncle during the ambassador's absences from his post at the Hague, discharging that trust with diligence and capacity.* He was knighted in 1626; was the King's Resident in Holland in 1630, as appears by Dorchester's will; and was appointed Clerk of the Council in 1637. Thenceforward, history knows no more of Sir Dudley Carleton, except that, in 1649, he conveyed the property of Imbercourt to one Mr. Knipe.†

For some years after his marriage Giles Vanbrugh resided in the parish of St. Nicholas Acons, in the city of London. In this parish was born, in the month of January, 1664, his son

---

* Kippis's *Biographia Britannica.*
Manning and Bray's *History of Surrey*, vol. i., p. 459*.

John, the future dramatist, and the subject of this memoir.
The following are the exact words of the entry, copied by
myself from the register of St. Nicholas Acons :—"John
Vanbrugh the sonn of Giles Vanbrugh and Elizabeth his
wife was Christned the 24 of January in the house by Mr.
John Meriton. 1663"—*i.e.*, 1664, N.S.   "The house" is, of
course, Giles Vanbrugh's : two of John Vanbrugh's sisters,
Dorothy and Lucy, were similarly christened in their father's
house.   Mr. John Meriton was the rector of St. Nicholas
Acons.*

The youngest child of Giles Vanbrugh, whose name appears
in the register of St. Nicholas, is a daughter—Elizabeth—who
was born on the 7th of January, 1665.   Between this date and
the autumn of 1667, when entries respecting the family begin to
appear in the register of Holy Trinity, Chester, there is a blank
which we are left to supply as well as we can, by inference.   It
is tolerably certain, however, that in this interim Giles Vanbrugh was made the father of two more children.   No
other period can well be assigned for the births of Anna Maria
and Carleton, to say nothing of the strong presumption afforded
by Mrs. Vanbrugh's extreme punctuality in these matters.
Meanwhile, from the absence of farther entries in the register
of St. Nicholas, we gather that Giles had quitted that parish ;
and it seems but a reasonable conjecture, that dread of the
plague had driven him, with his young family, altogether from
London in the spring of 1665.   He ultimately settled in

---

* I am indebted to Mr. J. P. Earwaker, F.S.A., for the important
information that the records of the births of John Vanbrugh, and others
of the family, were to be found in the register of St. Nicholas Acons.   The
church of St. Nicholas Acons no longer exists, not having been rebuilt
after its destruction by the fire of 1666.   It stood on the west side of
Nicholas Lane, near Lombard Street, where the little churchyard yet
remains.   The parish registers were transferred, after the fire, to the church
of St. Edmund, in Lombard Street.

Chester, but it is not likely that he was resident there before 1667, or the birth of one of his children, which must have occurred during that year, or, at the earliest, about the end of 1666, would have been recorded in a Chester register.

Giles Vanbrugh, then, settled in Chester in the year 1667, and established himself in business as a sugar-baker in Weaver Street. Here, there is no doubt, he passed the remainder of his life, and here were born the rest of his numerous family.*

---

* The following list of Giles Vanbrugh's children is compiled from the registers of St. Nicholas Acons, St. Stephen's, Walbrook, and Holy Trinity, Chester. The two London registers I have myself examined : the particulars from Chester were long since communicated to *Notes and Queries* (Second Series, vol. 1, pp. 116-7) by Mr. T. Hughes, of that city. The years are given according to New Style.

1.—Giles, born Oct. 6, 1660 : St. Nicholas. Buried at St. Stephen's, Mar. 31, 1661. His Christian name is not given in the register of St. Stephen's, where he is entered as "a yongue Childe of Mr. Giles Van Bruggs" : the entry, moreover, appears under the year 1660, but the dates of preceding and succeeding entries show that it belongs to 1661. 2.—Dorothy, born Feb. 14, 1662 : St. Nicholas. Buried at St. Stephen's, where she is described only as "a young Child of Mr. Giles Vanbroge," Sept. 27, 1663. 3.—Lucy, born Feb. 11, 1663 : St. Nicholas. 4.—John, bapt. Jan. 24, 1664 : St. Nicholas. 5.—Elizabeth, born Jan. 7, 1665 : St. Nicholas. Buried at Holy Trinity, Chester, Nov. 27, 1667. 6 and 7.—Carleton and Anna Maria. I have found no record of their births, and cannot tell which was the elder; but they come between Elizabeth and Mary. Carleton was buried at Holy Trinity, Chester, Oct. 13, 1667. Anna Maria is named in her father's will, and is mentioned by Le Neve as the second daughter, Lucy being the first in his table. The remainder of the list is from the Register of Holy Trinity, Chester. 8.—Mary, born Nov. 3, 1668. 9.—Victoria, bapt. Jan. 25, 1670. 10.—Elizabeth, bapt. May 4, 1671. 11.—Robina, bapt. Sept. 22, 1672. 12.—Carleton, bapt. Sept. 18, 1673. 13.—An infant son, buried Aug. 31, 1674. 14.—Giles, bapt. Sept. 3, 1675. 15.—Catherina, bapt. Oct. 9, 1676. Buried Mar. 22, 1677. 16.—Dudley, born Oct. 21, 1677. 17.—Kendrick, bapt. Nov. 21, 1678. 18.—Charles, bapt. Feb. 27, 1680. 19.—Philip, bapt. Jan. 31, 1681.

The thirteen, whose burials are not recorded above, were living at the date of Giles Vanbrugh's will,—1683.

The story of his returning to London, and obtaining the appointment of "Comptroller of the Treasury Chamber" (whatever
that may mean), is without foundation, and may be dismissed
as a pure fiction. He is said to have acquired a competent
fortune, and it is beyond question that he was a highly respectable citizen, and a person of consideration in Chester. In
Blome's *Britannia* (1673) he figures in the list of "Nobility and
Gentry related unto Cheshire," as "Giles Vanbrough of
Chester, Gent." But here is an actual glimpse of him, not
uninteresting, in his habit as he lived. In June, 1687, the
famous dissenting minister, Matthew Henry, went to reside in
Chester ; which city, writes his biographer, "was then very
happy in several worthy Gentlemen that had their Habitations
there ; they were not altogether Strangers to Mr. *Henry* before
he came to live among them, but now they came to be his very
intimate Acquaintance ; some of these, as Alderman *Main-
waring* and Mr. *Vanbrugh*, Father to Sir *John Vanbrugh*, were
in Communion with the Church of *England*, but they heard
Mr. *Henry* on the Week-day Lectures, and always treated him
with great and sincere Respect."*

We picture to ourselves Mr. Vanbrugh as a staid, serious
man, of a religious turn, and wonder whether John took after
his mother? In the summer of 1689 Giles Vanbrugh died,
and was buried in Holy Trinity Church, Chester, on the 19th
of July. His will, which is dated October 25, 1683, is preserved
in the Episcopal Registry at Chester. The following abstract of
it appeared in *Notes and Queries*† :—" Giles Vanbrugh, of the City
of Chester, by his will of this date, gave to his wife Elizabeth
the whole of his household furniture, &c., (plate excepted), and
what was due to her by marriage contract ; and directed the
whole of his real estate, &c., to be sold by his executor, and the

---

* Tong's *Life of Mr. Matthew Henry*, pp. 98-99. London, 1716.
† Second Series, vol. i., p. 117. Communicated by T. Hughes, Chester.

proceeds to be divided into fourteen parts, two of which he gave to his eldest son John, one part to Lucy, one to Anna Maria, one to Mary, one to Victoria, and one each to Elizabeth, Robina, Carleton, Giles, Dudley, Kendrick, Charles, and Philip. Appoints his wife sole executrix. Will proved by her, July 24, 1689."

The widow, Elizabeth Vanbrugh, lived to enjoy the successes of her famous son. She died at Chargate, in the parish of Esher, on the 13th of August, 1711, and was buried, on the 15th, in the church at Thames Ditton.* The register of that church being, unfortunately, defective about this date, I have been unable to discover the entry of her burial.

Of John Vanbrugh's education we know nothing but that it was "probably liberal." Mr. T. Hughes supposes him to have been educated at the King's School, Chester, "then a seminary of the highest repute"; † which is likely enough, but lacks confirmation. At an early age—at nineteen, one account has it— he was sent into France, where he continued several years. During this period, it may be presumed, he laid the foundation of that skill in architecture which he afterwards so eminently displayed : at least, there is no subsequent period of his life to which we can, with equal probability, ascribe his studies in that art. It is in France that we get our first authentic glimpse of Vanbrugh, in the enviable position of a prisoner in the Bastile. The story has been pronounced a myth by Disraeli,‡ but it is confirmed by the following passages from Narcissus Luttrell's *Diary :*—

"Thursday, 11th February [1691-2]. Last letters from France say, three English gentlemen, Mr. Vanbrook, Mr. Goddard, and

---

* Noble, p. 355.

† *Notes and Queries*, Second Series, vol. i., p. 117.

‡ *Curiosities of Literature : Secret History of the Building of Blenheim.*

Mr. North, were clapt up in the Bastile, suspected to be spyes."
France and England were then at war, and reprisals ensued.
On Tuesday, 15th March, Luttrell writes : " French merchants
were the other day sent to the Tower, to be used as Mr. North
and Mr. Vanbroke are in the Bastile."

Vanbrugh remained some time in the Bastile, says Voltaire,*
without ever learning what had procured him this attention on
the part of the French ministry. But the gaiety and good
humour for which he was afterwards noted, and to which his
writings so strongly testify, did not desert him. He employed
this period of leisure in sketching the scenes of a comedy, which
he some years later completed, and brought upon the stage,
under the title of *The Provok'd Wife*. It is generally added
that his liberation was due to the good offices of certain French
gentlemen, who visited him in prison, and, being charmed with
his wit and talent, represented the affair to the King in a favourable light.

We know not whether it was before or after his confinement
in the Bastile that Vanbrugh entered the army as an ensign ;
it is likely, however, to have been before, as he was twenty-eight
years of age at the date of his arrest. His military adventures
have never been recorded, but he was long known about town
as " Captain Vanbrugh." I find in Luttrell another little story, of
which there is a bare possibility that our Vanbrugh may be the
hero.—" Tuesday, 22nd November, 1692. Ostend letters say,
collonel Beveredge of the Scotts regiment being at dinner with
captain Vanbrook of the same, words arose and swords were
after drawn, and the collonel was killed, having given abusive
language to the captain first and shook him."

The " Mr. Vanbrugh," whom Evelyn mentions as secretary
to the Greenwich Commission in 1695, appears not to have
been John Vanbrugh, but a certain William Vanbrugh, who

---

* *Letters on the English People.*

died November 20, 1716 ;—possibly the son of Giles Vanbrugh's elder brother.*

II.

In the year 1696 Vanbrugh commenced, under the most favourable auspices, the career in which his genius fitted him chiefly to excel, and in which he was destined to outstrip all his contemporaries, Congreve alone excepted,—the career of comic dramatist. The fortunes of the theatre had been for some time in a declining way. Ill-management, resulting in pecuniary difficulties and disputes between the patentees and the actors, had nullified the advantages which had been so confidently anticipated from the union of the two companies at Drury Lane in 1682 ; and when Betterton, the greatest actor of the day, seceded from the Theatre Royal, he drew after him to his new theatre in Lincoln's Inn Fields most of the best performers in the service of the patentees. Fortune, as well as merit, was on the side of the malcontents. They opened, on the 30th of April, 1695, with the most successful new play which had been produced for many years—Congreve's *Love for Love;* and day after day crowded audiences assembled at Lincoln's Inn Fields to laugh and applaud, while at Drury Lane the dispirited patentees were paying double salaries to inexperienced actors from the profits of a half-filled house. But this sudden flood of popular favour presently subsided. The negligence consequent upon fancied security, aided by internal jealousies, brought about a result which a little prudence and forbearance might easily have obviated, and the new management found itself before long obliged to follow the example already set by the " provident patentees " of the Theatre Royal, and to withhold the wages of the actors except

---

* See *Notes and Queries*, Fourth Series, vol. ix, p. 499.

at such times as the financial condition of the house made it convenient to pay them.

The fortunes of the Theatre Royal were now at low water, and those of the rival company, though not yet so far reduced, a little on the ebb, when the patentees resolved, on the recommendation of Southern, to bring forward, in January, 1696, a new play, the first production of a young actor of their house. Colley Cibber, the young actor in question, was then rising in his profession somewhat more slowly than, in his own estimation, his merits warranted. The applause which had rewarded his happy mimicry of Dogget's manner in Alderman Fondlewife,* some months before, had failed to convince the managing patentee, Christopher Rich, and Cibber's fellow-actors at Drury Lane, that he was fitted equally to shine in other characters of importance. " There were few or no Parts, of the same kind, to be had," he himself tells us. " If I sollicited for any thing of a different Nature, I was answered, *That was not in my Way. And what *was* in my Way, it seems, was not, as yet, resolv'd upon."†

Under these circumstances, what remained for an aspiring young comedian but to write a part for himself? The play was in due course completed, submitted to Southern's judgment, and, on his recommendation, accepted by the patentees. Its success was such as completely to vindicate Southern's discernment. Without one stroke of inspiration, *Love's Last Shift; or, The Fool in Fashion*, displayed unquestionable talent : a well-constructed and effective comedy, it deserved the favour with which it was received. The plot turns upon the reclamation of a dissolute husband by the wife from whom he has been eight years parted. But the most diverting character in the piece is that of Sir Novelty Fashion, an affected fop, whose soul is everlastingly in pawn to his tailor ; and this part was imper-

---

* In Congreve's *Old Bachelor.*
† Cibber's *Apology for his Life*, chap. vi.

sonated, with great applause, by the author himself. Nor was
the applause that of the general public alone. The Earl of
Dorset—"Dorset, the grace of courts, the Muses' pride"—pronounced *Love's Last Shift* "the best first play that any author,
in his memory, had produced"; but either Dorset's memory was
very defective, or the "judge of Nature," as Pope called him,
was not equally a judge of art ; for the *Old Bachelor* had been
produced but three years previously, and between Congreve's
genius and Cibber's ingenuity no comparison can be admitted.
Congreve himself, the wittiest of a witty school, showed more
penetration when he averred that the new play "had only in it
a great many things that were *like* wit, that in reality were *not*
wit." Yet even Congreve seems to have been indebted to *Love's
Last Shift* for the hint of the famous couplet which concludes
the third act of the *Mourning Bride*. There is surely a nearer
connection than that of mere casual coincidence between Mrs.
Flareit's "He shall find no Fiend in Hell can match the fury
of a disappointed Woman," and Zara's often quoted lines—

> "Heaven has no Rage, like Love to Hatred turn'd,
> *Nor Hell a fury, like a Woman scorn'd.*"

But a greater honour yet was in store for Cibber. Among the
thousands who saw and approved *Love's Last Shift* was
Captain Vanbrugh. The gallant captain had long since, as we
have seen, made his private addresses to the Muse of Comedy,
and although his early attachment had for a time lain
dormant, it was ready to be revived now that he was at
leisure to indulge it. Cibber's play proved the breath which
re-kindled into flame the smouldering fire. Vanbrugh was
struck by the situation with which the piece closed. The
characters appeared to him capable of farther development.
He flung himself into the task with the ardour of a lover : the
short space of six weeks sufficed for its completion, and, in the
beginning of April, 1696, he presented to the management at

Drury Lane a sequel to *Love's Last Shift*, under the title of *The Relapse; or, Virtue in Danger*. From Cibber's comedy he had borrowed three characters, and the name of a fourth. The characters were those of Loveless, the libertine husband, his virtuous wife Amanda, and Sir Novelty Fashion, whom Vanbrugh created a peer by the style of Lord Foppington; the name was that of Worthy, the "fine gentleman" of *The Relapse*, who is, however, in other respects, like the remaining *dramatis personæ*, a new character.

The season being now too far advanced to afford time for the preparation and production of the new play, *The Relapse* was not acted until the succeeding winter.* Every measure had been taken to ensure the success of the piece, and its success was complete. There was scarce an actor of any eminence at Mr. Rich's disposal who had not some part in it. The three characters borrowed from *Love's Last Shift* were represented by the actors who had played the corresponding parts in Cibber's comedy. Jack Verbruggen, " that rough Diamond, who shone more bright than all the artful, polish'd Brilliants that ever sparkled on our Stage,"† appeared in the part of Loveless ; Mrs. Rogers in that of Amanda ; while Colley Cibber, as Lord Foppington, drew from the crowded audiences applause yet louder and more prolonged than that which had formerly rewarded his exertions in the character of Sir Novelty.

---

* There is no doubt that *The Relapse* was first produced in December, 1696. Plays, at this period, were commonly published within about a fortnight of their production, and so successful a piece as *The Relapse* would certainly not be an exception to the rule. The first edition bears the date of 1697 on the title-page, but it was actually issued before the end of 1696. The following announcement of its publication appeared in the *Post Boy* of December 26-29, 1696 :—"The Relapse : or, Vertue in Danger, being the Sequel of the Fool in Fashion. A Comedy. Acted at the Theatre-Royal in Drury-Lane. Printed for Sam. Briscoe at the corner of Charles Street, Covent Garden. 1697."

† Tony Aston's *Brief Supplement to Cibber's Lives of the Actors and Actresses*, p. 16.

Berinthia was played by the most finished comic actress of the day, the inimitable Mrs. Verbruggen ; and Powell, the leading gentleman of the Drury Lane company, imparted, on the first evening at least, more than necessary vigour to the part of Worthy, having been " drinking his Mistress's Health in Nants Brandy, from six in the Morning to the time he waddled on upon the Stage."*

Two of the minor parts were filled by actors whose posthumous fame has been greater than that of any of the above, except Cibber.   The few sentences allotted to the quack surgeon, Sirringe, were, no doubt, made the most of by that witty scapegrace, Joe Haines ; and, at the first performance, the part of Lory, Young Fashion's servant, was taken by the already renowned Irish comedian, Thomas Dogget.   Dogget had held a distinguished position among the mutineers who, under Betterton's lead, had defied Manager Rich, and shaken from their feet the dust of Drury Lane.   At Lincoln's Inn Fields he had gained fresh laurels by his creation of the part of Ben, in *Love for Love*, but his pragmatical and dogged disposition rendered it impossible for him to remain long content in any situation.   He quarrelled with Betterton upon the management of the theatre, mutinied again, and returned to the Theatre Royal, where, as we have said, he accepted the part of Lory, in *The Relapse*.   Still, however, he was not suited.   The part agreed " so ill with Dogget's dry and closely natural Manner of acting, that upon the second Day he desired it might be disposed of to another ; which the Author complying with, gave it to *Penkethman ;* who tho', in other Lights, much his Inferior, yet this Part he seem'd better to become."†   Penkethman had acted a similar part—that of Loveless's man, Snap—in *Love's Last Shift*.

---

* Preface to *The Relapse.*
† Cibber's *Apology*, chap. vii.

With characteristic generosity, Vanbrugh resigned to the patentees his own rights in the performance of the successful play.* Sir Thomas Skipwith, who owned a large share in the theatrical patent, had known Vanbrugh in early days, "when he was but an Ensign, and had a Heart above his Income ;" † and had conferred a particular obligation upon him, which the poet was now desirous to repay. The recent languishing condition of the Drury Lane exchequer had, of course, reduced the profits of the patentees, and, as Vanbrugh thought, a successful new piece would at once bring prosperity to the house, and raise the value of his friend's share. After all, Sir Thomas does not appear to have benefited greatly by Vanbrugh's generous endeavour to serve him. Utterly careless of his own interest, he left the management of the theatre entirely in the hands of his colleague, Rich ; than whom, if we may believe Cibber, "no Creature ever seem'd more fond of Power, that so little knew how to use it to his Profit and Reputation." The result was, that about ten years later, Sir Thomas, having, as he said, made nothing of it for years, fairly made a present of his whole right in the patent to Colonel Brett, whose exertions brought the stage, for a time, to a more prosperous condition.

III.

The Relapse, like its author's later productions, belongs to that school of comedy, called artificial, which was introduced into the English theatre by Sir George Etherege, and which, after a career of unexampled brilliancy, was slowly flogged to death by that "awful cat-a-nine-tails to the Stage," ‡ the Puritan inquisi-

---

* By the custom of the time, the poet was entitled to the profits of the third and sixth nights' performances of a new play.

† Cibber's *Apology*.

‡ Vanbrugh's Prologue to *The False Friend*.

tion of the times of William III. and Anne. Fostered by the favour of a Court of which the manners and tastes were inevitably influenced by the habits of a long exile, the Artificial Comedy, or, as it is better denominated, the Comedy of Manners, was naturally, in some of its features, an exotic. Its dominant idea—at least, as regards the works of its greatest masters—was Satire : its most indispensable attribute was Wit. The traditions of the Shakespearean comedy, the comedy of human life, as one might term it, were forgotten ; and it was now held

> "——the intent and business of the Stage,
> To copy out the Follies of the Age ;
> To hold to every man a faithful Glass,
> And show him of what Species he's an Ass." *

In these particulars we recognize the practice of the French theatre, of which the influence is strongly attested by the frequency with which, during the fifty years succeeding the Restoration, English comic poets of all grades, from Dryden down to Ravenscroft, translated, adapted, or borrowed from the works of Molière. Vanbrugh, indeed, has left us only two finished plays which are not directly founded upon French originals. In a less degree, the Spanish theatre, and especially the comedies of Calderon, with their scenes of complicated intrigue, may claim some share in the formation of the new English school.

But with all these alien influences the Comedy of Manners retained many characteristics of true British growth. Essentially, it owed more to Ben Jonson and *The Silent Woman,* than to all the dramatists of France and Spain united. In fact, it may even be said, that wide as was the impression made at this period by the French drama upon our own, it was also, for the most part, superficial. Even where they copied

---

* Prologue to *The Provok'd Wife.*

most directly, our playwrights generally managed to disguise their appropriations in a garb of unmistakable homespun. Molière was faithfully followed in his wit and satire, Calderon in his intrigue ; but the specifically national characteristics of these authors, the classic refinement of the Frenchman and the poetic dignity of the Spaniard, are commonly conspicuous by their absence from the English adaptations of their works ; and their place is but too often supplied by an extravagant and peculiarly English grossness of language and sentiment. In fine, if the body were French, not only the garb which clothed it, but the spirit which animated it, for better or for,worse, was usually altogether English.

Like most of his contemporaries and immediate predecessors, Vanbrugh has not escaped the charge of licentiousness of language and sentiment. It is a charge which has been, I believe, frequently overstated against the post-Restoration poets as a body ; though, of course, it cannot be denied that most of them, and even the most eminent among them, condescended at times to pander to the depraved taste of their audience, by the employment of language and incidents past the possibility of extenuation. But, on the other hand, it should be remembered, that much of the apparent licentiousness of these plays had a purpose expressly satirical, and was intended not to countenance, but to expose, the vices of the age. The times permitted plain speaking, and the poets availed themselves of the liberty, sometimes with a bad, but frequently also with a good motive ; in which case, I conceive, the charge of immorality belongs not to the poet, but the society which he portrayed. This observation, it may be remarked in passing, will be found particularly applicable to one of the best abused of Restoration dramatists, William Wycherley.

I cannot regard Vanbrugh as a great culprit in this respect. In two of his comedies—*The Relapse* and *The Provok'd Wife*— we may at once admit that there are occasional passages which

c

transgress the bounds of decorum, but it can hardly be contended that, in either of these pieces, the poet proves himself a deliberate advocate of immorality. The intrigue between Loveless and Berinthia, for example, is painted in colours perhaps too glowing, yet it is certain that the author's design was not to engage the sympathy of the audience on behalf of the criminals, but rather to enhance, by a lively contrast, their admiration for the pureminded, though cruelly tempted, Amanda. As to the remaining plays of Vanbrugh, the criticism which can find anything in them worthy of serious condemnation on the score of licentiousness, must be captious indeed.

The chief defect of *The Relapse* lies in its construction. It comprises two distinct plots, of almost equal importance, and very slightly connected. But this, perhaps its only considerable blemish, appears a trifle beside the beauties which outweigh it a thousandfold. The characters are delineated with so masterly a hand, the scenes are so happily contrived, the dialogue is so brimful of wit, the action proceeds, from beginning to end, with such unflagging animation, that the faults of the piece are forgotten in generous admiration of the author's genius. In the character of Lord Foppington, Vanbrugh has followed, to some extent, the design of his predecessor; but to say only that he has vastly improved upon Cibber, were to allow him far less than his due of honour. Sir Novelty Fashion is an amusing portrait of the beau of the period : Lord Foppington is one of the most inimitably drawn characters within the entire range of English comic drama. Vanbrugh has not merely remodelled the figure, he has endowed it with life, and is entitled to the full credit of the creation. The name of Lord Foppington recalls that of Etherege's Man of Mode, Sir Fopling Flutter, but there is no real resemblance between the two characters farther than the inevitable likeness of one fop to another. The Man of Mode is merely a "brisk blockhead," as Medley calls him in the play : Lord Foppington is not so much a fool by nature, as a coxcomb by caprice ; and his conversation, though affected to the last degree, displays occasional symptoms of wit and observation.

In quick succession to *The Relapse* followed the comedy of *Æsop,* which was produced at Drury Lane in the month of January, 1697,* with Colley Cibber in the title-rôle. It is a free translation, with considerable additions and alterations, of a French comedy by Boursault, entitled *Les Fables d'Ésope.* Like *The Relapse,* though in a different way, *Æsop* is somewhat faulty in construction. If, as it is said in *Tristram Shandy,* digressions are " the sunshine, the life, the soul of reading," the play needs no farther recommendation ; for it consists largely of digressions. The plot is of the simplest description, and is, in fact, little more than a thread upon which the author has strung together a series of independent episodes. Upon the whole, it must be allowed that Vanbrugh's comedy is greatly superior to Boursault's. In the more serious scenes, it is true, the French poet displays more pathos and dignity than his English adapter ; but in the comic episodes, which, after all, are the most vital portions of the play, Vanbrugh far surpasses him. The fables, moreover, which with Boursault are little more than outlines, destitute of life and colour, are enriched by Vanbrugh with strokes of wit and fancy which raise them to a respectable rank among compositions of this kind.

The morality of *Æsop* is unimpeachable, which probably accounts for the comparative coolness of its reception by English audiences of that day. It ran, however, for eight or nine nights, and was revived, both at Drury Lane and Lincoln's

---

* The date of *Æsop* is fixed by the following advertisement of its publica- tion, from the *London Gazette* of January 18-21, 1697 :—" Æsop. A Comedy. As it is acted at the Theatre Royal in Drury Lane. Printed for Tho. Bennet at the Half Moon in St. Paul's Church-Yard." The produc- tion of *Æsop* probably preceded its publication by a very brief interval,. as the author remarks in the preface,—" 'tis now but the second day of acting."

c 2

Inn Fields, on several occasions during the author's lifetime.*
As in the case of *The Relapse*, the poet assigned to the patentees
his rights in the performance.

Having thus presented the Theatre Royal with two master-
pieces in order to oblige Sir Thomas Skipwith, Vanbrugh next
proceeded to gratify another of his friends, by conferring a
similar favour upon the company in Lincoln's Inn Fields.
This friend was the Right Honourable Charles Montague,
Chancellor of the Exchequer, afterwards Earl of Halifax ; a
statesman of ability and repute, as well as a maker of mediocre
verses ; but best remembered as the great patron of poetry,
the Mæcenas of the age, although, if we may believe Pope,
"rather a pretender to taste than really possessed of it."†
Montague was "a great Favourer of *Betterton's* Company,
Cibber tells us ; and, "having formerly, by way of Family-
Amusement, heard the *Provok'd Wife* read to him, in its looser
Sheets, engag'd Sir *John Vanbrugh* to revise it, and give it to
the Theatre in *Lincoln's-Inn Fields*. This was a Request not
to be refus'd to so eminent a Patron of the Muses as the Lord
Hallifax, who was equally a Friend and Admirer of Sir *John*

---

* There is a passage in the prologue to *The Provok'd Wife* which can be
interpreted only, I think, as an allusion to the partial failure of *Æsop*.
The success of *The Relapse*, so recent and so complete, had probably
encouraged the author to anticipate an equally pronounced triumph for his
second essay, and his expectations were, no doubt, in a measure disappointed.
Yet *Æsop* appears to have been fairly successful. Cibber writes—"I was
equally approv'd in *Æsop*, as the *Lord Foppington*, allowing the Difference
to be no less than as Wisdom, in a Person deform'd, may be less entertaining to the general Taste, than Folly and Foppery, finely drest."
And in Gildon's *Comparison between the Two Stages* we read—"*Oroonoko*,
Æsop, and *Relapse* are Master-pieces, and subsisted Drury-lane House,
the first two or three years."

† Spence's *Anecdotes*, where a story is told of Lord Halifax which con-
firms Pope's judgment of him.

himself."* Accordingly, *The Provok'd Wife*, begun, as we have seen, in the Bastile, some years previously, was now completed, handed over to Betterton, and produced by his company about the end of April, or beginning of May, 1697.†

The cast was unexceptionable. Betterton himself—"an Actor, as *Shakespear* was an Author, both without Competitors"—took the part of Sir John Brute. Verbruggen, who had recently migrated from the rival house, appeared as Constant. Lady Brute was played by the famous Mrs. Barry ; Belinda by the not less famous, and still more fascinating, Mrs. Bracegirdle. With such actors, and such a comedy, success followed as a matter of course.

The Provok'd Wife is, upon the whole, superior in construction to either of its predecessors ; at least, the unity of action is better preserved. Its moral tone, however, is looser, nor does it contain a single character which even pretends to evoke, in the smallest degree, the reader's sympathy. For all this, it is a true masterpiece of wit and humour, and can hardly with justice be pronounced, in general, an immoral play. There is nothing in it of the earnestness of purpose which distinguishes the story of Loveless and Amanda, yet where the author does occasionally deviate into seriousness, the moral is good enough ; as, for example, when Constant exclaims—"Though Marriage be a Lottery, yet there is one inestimable Lot, in which the only Heaven on Earth is written"; and Heartfree responds—" To be

---

* Cibber's *Apology*, chap. vi. Montague was not Lord Halifax until 1700—he was created Baron Halifax in that year, and Earl in 1714. In the latter year Vanbrugh was knighted.

† The publication of *The Provok'd Wife* is thus announced in the *Post Man* of May 11-13, 1697 :—'' This day is published The Provok'd Wife, a Comedy, as it is Acted at the New Theatre in Little Lincolns Inn Fields, by the Author of a new Comedy of the Relapse, or Virtue in Danger, and Æzop. Printed for Rich. Wellington at the Lute in St. Paul's Church-yard."

capable of loving one, doubtless is better than to possess a Thousand." Briefly, *The Provok'd Wife* is a gay, lively satire upon the manners of a certain section of society, and is conducted exactly on the principle laid down by the author himself in the first four lines, already quoted, of the prologue.

IV.

WE are now approaching a turning point in the history of the English stage. The witty licentiousness of the comic drama, still flourishing in unabated luxuriance, was no longer so openly in accord with popular sentiment as in the days when the rage of revolt against Puritan intolerance led naturally into the opposite excess. Indeed, it can hardly be maintained that at any period since the Restoration the immorality of the drama had really reflected the feeling of the nation at large. Even in London, the play-going public formed but a small minority of the population. The stage was chiefly upheld by the "quality"; the poets, as Dryden wrote, "must live by Courts, or starve"; and the history of the London theatres, from 1660 to the time at which we have now arrived, is a record of continual struggles, on the part of the managers, to maintain two houses, for the entire metropolis, in a state of tolerable prosperity.

We have but to read the plays themselves to find convincing proofs as to the class to which they were intended to appeal. Beaux, it is true, were ridiculed and scoffed at with the utmost freedom of language,* yet the hero of the piece was always a man of fashion and of pleasure ; much the kind of man, in short, which the beau himself would have been, if he had had but the wit. Thus the beaux in the audience were under no necessity of applying to themselves the satire which the poet lavished upon

---

* See, for example, the prologues and epilogue to *The Relapse.*

their kind : when Dorimant went as fine as Sir Fopling, what was to hinder each admiring beau from taking Dorimant to himself, and writing his fellow down the ass? For the citizens, on the other hand, there were no such opportunities of escape. A "citizen," in the dialect of the playhouse, was but another term for a cuckold ; nor was it to be supposed that the sober citizens of London would themselves frequent, or allow their wives and daughters to frequent, entertainments in which they were invariably held up to contempt and derision.

But, as yet, no accumulated force of public reprobation had been directed against the licence of the theatres. They had been protected by the Stuart monarchs, uncensured by the Church; and the bulk of the nation was too loyal openly to condemn that which found favour in the eyes of its rulers. With the Revolution the situation of affairs was altered. Decorum prevailed at Court, and although the drama was as frankly licentious as ever, the temper of the people was no longer so tolerant. Decency was not now synonymous with disloyalty : a storm was brewing which, before long, was to overspread the whole sky, and to sweep away, in indiscriminate ruin, all that was reprehensible, and nearly all that was valuable, in the drama of the day.

The first low mutterings of the thunder were audible when, in 1695, the "everlasting Blackmore" published his preface to *Prince Arthur*. Three years later the tempest descended in full fury. In March, 1698, Jeremy Collier, a non-juring clergyman, put forth his *Short View of the Immorality and Profaneness of the English Stage*—a book written with some ingenuity, considerable learning, and an abundance of bitterness and pedantry. Its success was stupendous. Three editions appeared within the year ; a fourth was issued in 1699 ; and in its train pamphlet succeeded pamphlet, directed to the same end, by writers who rivalled Collier in bitterness, however far they fell short of him in ability. Public opinion was thoroughly aroused, and strong on the side of the assailants. The attack upon the playwrights was presently followed up by prosecutions of the players. On the 10th of May, 1698, Luttrell notes in his *Diary* that " the justices of Middlesex have presented the play-houses to be nurseries of debauchery and blasphemy." Two days later he writes : " The justices did not only present the playhouses, but also Mr. Congreve, for writing the *Double Dealer;* Durfey for *Don Quixot;* and Tonson and Brisco, book-sellers, for printing them : and that women frequenting the playhouses in masks tended much to debauchery and immorality." An Act of James I., against profane swearing, was put in force : informers were stationed in the theatres to take notes of any objectionable words which might be used upon the stage ; and although Queen Anne's intervention at length put a stop to these vexatious and absurd proceedings, it was not until several of the players, including Betterton and Mrs. Bracegirdle, had been convicted under the Act.

Threatened dramas, however, like threatened men, live long. Even the great storm of the 27th of November, 1703, did not entirely empty the playhouses, although carefully "improved," as a judgment, by the zealots. The anonymous author of a pamphlet published two or three years later, under the edifying title of *Hell upon Earth; or the Language of the Playhouse,* makes the mournful admission that "the horrid Comedies of *Love for Love, The Provok'd Wife,* and *The Spanish Fryar,* are frequently acted in all places to which the Players come. The more they have been expos'd by Mr. *Collier* and others, the more they seem to be admir'd ! " But the victory, after all, remained with the reformers, though less complete than the more violent among them had desired. The chief defendants themselves, Congreve and Vanbrugh (for Dryden's dramatic career was already closed), became more guarded in their writings after Collier's attack, and an era of decorum commenced for the stage. Not decorum alone, however, was the result of the popular outcry. By long association, wit and licence had become, as it seemed, inseparable, and the younger school of dramatists wrought uneasily in their newly imposed fetters. At a later period, indeed, it was shown by Goldsmith and Sheridan, that the most charming humour and the most brilliant wit could consist in comedy with perfect purity of thought and language ; but for the time the case seemed hopeless, and side by side with decorum, dulness fixed her seat in the deserted temple of wit and satire.

To return to the *Short View.* Collier opens his attack with temper and moderation. His purpose is the reformation, not the abolition, of the theatres. "The business of Plays," he writes, "is to recommend Virtue, and discountenance Vice ; To shew the Uncertainty of Humane Greatness, the suddain Turns of Fate, and the Unhappy Conclusions of Violence and Injustice : 'Tis to expose the Singularities of Pride and Fancy, to make Folly and Falsehood contemptible, and to bring every thing that is Ill under Infamy and Neglect. This Design," adds Collier, "has been oddly pursued by the English Stage ! "

We will waive the exceptions which might easily be made against Mr. Collier's view of the "business of plays." 'Tis indubitable that part, at least, of his design was pursued, however oddly, by some of the very poets whom he proceeds to condemn with so much acrimony. Those who imagine they perceive in the plays of Wycherley, Congreve, or Vanbrugh, only scenes of debauchery rendered more dangerously seductive by wit and fancy, are blind to their real purpose. These authors were essentially satirists. Even that *bête noire* of the Puritans, Wycherley's *Country Wife*, is in reality a powerful and scathing satire upon those very vices of which it has been popularly supposed a hot-bed. Indeed, Collier himself seems to have been dimly conscious that in assailing Wycherley he was upon dangerous ground. His references to the "Plain Dealer" are few, and singularly temperate, and on more than one occasion he pauses to conciliate the great dramatist by a well-deserved compliment. Perhaps Collier may have felt the force of that satire which is more unmistakable in the productions of this Hogarth of the drama than in those of most of his contemporaries, but it is difficult to reconcile such a supposition with his usual obtuseness in regard to irony. Because Vanbrugh and Congreve fail to conduct their fops and libertines to the gallows at the conclusion of the piece, he gravely charges them with intending these creatures as models for the imitation of the admiring spectators.

At the same time there is no denying that Collier's complaints of the immodesty of the stage were, in general, only too well founded. The audience—at least, the noisier section of the audience—delighted in obscenity ; and even the greatest poets, Dryden in particular, would sometimes sink to the level of those whose humour was all-powerful to save or to condemn. Yet there is need of discrimination. The plain language, permitted by the manners of the age, is not necessarily a proof of immorality. We may even go farther, and admit that in many of the comical passages of these old plays—"happy breathing-places from the burthen of a perpetual moral questioning "*—the wit and humour go far to redeem the indecorum ; that it were not amiss occasionally to lay aside our nineteenth-century prudishness, and to own ourselves diverted by a brilliant repartee or a ludicrous situation, though introduced with bolder licence than the manners of our own strictly moral time allow.

Many instances, however, are to be found, which it is impossible to palliate. Such are the grossly indecent lines often to be met with in the prologues and epilogues of seventeeth century plays, when the poet, addressing his audience directly, stoops thus to bid for the applause of the looser sort among them ; while, to make matters worse, the offending passages were

---

* Charles Lamb.

frequently 'placed in the mouths of women. In reprobating
such practices as these Collier stood upon his strongest ground,
and was sure of the sympathy of all decent persons. Unfortunately, his zeal could not rest here. The just censure which,
in his first chapter, he bestows upon that which was reprehensible in the poets of his day, is weakened by a tendency to
exaggeration and to the introduction of trivial or irrelevant
instances ; and these tendencies grow upon him as the work
progresses, until, before its close, he shows himself a mere
fanatic, devoid alike of judgment and of discrimination. He
cites the dramatists of past ages as evidence against his contemporaries, commending the morality of Terence and Plautus,
the modesty of Ben Jonson, and (oddly enough) of Beaumont
and Fletcher. Aristophanes and Shakespeare he puts
conveniently out of court ; for the former "discovers himself a
downright Atheist," while, "as for Shakespeare, he is too
guilty to make an Evidence."

So far, however, Collier has remained cool, if not always
discreet. But both discretion and coolness are flung to the
winds when he proceeds to deal with the profanity of the
dramatists, their "Cursing and Swearing," their abuse of
religion and the clergy. Every thoughtless ejaculation—my
Lord Foppington's "Gad," or poor Miss Hoyden's "Icod !"—
good Mr. Collier resents as a deliberate insult to the majesty of
the Deity. "They swear in Solitude and cool Blood," he
exclaims, "under Thought and Deliberation, for Business and
for Exercise ! This is a terrible Circumstance !"

When Amanda, smarting under the discovery of her
husband's repeated infidelity, very innocently cries—

> "What slippery Stuff are Men compos'd of !
> Sure the Account of their Creation's false, .
> And 'twas the Woman's Rib that they were form'd of "—

the 'irate clergyman declares that she "makes no Scruple to
charge the Bible with Untruths." Again, Sir John Brute's

masquerading in the garb of a parson is an affront to the cloth never to be forgiven. On this point, indeed, the reverend controvertist, with a fine sense of what is due to his profession, is particularly sore. He revives, in favour of the priesthood, the old theory of divine right, and claims for every minister of religion, not, indeed, exemption from the failings and follies of humanity, but entire immunity from the satire and ridicule for which, in the case of persons less sacred, such follies and failings would be admitted a proper subject. In fact, the contemptible figure which clergymen occasionally make upon the stage of the seventeenth century, was not without abundant warrant. "I by no means design this," writes Dennis, "as a reflection upon the Church of England, who I am satisfy'd may more justly boast of its Clergy, than any other Church whatsoever; yet may I venture to affirm that there are some among them, who can never be suppos'd to have been corrupted by Play-houses, who yet turn up a Bottle oft'ner than they do an Hour-glass, who box about a pair of Tables with more fervour than they do their cushions, contemplate a pair of Dice more frequently than the Fathers or Councils, and meditate and depend upon Hazard, more than they do upon Providence."* Against men of this stamp the satire of the stage was surely not ill-directed, although Mr. Collier, confounding their character with their cloth, prefers to regard them as the ambassadors of Heaven.

But not content with throwing his protecting ægis over the clergy, our Tory parson must needs extend its shelter to persons of quality among the laity. The Plain Dealer's sturdy assertion that "he would call a Rascal by no other Title, tho' his Father had left him a Duke's," Mr. Collier quotes, under the evident impression that a sentiment so abhorrent to good manners carries its own condemnation. He reverts to this

---

* *The Usefulness of the Stage*, London, 1698, p. 26.

subject later, in his *Defence of the Short View,* where he
maintains that "all Satire ought to have regard to Quality and
Condition," and that to expose a lord is to represent nobility
and folly as inseparable,—forgetting, or, more probably,
disregarding, the fact that this argument would apply with
equal force to every condition of men. Congreve's stern rebuke
had evidently failed to penetrate his antagonist. "When
Vice," the poet wrote, "shall be allowed as an Indication of
Quality and good Breeding, then it may also pass for a piece of
good Breeding to compliment Vice in Quality : But till then, I
humbly conceive, that to expose and ridicule it will altogether
do as well." *

Collier criticizes plays as he would criticize sermons, and
makes no distinction of persons. If Lord Foppington speak
irreverently of the church, or my Lady Brute lightly of virtue,
this acute critic is as indignant as if the words had been placed
in the mouths of characters intended as models of serious excel-
lence ; although in the former instance it must be clear, as
Vanbrugh pointed out, "even to the meanest capacity," that
what his lordship says of his church-behaviour is designed for
the contempt, and not for the imitation of the audience ; while
as to Lady Brute's words—"Virtue's an Ass, and a Gallant's
worth forty on't"—'tis equally obvious that it is "not Virtue she
exposes, but herself, when she says 'em : nor is it me he exposes,"
adds the poet, "but himself, when he quotes 'em."†

I will oblige the reader with one more chosen flower from the
Reverend Mr. Collier's garland of amenities. After a few short
excerpts from *The Relapse* (Tom Fashion's "Providence, thou
seest at last, takes care of men of merit"—Berinthia's "Mr.
Worthy used you like a text, he took you all to pieces"—and
the same lady's "Heaven give you grace to put it in practice ! "),

---

* *Amendments to Mr. Collier's False and Imperfect Citations,* p. 21.
† *A Short Vindication of* The Relapse *and* The Provok'd Wife, p. 48.

of which the worst is spoken in thoughtless levity, perfectly consistent with the character of the speaker, he bursts out: " There are few of these last Quotations, but what are plain Blasphemy, and within the *Law*. They look reeking as it were from *Pandæmonium*, and almost smell of Fire and Brimstone. This is an Eruption of Hell with a Witness ! I almost wonder the Smoak of it has not darken'd the Sun, and turn'd the Air to Plague and Poyson ! These are outrageous Provocations; enough to arm all Nature in Revenge ; to exhaust the Judgments of Heaven, and sink the *Island* in the Sea !"*

Vanbrugh's recent and brilliant successes in the theatre, to say nothing of his delightful witticism, in the preface to *The Relapse*, upon the Saints "who make debauches in piety, as Sinners do in wine," had given him a special claim upon the attention of the reverend reformer. References to *The Relapse* and *The Provok'd Wife* are, accordingly, scattered thickly throughout the *Short View*, and the former play is additionally favoured by the devotion of a long section of the fifth chapter to its examination. In this section Collier criticizes the construction as well as the morality of the play, with the evident determination to see no good in either. He sets up for a pedantic observance of the unities of time, place, and action, and, of course, has no difficulty in proving Vanbrugh guilty of great irregularities in respect to these. By his violation of the unity of action, in founding his drama upon two nearly unconnected plots, Vanbrugh had, indeed, laid himself fairly open to the attack of critics to whom the laws of the French theatre were as those of the Medes and Persians ; and Collier takes full advantage of the opportunity thus afforded him to treat Tom Fashion as the hero of the piece, and to ignore the more serious purpose of the poet in the story of Loveless and Amanda. Candour and discernment are equally conspicuous in his con-

---

* *Short View*, p. 85.

clusion. *The Relapse* "appears a Heap of Irregularities. There is neither Propriety in the *Name*, nor Contrivance in the *Plot*, nor Decorum in the *Characters*. 'Tis a thorough Contradiction to Nature, and impossible in *Time* and *Place*. Its *Shining Graces*, as the Author calls them, are *Blasphemy* and *Baudy*, together with a Mixture of *Oaths* and *Cursing*."

The extraordinary popularity of the *Short View* rendered it impossible to pass it over in silence. Of the poets particularly attacked by Collier, Dryden was, incomparably, the best fitted to reply. But Dryden was an old man, who had ceased to write for the stage, and was willing to devote the few years that might remain to him, to worthier work than that of engaging in a controversy with an antagonist behind whom was ranked the unreasoning fanaticism of a nation which, twenty years before, had gone mad over the Popish Plot, and whose sovereign had, but a few months previously, bestowed a handsome pension upon the infamous Titus Oates.* In Dryden's subsequent publications a few passing references to Collier may be found. The poet admitted, to some extent, the justice of his charge of immorality, and frankly avowed his penitence for his own transgressions. At the same time, he deprecated the reckless extravagance of much that Collier had advanced, and observed, with perfect truth, that "if the zeal for God's house had not eaten him up, it had at least devoured some part of his good manners and civility."†

But if Dryden declined the contest, there was no lack of younger authors ready to measure swords with the assailant. The summer of 1698 witnessed the publication of replies to the *Short View* by Vanbrugh, Congreve, Dennis, Wycherley, and

---

* "Tuesday, 28 Dec. 1697.—His majestie has given Dr. Oates 1,000l. to pay his debts, and 300l. per ann. during his life, in consideration of his former sufferings."—*Luttrell*.

† Preface to the *Fables*.

others of less note. In nearly all the replies, however, one common fault is observable; they partake too much of the nature of special pleading, and fail to argue the question on sufficiently broad grounds. Dennis's interesting little volume on the *Usefulness of the Stage* is the one considerable exception to this rule. The parts taken in the controversy by Congreve and Vanbrugh were scarcely commensurate with the expectations warranted by their high reputation and exceptional ability. They attempted little more than a bare reply to the charges which Collier had preferred against themselves; and so far, they were both, in some measure, successful, although Congreve, with strange indiscretion, seriously damaged his own cause by the ill-temper and scurrility which he vented upon his antagonist; and even, on one or two occasions, by his eagerness to prove too much, managed to place himself decidedly in the wrong, where he had before been as decidedly in the right.*

On the 8th of June appeared *A Short Vindication of the Relapse and the Provok'd Wife from Immorality and Profaneness. By the Author.* It is a pamphlet of seventy-nine pages, anonymous, like all Vanbrugh's previous publications. The tone is by no means apologetic. "What I have done," writes the Author, "is in general a Discouragement to Vice and Folly; I am sure I intended it, and I hope I have performed it." The words "in general" require a little emphasis, but, this granted, I believe we shall find no very solid reason for quarrelling with Vanbrugh's estimate of his performances. He then proceeds to examine the particular passages quoted by Collier from his works, and clearly shows that the latter's objections are, for the most part, in their nature frivolous, or based upon misapprehension. Collier's claim, on behalf of the clergy, to temporal honours and distinction, is treated by Vanbrugh

---

* It is probably unnecessary to remind the reader that he will find an admirable account of the entire controversy in Mr. Gosse's *Life of Congreve.*

in a spirit certainly more in accordance with the teaching of
Christ than that which inspired the churchman to put it forth.
" He is of Opinion," the poet writes, "that Riches and Plenty,
Title, State and Dominion, give a Majesty to Precept, and cry
Place for it wherever it comes ; That Christ and his Apostles
took the thing by the wrong Handle ; and that the Pope and
his Cardinals have much refin'd upon 'em in the Policy of
Instruction." And he shrewdly adds, " I'm afraid those very
Instances Mr. *Collier* gives us of the Grandeur of the Clergy,
are the things that have destroy'd both them and their
Flocks."

Upon another argument he writes : " I cou'd say a great deal
against the too exact observance of what's call'd the Rules of
the Stage, and the crowding a Comedy with a great deal of
Intricate Plot. I believe I cou'd shew, that the chief entertainment, as well as the Moral, lies much more in the Characters
and the Dialogue, than in the Business and the Event." The
latter sentence contains the expression of a principle uniformly
pursued by writers of the school to which Vanbrugh belonged,
and entirely opposed to the usual practice of playwrights at
the present day. With especial reference to *The Relapse*, the
author observes: " Whether it be right to have two distinct
Designs in one Play ; I'll only say, I think when there are so,
if they are both entertaining, then 'tis right ; if they are not, 'tis
wrong."

Finally, Vanbrugh defends the general tendency of the
aspersed comedies. Of *The Provok'd Wife* he submits that that
is surely "a good End, which puts the Governor in mind, let
his Soldiers be ever so good, 'tis possible he may provoke 'em
to a Mutiny"; while in *The Relapse* he declares his purpose
was to present "a natural Instance of the Frailty of Mankind,
without that necessary Guard of keeping out of Temptation."
He claims a useful moral in this, and is, not unreasonably,
indignant that Collier refuses to recognize it. He concludes

a

his *Vindication* with a touch of characteristic humour. In commenting upon *The Relapse*, Collier had, rather unfortunately ridiculed Worthy's sudden reformation in his scene with Amanda. "He is refin'd into a Platonick Admirer," sneered the divine, "and goes off as like a Town Spark as you would wish. And so much for the Poet's fine Gentleman!" Vanbrugh turns upon him, not quite fairly it must be owned; but the temptation was irresistible. "The World may see by this what a Contempt the Doctor has for a Spark that can make no better use of his Mistress than to admire her for her Virtue. This methinks is something so very extraordinary in a Clergyman, that I almost fancy when He and I are fast asleep in our Graves, those who shall read what we both have produc'd, will be apt to conclude there's a Mistake in the Tradition about the Authors ; and that 'twas the Reforming Divine writ the Play, and the Scandalous Poet the Remarks upon't."

There is a curious passage in the *Vindication*, in which Vanbrugh makes mention of a gentleman who, he says, had assisted him in writing *The Relapse*, and who had since "gone away with the Czar, who has made him Poet Laureate of Muscovy." I am unable to explain this assertion. It bears the stamp of improbability upon its face, although what could have induced the poet to invent such a story, if he did invent it, is beyond conjecture. Peter the Great arrived in England in the month of January, 1698, and remained here until late in the following April. On his departure he was accompanied by a number of Englishmen whom he had enlisted in his service— mathematicians, shipbuilders, and other artificers. But a Poet Laureate ! and, apparently, an English Poet Laureate, for the Muscovites ! *Que diable allait-il faire dans cette galère ?*

Collier did not improve his position by the *Defence of the Short View*, which he published in November, 1698, as a rejoinder to the replies of Congreve and Vanbrugh. He scores a few points, it is true; but much that he urges, is

merely feeble and frivolous. To Vanbrugh's remarks upon
the grandeur of the *clergy, his opponent has no better
answer than that the Apostles possessed the power of
working miracles, and that, this power being withdrawn,
it was necessary to have recourse to worldly expedients
to supply its place. "Appearance," he naively observes,
"goes a great way in the Expediting of Affairs." With
Collier's *Defence*, the interest of the controversy, so far as
Vanbrugh is concerned, comes to an end. Unless we reckon
an ironical touch or two in the prologues to *The False Friend*
and *The Confederacy*, the poet was henceforth silent on the
subject.

He probably felt that he had said enough for his own vindication ; and, indeed, an impartial judgment must needs
pronounce, that if he had not come wholly unscathed from the
encounter, his wounds were little more than skin-deep. But
from the fury of popular fanaticism, of which Collier had made
himself the mouthpiece, no impartial judgment was to be
expected. The fierce satire of Wycherley, the polished
sarcasm of Congreve, the broadly humorous raillery of
Vanbrugh, were, in the eyes of their infatuated opponents,
offences against public morality equally obnoxious with the bold
indecencies of the brilliant Mrs. Behn, or the deliberate
foulness of the low-minded Ravenscroft. A reform in the
the theatres was certainly needed, a reform in the audiences
yet more incontestably. But popular uprisings, of whatever
nature, are enemies to moderation. The tree needed pruning,
and the axe was laid to its roots. For some years the poets
maintained the unequal struggle. Their party was influential
and enthusiastic, and in the year following that of Collier's
attack, a new recruit to the theatre, George Farquhar, produced
a first play which promised a career of exceptional brilliancy.
But the death-blow had been struck, and if English comedy
was long a-dying, the end came none the less surely. A

generation passed away, and the walls which had so often re-echoed the laughter and applause which greeted the master-pieces of Wycherley and Congreve, of Vanbrugh and Farquhar, now looked down on reformed audiences weeping for the sentimental sorrows of the *Conscious Lovers*, or glutting their political spite with the partisan scenes of *The Nonjuror*.

V.

VANBRUGH'S next contribution to the theatre, inconsiderable on his own account, was made for ever memorable by its connection with the last published words of Dryden. The piece itself was an alteration by Vanbrugh of Fletcher's fine comedy, *The Pilgrim;* the alterations, which can hardly be said to improve the play, consisting in the reduction of Fletcher's blank verse to prose, and a few trivial additions to the dialogue. Thus transformed, *The Pilgrim* was produced at Drury Lane on New Year's Day, the 25th of March, 1700.* The third night was assigned to Dryden's benefit, and the great poet contributed to the performance a prologue and epilogue, a "Song of a Scholar and his Mistress," introduced in the mad-house scene, and a "Secular Masque," set to music and tacked to the end of the comedy. Age and infirmity had not impaired Dryden's literary powers, and the prologue and epilogue, which were both spoken by Colley Cibber, are perhaps unsurpassed, in their kind, for vigorous thought and trenchant satire.

---

* There is some uncertainty as to the exact date of this production, but it was most probably as given above. The "Secular Masque," contributed by Dryden, bears internal evidence of having been designed to celebrate the beginning of a new century (the year 1700 being taken as the first of the century.) As to the reference to Dryden as "the *late* great Poet of our Age," which appears in the printed copy, there is no difficulty in supposing that to have been inserted after the production of the play. Dryden died on the 1st of May, 1700, and *The Pilgrim*, in its new dress, was not published until the following June.

The Pilgrim enjoyed a long run. Its success was largely due to the impression made by a young and hitherto unknown actress, who, in the character of Alinda, "charm'd the Play into a Run of many succeeding Nights."* Anne Oldfield, who subsequently became the most celebrated actress of her time, had been discovered, about a year previously, by Farquhar, who chanced to overhear her reading a comedy to herself, in a room behind the bar of a tavern kept by a relative of hers. Struck by the girl's beauty and intelligence, Farquhar "took some Pains to acquaint Sir John Vanbrugh with the Jewel he had found thus by Accident," and upon Vanbrugh's recommendation Mrs. Oldfield obtained an engagement at the Theatre Royal. There, however, she remained about a twelvemonth "almost a Mute, and unheeded,"† until Vanbrugh gave her, with the part of Alinda, the opportunity, which was all she required, of recommending herself to the public. She played this part on the occasion of her benefit, July 6, 1700.

Early in 1702 a new comedy by Vanbrugh, entitled *The False Friend*, was produced at Drury Lane.‡ The prologue is an ironical appeal to the reformers of the stage, whose good-will the poet hopes to gain by presenting them, on this occasion, with a moral piece—"so moral, we're afraid 'twill damn the Play !" he slyly adds. This line, as it proved, was prophetic, but there were other sufficient reasons for the failure of *The False Friend*. Vanbrugh's genius was little adapted to deal with subjects of so sombre a cast. The

---

* Chetwood's *History of the Stage*, 1749, p. 201.

† Cibber.

‡ It was produced about the end of January, or beginning of February, 1702. The following announcement of its publication appeared in the *Post Man* of Feb. 7-10, 1702 :—"This day is published The False Friend : a Comedy, as it is Acted at the Theatre Royal in Drury-lane. By his Majesties Servants. Printed for Jacob Tonson, within Gray's Inn Gate, next Gray's Inn Lane." A nearly similar announcement in the *Flying Post* of the same date, reads "as 'twas acted," instead of "as it is acted."

plot, moreover, is ill contrived in several important respects. Even the most powerful part of the play, the really fine scene which concludes the third act, loses something of its effectiveness by reason of the utter improbability of Don Pedro's sudden re-appearance. In the catastrophe, the principal character meets with a violent end, which, however deserved, is hardly of the nature of comedy ; the lovers are parted for ever, and Don Pedro is left in possession of a wife, whose heart, as he well knows, is wholly occupied by his rival : in fine, the piece is so far from justifying its title of comedy, that Gildon (a friendly critic) actually suggested that it had been so called by a mistake of the printer. The same critic takes notice of a mishap which befell *The False Friend* on the fourth night, when Cibber, who played Don John, was accidentally hurt, and could not continue his part.*

We may here mention a rather trivial farce, called *The Country House*, which Vanbrugh translated from d'Ancourt's *La Maison de Campagne*. The first performance of this piece recorded by Genest took place at Drury Lane on the 16th of June, 1705, but it appears to have been produced earlier—Genest supposes, at some date between 1697 and 1703.

The year 1702 presents our author in a new character. Of his architectural studies we know absolutely nothing, unless we may accept Swift's account, who pretends that Vanbrugh acquired the rudiments of the art by watching children building houses of cards or clay.† But this was probably ironical. However he came by his skill, in 1702 he stepped into sudden fame as the architect of Castle

---

* *A Comparison between the two Stages*, London, 1702, p. 178. This lively and entertaining little dialogue upon plays and players is generally attributed to Charles Gildon.

† Miscellaneous Poems : *The History of Vanbrugh's House*. Written in 1708.

Howard, the Earl of Carlisle's seat in Yorkshire. I borrow from Allan Cunningham the following description of the building.

"The design is at once simple and grand. A lofty portico with six columns, rising two stories, occupies the centre ; on either side are long galleries, terminating in advancing wings with pavilions ; while a cupola, rising to the height of a hundred feet, and proportioned, in every respect, to the body of the building, is seen far and wide. The whole is of the Corinthian order, and though very lofty, there are no double stories of columns, as in Whitehall. The interior is every way worthy of the exterior. The hall, thirty-five feet square, and sixty feet high, adorned with columns of the Corinthian and Composite orders, is surmounted by a spacious dome. The whole house is upon the same magnificent scale, and is filled with statues and paintings. For picturesque splendour, we know of no English mansion to compare with it—nor is it more splendid than solid. The number of roofs, cupolas, statues, vases, and massy-clustered chimneys, give to the horizontal profile of the structure a richness of effect, which is nowhere surpassed in British art." *

---

* *Lives of British Architects:* VANBRUGH. The first volume of Campbell's *Vitruvius Britannicus*, published in 1717, contains plans and elevations of Castle Howard and Blenheim, executed from Vanbrugh's own drawings. The author states that Castle Howard was built in 1714 ; meaning, of course, that it was completed in that year. An obelisk in the park at Castle Howard bears an inscription to the effect that the Earl of Carlisle began those works in the year 1702—*not* 1712, as it has been wrongly printed elsewhere. The date is confirmed by a manuscript book in the possession of the present Earl, which I have been kindly permitted to examine. This book, which is in the autograph of the third Earl of Carlisle, contains an exact account of the expenditure upon Castle Howard, made up half-yearly, from the commencement of the building until Lady-day, 1713. The first entry in the book is as follows : "Disbursed upon account of ye building from ye 31st of March, 1701, til ye 29th of Sept., 1702,—£3032 : 15 : 6." The disbursements in the year 1701 were, no doubt, for preliminary work, such as quarrying.

To the fame of this important undertaking were doubtless in great measure due the reputation, honours, and employment which now fell to the share of the successful architect. The Earl of Carlisle, then deputy Earl-Marshal, testified his satisfaction by procuring for Vanbrugh a place in the College of Arms : on the 26th of June, 1703, he was appointed " Carlisle Herald Extraordinary," * and on the 30th of March following, a warrant was passed for creating him Clarenceux King of Arms, and the ceremony was performed at the College by the Earl of Essex, substitute to the Earl of Carlisle.† It was an odd appointment, for Vanbrugh not only knew nothing of heraldry, but had openly ridiculed that grave science in his comedy of *Æsop*. But the indignant College protested in vain, and the poet stuck to his post. We know not at what period he received the appointment of Comptroller of her Majesty's Works : it was possibly before the year 1702, for Le Neve styles him " Comptroller of the Works, Surveyor of the Gardens to King William, Queen Anne, and King George."‡ It is certain, however, that he held this office when he undertook the building of Blenheim, in the summer of 1705.

A list of some of the mansions erected by Vanbrugh during these years may be found in Allan Cunningham's Life of the poet-architect. They were none of them, according to the biographer, equal to his first essay. A small house, which he built for himself at Whitehall, was immortalized by Swift in two witty pieces of satirical verse, written in 1706 and 1708. In the earlier of these pieces Swift recounts the building of the house, which, it seems, Vanbrugh, like another Amphion, raised entirely by the magical power of his poetry.

---

* Noble's *History of the College of Arms*, p. 346.
† *Ibid*, p. 356.
‡ *Pedigrees of the Knights, &c.*, p. 512. Harleian Soc. Pub. 1873.

" ' Great Jove ! ' he cry'd, ' the art restore
To build by verse as heretofore,
And make my Muse the architect ;
What palaces shall we erect !
No longer shall forsaken Thames
Lament his old Whitehall in flames ; *
A pile shall from its ashes rise
Fit to invade or prop the skies.'
Jove smil'd, and like a gentle god,
Consenting with the usual nod,
Told Van he knew his talent best,
And left the choice to his own breast :
So Van resolv'd to write a farce ;
But, well perceiving wit was scarce,
With cunning that defect supplies,
Takes a French play as lawful prize,
Steals thence his plot and every joke,
Not once suspecting Jove would smoke.

. . . .

Jove saw the cheat, but thought it best
To turn the matter to a jest ;
Down from Olympus' top he slides,
Laughing as if he'd burst his sides.
' Ay,' thought the god, ' are these your tricks ?
Why, then old plays deserve old bricks ;
And since you're sparing of your stuff,
Your building shall be small enough.' "

As the farce proceeds, the house rises in proportion, and
both are at length completed.

" Now Poets from all quarters ran
To see the House of Brother Van ;
Look'd high and low, walk'd often round,
But no such House was to be found.
One asks the waterman hard by,
Where may the poet's palace lie ?
Another of the Thames inquires
If he has seen its gilded spires ?
At length they in the rubbish spy
A thing resembling a goose-pie "—

which turns out, upon closer investigation, to be the edifice in
question.

---

* Whitehall was destroyed by fire in January, 1698.

This lively banter set all the world in a roar, except the unfortunate butt, who was not allowed to forget it, had he been ever so willing. In the Journal to Stella, Swift writes (Nov. 7, 1710) : "I dined to-day at Sir Richard Temple's with Congreve, Vanbrugh, Lieutenant-General Farrington, &c. Vanbrugh, I believe I told you, had a long quarrel with me about those verses on his house ; but we were very civil and cold. Lady Marlborough used to tease him with them, which had made him angry, though he be a good-natured fellow." The year after Vanbrugh's death, Swift publicly expressed his regret for having satirized "a man of wit and of honour."*

After all, it was not a poet, but a doctor of divinity, who wrote the most famous satire on Vanbrugh's architecture. Dr. Abel Evans is now remembered only as a *name* in the *Dunciad*, where Pope, who seems to have been his friend, has placed him in the company of Swift and Young; and as the author (or reputed author) of the following ingenious lines :

> " Under this stone, reader, survey
> Dead Sir John Vanbrugh's house of clay :
> Lie heavy on him, earth ! for he
> Laid many heavy loads on thee ! " †

In the year 1704, Vanbrugh was a collaborator with Congreve and Walsh in a translation of Molière's *comédie-ballet* of *Monsieur de Pourceaugnac*, which, under the title of *Squire Trelooby*, was produced at Lincoln's Inn Fields with great applause, on the 30th of March of that year. It does not appear that this piece was ever published. Within a month, however, of the performance, there was issued an anonymous translation of Molière's play, entitled *Monsieur de Pourceaugnac,*

---

* In the Preface to the *Miscellanies*, published by Swift and Pope, 1727.

† These lines may be found in Nichols's *Select Collection of Poems*, 1780, vol. iii, p. 161. The same volume contains some further specimens of Dr. Evans's muse, including two or three short pieces on Vanbrugh, not worth quoting.

or, Squire Trelooby. Acted at the Subscription Musick at the Theatre Royal in Lincoln's-Inn-Fields, March 30, 1704. *By select Comedians from both Houses.* The scene is changed from Paris to London, and the advocate of Limoges becomes a Cornish squire : in other respects the translation is pretty faithful—so faithful indeed, that one of the characters, of the very English name of Wimble, who answers to Molière's Sbrigani, is made to describe himself as a Neapolitan ! With this translation were printed, not only the prologue by Garth, and the epilogue by Congreve, which were spoken at Lincoln's Inn Fields, but the names of the actors who took part in the performance. Nevertheless, it was put forth expressly as an independent version, which the author "design'd for the English Stage, had he not been prevented by a Translation of the same Play, done by other Hands, and presented at the New Play-house the 30th of last Month."* "I was assured," he writes further, "(after due Inquiry made) that their Transla- tion was not likely to be printed, tho' there have been great Demands made for it, by the whole Town, who have taken up with wrong Conceptions cf it as it was acted ; some thinking it was a Party-Play made on purpose to ridicule the whole Body of *West-Country* Gentlemen, others averring that it was wrote to expose some eminent Doctors of Physick in this Town." This seems sufficiently explicit, and it is corroborated by Congreve's positive declaration that the published *Squire Trelooby* was "none of ours,"—alluding, of course, to himself and his two collaborators. † At the same time it is remarkable, as Mr. Gosse has pointed out, that the translations were both entitled *Squire Trelooby*, and one does not see why Pour- ceaugnac and Limoges should "suggest to two independent minds Trelooby and Cornwall." ‡ Mr. Gosse thinks it "not at

---

* Preface to *Squire Trelooby.* The preface is dated April the 19th, 1704.
† Gosse's *Life of Congreve*, p. 148.
‡ *Life of Congreve*, p. 149.

all certain that this *Squire Trelooby* of 1704 does not virtually
represent the play which the joint authors thought it wise to
disown." At all events, it is a rather poor translation of a play
which, in the original, is by no means one of its great author's
masterpieces ; nor is there anything in the piece, as it stands,
which very strongly recalls the style of either Vanbrugh or
Congreve, or which is worthy of the pen of either of those
accomplished dramatists.

We have not quite done with *Squire Trelooby*. In 1734 a
translation of *Monsieur de Pourceaugnac* was published under
the title of *The Cornish Squire*. This piece directly claims to
be the production of Vanbrugh. The title-page bears the
words : "Done from the French by the late Sir John
Vanbrugh" ; and the editor, J. Ralph, in his preface declares
"that, tho' Sir John Vanbrugh was by many reputed the sole
Author of it, yet it was currently reported at the Time of its
Representation, that he wrote it in conjunction with Mr. Walsh
and Mr. Congreve : Each of them being suppos'd to have done
an Act a piece." Ralph admits his inability to explain "how
the Publication of this Piece came to be delay'd so long, or the
Piece itself to be so little known." Indeed, his account of it is
altogether unsatisfactory. The book had disappeared in some
mysterious way from the play-house, after the run was over,
and an imperfect copy had been sent to Ralph by a gentleman
who had had it several years in his library : Ralph, having
himself supplied the omissions and altered certain passages,
caused the play to be published and brought upon the stage.
A comparison of the two versions puts it beyond doubt that
The Cornish Squire of 1734 is simply the anonymous *Squire
Trelooby* of 1704, revised, altered, as to the dialogue, in many
trivial instances, and with the very needless addition of some
three or four pages of new matter at the end of the last
act.

To Vanbrugh hitherto fortune had been prodigal of her
favours : he was soon to taste the uses of adversity in the fruit
of his own rash enterprise. Betterton's star was no longer in
the ascendant, and the popular applause which had once been
almost a monopoly of the players in Lincoln's Inn Fields, was
now lavished on the younger actors of the Theatre Royal. "To
this Decline of the Old Company," says Cibber, "many
accidents might contribute " : in the meantime, the smallness
and inconvenience of their theatre was an obvious disadvantage,
which it were perhaps possible to remedy. " To recover them,
therefore, to their due Estimation, a new Project was form'd, of
building them a stately Theatre, in the *Hay-Market*,* by Sir
John Vanbrugh, for which he raised a Subscription of thirty
Persons of Quality, at one Hundred Pounds each, in Consideration whereof every Subscriber, for his own Life, was to be
admitted to whatever Entertainments should be publickly
perform'd there, without farther Payment for his Entrance. Of
this Theatre I saw the first Stone laid, on which was inscrib'd,
The little Whig, in Honour to a Lady† of extraordinary
Beauty, then the celebrated Toast, and Pride of that Party." ‡
The building being completed, Betterton and his co-partners
at Lincoln's Inn Fields dissolved their own agreement, and
engaged themselves to act at the Haymarket, under the
direction of Vanbrugh and Congreve. On the 9th of April
1705, the new theatre was opened with a translated Italian
opera, entitled *The Triumph of Love*. It was an inauspicious
beginning, for the *Triumph of Love* proved anything but a
triumph on the stage, being "perform'd but three Days
and those not crowded." No new piece of importance was
produced during the remainder of the season, which closed at

---

* On the site of the present opera-house.
† Marlborough's daughter, the Countess of Sunderland.
‡ Cibber's *Apology*, ch. ix.

the end of June, when Congreve, whose single contribution to the company had been an epilogue spoken by Mrs. Bracegirdle on the opening night, resigned his connection with the theatre, and Vanbrugh was left sole proprietor.

But if Congreve had disappointed the players' hopes, Vanbrugh worked with a will to bring success to the house, and before the year expired, two new plays by his hand were produced at the Haymarket. The first of these to appear was *The Confederacy*, translated from d'Ancourt's comedy, *Les Bourgeoises à la Mode*. This delightful comedy is not only by far the happiest of Vanbrugh's translations from the French, but ranks indisputably among the most brilliant of his performances. It is a pure comedy of manners, alive with wit and instinct with satire. The subject was entirely suited to Vanbrugh's taste, and, although he has followed closely the general plan of the original, there is not a scene in the play which he has left unimproved, and the improvements are uniformly conceived in his most felicitous vein.

The Confederacy was produced on the 30th of October, 1705, with an excellent cast, including Mrs. Barry and Mrs. Bracegirdle, Dogget, and a young actor of great promise and future celebrity, Barton Booth. Betterton, however, took no part in the performance, perhaps from infirmity ; for the great actor, though still without a rival in his profession, was now seventy years of age, and a martyr to the gout. Had the success of the piece been proportioned to its deserts, Vanbrugh would have added one more to the list of his theatrical triumphs ; but, although it ran for ten nights, it was played under circumstances which precluded the possibility of enthusiasm on the part of the audience. The fact was, Vanbrugh, in building his theatre, had indulged his architec-tural tastes to the serious detriment of his prospects as a manager. His lofty columns, his gilded cornices, and spacious dome, made, doubtless, a very splendid appearance, but the acoustic requirements of the house had been totally neglected. Scarcely one word in ten which were spoken on the stage, could be heard distinctly by the audience : the voices of the actors "sounded like the Gabbling of so many People, in the lofty Aisles in a Cathedral." *

This was not the only drawback. The theatre was situated at an inconvenient distance from the town, for as yet the Haymarket was surrounded by green meadows, from whence, as Cibber facetiously observes, the actors "could draw little or no Sustenance, unless it were that of a Milk-Diet." And lastly, by the death of some of the actors, and the advanced age of others, the effective strength of the company had been gradually declining during the ten years which had elapsed since they achieved their independence of the patentees of Drury Lane.

Such were the disadvantages against which Vanbrugh struggled for some months to make head. On the 27th of December, 1705, he produced his translation of Molière's *Dépit Amoureux*, under the ominous title of *The Mistake*, with Betterton in the part of Don Alvarez. This ran for nine nights. On the 19th of January was revived one of his most popular plays, *The Provok'd Wife*, with a new masquerade scene for Sir John Brute, who was now made to swagger in female attire, by way, it would seem, of a sop to the reformers, who were less sensitive to the exposure of a drunken woman than to that of a drunken parson. *The Provok'd Wife* was withdrawn after three performances only. A few days later (January 28) *Squire Trelooby* was revived. But the old successes were not repeated ; for, in Cibber's words, "what few could plainly hear, it was not likely a great many could applaud."

This unfortunate speculation appears to have proved a heavy drain upon Vanbrugh's resources. As long afterwards as July,

---

* Cibber.

1708, Maynwaring wrote with reference to Vanbrugh, in a letter to the Duchess of Marlborough,—" I am sorry for him, because I believe he is unhappy through his own folly, and I can see no reasonable way to help him. What I mean by his folly, is his building the playhouse, which certainly cost him a great deal more than was subscribed; and his troubles arise from the workmen that built it, and the tradesmen that furnished the cloaths, &c., for the actors."* In the autumn of 1706, about a year after Congreve's retirement, Vanbrugh also withdrew from the management of the theatre, handing over house, actors, and licence, to Mr. Owen Swiney, who undertook to pay him a rental of £5 for every acting day, the whole not to exceed £700 in the year. Swiney was a kind of unofficial agent and right-hand man of Rich, the patentee of Drury Lane, with whose consent he reinforced the company at the Haymarket with all the best actors of the Theatre Royal; Mr. Rich, at this time, depending chiefly upon singers and dancers for the delectation of his supporters. Under the new management the Haymarket Theatre was re-opened on the 15th of October, 1706, with improved prospects. Despite the unfitness of the building, the strengthened company drew larger audiences, and the actors " were all paid their full Sallaries, a Blessing they had not felt, in some Years, in either House before."†

To finish at once with Vanbrugh's theatrical record, it may be added that on the 22nd of March, 1707, there was produced at the Haymarket a translation of Molière's *Cocu Imaginaire*, entitled *The Cuckold in Conceit*, which Cibber attributes to our poet. It was never printed, and Vanbrugh's claim to the authorship is considered doubtful by Genest; but, if Cibber's statement

---

* *Private Correspondence of Sarah, Duchess of Marlborough* : Vol. i., 140.

† Cibber.

be correct, *The Cuckold in Conceit* was the last of his completed plays.

In the summer of 1706 Vanbrugh was charged with the execution of an important duty in his capacity of herald. Lord Halifax was dispatched to Hanover in the spring of that year, to convey the Naturalization and Regency Acts to the Princess Sophia, and the order of the Garter to her grandson, the Electoral Prince, afterwards George II. The young prince was invested with the order at Hanover, on the 13th of June, by Halifax and Vanbrugh ; the latter acting as substitute for Garter, Sir Henry St. George, whom extreme old age prevented from fulfilling the duties of his office.*

VI.

ALLUSION has been already made to the palace of Blenheim, which Vanbrugh erected for the Duke of Marlborough. It is time to give a particular account of this great work, the most considerable and the most famous of his performances as an architect.

When, in December, 1704, at the close of the campaign immortalized by the victory of Blenheim, the Duke of Marlborough returned to England, he was received by the people with enthusiasm, and with unbounded favour by the Queen. Early in the following year the House of Commons "presented an address, soliciting her majesty to consider of proper means for perpetuating the memory of the great services performed by the Duke of Marlborough." On the 17th of February the Queen

---

* Beltz's *Memorials of the Order of the Garter*, 1841, p. cxxiii. In the same work may be found an account of a more memorable ceremony, in which Vanbrugh took part, on the occasion of the degradation of the gallant Duke of Ormond, who had been attainted for high treason. The ceremony was performed at Windsor, on the 12th of July, 1716, "after morning prayers," Clarenceux King of Arms (Sir John Vanbrugh) exercising the office of Garter, which was then vacant, pending the dispute between the two claimants, Vanbrugh and Anstis. See later, p. lxvii., *note*.

e

"informed the House, that in conformity with their application, she purposed to convey to the Duke and his heirs the interest of the Crown in the manor and honour of Woodstock, with the hundred of Wootton, and requested supplies for clearing off the incumbrances on that domain. A bill for the purpose was immediately introduced; passed both houses without opposition; and received the royal sanction on the 14th of March. . . . . Not satisfied that the nation alone should testify its gratitude, the Queen accompanied the grant with an order to the board of works to erect, at the royal expense, a splendid palace, which, in memory of the victory, was to be called the Castle of Blenheim."*

A design was accordingly prepared by John Vanbrugh, Comptroller of her Majesty's Works, and, being approved, the building was presently commenced. Vanbrugh's position in the undertaking was made perfectly clear by a warrant, empowering him to act on behalf of the Duke, and signed by the Lord High Treasurer, Godolphin.† It is true, at the date of this warrant, the Duke was prosecuting the war on the Continent; but it is absurd to pretend (as it was afterwards pretended) that Godolphin, his intimate friend, placed in Vanbrugh's hands an instrument of such importance, grounded so unequivocally upon

---

* Coxe's *Memoirs of John, Duke of Marlborough* : vol i., pp. 363-4.

† This document is so important to a right understanding of the case, that I quote it in full, as it is printed in Vanbrugh's *Justification*, a paper which I shall hereafter have occasion to refer.

"To all to whom these Presents shall come, The Right Honourable Sidney, Lord Godolphin, Lord High Treasurer of England, sendeth greeting. Whereas his Grace, John, Duke of Marlborough, hath resolv'd to erect a large Fabrick, for a Mansion House, at Woodstock, in the County of Oxon. Know ye, that I the said Sidney, Lord Godolphin, At the request and desire of the said Duke of Marlborough, have constituted and appointed, and do hereby, for and on the behalf of the said Duke, constitute and appoint John Vanbrugh, Esq; to be Surveyor of all the Works and Buildings so intended to be erected or made at Woodstock aforesaid; And do hereby Authorize and Impower him, the said John Vanbrugh, to make

the Duke's authority, without his knowledge or consent. And further, although the Crown was indeed responsible to the Duke for the outlay upon Blenheim, yet if the warrant have any meaning at all, it certainly implies that the Duke himself was responsible to Vanbrugh for his own expenses and the charges of his workmen.

The great work was begun with festivities and rejoicings. A contemporary journal supplies the following interesting account of the opening ceremony. "Woodstock, June 19th [1705]. Yesterday being Monday, about six o'clock in the evening, was laid the first stone of the Duke of Marlborough's House, by Mr. Vanbrugge, and then seven gentlemen gave it a stroke with a hammer, and threw down each of them a guinea ; Sir Thomas Wheate was the first, Dr. Bouchell the second, Mr. Vanbrugge the third ; I know not the rest. There were several sorts of musick ; three morris dances ; one of young fellows, one of maidens, and one of old beldames. There were about a hundred buckets, bowls, and pans, filled with wine, punch, cakes, and ale. From my lord's house all went to the Town-hall, where plenty of sack, claret, cakes, &c., were prepared for the gentry and better sort ; and under the Cross eight barrels of ale, with abundance of cakes, were placed for the common people. The stone laid by Mr. Vanbrugge was eight square, finely

---

and sign Contracts with any Persons for Materials, And also with any Artificers or Workmen to be employ'd about the said Buildings, in such manner as he shall judge proper for carrying on the said Work, in the best and most advantageous manner that may be, And likewise to employ such day Labourers and Carryages from time to time, as he shall find necessary for the said Service, and to do all other matters and things, as may be any ways conducive to the effectual Performance of what is directed by the said Duke of Marlborough in relation to the said Works, And I do hereby authorize and require the said John Vanbrugh to lay before me from time to time (in the absence of the said Duke) an Account of his proceedings herein, together with what he shall think necessary to be observ'd, or wherein any further Instructions may be wanting. To the end the same may be given accord-ingly. Dated June the 9th, 1705.

"(Signed) GODOLPHIN."

e 2

polished, about eighteen inches over, and upon it were these words inlayed in pewter—*In memory of the battel of Blenheim, June* 8, 1705, *Anna Regina.*" *

For some years supplies, which were charged upon the civil list, came in with regularity, and the work steadily proceeded. But the wind was changing, that had fanned the fortunes of the great Duke : intrigues of Court and State threatened him on all sides ; with the Queen's favour the payments from the Treasury also diminished ; and when, in 1710, the Whig ministry, including his friend Godolphin, was thrown out of office, a considerable amount of arrears was already due to the workmen and the unfortunate architect. Nor were difficulties such as these the only hardships with which Vanbrugh had to contend. Almost from the commencement of the building, he had been, from time to time, engaged in disputes with the Duchess, who was ever on the watch to restrain what she regarded as Vanbrugh's extravagance in the matter of expenditure. The colossal splendour of the design involved an outlay proportionately colossal. The original estimate of the cost had proved inadequate, and by the month of October, 1710, not less than £200,000 had already been received from the Treasury, while the work was yet far from completion.

Vanbrugh's relations with the Duchess had been further strained by a circumstance which befell in the year 1709. Her Grace had resolved upon levelling the ancient manor-house of Woodstock, which Vanbrugh was anxious to preserve, equally on account of its picturesqueness and its interesting historical associations. His remonstrances, however, were of no avail, and only induced the Duchess to surmise that he entertained the project of fitting up the old house for his own

---

* Quoted in Mrs. Thomson's *Memoirs of Sarah, Duchess of Marl-borough*, vol. ii., p. 443, *note.* June 8 is doubtless a misprint for June 18, the date of the ceremony.

residence. This imputation he, of course, denied, in terms which show him to have been stung to the quick : " I am much discouraged," he wrote to Godolphin, "to find I can be suspected of so poor a contrivance." But the charms with which antiquity and association had invested the old manor-house in the eyes of the poet and artist, appealed in vain to the sternly practical mind of the Duchess. She remained inflexible, and the act of Vandalism was accomplished.

In the autumn of 1710 a fresh blow, severe as unexpected, fell upon Vanbrugh from the same quarter. The story is best told in his own words, in a letter to the Duke of Marlborough, dated "Oxford, Oct. 3, 1710."

"By last post I gave your Grace an account from Blenheim, in what condition the building was, how near a close of this year's work, and how happy it was that after being carried up in so very dry a season, it was like to be covered before any wet fell upon it to soak the walls. My intention was to stay there till I saw it effectually done ; the great arch of the bridge likewise compleated and safe covered, and the centers struck from under it. But this morning Joynes and Bobart* told me they had recd. a letter from the Duchess of Marlborough to put a stop at once to all sorts of work till your Grace came over, not suffering one man to be employed a day longer. I told them there was nothing more now to do in effect but just what was necessary towards covering and securing the work, which would be done in a week or ten days, and that there was so absolute a necessity for it, that to leave off without it would expose the whole summer's work to unspeakable mischiefs : that there was likewise another reason not to discharge all the people thus at one stroke together, which was, that though the principal workmen that work by the great, such as masons, carpenters, &c.,

---

* Joynes and Bobart were joint "comptrollers" of the works at Blenheim, Vanbrugh being "surveyor."

would perhaps have regard to the promises made them that they should lose nothing, and so not be disorderly; yet the labourers, carters, and other country people, who used to be regularly paid, but were now in arrear, finding themselves disbanded in so surprising a manner without a farthing, would certainly conclude their money lost, and finding themselves distressed by what they owed to the people where they lodged, &c., and numbers of them having their familys and homes at great distances in other countys, 'twas very much to be feared such a general meeting might happen, that the building might feel the effects of it; which I told them I the more apprehended, knowing there were people not far off who would be glad to put 'em upon it; and that they themselves, as well as I, had for some days past observed 'em grown very insolent, and in appearance kept from meeting only by the assurances we gave them from one day to another that money was coming. But all I had to say was cut short by Mr. Joynes's shewing me a post-script my Lady Duchess had added to her letter, forbidding any regard to whatever I might say or do.

"Your Grace wont blame me if, ashamed to continue there any longer on such a foot, as well as seeing it was not in my power to do your Grace any farther service, I immediately came away."*

It is not to be doubted that the ill-temper consequent upon her disgrace with the Queen had some share in occasioning this sudden outbreak on the part of the Duchess. But it is equally certain that she was alarmed at the ever-increasing cost of the building, and apprehensive (not without reason, as matters were going at Court,) of the failure of supplies from the Treasury. Vanbrugh, it may well be supposed, had been throughout more intent upon giving full play to his architectural genius, than

---

* Quoted in Mrs. Thomson's *Memoirs of Sarah, Duchess of Marlborough:* vol. ii., *appendix.*

upon reducing expenses to a minimum ; but we have no reason to discredit his own express declaration, that he did nothing without the Duke's approval. The breach, though violent, proved not irreparable. A fresh instalment was presently obtained from the Treasury, and, on the strength of this, Vanbrugh induced his men to resume work in the following spring. But a more serious calamity was in store. On the last day of 1711, the hero of Blenheim was dismissed from all his appointments : in the summer of 1712, the building, intended to commemorate his great victory, was abandoned by the Queen's command.

With the new reign, new hopes sprang into life. King George landed at Greenwich on the 18th of September, 1714, and the next day Vanbrugh was knighted at Greenwich House, being introduced to his majesty by the Duke of Marlborough.* On the 10th of January following, he was re-appointed Comptroller of his majesty's Works, from which office he had been dismissed by the late Queen ; † and (to finish at once with these Court appointments) on the 17th of August, 1716, he was made Surveyor of the Works at Greenwich Hospital. In pursuance of an act of Parliament, providing that the arrears of the debt incurred at Blenheim, before the discontinuance of the works in 1712, should be " liquidated out of the sum of £500,000, which had previously been granted for the payment of the debts on the civil list, and the arrears of the revenues belonging to her late majesty,"‡ a commission was appointed to investigate the

---

* Le Neve's *Pedigrees of the Knights*, &c., p. 511.

† A letter from Vanbrugh to the Mayor of Woodstock, dated January 25, 1713, and copied from the *Post Boy* of March 24, 1713, may be found in the *Gentleman's Magazine* of May, 1804. This letter, in which he refers, with generous indignation, to the persecution suffered by the Duke of Marlborough, appears to have been, at least in part, the cause of his dismissal from the place of Comptroller of the Works.

‡ Coxe's *Memoirs of John, Duke of Marlborough :* vol. iii., p. 636.

claims, and the creditors received, in January, 1715, about £16,000 in all, being one third part of the sum actually due. This was the last grant made by the Treasury for the work at Blenheim.

The vast undertaking was now resumed, under altered conditions, of which we possess a relation in Vanbrugh's own words. He writes : "As soon as the Duke of Marlborough arrived in England,* I received his commands to attend him at Blenheim, where he was pleased to tell me, that when the government took care to discharge him from the claim of the workmen for the debt in the Queen's time, he intended to finish the building at his own expense. And, accordingly, from that time forwards, he was pleased to give me his orders as occasion required, in things preparatory to it ; till, at last, the affair of the debt being adjusted with the Treasury and owned to be the Queen's, he gave me directions to set people actually to work, after having considered an estimate he ordered me to prepare of the charge, to finish the house, offices, bridges, and out-walls of courts and gardens, which amounted to fifty-four thousand pounds. . . . . I made no step without the Duke's knowledge while he was well ; and I made none without the Duchess's after he fell ill ; and was so far, I thought, from being in her ill opinion, that even the last time I waited on her and my Lord Duke at Blenheim, she showed no sort of dissatisfaction on anything I had done."†

Vanbrugh had little reason to complain of the Duchess's want of interest in the work : "she was pleas'd," he writes, subsequently, "to value no trouble she gave herself (or other people) in what related to that building." During the two years preceding the Duke's illness (a paralytic stroke, in May, 1716) she had

---

* August 1, 1714, the day of Queen Anne's death.

† From a paper written by Vanbrugh, and printed in Mrs. Thomson's *Memoirs of the Duchess of Marlborough :* vol. ii., *appendix.*

been on terms of civility, at least, with Vanbrugh, who was employed, on her behalf, in conducting the negociations which eventually led to the marriage of her grand-daughter, Lady Harriet Godolphin, with the Duke of Newcastle. This favourable turn had been due, possibly, to the Duke's influence. At all events, his malady had not long removed him from active life, before she threw off, now finally, the mask of friendship. Suddenly, and without, apparently, the smallest provocation, she discarded Vanbrugh's services in the affair of the marriage, entrusting the conduct of that business to a new agent, one Mr. Walters. Upon this indignity Vanbrugh sent her a respectful remonstrance, to which he had not yet received an answer, when he learned that to insult she was preparing to add injury, and that of the most grievous nature, in consigning to another person the completion of Blenheim. Irritated now beyond endurance, he wrote to the Duchess a curt and angry letter, commenting in strong terms upon her behaviour to him, and assuring her that he " would never trouble her more, unless the Duke of Marlborough recovered so far as to shelter him from such intolerable treatment." This letter, which is dated " Whitehall, Nov. 8, 1716," may be taken as marking the termination of Vanbrugh's services at Blenheim, though not of the annoyances to which those services had subjected him.

We have already seen that the final payment from the Treasury left two thirds of the old arrears still undischarged. The creditors applied, from time to time, to the Duke for a settlement, but to no purpose. At length, in Easter term, 1718, a suit was instituted by two of the contractors, in the Court of Exchequer, against John, Duke of Marlborough, and Sir John Vanbrugh, for the sum of £7314 : 16 : 4, due to them for stone supplied and for masons' work, together with the interest on that amount since the year 1710. The Duchess (for, owing to the Duke's infirmity, Vanbrugh regarded her as the real defendant) endeavoured, with a nice sense of honour, to turn upon the architect the entire burden of the debt; and Godolphin's warrant, produced by him, was disallowed by the Duke, or by those who acted on his behalf. Godolphin was no longer living, but it is satisfactory to find that the warrant was upheld by the Court. A decree was pronounced, absolving Vanbrugh, and rendering the Duke of Marlborough solely responsible for the debt; and this judgment was confirmed, on appeal, by the House of Lords. Vanbrugh writes, about this time, to his friend Tonson, the publisher : " I have the misfortune of losing, for I now see little hopes of ever getting it, near two thousand pounds, due to me for many years' service, plague, and trouble at Blenheim, which that *wicked woman* of Marlborough is so far from paying me, that, the Duke being sued by some of the workmen for work done there, she has tried to turn the due to them upon me, for which, I think, she ought to be hanged."

Foiled in her attempt upon the architect's purse, the angry Duchess now directed her attack against his reputation. She privately circulated an anonymous statement, entitled *The Case of the Duke of Marlborough and Sir John Vanbrugh*, by which it was endeavoured to discredit his evidence, and to malign his character. In the meantime, Vanbrugh had written, and was about printing, a *Justification of what he depos'd in the Duchess of Marlborough's late Tryal*, when the *Case* was put into his hands. To his *Justification* he accordingly appended a reply to the *Case*, which, he observes, contained "so much decent Language, fair stating of Facts, and right sound Reasoning from them, that one would almost swear it had been writ by a woman." He recapitulates the circumstances of the dispute, and prints letters from the Duchess to himself, proving that the Duke had given assurances that the payments should be continued. The *Case* concluded with a bitter taunt : " And if, at last, the Charge run into by Order of the Crown, must lie upon him [the Duke]; yet the Infamy of it must lie upon another, who was perhaps the only Architect in the World

capable of building such a House, and the only Friend in the
World capable of contriving to lay the Debt upon one to whom
he was so highly oblig'd." Upon this Vanbrugh retorts by
enumerating his obligations to the Duke. His recompense for
twelve years' service has been—many professions of obligation
and of resolution to reward him—" the Misfortune of being
turn'd out of his Place of Comptroller of the Works, and losing
that of Garter * by offending the Queen, on the Duke's
account "—not one Court favour obtained for him by the Duke,
" or any allowance or Present from his Grace ever made him
(except a Trifle, I believe he would not have him name)." "He
has been left," he continues, " to work upon his own Bottom, at
the tedious Treasury, for a Recompense for his Services ; where
through a tiresome Application of many Years, he has to this
Hour prevail'd for very little more than his necessary
Expenses, and instead of any Reward from the Duke, finds his
Authority for acting in his Service disclaim'd, and himself
thrown among the Workmen to be torn to pieces, for what his
Grace possesses and enjoys, in the midst of an immense
Fortune. These," he concludes, "these, and no other, are the
Friendships and the Obligations laid by the Duke of
Marlborough upon his Faithful and Zealous Servant, John
Vanbrugh."

The next step was an application on the part of the Duke to

---

* Queen Anne gave a reversionary grant of the office of Garter, principal
King of Arms, to John Anstis, on the 2nd of April, 1714. Garter, at that
date, was Sir Henry St. George, who died in August of the following year,
aged ninety. Anstis thereupon claimed the appointment, but, being in
prison on suspicion of Jacobitism, his claim was disregarded, and the
appointment was given to Vanbrugh, Oct. 26, 1715. Anstis, having
established his innocence, contested Vanbrugh's right, and the controversy
lasted until the 20th of April, 1718, when it was decided in favour of
Anstis, who was created Garter. (See *Noble.*) Vanbrugh continued to
hold the place of Clarenceux until Feb 9, 1726, when he disposed of it to
Knox Ward, Esq., for the sum of £2,000.

the Court of Chancery, "to compel the several creditors to submit to an examination of their claims."* A speedy settlement was now hardly to be hoped for. On the 16th of June, 1722, the Duke was acquitted of further responsibility—by death ; but still the suit dragged its slow length along. He left £50,000 to be expended by the Duchess, at the rate of £10,000 a year for five years, in completing the building. Writing again to Tonson, Vanbrugh states particulars of the Duke's enormous wealth ; "and yet this man could neither pay his workmen their bills, nor his architect his salary. He has given his widow—*may a Scotch ensign get her !*—ten thousand pounds a year to spoil Blenheim in her own way, and twelve thousand a year to keep herself clean and go to law."

Under the management of the Duchess the work was again resumed, and the building was finished within the stipulated period, and for half the allotted sum.† Her vindictiveness towards the architect did not hinder her from following his design, at the same time that, not content with denying him his due, she jealously excluded him from the scene of his long and thankless labour. A petty piece of insolent malice worthily capped the climax of indignities to which he had been subjected. He visited Woodstock in the company of his wife and the Countess of Carlisle, with some ladies of her family. "We staid," he writes, "two nights in Woodstock, but there was an order to the servants, under her Grace's own hand, not to let me enter Blenheim ; and, lest that should not mortify me enough, she having somehow learned that my wife was of the

---

* Coxe ; vol. iii., p. 637.

† Archdeacon Coxe estimates roughly, that Blenheim cost the nation £240,000, and the Duke and Duchess £60,000. The representatives of the Duke were finally made responsible for the arrears, "but we have not the means of tracing the progress of the investigation, or ascertaining the exact sums with which his estate was finally charged" (*Coxe*, vol. iii., p. 638).

company, sent an express the night before we came there, with
orders that if she came with the Castle Howard ladies, the
servants should not suffer her to see either house, gardens, or
even to enter the park ; so she was forced to sit all day long,
and keep me company at the inn."

A settlement was ultimately made in Vanbrugh's favour.   In
1725 he writes, with more emphasis than elegance : " I have
been forced into Chancery by that B. B. B. the Duchess of
Marlborough, where she has got an injunction upon me by her
friend the late good Chancellor [the Earl of Macclesfield], who
declared that I was never employed by the Duke, and therefore
had no demand upon his estate for my services at Blenheim.
Since my hands were thus tied up from trying by law to
recover my arrear, I have prevailed with Sir Robert Walpole to
help me in a scheme which I proposed to him, *by which I got
my money* in spite of the hussey's teeth.   My carrying this
point enrages her much, and the more because it is of
considerable weight in my small fortune, which she has
heartily endeavoured so to destroy as to throw me into an
English Bastile, there to finish my days as I began them in a
French one." *   The nature of the scheme referred to we have
no means of ascertaining, but it is some small satisfaction to
find that, even at the eleventh hour, Vanbrugh was relieved
from this miserable aggravation of greater hardships—of
disappointed hopes and the memory of services embittered by
insult and ingratitude.

It is no part of our present plan to enter upon an investigation of the merits or defects of Vanbrugh's architectural works.
They have been frequently censured, but frequently, also,
applauded : no worse a judge than Sir Joshua Reynolds has
spoken in terms of warm commendation of the design and

---

* Alluding to his imprisonment in the Bastile when a young man.

picturesque effect of Blenheim.* I shall conclude this section with the ensuing apt remarks upon some of the principal features of that famous building. "It appears to me that at Blenheim Vanbrugh conceived and executed a very bold and difficult design ; that of uniting in one building the beauty and magnificence of Grecian architecture, the picturesqueness of the Gothic, and the massive grandeur of a castle ; and that in spite of the many faults with which he is very justly reproached, he has formed, in a style truly his own, a well-combined whole, a mansion worthy of a great prince and warrior. His first point seems to have been massiveness, as the foundation of grandeur. Then, to prevent that mass from being a lump, he has made various bold projections of various heights, which from different points serve as foregrounds to the main building. And lastly, having probably been struck with the variety of outline against the sky in many Gothic and other ancient buildings, he has raised, on the top of that part where the slanting roof begins in many houses of the Italian style, a number of decorations of various characters. These, if not new in themselves, have at least been applied and combined by him in a new and peculiar manner ; and the union of them gives a surprising splendour and magnificence, as well as variety, to the summit of that princely edifice." †

VII.

THE last years of Vanbrugh's life were devoted mainly to architectural employments, and the performance of his official duties as Comptroller of the Works. For himself he built two or three houses, besides the " goose-pie " house at Whitehall.

---

* In his thirteenth Discourse to the students of the Royal Academy.
† Sir Uvedale Price : *Essays on the Picturesque*, 1798 : *An Essay on Architecture and Buildings as connected with Scenery.*

" His country residence," says Noble, " was Vanbrugh-Fields at Greenwich, where he built two seats, one called the Bastile, standing on Maize, or Maze Hill, on the east side of the Park. Lady Vanbrug, his relict, sold it to Lord Trelawny, who made it his residence : the name was taken from the French prison of which it was a model. His other house, built in the same kind of style, is called the Mince-pie house, now [1804] possessed and occupied by Edward Vanbrugh, Esq."*

Moreover, on a piece of ground which he purchased at Esher, in Surrey, he erected a low brick house. This property, how-ever, he sold to Thomas Pelham, Earl of Clare (created Duke of Newcastle in 1718), who added largely to the estate, and raised thereon a mansion, which he called, from his title, Claremont.†

Vanbrugh's correspondence with the Duke of Newcastle, which is preserved in the British Museum, shows him to have been frequently employed by that nobleman ; building at Claremont, altering Nottingham Castle for his Grace's residence, or otherwise engaged in his service. Occasionally we find him at Castle Howard, on a visit to his old friend and patron, the Earl of Carlisle. From Castle Howard is dated, the 25th of December, 1718, the letter which contains the first hint of his approaching marriage.

" Your Grace's Letter to meet you at Nottingham to-morrow," he writes, " I found here yesterday. And had been three days getting from thence to York, through such difficulty as the Stage Coach cou'd not pass, which I left overset and quite disabled upon the way. There has now fallen a Snow up to one's neck, to mend it, wch may possibly fix me here as long as it did at the Bath this time two years : wch was no less than five Weeks. In short, 'tis so bloody Cold, I have almost a mind to marry to keep myself warm, And if I do, I'm sure it will be a Wiser

---

* *History of the College of Arms*, p. 356.
† Manning and Bray's *History of Surrey*, vol. ii., p. 742.

thing than your Grace has done, if you have been at Notting-ham."*

The last sentence needs a few words of explanation. Vanbrugh had been anxious that the Duke should not visit Nottingham until the alterations at the castle had been carried out, lest, by seeing it in its unfinished condition, and, especially, under the gloom of a winter aspect, he should conceive some disgust at the place. The Duke paid his visit, nevertheless, as we learn by a subsequent letter, but without the ill consequences apprehended by the architect.

I have already mentioned Vanbrugh's wife. This lady was Henrietta Maria, eldest child of Lieutenant-colonel James Yarburgh, of Snaith Hall, near York. The family was of some consideration. Henrietta's grandfather, Sir Thomas Yarburgh, of Snaith Hall, was Member of Parliament for Pontefract in 1685 and 1688. His eldest son, James, who was born in 1664, was godson to the Duke of York, and one of the royal pages. He entered the army, where he rose to the rank of lieutenant-colonel of horse, and aide-de-camp to the Duke of Marlborough. This James married, on the 31st of October, 1692, Ann, daughter and co-heir of Thomas Hesketh of Heslington : their first child, Henrietta Maria, was baptized, on the 13th of October of the following year, at the church of St. Lawrence, in York.†

Vanbrugh appears to have been acquainted with the Yarburgh family for some years before his marriage. A letter written from York, about November, 1713, by that very lively young woman, Lady Mary Wortley Montagu, contains an amusing picture of his love-making.

---

* British Museum. Add. MSS. 33,064.

† These details respecting the Yarburgh family are taken from C. B. Robinson's *History of the Priory and Peculiar of Snaith :* London and York, 1861.

" I can't forbear entertaining you with our York lovers.
(Strange monsters, you'll think, love being as much forced up
here as melons.) In the first form of these creatures is even
Mr. Vanbrugh. Heaven, no doubt, compassionating our
dulness, has inspired him with a passion that makes us all
ready to die with laughing : 'tis credibly reported that he is
endeavouring at the honourable state of matrimony, and vows
to lead a sinful life no more. Whether pure holiness inspires
his mind, or dotage turns his brain, is hard to find. 'Tis
certain he keeps Mondays and Thursdays market (assembly-day)
constant ; and for those that don't regard worldly muck,
there's extraordinary good choice indeed. I believe last
Monday there were two hundred pieces of woman's flesh (fat
and lean) : but you know Van's taste was always odd : his
inclination to ruins* has given him a fancy for Mrs.
Yarborough : he sighs and ogles that it would do your
heart good to see him ; and she is not a little pleased, in so
small a proportion of men amongst such a number of women,
a whole man should fall to her share.—My dear, adieu. My
service to Mr. Congreve." †

The marriage took place at the church of St. Lawrence,
York, on the 14th of January, 1719. ‡ The honeymoon was of
brief duration, for within a week of the marriage we find
Vanbrugh back at Nottingham on the Duke of Newcastle's
business. In a letter to the Duke, dated "Nottingham,
January the 24th," after recounting what order he has taken
with regard to the fitting up of the castle, he continues, in the

---

* The reader must put his own construction upon this expression.
At the date of this letter, Henrietta Yarburgh was twenty years of age.

† *Letters and Works of Lady Mary Wortley Montagu*, vol. i, pp. 83-4.
Bohn's edition, 1887.

‡ Robinson's *History of Snaith*, p. 77.

strain of exaggerated compliment which was then a matter of course in addressing persons of quality :

"I have no care now left, but to see the Duchess of Newcastle* as well pleas'd with it as your Grace is. I hope she won't have the less expectation from my judgment in chusing a Seat, from my having chosen a Wife, whose principal merit in my Eye, has been some small distant Shadow of those valuable Qualifications in her, your Grace has formerly with so much pleasure heard me talk of. The honour she likewise has, of being pretty nearly related to the Duchess, gives me the more hopes I may not have been mistaken. If I am, 'tis better however to make a Blunder towards the end of one's Life, than at the beginning of it. But I hope all will be well ; it can't at least be worse than most of my neighbours, which every modest man ought to be content with : And so I'm easy." †

An amusing reference to Tonson, the publisher, occurs in a postscript : " Jacob will be fright'ned out of his Witts and his Religion too, when he hears I'm gone at last. If he is still in France, he'll certainly give himself to God, for fear he shou'd now be ravish'd by a Gentlewoman. I was the last man left between him and Ruin."

In spite of the great disparity of age between husband and wife, the marriage appears to have been a happy one. Three children were born to them,‡ of whom two, however, lived not to be baptized. I find in one of Vanbrugh's letters to the Duke of Newcastle, a brief reference to his first-born child. In 1719, building was still going on at Claremont under his direction, and he mentions, in a letter of August the 6th, his intention of

---

* The Duchess was Lady Harriet Godolphin, whose marriage Vanbrugh had been instrumental in promoting. See *ante*, p. lxv.

† Add. MSS., 33,064.

‡ Le Neve, p. 512.

taking his wife down to Claremont for two or three days. But on the eleventh of August he writes : " I have been two days at Claremount, but not en Famille, a Bit of a Girle popping into the world three months before its time."

Besides this girl, and a son named Charles, Le Neve mentions a second son, who died without baptism. Of Charles Vanbrugh, the poet's son and heir, all that is told is, that he joined the army as an ensign in the second regiment of footguards, served in Flanders, and got his death-wound in the battle of Fontenoy, April the 30th, 1745.* The British Museum possesses an autograph letter of his, addressed to the Duke of Newcastle, and dated, "From the Head Quarters at Avelgem, Oct. 3, 1744, *N.S.*"† The young man was about purchasing a lieutenancy, when an older ensign, the brother of Lord Cathcart, made offers for the same appointment, and, by his superior interest, seemed likely to carry it. Young Vanbrugh thereupon writes to the Duke to solicit his support in the matter. In the same volume is preserved a letter of Lady Vanbrugh's to the Duke, dated Greenwich, September the 30th, on the same business. How the matter ended, we know not, but the letters, at least, are a proof that the Duke's kindness was continued to the widow and son of his friend.

Sir John Vanbrugh died, of quinsy, it is said, at his house at Whitehall, on the 26th of March, 1726, and was buried in the family vault beneath the church of St. Stephen. By his will, which is dated August the 30th, 1725, he left small legacies to his unmarried sisters, Mary, Victoria, and Robina; to his brothers, Charles and Philip; his nieces, Elizabeth and Robina Vanbrugh ; a married sister, and her daughter. To his

---

* Noble's words are, "a battle fought near Tournay, in 1745." The " Captain Charles Vanbrugh," whose burial at St. Stephen's was registered on the 9th of November, 1740, was possibly Sir John Vanbrugh's brother.

† Add. MSS. 32,703.

f 2

son Charles he bequeathed all his houses at Greenwich, together with the lease of the ground on which they stood, the tenement and vaults under and adjoining the Opera House in the Hay-market, and one thousand pounds in money. This bequest was to take effect upon Charles Vanbrugh's coming of age: in the meantime, the income accruing from the property was to be applied to the boy's education, at the discretion of his mother, who was appointed sole executrix. There is one codicil to the will, dated August the 31st, 1725. By this codicil, Charles Vanbrugh was empowered, on attaining the age of fifteen, to bequeath by will the sum of one thousand pounds; but in the event of his death before coming of age, the property bequeathed him was to go to his mother, with the exception of the house at Greenwich then occupied by Sir John Vanbrugh's brother Philip, and the two " white towers " adjoining it. The house, in this event, was to become the property of Philip, while the two towers passed to the testator's sisters, Victoria and Robina.

From the fact that no provision is made by the will for Lady Vanbrugh, it must be inferred that an independency had already been secured to her by the marriage-settlements. Her own will, which is dated June the 15th, 1769, shows her to have been in very comfortable circumstances ; and the house at Whitehall, which is not mentioned in Sir John Vanbrugh's will, formed part of the property bequeathed by her. She died, in the eighty-third year of her age, on the 26th of April, 1776, and was interred in the vault which, half a century before, had received the remains of her distinguished husband.*

---

* I copy here the exact words of the entries, in the register of St. Stephen's, Walbrook, which record the burial of Sir John Vanbrugh and his wife.—"March 31 [1726] was buried Sr. John Vanbrough in ye North Isle."—"May 3d. [1776] Was Buried Dame Henrietta Maria Vanbrugh in the Vanbrugh's Familey Vault in the North Ile. brought from Whitehall aged 84 years."

Of Vanbrugh's character, all that we are able to gather from
stray remarks, and the hints furnished by his own writings, gives
us an agreeable impression.   That he was generous and good-
natured is beyond dispute, nor does he seem to have had
an enemy, except the Duchess of Marlborough.   He was a
Whig in politics, and a member of the famous Kit-cat club :
" Garth, Vanbrugh, and Congreve, were the three most honest-
hearted, real good men of the poetical members of the Kit-cat
club," said Pope.*   As to his wit in conversation, nothing can
be more striking than the testimony of Cibber, who declares
that the most entertaining scenes of his plays " seem'd to be
no more than his common Conversation committed to Paper."

He left an unfinished comedy—*A Journey to London*—which,
had it been completed by the hand which began it, would
certainly have ranked high among his masterpieces.   Besides
the works already mentioned, he published but one piece—the
following short copy of verses, which originally appeared in the
Fifth Part of Miscellany Poems, published by Tonson in 1704.

To a LADY *more Cruel than Fair.   By Mr.* VANBROOK.

Why d'ye with such Disdain refuse
    An humble Lover's Plea ?
Since Heav'n denies you Pow'r to chuse,
    You ought to value me.

Ungrateful Mistress of a Heart,
    Which I so freely gave ;
Tho' weak your Bow, tho' blunt your Dart,
    I soon resign'd your Slave.

Nor was I weary of your Reign,
    Till you a Tyrant grew,
And seem'd regardless of my Pain,
    As Nature seem'd of you.

* Spence's *Ancedotes.*

When thousands with unerring Eyes
Your Beauty would decry,
What Graces did my Love devise,
To give their Truths the Lie?

To ev'ry Grove I told your Charms,
In you my Heav'n I plac'd,
Proposing Pleasures in your Arms,
Which none but I cou'd taste.

For me t' admire, at such a rate,
So damn'd a Face, will prove
You have as little Cause to hate,
As I had Cause to Love.

NOTE.

THE text of Vanbrugh's plays has remained substantially unaltered throughout the editions. Such variations as occur are, almost without exception, either differences of punctuation, often due to mere carelessness, or verbal changes of the slightest importance. In such cases, I have usually relied upon the text of the first editions, amending the punctuation where necessary, and correcting occasional misprints. I have partly followed Leigh Hunt in supplying, here and there, the omissions of the original text in regard to the headings of scenes, and, in a few instances, the indications of exits or entrances. The names of the actors who took part in the first performance of each play, are here given, facing the *dramatis personæ*, as in the original editions.

THE RELAPSE.

The Relapse, the first in order of performance of Vanbrugh's comedies, was written in the spring of 1696, as a sequel to Colley Cibber's play of *Love's Last Shift; or, The Fool in Fashion.* It was produced at the Theatre Royal, Drury Lane, in December, 1696, and published the same month, with the date 1697 on the title-page. Yet it was entered at Stationers' Hall by Richard Wellington, the bookseller, on the 21st of September, 1697.* The first edition is in 4to, and has the following title-page: " *The Relapse; or, Virtue in Danger: Being the Sequel of The Fool in Fashion, a Comedy. Acted at the Theatre-Royal in Drury-lane; Printed for Samuel Briscoe at the corner of Charles-street in Russel-street Covent-garden.* 1697."

The circumstances connected with the production of this play have already been recounted in the general introduction: a few details may be added concerning the relation between Vanbrugh's comedy and *Love's Last Shift.*

Cibber's *Loveless* is a dissolute scamp, who deserts his

---

* Wellington's name appears on the title-page of *The Relapse*, in the 4to edition of 1698: " *London, Printed for S. B. and Sold by R. Wellington, at the Lute, in St. Paul's Church-yard,* 1698." *The Relapse* is the only play of Vanbrugh's which I find entered at Stationers' Hall.

The British Museum does not possess copies of the first editions of *The Relapse, Æsop,* and *The Mistake.* For the loan of these plays, as well as for many other kindnesses, I am indebted to Mr. Edmund Gosse.

B 2

innocent wife, and wanders for eight years in pursuit of pleasure ; returning at last, penniless, to receive her forgiveness, and to enjoy the treasure of her unshaken constancy. The play ends conventionally, with Amanda's happiness, and the supposed reformation of the prodigal ; but, in point of fact, a character such as Loveless would be incapable of true reformation, and, in depicting his relapse, Vanbrugh has given but a natural sequel to the fable of his predecessor.

In both comedies the capital part is that of the fop. In Cibber's, Sir Novelty Fashion is described as " One that Heaven intended for a man ; but the whole business of his Life is, to make the World believe he is of another species. A Thing that affects mightily to ridicule himself, only to give others a kind of Necessity of praising him."

The following fragment is extracted from one of the best scenes of *The Fool in Fashion*, that the reader may, with entire justice to Cibber, compare the character of Sir Novelty with that of Lord Foppington. The persons introduced are Narcissa, Hillaria, and Sir Novelty. It should be premised that Worthy is suitor to Hillaria, to whom Sir Novelty makes love at the beginning of the scene. He now turns to her sister.

Sir Nov. Pray, Madam, how do I look to-day ?—What, cursedly ? I'll warrant ; with a more hellish Complexion than a stale Actress in a Morning.—I don't know, Madam,—'tis true—the Town does talk of me, indeed ;—but the Dev'l take me, in my mind, I am a very ugly Fellow !

Nar. Now you are too severe, Sir *Novelty !*

Sir Nov. Not I, burn me :—For Heaven's sake deal freely with me, Madam; and if you can, tell me—one tolerable thing about me!

Hil. (*Aside.*) 'Twould pose me, I'm sure.

Nar. Oh! Sir *Novelty*, this is unanswerable; 'tis hard to know the brightest part of a diamond.

Sir Nov. You'll make me blush, stop my Vitals, Madam.—(*Aside.*) I'gad, I always said she was a Woman of Sense. Strike me dumb, I am in Love with her! I'll try her farther.—But, Madam, is it possible I may vie with Mr. *Worthy?*—Not that he is any Rival of mine, Madam; for, I can assure you, my Inclinations lie where, perhaps, your Ladyship little thinks.

Hil. (*Aside.*) So! now I am rid of him.

Sir Nov. But pray tell me, Madam; for I really love a severe Critick : I am sure you must believe he has a more happy Genius in Dress : For my part, I am but a Sloven.

Nar. He a Genius! insufferable! Why, he dresses worse than a Captain of the Militia! . . . . He's a mere *Valet de Chambre* to all Fashion; and never is in any, till his betters have left them off.

Sir Nov. Nay, Ged, now I must laugh; for the Dev'l take me, if I did not meet him, not above a Fortnight ago, in a Coat with Buttons no bigger than Nutmegs.

Hil. There, I must confess, you out-do him, Sir *Novelty*.

Sir Nov. Oh, dear Madam, why mine are not above three Inches diameter! . . .

THE PREFACE.

To go about to excuse half the defects this abortive brat is come into the world with, would be to provoke the town with a long useless preface, when 'tis, I doubt, sufficiently soured already by a tedious play.

I do therefore (with all the humility of a repenting sinner) confess, it wants everything—but length; and in that, I hope, the severest critic will be pleased to acknowledge I have not been wanting. But my modesty will sure atone for everything, when the world shall know it is so great, I am even to this day insensible of those two shining graces in the play (which some part of the town is pleased to compliment me with)—blasphemy and bawdy.

For my part, I cannot find 'em out. If there were any obscene expressions upon the stage, here they are in the print; for I have dealt fairly, I have not sunk a syllable that could (though by racking of mysteries) be ranged under that head; and yet I believe with a steady faith, there is not one woman of a real reputation in town, but when she has read it impartially over in her closet, will find it so innocent, she'll think it no affront to her prayer-book, to lay it upon the same shelf. So to them (with all manner of deference) I entirely refer my cause; and I'm confident they'll justify me against those pretenders to good manners, who, at the same time, have so little respect for the ladies, they would extract a bawdy jest from an ejaculation, to put 'em out of countenance. But I expect to have these well-bred persons always my enemies, since I'm sure I shall never write anything lewd enough to make 'em my friends.

As for the saints (your thorough-paced ones, I mean, with screwed faces and wry mouths) I despair of them, for they are friends to nobody. They love nothing but their altars and themselves. They have too much zeal to have any charity : they make debauches in piety, as sinners do in wine; and are as quarrelsome in their religion, as other people are in their drink ; so I hope nobody will mind what they say. But if any man (with flat plod shoes, a little band, greasy hair, and a dirty face, who is wiser than I, at the expense of being forty years older) happens to be offended at a story of a cock and a bull, and a priest and a bull-dog, I beg his pardon with all my heart; which, I hope, I shall obtain, by eating my words, and making this public recantation. I do therefore, for his satisfaction, acknowledge I lied, when I said, they never quit their hold; for in that little time I have lived in the world, I thank God I have seen 'em forced to it more than once; but next time I'll speak with more caution and truth, and only say, they have very good teeth.

If I have offended any honest gentlemen of the town, whose friendship or good word is worth the having, I am very sorry for it ; I hope they'll correct me as gently as they can, when they consider I have had no other design, in running a very great risk, than to divert (if possible) some part of their spleen, in spite of their wives and their taxes.

One word more about the bawdy, and I have done. I

own the first night this thing was acted, some indecencies had like to have happened, but 'twas not my fault.

The fine gentleman of the play,* drinking his mistress's health in Nantes brandy, from six in the morning to the time he waddled on upon the stage in the evening, had toasted himself up to such a pitch of vigour, I confess I once gave Amanda for gone, and I am since (with all due respect to Mrs. Rogers) very sorry she scaped ; for I am confident a certain lady (let no one take it to herself that's handsome) who highly blames the play, for the barrenness of the conclusion, would then have allowed it a very natural close.

---

* Powell, who acted the part of Worthy.

DRAMATIS PERSONÆ.

MEN.

Sir *Novelty Fashion*, newly created Lord *Foppington*	Mr. *Cibber*.
Young *Fashion*, his Brother	Mrs. *Kent*.*
Loveless, Husband to *Amanda*	Mr. *Verbruggen*.
Worthy, a Gentleman of the Town	Mr. *Powell*.
Sir *Tunbelly Clumsey*, a Country Gentleman...	Mr. *Bullock*.
Sir *John Friendly*, his Neighbour ...	Mr. *Mills*.
Coupler, a Match-maker	Mr. *Johnson*.
Bull, Chaplain to Sir *Tunbelly*	Mr. *Simson*.
Syringe, a Surgeon...	Mr. *Haynes*.
Lory, Servant to young *Fashion*	Mr. *Dogget*.

Shoemaker, Tailor, Periwig-maker, &c.

WOMEN.

Amanda, Wife to *Loveless*	Mrs. *Rogers*.
Berinthia, her Cousin, a young Widow	Mrs. *Verbruggen*.
Miss *Hoyden*, a great Fortune, Daughter to Sir *Tunbelly* ...	Mrs. *Cross*.
Nurse, her Governante	Mrs. *Powell*.

[SCENE.—Sometimes in *London*, sometimes in the Country.]

---

* "Mrs. Kent" is the reading of the earliest editions—those of 1697, 1698, and 1708 : her name also stands to the part of young Fashion in the Drury-lane play-bill for October 26, 1708, as Genest informs us. In some later editions of *The Relapse* the name is altered to "Mr. Kent," but there is no doubt that the original reading is the correct one. An actress performing the part of a young man was by no means so rare a spectacle at this time that we need hesitate to accept it. Of Mrs. Mountfort—by her second marriage, Mrs. Verbruggen, the Berinthia of *The Relapse*—Cibber writes : "People were so fond of seeing her a Man, that when the part of *Bays*, in the *Rehearsal*, had, for some time, lain dormant, she was desired to take it up, which I have seen her act with all the true, coxcombly Spirit, and Humour, that the Sufficiency of the Character required." Mrs. Kent, though not a leading lady, habitually played good parts : Mr. Kent, for there *was* such an actor, appeared in such characters as "one of the Ruffians in *King Lear*," and was not at all likely to be entrusted with such a part as that of young Fashion. See *Genest*, II., p. 408.

FIRST PROLOGUE.

SPOKEN BY MISS CROSS.*

LADIES, this Play in too much haste was writ,
To be o'ercharg'd with either plot or wit ;
'Twas got, conceiv'd, and born in six weeks' space,
And wit, you know, 's as slow in growth—as grace.
Sure it can ne'er be ripen'd to your taste ;
I doubt 'twill prove, our author bred too fast :
For mark 'em well, who with the Muses marry,
They rarely do conceive, but they miscarry.
'Tis the hard fate of those who are big with rhyme,
Still to be brought to bed before their time.   10
Of our late poets Nature few has made ;
The greatest part—are only so by trade.
Still want of something brings the scribbling fit ;
For want of money some of 'em have writ,
And others do't, you see—for want of wit.
Honour, they fancy, summons 'em to write,
So out they lug in wresty Nature's spite,
As some of you spruce beaux do—when you fight.
Yet let the ebb of wit be ne'er so low,
Some glimpse of it a man may hope to show,   20

---

* The actress who performed the part of Miss Hoyden. The " Miss "
prefixed to her name, instead of the customary " Mrs.," implies that
she was a very young girl. Her first appearance, recorded by Genest,
was in the part of Altesidora, in Durfey's *Don Quixote*, Part III., early
in 1696.

Upon a theme so ample—as a beau.
So, howsoe'er true courage may decay,
Perhaps there's not one smock-face here to-day,
But's bold as Cæsar—to attack a play.
Nay, what's yet more, with an undaunted face,
To do the thing with more heroic grace,
'Tis six to four y' attack the strongest place.
You are such Hotspurs in this kind of venture,
Where there's no breach, just there you needs must enter :
But be advised—   30
E'en give the hero and the critic o'er,
For Nature sent you on another score ;—
She form'd her beau, for nothing but her whore.

PROLOGUE ON THE THIRD DAY.

SPOKEN BY MRS. VERBRUGGEN.

APOLOGIES for Plays, experience shows,
Are things almost as useless—as the beaux.
Whate'er we say (like them) we neither move
Your friendship, pity, anger, nor your love.
'Tis interest turns the globe : let us but find
The way to please you, and you'll soon be kind :
But to expect, you'd for our sakes approve,
Is just as though you for their sakes should love ;
And that, we do confess, we think a task,
Which (though they may impose) we never ought to ask. 10
    This is an age, where all things we improve,
But, most of all, the art of making love.
In former days, women were only won
By merit, truth, and constant service done ;
But lovers now are much more expert grown ;
They seldom wait, t' approach by tedious form ;
They're for dispatch, for taking you by storm :
Quick are their sieges, furious are their fires,
Fierce their attacks, and boundless their desires.
Before the Play's half ended, I'll engage   20
To show you beaux come crowding on the stage,
Who with so little pains have always sped,
They'll undertake to look a lady dead.

How have I shook, and trembling stood with awe,
When here, behind the scenes, I've seen 'em draw
—A comb; that dead-doing weapon to the heart,
And turn each powder'd hair into a dart !*
When I have seen 'em sally on the stage,
Dress'd to the war, and ready to engage,
I've mourn'd your destiny—yet more their fate,   30
To think, that after victories so great,
It should so often prove their hard mishap
To sneak into a lane—and get a clap.
But, hush ! they're here already ; I'll retire,
And leave 'em to you ladies to admire.
They'll show you twenty thousand airs and graces,
They'll entertain you with their soft grimaces,
Their snuff-box, awkward bows,—and ugly faces.
In short, they're after all so much your friends,
That lest the Play should fail the author's ends,   40
They have resolv'd to make you some amends.
Between each act (perform'd by nicest rules)
They'll treat you—with an Interlude of fools :
Of which, that you may have the deeper sense,
The entertainment's—at their own expense.

---

* To comb their wigs in public was a common practice of gentlemen
in the seventeenth century. We find occasional allusions to this odd
custom in the dramatists of the time. Thus in *The Parson's Wedding*,
by Thomas Killegrew (Act I, Scene 3): "Enter Jack Constant, Will
Sad, Jolly, and a Footman : they comb their heads and talk." And
in the prologue to the second part of Dryden's *Conquest of Granada :*

" But, as when Vizard-Mask appears in Pit,
   Straight ev'ry Man, who thinks himself a Wit,
   Perks up ; and, managing his Comb with Grace,
   With his white Wigg sets off his Nut-brown Face."

THE RELAPSE;

OR, VIRTUE IN DANGER.

ACT I.

SCENE I.—*A Room in* LOVELESS'S *Country House.*

Enter LOVELESS *reading.*

Love. How true is that philosophy, which says
Our heaven is seated in our minds !
Through all the roving pleasures of my youth,
(Where nights and days seem'd all consum'd in joy,
Where the false face of luxury
Display'd such charms,
As might have shaken the most holy hermit,
And made him totter at his altar,)
I never knew one moment's peace like this.
Here, in this little soft retreat,   10
My thoughts unbent from all the cares of life,
Content with fortune,
Eas'd from the grating duties of dependence,
From envy free, ambition under foot,
The raging flame of wild destructive lust
Reduc'd to a warm pleasing fire of lawful love,

My life glides on, and all is well within.

Enter AMANDA.

How does the happy cause of my content,

[*Meeting her kindly.*

My dear Amanda?
You find me musing on my happy state,   20
And full of grateful thoughts to Heaven, and you.

   Aman.   Those grateful offerings Heaven can't receive
With more delight than I do :
Would I could share with it as well
The dispensations of its bliss !
That I might search its choicest favours out,
And shower 'em on your head for ever.

   Love.   The largest boons that Heaven thinks fit to grant,
To things it has decreed shall crawl on earth,
Are in the gift of women form'd like you.   30
Perhaps, when time shall be no more,
When the aspiring soul shall take its flight,
And drop this pond'rous lump of clay behind it,
It may have appetites we know not of,
And pleasures as refin'd as its desires—
But till that day of knowledge shall instruct me,
The utmost blessing that my thought can reach,

[*Taking her in his arms.*

Is folded in my arms, and rooted in my heart.

   Aman.   There let it grow for ever !

   Love.   Well said, Amanda—let it be for ever—   40
Would Heaven grant that—

   Aman.   'Twere all the heaven I'd ask.
But we are clad in black mortality,

And the dark curtain of eternal night
At last must drop between us.
 Love.   It must :
That mournful separation we must see.
A bitter pill it is to all ; but doubles its ungrateful taste,
When lovers are to swallow it.
 Aman. Perhaps that pain may only be my lot,
You possibly may be exempted from it.
Men find out softer ways to quench their fires.   50
 Love. Can you then doubt my constancy, Amanda ?
You'll find 'tis built upon a steady basis—
The rock of reason now supports my love,
On which it stands so fix'd,
The rudest hurricane of wild desire
Would, like the breath of a soft slumbering babe,
Pass by, and never shake it.
 Aman. Yet still 'tis safer to avoid the storm ;
The strongest vessels, if they put to sea,
May possibly be lost.   60
Would I could keep you here, in this calm port, for ever !
Forgive the weakness of a woman,
I am uneasy at your going to stay so long in town ;
I know its false insinuating pleasures ;
I know the force of its delusions ;
I know the strength of its attacks ;
I know the weak defence of nature ;
I know you are a man—and I—a wife.
 Love. You know then all that needs to give you rest,
For wife's the strongest claim that you can urge. 70
When you would plead your title to my heart,
On this you may depend. Therefore be calm,

          C

Banish your fears, for they
Are traitors to your peace : beware of 'em,
They are insinuating busy things
That gossip to and fro,
And do a world of mischief where they come.
But you shall soon be mistress of 'em all ;
I'll aid you with such arms for their destruction,
They never shall erect their heads again.   80
You know the business is indispensable, that obliges me to
  go for London ; and you have no reason, that I know of,
  to believe I'm glad of the occasion. For my honest
  conscience is my witness,
I have found a due succession of such charms
In my retirement here with you,
I have never thrown one roving thought that way ;
But since, against my will, I'm dragg'd once more
To that uneasy theatre of noise,
I am resolv'd to make such use on't,   90
As shall convince you 'tis an old cast mistress,
Who has been so lavish of her favours,
She's now grown bankrupt of her charms,
And has not one allurement left to move me.
    Aman.   Her bow, I do believe, is grown so weak,
Her arrows (at this distance) cannot hurt you ;
But in approaching 'em, you give 'em strength.
The dart that has not far to fly, will put
The best of armour to a dangerous trial.
    Love.   That trial past, and y'are at ease for ever ;   100
When you have seen the helmet prov'd,
You'll apprehend no more for him that wears it.
Therefore to put a lasting period to your fears,

I am resolv'd, this once, to launch into temptation :
I'll give you an essay of all my virtues ;
My former boon companions of the bottle
Shall fairly try what charms are left in wine :
I'll take my place amongst 'em,
They shall hem me in,
Sing praises to their god, and drink his glory :   110
Turn wild enthusiasts for his sake,
And beasts to do him honour :
Whilst I, a stubborn atheist,
Sullenly look on,
Without one reverend glass to his divinity.
That for my temperance,
Then for my constancy—
  Aman.   Ay, there take heed.
  Love.   Indeed the danger's small.
  Aman.   And yet my fears are great.
  Love.   Why are you so timorous ?
  Aman.   Because you are so bold.
  Love.   My courage should disperse your apprehensions. 120
  Aman.   My apprehensions should alarm your courage.
  Love.   Fy, fy, Amanda ! it is not kind thus to distrust me
  Aman.   And yet my fears are founded on my love.
  Love.   Your love then is not founded as it ought;
For if you can believe 'tis possible
I should again relapse to my past follies,
I must appear to you a thing
Of such an undigested composition,
That but to think of me with inclination,
Would be a weakness in your taste,   130
Your virtue scarce could answer.

Aman. 'Twould be a weakness in my tongue,
My prudence could not answer,
If I should press you farther with my fears ;
I'll therefore trouble you no longer with ''em.

Love.   Nor shall they trouble you much longer,
A little time shall show you they were groundless :
This winter shall be the fiery trial of my virtue ;
Which, when it once has pass'd,
You'll be convinc'd 'twas of no false allay,   140
There all your cares will end.

Aman.   Pray Heaven they may.

                              [*Exeunt, hand in hand.*

SCENE II.—*Whitehall.*

Enter Young FASHION, LORY, *and* Waterman.

Fash.   Come, pay the waterman, and take the portmantle.

Lory.   Faith, sir, I think the waterman had as good take
the portmantle, and pay himself.

Fash.   Why, sure there's something left in't !

Lory.   But a solitary old waistcoat, upon honour, sir.

Fash.   Why, what's become of the blue coat, sirrah ?

Lory.   Sir, 'twas eaten at Gravesend ; the reckoning
came to thirty shillings, and your privy purse was worth but
two half-crowns.   10

Fash.   'Tis very well.

Wat.   Pray, master, will you please to dispatch me ?

Fash.   Ay, here, a—canst thou change me a guinea ?

Lory. [*Aside.*]   Good !

Wat. Change a guinea, master ! Ha ! ha ! your honour's pleased to compliment.

Fash. Egad, I don't know how I shall pay thee then, for I have nothing but gold about me.

Lory. [*Aside.*]   Hum, hum !

Fash. What dost thou expect, friend ?   20

Wat. Why, master, so far against wind and tide is richly worth half a piece.*

Fash. Why, faith, I think thou art a good conscionable fellow. Egad, I begin to have so good an opinion of thy honesty, I care not if I leave my portmantle with thee, till I send thee thy money.

Wat. Ha ! God bless your honour; I should be as willing to trust you, master, but that you are, as a man may say, a stranger to me, and these are nimble times ; there are a great many sharpers stirring.—[*Taking up the portmantle.*] Well, master, when your worship sends the money, your portmantle shall be forthcoming ; my name's Tug ; my wife keeps a brandy-shop in Drab-Alley, at Wapping.

Fash. Very well; I'll send for't to-morrow.   34

[*Exit* Waterman.

Lory. So.—Now, sir, I hope you'll own yourself a happy man, you have outlived all your cares.

Fash. How so, sir ?

Lory. Why, you have nothing left to take care of.

Fash. Yes, sirrah, I have myself and you to take care of still.

Lory. Sir, if you could but prevail with somebody else to do that for you, I fancy we might both fare the better for't.

---

* " Piece.   A coin worth twenty-two shillings."—Wright.

Fash.   Why, if thou canst tell me where to apply myself,
I have at present so little money and so much humility
about me, I don't know but I may follow a fool's advice.

Lory.   Why then, sir, your fool advises you to lay aside
all animosity, and apply to sir Novelty, your elder brother.

Fash.   Damn my elder brother !

Lory.   With all my heart ; but get him to redeem your
annuity, however.   50

Fash.   My annuity ! 'Sdeath, he's such a dog, he would
not give his powder-puff to redeem my soul.

Lory.   Look you, sir, you must wheedle him, or you
must starve.

Fash.   Look you, sir, I will neither wheedle him, nor
starve.

Lory.   Why, what will you do then ?

Fash.   I'll go into the army.

Lory.   You can't take the oaths ; you are a Jacobite.

Fash.   Thou may'st as well say I can't take orders
because I'm an atheist.   61

Lory.   Sir, I ask your pardon ; I find I did not know the
strength of your conscience so well as I did the weakness of
your purse.

Fash.   Methinks, sir, a person of your experience should
have known that the strength of the conscience proceeds
from the weakness of the purse.

Lory.   Sir, I am very glad to find you have a conscience
able to take care of us, let it proceed from what it will ; but
I desire you'll please to consider, that the army alone will
be but a scanty maintenance for a person of your generosity
(at least as rents now are paid).   I shall see you stand in
damnable need of some auxiliary guineas for your *menus*

plaisirs; I will therefore turn fool once more for your service, and advise you to go directly to your brother.   75

Fash. Art thou then so impregnable a blockhead, to believe he'll help me with a farthing?

Lory. Not if you treat him *de haut en bas,* as you use to do.

Fash. Why, how wouldst have me treat him?

Lory. Like a trout—tickle him.

Fash. I can't flatter.

Lory. Can you starve?

Fash. Yes.

Lory. I can't.—Good-by t'ye, sir—   [*Going.*

Fash. Stay; thou wilt distract me ! What wouldst thou have me say to him?   87

Lory. Say nothing to him, apply yourself to his favourites, speak to his periwig, his cravat, his feather, his snuff-box, and when you are well with them—desire him to lend you a thousand pounds. I'll engage you prosper.

Fash. 'Sdeath and furies ! why was that coxcomb thrust into the world before me? O Fortune! Fortune !—thou art a bitch, by Gad.   [*Exeunt.*

SCENE III.—*A Dressing-room.*

Enter Lord Foppington *in his nightgown.*

Lord Fop. Page !

Enter Page.

Page. Sir !

Lord Fop. Sir!— Pray, sir, do me the favour to teach your tongue the title the king has thought fit to honour me with.

Page. I ask your lordship's pardon, my lord.

Lord Fop. O, you can pronounce the word then? I thought it would have choked you.—D'ye hear ?

Page. My lord !   8

Lord Fop. Call La Vérole: I would dress.—[*Exit* Page.]— Well, 'tis an unspeakable pleasure to be a man of quality, strike me dumb !—My lord.—Your lordship! My lord Foppington !—Ah ! *c'est quelque chose de beau, que le diable m'emporte !*—Why, the ladies were ready to puke at me whilst I had nothing but sir Navelty to recommend me to 'em.—Sure, whilst I was but a knight, I was a very nauseous fellow.—Well, 'tis ten thousand pawnd well given, stap my vitals !—

Enter LA VÉROLE.

La Vér. Me Lord, de shoemaker, de tailor, de hosier, de sempstress, de barber, be all ready, if your lordship please to be dress.   20

Lord Fop. 'Tis well, admit 'em.

La Vér. Hey, *messieurs, entrez.*

Enter Tailor, &c.

Lord Fop. So, gentlemen, I hope you have all taken pains to show yourselves masters in your professions.

Tailor. I think I may presume to say, sir—

La Vér. My lord—you clawn, you !

Tailor. Why, is he made a lord?—My lord, I ask your lordship's pardon, my lord ; I hope, my lord, your lordship will please to own I have brought your lordship as accomplished a suit of clothes as ever peer of England trod the

stage in, my lord. Will your lordship please to try 'em
now?   32

Lord Fop. Ay; but let my people dispose the glasses so
that I may see myself before and behind, for I love to see
myself all raund.

Whilst he puts on his clothes, enter Young FASHION
and LORY.

Fash. Heyday, what the devil have we here? Sure my
gentleman's grown a favourite at court, he has got so many
people at his levee.

Lory. Sir, these people come in order to make him a favourite at court; they are to establish him with the ladies. 40

Fash. Good God! to what an ebb of taste are women
fallen, that it should be in the power of a laced coat to
recommend a gallant to 'em!

Lory. Sir, tailors and periwig-makers are now become
the bawds of the nation; 'tis they debauch all the women.

Fash. Thou sayest true; for there's that fop now has
not by nature wherewithal to move a cook-maid, and by that
time these fellows have done with him, egad he shall melt
down a countess!—But now for my reception; I'll engage
it shall be as cold a one as a courtier's to his friend, who
comes to put him in mind of his promise.   51

Lord Fop. [*To his* Tailor.] Death and eternal tartures!
Sir, I say the packet's too high by a foot.

Tailor. My lord, if it had been an inch lower, it would
not have held your lordship's pocket-handkerchief.

Lord Fop. Rat my pocket-handkerchief! have not I a page
to carry it? You may make him a packet up to his chin a
purpose for it; but I will not have mine come so near my face.

Tailor. 'Tis not for me to dispute your lordship's fancy.

Fash. [*To* LORY.]   His   lordship !   Lory, did   you observe that ?   61

Lory. Yes, sir ; I always thought 'twould end there. Now, I hope, you'll have a little more respect for him.

Fash. Respect !—Damn him for a coxcomb ! now has he ruined his estate to buy a title, that he may be a fool of the first rate ;—but let's accost him.—[*To* Lord FOPPING-TON.]   Brother, I'm your humble servant.

Lord Fop. O Lard, Tam ! I did not expect you in England.—Brother, I am glad to see you.—[*Turning to his* Tailor.]   Look you, sir ; I shall never be reconciled to this nauseous packet ; therefore pray get me another suit with all manner of expedition, for this is my eternal aversion.— Mrs. Calico, are not you of my mind ?   .   73

Sempstress. O, directly, my lord ! it can never be too low.

Lord Fop. You are pasitively in the right on't, for the packet becomes no part of the body but the knee.

                                        [*Exit* Tailor.

Semps. I hope your lordship is pleased with your steenkirk.*

Lord Fop. In love with it, stap my vitals !—Bring your bill, you shall be paid to-marrow.   80

Semps. I humbly thank your honour.   [*Exit.*

Lord Fop. Hark thee, shoemaker ! these shoes an't ugly, but they don't fit me.

Shoemaker. My lord, my thinks they fit you very well.

---

* Cravat.   The word " steenkirk " was brought from Paris, where it had come into fashion as a name for cravats, and other small articles of apparel, during the excitement which followed the battle of Steenkirk, where William III. was defeated by the French, July 24, 1692.

Lord Fop. They hurt me just below the instep.

Shoe. [*Feeling his foot.*] My lord, they don't hurt you there.*

Lord Fop. I tell thee, they pinch me execrably.

Shoe. My lord, if they pinch you, I'll be bound to be hanged, that's all. 90

Lord Fop. Why, wilt thou undertake to persuade me I cannot feel ?

Shoe. Your lordship may please to feel what you think fit ; but that shoe does not hurt you ; I think I understand my trade.

Lord Fop. Now by all that's great and powerful, thou art an incomprehensible coxcomb ! but thou makest good shoes and so I'll bear with thee.

Shoe. My lord, I have worked for half the people of quality in town these twenty years ; and 'twere very hard I should not know when a shoe hurts, and when it don't. 101

Lord Fop. Well, prithee be gone about thy business.—
[*Exit* Shoemaker.

[*To the* Hosier.] Mr. Mendlegs, a word with you : the calves of these stockings are thickened a little too much. They make my legs look like a chairman's.

Mend. My lord, my thinks they look mighty well.

Lord Fop. Ay, but you are not so good a judge of these things as I am, I have studied 'em all my life ; therefore pray let the next be the thickness of a crawn-piece less.—
[*Aside.*] If the town takes notice my legs are fallen away, 'twill be attributed to the violence of some new intrigue.—
[*Exit* Mendlegs. [111

---

* This little dispute with the shoemaker appears to have been suggested by *Le Bourgeois Gentilhomme*, Act II., Scene VIII.

[*To the* Periwig-maker.] Come, Mr. Foretop, let me see what you have done, and then the fatigue of the marning will be over.

Fore. My lord, I have done what I defy any prince in Europe to outdo ; I have made you a periwig so long, and so full of hair, it will serve you for hat and cloak in all weathers.

Lord Fop. Then thou hast made me thy friend to eternity. Come, comb it out.

Fash. [*Aside to* LORY.] Well, Lory, what dost think on't ? A very friendly reception from a brother after three years' absence !   122

Lory. Why, sir, it's your own fault ; we seldom care for those that don't love what we love : if you would creep into his heart, you must enter into his pleasures.—Here have you stood ever since you came in, and have not commended any one thing that belongs to him.

Fash. Nor never shall, whilst they belong to a coxcomb.

Lory. Then, sir, you must be content to pick a hungry bone.   130

Fash. No, sir, I'll crack it, and get to the marrow before I have done.

Lord Fop. Gad's curse, Mr. Foretop ! you don't intend to put this upon me for a full periwig ?

Fore. Not a full one, my lord ? I don't know what your lordship may please to call a full one, but I have crammed twenty ounces of hair into it.

Lord Fop. What it may be by weight, sir, I shall not dispute ; but by tale, there are not nine hairs of a side.

Fore. O lord ! O lord ! O lord ! Why, as Gad shall judge me, your honour's side-face is reduced to the tip of your nose !   142

Lord Fop. My side-face may be in eclipse for aught I know; but I'm sure my full-face is like the full-moon.

Fore. Heavens bless my eye-sight—[*Rubbing his eyes.*] Sure I look through the wrong end of the perspective; for by my faith, an't please your honour, the broadest place I see in your face does not seem to me to be two inches diameter.   150

Lord Fop. If it did, it would be just two inches too broad; for a periwig to a man should be like a mask to a woman, nothing should be seen but his eyes.

Fore. My lord, I have done; if you please to have more hair in your wig, I'll put it in.

Lord Fop. Pasitively, yes.

Fore. Shall I take it back now, my lord?

Lord Fop. No: I'll wear it to-day, though it show such a manstrous pair of cheeks, stap my vitals, I shall be taken for a trumpeter.   [*Exit* Foretop. 160

Fash. Now your people of business are gone, brother, I hope I may obtain a quarter of an hour's audience of you.

Lord Fop. Faith, Tam, I must beg you'll excuse me at this time, for I must away to the House of Lards immediately; my lady Teaser's case is to come on to-day, and I would not be absent for the salvation of mankind.—Hey, page!

Enter Page.

Is the coach at the door?

Page. Yes, my lord.

Lord Fop. You'll excuse me, brother.   [*Going.* 170

Fash. Shall you be back at dinner?

Lord Fop. As Gad shall jidge me, I can't tell; for 'tis passible I may dine with some of aur House at Lacket's.*

Fash. Shall I meet you there? For I must needs talk with you.

Lord Fop. That I'm afraid mayn't be so praper ; far the lards I commonly eat with, are people of a nice conversation ; and you know, Tam, your education has been a little at large : but, if you'll stay here, you'll find a family dinner. —[*To* Page.] Hey, fellow ! What is there for dinner? There's beef : I suppose my brother will eat beef.—Dear Tam, I'm glad to see thee in England, stap my vitals !   183

[*Exit with his equipage.*

Fash. Hell and furies ! is this to be borne ?

Lory. Faith, sir, I could almost have given him a knock o' th' pate myself.

Fash. 'Tis enough ; I will now show thee the excess of my passion by being very calm. Come, Lory, lay your loggerhead to mine, and in cool blood let us contrive his destruction.   190

Lory. Here comes a head, sir, would contrive it better than us both, if he would but join in the confederacy.

Enter COUPLER.

Fash. By this light, old Coupler alive still !—Why, how now, matchmaker, art thou here still to plague the world with matrimony? You old bawd, how have you the impudence to be hobbling out of your grave twenty years after you are rotten ?

---

* Locket's : a fashionable ordinary near Charing Cross, on the site of Drummond's Bank.

Coup. When you begin to rot, sirrah, you'll go off like a pippin; one winter will send you to the devil. What mischief brings you home again? Ha! you young lascivious rogue you. Let me put my hand in your bosom, sirrah.   202

Fash. Stand off, old Sodom!

Coup. Nay, prithee now, don't be so coy.

Fash. Keep your hands to yourself, you old dog you, or I'll wring your nose off.

Coup. Hast thou then been a year in Italy, and brought home a fool at last? By my conscience, the young fellows of this age profit no more by their going abroad than they do by their going to church. Sirrah, sirrah, if you are not hanged before you come to my years, you'll know a cock from a hen. But, come, I'm still a friend to thy person, though I have a contempt of thy understanding; and therefore I would willingly know thy condition, that I may see whether thou stand'st in need of my assistance: for widows swarm, my boy, the town's infected with 'em.   217

Fash. I stand in need of anybody's assistance, that will help me to cut my elder brother's throat, without the risk of being hanged for him.

Coup. Egad, sirrah, I could help thee to do him almost as good a turn, without the danger of being burned in the hand for't.

Fash. Sayest thou so, old Satan? Show me but that, and my soul is thine.

Coup. Pox o' thy soul! give me thy warm body, sirrah I shall have a substantial title to't when I tell thee my project.

Fash. Out with it then, dear dad, and take possession as soon as thou wilt. 230

Coup. Sayest thou so, my Hephestion ? Why, then thus lies the scene.—But hold ; who's that ? if we are heard we are undone.

Fash. What, have you forgot Lory ?

Coup. Who, trusty Lory, is it thee ?

Lory. At your service, sir.

Coup. Give me thy hand, old boy. Egad, I did not know thee again ; but I remember thy honesty, though I did not thy face ; I think thou hadst like to have been hanged once or twice for thy master. 240

Lory. Sir, I was very near once having that honour.

Coup. Well, live and hope ; don't be discouraged ; eat with him, and drink with him, and do what he bids thee, and it may be thy reward at last, as well as another's.— [*To* Young FASHION.] Well, sir, you must know I have done you the kindness to make up a match for your brother.

Fash. I am very much beholding to you, truly.

Coup. You may be, sirrah, before the wedding-day yet. The lady is a great heiress ; fifteen hundred pound a year, and a great bag of money ; the match is concluded, the writings are drawn, and the pipkin's to be cracked in a fortnight. Now you must know, stripling (with respect to your mother), your brother's the son of a whore. 253

Fash. Good !

Coup. He has given me a bond of a thousand pounds for helping him to this fortune, and has promised me as much more in ready money upon the day of marriage, which, I understand by a friend, he ne'er designs to pay me. If therefore you will be a generous young dog, and secure me five thousand pounds, I'll be a covetous old rogue, and help you to the lady.

Fash. Egad, if thou canst bring this about, I'll have thy statue cast in brass. But don't you dote, you old pander you, when you talk at this rate ? 264

Coup. That your youthful parts shall judge of. This plump partridge, that I tell you of, lives in the country, fifty miles off, with her honoured parents, in a lonely old house which nobody comes near ; she never goes abroad, nor sees company at home. To prevent all misfortunes, she has her breeding within doors ; the parson of the parish teaches her to play upon the bass-viol, the clerk to sing, her nurse to dress, and her father to dance. In short, nobody can give · you admittance there but I ; nor can I do it any other way than by making you pass for your brother.

Fash. And how the devil wilt thou do that ? 275

Coup. Without the devil's aid, I warrant thee. Thy brother's face not one of the family ever saw, the whole business has been managed by me, and all the letters go through my hands. The last that was writ to sir Tunbelly Clumsey (for that's the old gentleman's name), was to tell him, his lordship would be down in a fortnight to consum-mate. Now, you shall go away immediately, pretend you writ that letter only to have the romantic pleasure of surprising your mistress ; fall desperately in love, as soon as you see her ; make that your plea for marrying her immedi-ately, and, when the fatigue of the wedding-night's over, you shall send me a swinging purse of gold, you dog you.

Fash. Egad, old dad, I'll put my hand in thy bosom now. 290

Coup. Ah, you young hot lusty thief, let me muzzle you !
—[*Kissing.*]   Sirrah, let me muzzle you.

Fash. [*Aside.*] Psha, the old lecher !

Coup. Well ; I'll warrant thou hast not a farthing of
money in thy pocket now ; no, one may see it in thy face.

Fash. Not a souse, by Jupiter !

Coup. Must I advance then ?—Well, sirrah, be at my
lodgings in half an hour, and I'll see what may be done ;
we'll sign, and seal, and eat a pullet, and when I have
given thee some farther instructions, thou shalt hoist sail
and be gone.—[*Kissing.*]   T'other buss, and so adieu.

Fash. Um ! psha !   312

Coup. Ah, you young warm dog you, what a delicious
night will the bride have on't !   [*Exit.*

Fash. So, Lory ; Providence, thou seest at last, takes
care of men of merit : we are in a fair way to be great
people.

Lory. Ay, sir, if the devil don't step between the cup
and the lip, as he uses to do.

Fash. Why, faith, he has played me many a damned
trick to spoil my fortune, and egad I'm almost afraid he's at
work about it again now ; but if I should tell thee how,
thou'dst wonder at me.

Lory. Indeed, sir, I should not.

Fash. How dost know ?   325

Lory. Because, sir, I have wondered at you so often, I
can wonder at you no more.

Fash. No ! what wouldst thou say if a qualm of
conscience should spoil my design ?

Lory. I would eat my words, and wonder more than
ever.

Fash. Why, faith, Lory, though I am a young rake-hell, and have played many a roguish trick ; this is so full-grown a cheat, I find I must take pains to come up to't, I have scruples—

Lory. They are strong symptoms of death ; if you find they increase, pray, sir, make your will.   337

Fash. No, my conscience shan't starve me neither. But thus far I will hearken to it ; before I execute this project, I'll try my brother to the bottom, I'll speak to him with the temper of a philosopher ; my reasons (though they press him home) shall yet be clothed with so much modesty, not one of all the truths they urge shall be so naked to offend his sight. If he has yet so much humanity about him as to assist me (though with a moderate aid), I'll drop my project at his feet, and show him I can do for him much more than what I ask he'd do for me. This one conclusive trial of him I resolve to make—

> Succeed or no, still victory's my lot ;
> If I subdue his heart, 'tis well ; if not,
> I shall subdue my conscience to my plot.

[*Exeunt.*

ACT II.

SCENE I.—*London.*—*A Room in* LOVELESS'S *Lodgings.*

Enter LOVELESS *and* AMANDA.

Love. How do you like these lodgings, my dear? For my part, I am so well pleased with 'em, I shall hardly remove whilst we stay in town, if you are satisfied.

Aman. I am satisfied with everything that pleases you; else I had not come to town at all.

Love. Oh! a little of the noise and bustle of the world sweetens the pleasures of retreat. We shall find the charms of our retirement doubled, when we return to it.

Aman. That pleasing prospect will be my chiefest entertainment, whilst (much against my will) I am obliged to stand surrounded with these empty pleasures, which 'tis so much the fashion to be fond of.   12

Love. I own most of them are indeed but empty; nay, so empty, that one would wonder by what magic power they act, when they induce us to be vicious for their sakes. Yet some there are we may speak kindlier of. There are delights (of which a private life is destitute) which may divert an honest man, and be a harmless entertainment to a virtuous woman. The conversation of the town is one; and truly (with some small allowances), the plays, I think, may be esteemed another.

Aman. The plays, I must confess, have some small charms; and would have more, would they restrain that loose obscene encouragement to vice, which shocks, if not the virtue of some women, at least the modesty of all.*   26

Love. But till that reformation can be made, I would not leave the wholesome corn for some intruding tares that grow amongst it. Doubtless the moral of a well-wrought scene is of prevailing force.—Last night there happened one that moved me strangely.

Aman. Pray, what was that?

Love. Why 'twas about—but 'tis not worth repeating.

Aman. Yes, pray let me know it.

Love. No; I think 'tis as well let alone.   35

Aman. Nay, now you make me have a mind to know.

Love. 'Twas a foolish thing. You'd perhaps grow jealous should I tell it you, though without cause, Heaven knows.

Aman. I shall begin to think I have cause, if you persist in making it a secret.

Love. I'll then convince you you have none, by making it no longer so. Know then, I happened in the play to find my very character, only with the addition of a relapse; which struck me so, I put a sudden stop to a most harmless entertainment, which till then diverted me between the acts. 'Twas to admire the workmanship of nature, in the face of a

---

* The "reforming Divine," one would think, might have felt at home here, but he probably suspected the "scandalous Poet" of laughing in his sleeve when he wrote this passage. I see no reason to doubt that Vanbrugh intended it as an expression of his own opinion on the matter.

young lady that sat some distance from me, she was so
exquisitely handsome !—

Aman. So exquisitely handsome !   50

Love. Why do you repeat my words, my dear ?

Aman. Because you seemed to speak 'em with such
pleasure, I thought I might oblige you with their echo.

Love. Then you are alarmed, Amanda ?

Aman. It is my duty to be so, when you are in danger.

Love. You are too quick in apprehending for me ; all
will be well when you have heard me out. I do confess I
gazed upon her ; nay, eagerly I gazed upon her.

Aman. Eagerly ! that's with desire.

Love. No, I desired her not : I viewed her with a world
of admiration, but not one glance of love.   61

Aman. Take heed of trusting to such nice distinctions.

Love. I did take heed ; for observing in the play that
he who seemed to represent me there was, by an accident
like this, unwarily surprised into a net, in which he lay a
poor entangled slave, and brought a train of mischiefs on
his head, I snatched my eyes away ; they pleaded hard for
leave to look again, but I grew absolute, and they obeyed.

Aman. Were they the only things that were inquisitive ?
Had I been in your place, my tongue, I fancy, had been
curious too ; I should have asked her name, and where she
lived (yet still without design).—Who was she, pray ?

Love. Indeed I cannot tell.

Aman. You will not tell.

Love. By all that's sacred then, I did not ask.   75

Aman. Nor do you know what company was with her ?

Love. I do not.

Aman. Then I am calm again.

Love. Why were you disturbed?

Aman. Had I then no cause?

Love. None, certainly.

Aman. I thought I had.

Love. But you thought wrong, Amanda: for turn the case, and let it be your story; should you come home, and tell me you had seen a handsome man, should I grow jealous because you had eyes? 86

Aman. But should I tell you he were exquisitely so; that I had gazed on him with admiration; that I had looked with eager eyes upon him; should you not think 'twere possible I might go one step farther, and inquire his name?

Love. [*Aside.*] She has reason on her side: I have talked too much; but I must turn it off another way.— [*Aloud.*] Will you then make no difference, Amanda, between the language of our sex and yours? There is a modesty restrains your tongues, which makes you speak by halves when you commend; but roving flattery gives a loose to ours, which makes us still speak double what we think. You should not, therefore, in so strict a sense, take what I said to her advantage. 101

Aman. Those flights of flattery, sir, are to our faces only: when women once are out of hearing, you are as modest in your commendations as we are. But I shan't put you to the trouble of farther excuses, if you please this business shall rest here. Only give me leave to wish, both for your peace and mine, that you may never meet this miracle of beauty more.

Love. I am content.

Enter Servant.

Ser.   Madam, there's a young lady at the door in a chair, desires to know whether your ladyship sees company.   I think her name is Berinthia.   112

Aman.   O dear ! 'tis a relation I have not seen these five years.   Pray her to walk in.—[*Exit* Servant.] Here's another beauty for you.   She was young when I saw her last ; but I hear she's grown extremely handsome.

Love.   Don't you be jealous now ; for I shall gaze upon her too.

Enter BERINTHIA.

[*Aside.*]—Ha ! by Heavens the very woman !   120

Ber. [*Saluting* AMANDA.]   Dear Amanda, I did not expect to meet with you in town.

Aman.   Sweet cousin, I'm overjoyed to see you.—Mr. Loveless, here's a relation and a friend of mine, I desire you'll be better acquainted with.

Love. [*Saluting* BERINTHIA.]   If my wife never desires a harder thing, madam, her request will be easily granted.

Ber.   I think, madam, I ought to wish you joy.

Aman.   Joy ! Upon what ?   130

Ber.   Upon your marriage : you were a widow when I saw you last.

Love.   You ought rather, madam, to wish me joy upon that, since I am the only gainer.

Ber.   If she has got so good a husband as the world reports, she has gained enough to expect the compliments of her friends upon it.

Love. If the world is so favourable to me, to allow I deserve that title, I hope 'tis so just to my wife to own I derive it from her.   140

Ber. Sir, it is so just to you both, to own you are (and deserve to be) the happiest pair that live in it.

Love. I'm afraid we shall lose that character, madam, whenever you happen to change your condition.

Re-enter Servant.

Ser. Sir, my lord Foppington presents his humble service to you, and desires to know how you do.   He but just now heard you were in town.   He's at the next door; and if it be not inconvenient, he'll come and wait upon you.

Love. Lord Foppington !—I know him not.   150

Ber. Not his dignity, perhaps, but you do his person. 'Tis sir Novelty; he has bought a barony, in order to marry a great fortune.   His patent has not been passed eight-and-forty hours, and he has already sent how-do-ye's to all the town, to make 'em acquainted with his title.

Love. Give my service to his lordship, and let him know I am proud of the honour he intends me.—[*Exit* Servant.] Sure this addition of quality must have so improved his coxcomb, he can't but be very good company for a quarter of an hour.   161

Aman. Now it moves my pity more than my mirth, to see a man whom nature has made no fool, be so very industrious to pass for an ass.

Love. No, there you are wrong, Amanda ; you should never bestow your pity upon those who take pains for your contempt.   Pity those whom nature abuses, but never those who abuse nature.

Ber. Besides, the town would be robbed of one of its chief diversions, if it should become a crime to laugh at a fool.   171

Aman. I could never yet perceive the town inclined to part with any of its diversions, for the sake of their being crimes ; but I have seen it very fond of some I think had little else to recommend 'em.

Ber. I doubt, Amanda, you are grown its enemy, you speak with so much warmth against it.

Aman. I must confess I am not much its friend.

Ber. Then give me leave to make you mine, by not engaging in its quarrel.   180

Aman. You have many stronger claims than that, Berinthia, whenever you think fit to plead your title.

Love. You have done well to engage a second, my dear ; for here comes one will be apt to call you to an account for your country principles.

Enter Lord FOPPINGTON.

Lord Fop. Sir, I am your most humble servant.

Love. I wish you joy, my lord.

Lord Fop. O Lard, sir ! — Madam, your ladyship's welcome to tawn.

Aman. I wish your lordship joy.   190

Lord Fop. O Heavens, madam—

Love. My lord, this young lady is a relation of my wife's.

Lord Fop. [*Saluting* BERINTHIA.] The beautifullest race of people upon earth, rat me ! Dear Loveless, I'm

overjoyed to see you have brought your family to tawn
again ; I am, stap my vitals !—[*Aside.*]   Far I design to lie
with your wife.—[*To* Amanda.]   Far Gad's sake, madam,
haw has your ladyship been able to subsist thus long, under
the fatigue of a country life ?   200

Aman.   My life has been very far from that, my lord ;
it has been a very quiet one.

Lord Fop.   Why, that's the fatigue I speak of, madam.
For 'tis impossible to be quiet, without thinking : now thinking is to me the greatest fatigue in the world.

Aman.   Does not your lordship love reading then ?

Lord Fop.   Oh, passionately, madam.—But I never think
of what I read.

Ber.   Why, can your lordship read without thinking ?

Lord Fop.   O Lard !—can your ladyship pray without
devotion, madam ?   211

Aman.   Well, I must own I think books the best entertainment in the world.

Lord Fop.   I am so much of your ladyship's mind,
madam, that I have a private gallery, where I walk sometimes ; it is furnished with nothing but books and looking-
glasses.   Madam, I have gilded 'em, and ranged 'em so
prettily, before Gad, it is the most entertaining thing in the
world to walk and look upon 'em.

Aman.   Nay, I love a neat library too ; but 'tis, I think,
the inside of a book should recommend it most to us.   221

Lord Fop.   That, I must confess, I am nat altogether so
fand of.   Far to mind the inside of a book, is to entertain one's self with the forced product of another man's
brain.   Naw I think a man of quality and breeding may be
much better diverted with the natural sprauts of his own.

But to say the truth, madam, let a man love reading never so well, when once he comes to know this tawn, he finds so many better ways of passing the four-and-twenty hours, that 'twere ten thousand pities he should consume his time in that.   Far example, madam, my life; my life, madam, is a perpetual stream of pleasure, that glides through such a variety of entertainments, I believe the wisest of our ancestors never had the least conception of any of 'em.   I rise, madam, about ten a-clack.   I don't rise sooner, because 'tis the worst thing in the world for the complexion ; nat that I pretend to be a beau; but a man must endeavour to look wholesome, lest he make so nauseous a figure in the side-bax, the ladies should be compelled to turn their eyes upon the play.   So at ten a-clack, I say, I rise.   Naw, if I find 'tis a good day, I resalve to take a turn in the Park, and see the fine women ; so huddle on my clothes, and get dressed by one.   If it be nasty weather, I take a turn in the chocolate-house : where, as you walk, madam, you have the prettiest prospect in the world ; you have looking-glasses all raund you.—But I'm afraid I tire the company.

Ber.   Not at all.   Pray go on.   247

Lord Fop.   Why then, ladies, from thence I go to dinner at Lacket's, where you are so nicely and delicately served, that, stap my vitals ! they shall compose you a dish no bigger than a saucer, shall come to fifty shillings. Between eating my dinner (and washing my mouth, ladies) I spend my time, till I go to the play ; * where, till nine a-clack, I entertain myself with looking upon the company ; and usually dispose of one hour more in leading 'em aut.

---

* The hour for beginning the play was at this time five o'clock.

So there's twelve of the four-and-twenty pretty well over. The other twelve, madam, are disposed of in two articles : in the first four I toast myself drunk, and in t'other eight I sleep myself sober again. Thus, ladies, you see my life is an eternal raund O of delights.   260

Love. 'Tis a heavenly one indeed.

Aman. But I thought, my lord, you beaux spent a great deal of your time in intrigues : you have given us no account of them yet.

Lord Fop. [*Aside.*] Soh ; she would inquire into my amours.—That's jealousy :—she begins to be in love with me.—[*To* Amanda.] Why, madam,—as to time for my intrigues, I usually make detachments of it from my other pleasures, according to the exigency.   Far your ladyship may please to take notice, that those who intrigue with women of quality, have rarely occasion for above half an hour at a time : people of that rank being under those decorums, they can seldom give you a langer view than will just serve to shoot 'em flying. So that the course of my other pleasures is not very much interrupted by my amours.

Love. But your lordship is now become a pillar of the state; you must attend the weighty affairs of the nation.   279

Lord Fop. Sir,—as to weighty affairs—I leave them to weighty heads.   I never intend mine shall be a burden to my body.

Love. O but you'll find the House will expect your attendance.

Lord Fop. Sir, you'll find the House will compound for my appearance.

Love. But your friends will take it ill if you don't attend their particular causes.

Lord Fop. Not, sir, if I come time enough to give 'em my particular vote.　　290

Ber. But pray, my lord, how do you dispose of yourself on Sundays? for that, methinks, is a day should hang wretchedly upon your hands.

Lord Fop. Why, faith, madam—Sunday—is a vile day, I must confess. I intend to move for leave to bring in a bill, that players may work upon it, as well as the hackney coaches. Though this I must say for the government, it leaves us the churches to entertain us.—But then again, they begin so abominable early, a man must rise by candle-light to get dressed by the psalm.　　300

Ber. Pray which church does your lordship most oblige with your presence?

Lord Fop. Oh, St James's, madam :—there's much the best company.

Aman. Is there good preaching too?

Lord Fop. Why, faith, madam—I can't tell. A man must have very little to do there that can give an account of the sermon.

Ber. You can give us an account of the ladies at least?　　310

Lord Fop. Or I deserve to be excommunicated.—There is my lady Tattle, my lady Prate, my lady Titter, my lady Leer, my lady Giggle, and my lady Grin. These sit in the front of the boxes, and all church-time are the prettiest company in the world, stap my vitals !—[*To* AMANDA.] Mayn't we hope for the honour to see your ladyship added to our society, madam?

Aman. Alas, my lord! I am the worst company in the world at church : I'm apt to mind the prayers, or the sermon, or—   320

Lord Fop. One is indeed strangely apt at church to mind what one should not do. But I hope, madam, at one time or other, I shall have the honour to lead your ladyship to your coach there.—[*Aside.*]   Methinks she seems strangely pleased with everything I say to her.—'Tis a vast pleasure to receive encouragement from a woman before her husband's face.—I have a good mind to pursue my conquest, and speak the thing plainly to her at once. Egad, I'll do't, and that in so cavalier a manner, she shall be surprised at it.—[*Aloud.*]   Ladies, I'll take my leave ; I'm afraid I begin to grow troublesome with the length of my visit.

Aman. Your lordship's too entertaining to grow trouble-some anywhere.   334

Lord Fop. [*Aside.*]   That now was as much as if she had said—pray lie with me. I'll let her see I'm quick of apprehension.—[*To* AMANDA.] O Lard, madam ! I had like to have forgot a secret, I must needs tell your lady-ship.—[*To* LOVELESS.] Ned, you must not be so jealous now as to listen.

Love. Not I, my lord ; I am too fashionable a husband to pry into the secrets of my wife.

Lord Fop. [*To* AMANDA, *squeezing her hand.*]   I am in love with you to desperation, strike me speechless !

Aman. [*Giving him a box o' the ear.*]   Then thus I return your passion.—An impudent fool !

Lord Fop. Gad's curse, madam, I'm a peer of the realm !

Love. Hey; what the devil do you affront my wife, sir? Nay then—   350

 [*They draw and fight. The women run shrieking for help.*

Aman. Ah! What has my folly done? Help! murder! help! part 'em, for Heaven's sake!

Lord Fop. [*Falling back, and leaning upon his sword.*] Ah—quite through the body!—stap my vitals!

Enter Servants.

Love. [*Running to him.*] I hope I han't killed the fool however.—Bear him up!—Where's your wound?

Lord Fop. Just through the guts.

Love. Call a surgeon there.—Unbutton him quickly.

Lord Fop. Ay, pray make haste.   [*Exit* Servant.

Love. This mischief you may thank yourself for.

Lord Fop. I may so—love's the devil indeed, Ned. 360

Re-enter Servant *with* SYRINGE.

Ser. Here's Mr. Syringe, sir, was just going by the door.

Lord Fop. He's the welcomest man alive.

Syr. Stand by, stand by, stand by! Pray, gentlemen, stand by. Lord have mercy upon us! did you never see a man run through the body before? pray, stand by.

Lord Fop. Ah, Mr. Syringe—I'm a dead man!

Syr. A dead man and I by!—I should laugh to see that, egad!

Love. Prithee don't stand prating, but look upon his wound.   370

Syr. Why, what if I won't look upon his wound this hour, sir?

Love.   Why, then he'll bleed to death, sir.

Syr.   Why, then I'll fetch him to life again, sir.

Love.   'Slife, he's run through the guts, I tell thee.

Syr.   Would he were run through the heart, I should get the more credit by his cure.   Now I hope you're satisfied? —Come, now let me come at him ; now let me come at him. —[*Viewing his wound.*]   Oons, what a gash is here !—Why, sir, a man may drive a coach and six horses into your body.

Lord Fop.   Ho!   381

Syr.   Why, what the devil, have you run the gentleman through with a scythe ?—[*Aside.*]   A little prick between the skin and the ribs, that's all.

Love.   Let me see his wound.

Syr.   Then you shall dress it, sir ; for if anybody looks upon it, I won't.

Love.   Why, thou art the veriest coxcomb I ever saw.

Syr.   Sir, I am not master of my trade for nothing.

Lord Fop.   Surgeon !   390

Syr.   Well, sir.

Lord Fop.   Is there any hopes ?

Syr.   Hopes ?—I can't tell.—What are you willing to give for your cure ?

Lord Fop.   Five hundred paunds with pleasure.

Syr.   Why, then perhaps there may be hopes.   But we must avoid farther delay.—Here ; help the gentleman into a chair, and carry him to my house presently, that's the properest place—[*Aside.*] to bubble him out of his money.— [*Aloud.*] Come, a chair, a chair quickly—there, in with him.   [*They put him into a chair.*   401

Lord Fop.   Dear Loveless—adieu !   If I die—I forgive thee ; and if I live—I hope thou'lt do as much by me. . I'm

                                                       E

very sorry you and I should quarrel ; but I hope here's an end on't, for if you are satisfied—I am.

Love. I shall hardly think it worth my prosecuting any farther, so you may be at rest, sir.

Lord Fop. Thou art a generous fellow, strike me dumb ! —[*Aside.*] But thou hast an impertinent wife, stap my vitals !   410

Syr. So, carry him off ! carry him off ! we shall have him prate himself into a fever by and by ; carry him off.

[*Exit with* Lord FOPPINGTON.

Aman. Now on my knees, my dear, let me ask your pardon for my indiscretion, my own I never shall obtain.

Love. Oh, there's no harm done : you served him well.

Aman. He did indeed deserve it. But I tremble to think how dear my indiscreet resentment might have cost you.

Love. Oh, no matter, never trouble yourself about that. 420

Ber. For Heaven's sake, what was't he did to you?

Aman. O nothing ; he only squeezed me kindly by the hand, and frankly offered me a coxcomb's heart. I know I was to blame to resent it as I did, since nothing but a quarrel could ensue. But the fool so surprised me with his insolence, I was not mistress of my fingers.

Ber. Now, I dare swear, he thinks you had 'em at great command, they obeyed you so readily.

Enter WORTHY.

Wor. Save you, save you, good people : I'm glad to find you all alive ; I met a wounded peer carrying off. For Heaven's sake, what was the matter?   431

Love. Oh, a trifle! He would have lain with my wife before my face, so she obliged him with a box o' th' ear, and I run him through the body : that was all.

Wor. Bagatelle on all sides. But, pray madam, how long has this noble lord been a humble servant of yours?

Aman. This is the first I have heard on't. So I suppose 'tis his quality more than his love, has brought him into this adventure. He thinks his title an authentic passport to every woman's heart below the degree of a peeress.

Wor. He's coxcomb enough to think anything. But I would not have you brought into trouble for him : I hope there's no danger of his life? 443

Love. None at all. He's fallen into the hands of a roguish surgeon ; I perceive designs to frighten a little money out of him. But I saw his wound, 'tis nothing ; he may go to the play to-night, if he pleases.

Wor. I am glad you have corrected him without farther mischief. And now, sir, if these ladies have no farther service for you, you'll oblige me if you can go to the place I spoke to you of t'other day.

Love. With all my heart.—[*Aside.*] Though I could wish, methinks, to stay and gaze a little longer on that creature. Good gods, how beautiful she is !—But what have I to do with beauty? I have already had my portion, and must not covet more.—[*Aloud.*] Come, sir, when you please.

Wor. Ladies, your servant.

Aman. Mr. Loveless, pray one word with you before you go. 460

Love. [*To* WORTHY.] I'll overtake you, sir.—[*Exit* WORTHY.] What would my dear?

Aman.   Only a woman's foolish question,—how do you like my cousin here?

Love.   Jealous already, Amanda?

Aman.   Not at all, I ask you for another reason.

Love.   [*Aside.*] Whate'er her reason be, I must not tell her true.—[*To* AMANDA.] Why, I confess she's handsome. But you must not think I slight your kinswoman, if I own to you, of all the women who may claim that character, she is the last would triumph in my heart.   471

Aman.   I'm satisfied.

Love.   Now tell me why you asked?

Aman.   At night I will.   Adieu.

Love.   I'm yours.   [*Kisses her and exit.*

Aman.   [*Aside.*] I'm glad to find he does not like her; for I have a great mind to persuade her to come and live with me.—[*Aloud.*] Now, dear Berinthia, let me inquire a little into your affairs : for I do assure you, I am enough your friend to interest myself in everything that concerns you.   481

Ber.   You formerly have given me such proofs on't, I should be very much to blame to doubt it.   I am sorry I have no secrets to trust you with, that I might convince you how entire a confidence I durst repose in you.

Aman.   Why, is it possible that one so young and beautiful as you should live and have no secrets?

Ber.   What secrets do you mean?

Aman.   Lovers.

Ber.   Oh, twenty ! but not one secret one amongst 'em. Lovers in this age have too much honour to do anything underhand ; they do all above board.   492

Aman.   That now, methinks, would make me hate a man.

Ber. But the women of the town are of another mind: for by this means a lady may (with the expense of a few coquette glances) lead twenty fools about in a string for two or three years together. Whereas, if she should allow 'em greater favours, and oblige 'em to secrecy, she would not keep one of 'em a fortnight.

Aman. There's something indeed in that to satisfy the vanity of a woman, but I can't comprehend how the men find their account in it.   502

Ber. Their entertainment, I must confess, is a riddle to me. For there's very few of 'em ever get farther than a bow and an ogle. I have half a score for my share, who follow me all over the town ; and at the play, the Park, and the church, do (with their eyes) say the violentest things to me.—But I never hear any more of 'em.

Aman. What can be the reason of that ?

Ber. One reason is, they don't know how to go farther. They have had so little practice, they don't understand the trade. But, besides their ignorance, you must know there is not one of my half score lovers but what follows half a score mistresses. Now, their affections being divided amongst so many, are not strong enough for any one to make 'em pursue her to the purpose. Like a young puppy in a warren, they have a flirt at all, and catch none.

Aman. Yet they seem to have a torrent of love to dispose of.   519

Ber. They have so. But 'tis like the river of a modern philosopher, (whose works, though a woman, I have read,) it sets out with a violent stream, splits in a thousand branches, and is all lost in the sands.

Aman. But do you think this river of love runs all its

course without doing any mischief ?   Do you think it overflows nothing ?

Ber.   O yes ; 'tis true, it never breaks into anybody's
ground that has the least fence about it ; but it overflows all
the commons that lie in its way.   And this is the utmost
achievement of those dreadful champions in the field of
love—the beaux.   531

Aman.   But prithee, Berinthia, instruct me a little farther;
for I'm so great a novice I am almost ashamed on't.   My
husband's leaving me whilst I was young and fond threw me
into that depth of discontent, that ever since I have led so
private and recluse a life, my ignorance is scarce conceivable.
I therefore fain would be instructed.   Not (Heaven knows)
that what you call intrigues have any charms for me; my
love and principles are too well fixed.   The practic part of
all unlawful love is—   540

Ber.   Oh, 'tis abominable !   But for the speculative; that
we must all confess is entertaining.   The conversation of all
the virtuous women in the town turns upon that and new
clothes.

Aman.   Pray be so just then to me, to believe, 'tis with a
world of innocency I would inquire, whether you think those
women we call women of reputation, do so really 'scape all
other men, as they do those shadows of 'em, the
beaux.   549

Ber.   O no, Amanda ; there are a sort of men make
dreadful work amongst 'em : men that may be called the
beaux' antipathy ; for they agree in nothing but walking
upon two legs.—These have brains : the beau has none.
These are in love with their mistress : the beau with himself.
They take care of her reputation : he's industrious to destroy

it. They are decent : he's a fop. They are sound : he's
rotten. They are men : he's an ass.

Aman. If this be their character, I fancy we had here e'en
now a pattern of 'em both.

Ber. His lordship and Mr Worthy ?   560

Aman. The same.

Ber. As for the lord, he's eminently so ; and for the
other, I can assure you, there's not a man in town who has
a better interest with the women, that are worth having an
interest with. But 'tis all private : he's like a back-stair
minister at court, who, whilst the reputed favourites are
sauntering in the bedchamber, is ruling the roast in the closet.

Aman. He answers then the opinion I had ever of him.
Heavens ! What a difference there is between a man like
him, and that vain nauseous fop, sir Novelty.— [*Taking her
hand.*] I must acquaint you with a secret, cousin. 'Tis
not that fool alone has talked to me of love. Worthy has
been tampering too. 'Tis true, he has done't in vain : not
all his charms or art have power to shake me. My love,
my duty, and my virtue, are such faithful guards, I need
not fear my heart should e'er betray me. But what I
wonder at is this : I find I did not start at his proposal, as
when it came from one whom I contemned. I therefore
mention his attempt, that I may learn from you whence it
proceeds ; that vice (which cannot change its nature)
should so far change at least its shape, as that the self-same
crime proposed from one shall seem a monster gaping at
your ruin ; when from another it shall look so kind, as
though it were your friend, and never meant to harm you.
Whence, think you, can this difference proceed ? For 'tis
not love, Heaven knows.   586

Ber. O no; I would not for the world believe it were. But possibly, should there a dreadful sentence pass upon you, to undergo the rage of both their passions; the pain you apprehend from one might seem so trivial to the other, the danger would not quite so much alarm you.

Aman. Fy, fy, Berinthia! you would indeed alarm me, could you incline me to a thought, that all the merit of mankind combined could shake that tender love I bear my husband. No! he sits triumphant in my heart, and nothing can dethrone him.

Ber. But should he abdicate again, do you think you should preserve the vacant throne ten tedious winters more in hopes of his return?   599

Aman. Indeed, I think I should. Though I confess, after those obligations he has to me, should he abandon me once more, my heart would grow extremely urgent with me to root him thence, and cast him out for ever.

Ber. Were I that thing they call a slighted wife, somebody should run the risk of being that thing they call—a husband.

Aman. O fy, Berinthia! no revenge should ever be taken against a husband. But to wrong his bed is a vengeance, which of all vengeance—   609

Ber. Is the sweetest, ha! ha! ha! Don't I talk madly?

Aman. Madly, indeed.

Ber. Yet I'm very innocent.

Aman. That I dare swear you are. I know how to make allowances for your humour: you were always very entertaining company; but I find since marriage and widowhood have shown you the world a little, you are very much improved.

Ber. [*Aside.*] Alack a-day, there has gone more than
that to improve me, if she knew all !　　　　　　　619

Aman. For Heaven's sake, Berinthia, tell me what way
I shall take to persuade you to come and live with me ?

Ber. Why, one way in the world there is—and but one.

Aman. Pray which is that ?

Ber. It is, to assure me—I shall be very welcome.

Aman. If that be all, you shall e'en lie here to-night.

Ber. To-night !

Aman. Yes, to-night.

Ber. Why, the people where I lodge will think me mad.

Aman. Let 'em think what they please.　　　　　629

Ber. Say you so, Amanda? Why, then they shall think
what they please : for I'm a young widow, and I care not
what anybody thinks. Ah, Amanda, it's a delicious thing
to be a young widow !

Aman. You'll hardly make me think so.

Ber. Puh ! because you are in love with your husband :
but that is not every woman's case.

Aman. I hope 'twas yours, at least.

Ber. Mine, say ye ? Now I have a great mind to tell
you a lie, but I should do it so awkwardly you'd find me
out.　　　　　　　　　　　　　　　640

Aman. Then e'en speak the truth.

Ber. Shall I ?—Then after all I did love him, Amanda
—as a nun does penance.

Aman. Why did not you refuse to marry him, then?

Ber. Because my mother would have whipped me.

Aman. How did you live together?

Ber. Like man and wife, asunder. He loved the
country, I the town. He hawks and hounds, I coaches and

equipage. He eating and drinking, I carding and playing. He the sound of a horn, I the squeak of a fiddle. We were dull company at table, worse a-bed. Whenever we met, we gave one another the spleen ; and never agreed but once, which was about lying alone.

Aman. But tell me one thing, truly and sincerely.

Ber. What's that ? 655

Aman. Notwithstanding all these jars, did not his death at last extremely trouble you ?

Ber. O yes. Not that my present pangs were so very violent, but the after-pains were intolerable. I was forced to wear a beastly widow's band a twelvemonth for't.

Aman. Women, I find, have different inclinations.

Ber. Women, I find, keep different company. When your husband ran away from you, if you had fallen into some of my acquaintance, 'twould have saved you many a tear. But you go and live with a grandmother, a bishop, and an old nurse; which was enough to make any woman break her heart for her husband. Pray, Amanda, if ever you are a widow again, keep yourself so, as I do.

Aman. Why ! do you then resolve you'll never marry ?

Ber. O no; I resolve I will. 670

Aman. How so ?

Ber. That I never may.

Aman. You banter me.

Ber. Indeed I don't. But I consider I'm a woman, and form my resolutions accordingly.

Aman. Well, my opinion is, form what resolution you will, matrimony will be the end on't.

Ber. Faith it won't.

Aman. How do you know ?

Ber.   I'm sure on't.   680

Aman.   Why, do you think 'tis impossible for you to fall in love?

Ber.   No.

Aman.   Nay, but to grow so passionately fond, that nothing but the man you love can give you rest.

Ber.   Well, what then?

Aman.   Why, then you'll marry him.

Ber.   How do you know that?

Aman.   Why, what can you do else?

Ber.   Nothing—but sit and cry.

Aman.   Psha!

Ber.   Ah, poor Amanda! you have led a country life: but if you'll consult the widows of this town, they'll tell you you should never take a lease of a house you can hire for a quarter's warning.   [*Exeunt.*

ACT III.

SCENE I.—*A Room in* Lord FOPPINGTON's *House.*

Enter Lord FOPPINGTON *and* Servant.

Lord Fop. Hey, fellow, let the coach come to the door.

Ser. Will your lordship venture so soon to expose your-self to the weather ?

Lord Fop. Sir, I will venture as soon as I can, to expose myself to the ladies; though give me my cloak, however; for in that side-box, what between the air that comes in at the door on one side, and the intolerable warmth of the masks on t'other, * a man gets so many heats and colds, 'twould destroy the canstitution of a harse.

Ser. [*Putting on his cloak.*] I wish your lordship would please to keep house a little longer; I'm afraid your honour does not well consider your wound. 12

Lord Fop. My wound!—I would not be in eclipse another day, though I had as many wounds in my guts as I have had in my heart. [*Exit* Servant.

---

* Soon after the Restoration, masks were commonly worn at the theatre by ladies of reputation (See *Pepys*, June 12, 1663), but the custom appears to have been quickly abandoned to women of the town. In Dryden's prologues and epilogues, for example, the term "vizard-mask " is always synonymous with prostitute.

Enter Young Fashion.

Fash. Brother, your servant. How do you find yourself to-day?

Lord Fop. So well, that I have ardered my coach to
the door: so there's no great danger of death this baut,
Tam.   20

Fash. I'm very glad of it.

Lord Fop. [*Aside.*] That I believe's a lie.—[*Aloud.*]
Prithee, Tam, tell me one thing: did nat your heart cut a
caper up to your mauth, when you heard I was run through
the bady?

Fash. Why do you think it should?

Lord Fop. Because I remember mine did so, when I
heard my father was shat through the head.

Fash. It then did very ill.

Lord Fop. Prithee, why so?   30

Fash. Because he used you very well.

Lord Fop. Well?—naw, strike me dumb! he starved
me. He has let me want a thausand women for want of a
thausand paund.

Fash. Then he hindered you from making a great many
ill bargains, for I think no woman is worth money that will
take money.

Lord Fop. If I were a younger brother, I should think
so too.

Fash. Why, is it possible you can value a woman that's
to be bought?   41

Lord Fop. Prithee, why not as well as a padnag?

Fash. Because a woman has a heart to dispose of; a
horse has none.

Lord Fop. Look you, Tam, of all things that belang to a woman, I have an aversion to her heart. Far when once a woman has given you her heart—you can never get rid of the rest of her bady.

Fash. This is strange doctrine. But pray in your amours how is it with your own heart ? 50

Lord Fop. Why, my heart in my amours—is like—my heart aut of my amours ; *à la glace.* My bady, Tam, is a watch ; and my heart is the pendulum to it ; whilst the finger runs raund to every hour in the circle, that still beats the same time.

Fash. Then you are seldom much in love ?

Lord Fop. Never, stap my vitals !

Fash. Why then did you make all this bustle about Amanda ?

Lord Fop. Because she was a woman of an insolent virtue, and I thought myself piqued in honour to debauch her. 62

Fash. Very well.—[*Aside.*] Here's a rare fellow for you, to have the spending of five thousand pounds a year ! But now for my business with him.—[*Aloud.*] Brother, though I know to talk to you of business (especially of money) is a theme not quite so entertaining to you as that of the ladies ; my necessities are such, I hope you'll have patience to hear me.

Lord Fop. The greatness of your necessities, Tam, is the worst argument in the world for your being patiently heard. I do believe you are going to make me a very good speech, but, strike me dumb ! it has the worst beginning of any speech I have heard this twelvemonth.

Fash. I'm very sorry you think so. 75

Lord Fop. I do believe thou art. But come, let's know thy affair quickly; far 'tis a new play, and I shall be so rumpled and squeezed with pressing through the crawd, to get to my servant, the women will think I have lain all night in my clothes.

Fash. Why then, (that I may not be the author of so great a misfortune) my case in a word is this. The necessary expenses of my travels have so much exceeded the wretched income of my annuity, that I have been forced to mortgage it for five hundred pounds, which is spent; so that unless you are so kind to assist me in redeeming it, I know no remedy but to go take a purse.

Lord Fop. Why, faith, Tam—to give you my sense of the thing, I do think taking a purse the best remedy in the the world : for if you succeed, you are relieved that way; if you are taken—you are relieved t'other.

Fash. I'm glad to see you are in so pleasant a humour, I hope I shall find the effects on't.   93

Lord Fop. Why, do you then really think it a reasonable thing I should give you five hundred paunds ?

Fash. I do not ask it as a due, brother, I am willing to receive it as a favour.

Lord Fop. Thau art willing to receive it any haw, strike me speechless ! But these are damned times to give money in, taxes are so great, repairs so exorbitant, tenants such rogues, and periwigs so dear, that the devil take me, I am reduced to that extremity in my cash, I have been forced to retrench in that one article of sweet pawder, till I have braught it dawn to five guineas a manth. Naw judge, Tam, whether I can spare you five hundred paunds.   106

Fash. If you can't, I must starve, that's all.—[*Aside.*] Damn him !

Lord Fop. All I can say is, you should have been a better husband.

Fash. Oons, if you can't live upon five thousand a year, how do you think I should do't upon two hundred ?

Lord Fop. Don't be in a passion, Tam ; far passion is the most unbecoming thing in the world—to the face. Look you, I don't love to say anything to you to make you melancholy ; but upon this occasion I must take leave to put you in mind that a running horse does require more attendance than a coach-horse. Nature has made some difference 'twixt you and I.   119

Fash. Yes, she has made you older.—[*Aside.*] Pox take her !

Lord Fop. That is nat all, Tam.

Fash. Why, what is there else ?

Lord Fop. [*Looking first upon himself, then upon his brother.*] Ask the ladies.

Fash. Why, thou essence bottle ! thou musk cat ! dost thou then think thou hast any advantage over me but what Fortune has given thee ?

Lord Fop. I do—stap my vitals !

Fash. Now, by all that's great and powerful, thou art the prince of coxcombs !   130

Lord Fop. Sir—I am praud of being at the head of so prevailing a party.

Fash. Will nothing then provoke thee ? Draw, coward !

Lord Fop. Look you, Tam, you know I have always taken you for a mighty dull fellow, and here is one of the foolishest plats broke out that I have seen a long time.

Your paverty makes your life so burdensome to you, you would provoke me to a quarrel, in hopes either to slip through my lungs into my estate, or to get yourself run through the guts, to put an end to your pain.   But I will disappoint you in both your designs; far, with the temper of a philasapher, and the discretion of a statesman—I will go to the play with my sword in my scabbard.   [*Exit.*

Fash. So!   Farewell, snuff-box! and now, conscience, I defy thee.—Lory!   145

Enter LORY.

Lory. Sir!

Fash. Here's rare news, Lory; his lordship has given me a pill has purged off all my scruples.

Lory. Then my heart's at ease again.   For I have been in a lamentable fright, sir, ever since your conscience had the impudence to intrude into your company.

Fash. Be at peace, it will come there no more: my brother has given it a wring by the nose, and I have kicked it down stairs.   So run away to the inn; get the horses ready quickly, and bring 'em to old Coupler's, without a moment's delay.   156

Lory. Then, sir, you are going straight about the fortune?

Fash. I am.   Away! fly, Lory!

Lory. The happiest day I ever saw.   I'm upon the wing already.   [*Exeunt several ways.*

———

SCENE II.—*A Garden.*
Enter LOVELESS *and* Servant.

Love. Is my wife within?

Ser. No, sir, she has been gone out this half hour.

F

Love. 'Tis well, leave me. [*Exit* Servant.
Sure fate has yet some business to be done,
Before Amanda's heart and mine must rest ;
Else, why amongst those legions of her sex,
Which throng the world,
Should she pick out for her companion
The only one on earth
Whom nature has endow'd for her undoing ? 10
Undoing, was't, I said !—who shall undo her?
Is not her empire fix'd ? am I not hers ?
Did she not rescue me, a grovelling slave,
When chain'd and bound by that black tyrant vice,
I labour'd in his vilest drudgery ?
Did she not ransom me, and set me free?
Nay more : when by my follies sunk
To a poor tatter'd despicable beggar,
Did she not lift me up to envied fortune ?
Give me herself, and all that she possess'd, 20
Without a thought of more return,
Than what a poor repenting heart might make her ?
Han't she done this ? And if she has,
Am I not strongly bound to love her for it ?
To love her !—why, do I not love her then ?
By earth and heaven I do !
Nay, I have demonstration that I do:
For I would sacrifice my life to serve her.
Yet hold—if laying down my life
Be demonstration of my love, 30
What is't I feel in favour of Berinthia?
For should she be in danger, methinks I could incline to
risk it for her service too ; and yet I do not love her. How

then subsists my proof?—Oh, I have found it out ! What I would do for one, is demonstration of my love ; and if I'd do as much for t'other : it there is demonstration of my friendship.—Ay—it must be so.   I find I'm very much her friend.—Yet let me ask myself one puzzling question more : Whence springs this mighty friendship all at once ? For our acquaintance is of later date.   Now friendship's said to be a plant of tedious growth ; its root composed of tender fibres, nice in their taste, cautious in spreading, check'd with the least corruption in the soil ; long ere it take, and longer still ere it appear to do so : whilst mine is in a moment shot so high, and fix'd so fast, it seems beyond the power of storms to shake it.   I doubt it thrives too fast.   [*Musing*.

Enter Berinthia.

Ha, she here !—Nay, then take heed, my heart, for there are dangers towards.   48

Ber. What makes you look so thoughtful, sir ? I hope you are not ill.

Love. I was debating, madam, whether I was so or not ; and that was it which made me look so thoughtful.

Ber. Is it then so hard a matter to decide ? I thought all people had been acquainted with their own bodies, though few people know their own minds.

Love. What if the distemper, I suspect, be in the mind ?

Ber. Why then I'll undertake to prescribe you a cure.

Love. Alas ! you undertake you know not what.   59

Ber. So far at least then allow me to be a physician.

Love. Nay, I'll allow you so yet farther : for I have

reason to believe, should I put myself into your hands, you would increase my distemper.

Ber. Perhaps I might have reasons from the college not to be too quick in your cure ; but 'tis possible I might find ways to give you often ease, sir.

Love. Were I but sure of that, I'd quickly lay my case before you.

Ber. Whether you are sure of it or no, what risk do you run in trying ?   70

Love. Oh ! a very great one.

Ber. How ?

Love. You might betray my distemper to my wife.

Ber. And so lose all my practice.

Love. Will you then keep my secret ?

Ber. I will, if it don't burst me.

Love. Swear.

Ber. I do.

Love. By what ?

Ber. By woman.   80

Love. That's swearing by my deity. Do it by your own, or I shan't believe you.

Ber. By man then.

Love. I'm satisfied. Now hear my symptoms, and give me your advice. The first were these :
When 'twas my chance to see you at the play,
A random glance you threw at first alarm'd me,
I could not turn my eyes from whence the danger came :
I gaz'd upon you till you shot again,
And then my fears came on me.   90
My heart began to pant, my limbs to tremble,
My blood grew thin, my pulse beat quick, my eyes

Grew hot and dim, and all the frame of nature
Shook with apprehension.
'Tis true, some small recruits of resolution
My manhood brought to my assistance ;
And by their help I made a stand a while,
But found at last your arrows flew so thick,
They could not fail to pierce me ; so left the field,
And fled for shelter to Amanda's arms.   100
What think you of these symptoms, pray ?
    Ber.   Feverish every one of 'em.
But what relief pray did your wife afford you ?
    Love.   Why, instantly she let me blood ;
Which for the present much assuag'd my flame.
But when I saw you, out it burst again,
And rag'd with greater fury than before.
Nay, since you now appear, 'tis so increas'd,
That in a moment, if you do not help me,
I shall, whilst you look on, consume to ashes.   110
                            [*Taking hold of her hand.*
    Ber.   [*Breaking from him.*]   O Lard, let me go! 'Tis the
plague, and we shall all be infected.
    Love.   [*Catching her in his arms, and kissing her.*]
Then we'll die together, my charming angel !
    Ber.   O Ged—the devil's in you!—Lord, let me go,
here's somebody coming.

                    Enter Servant.

    Ser.   Sir, my lady's come home, and desires to speak
with you : she's in her chamber.
    Love.   Tell her I'm coming.—[*Exit* Servant.]   But
before I go, one glass of nectar more to drink her health.

Ber.   Stand off, or I shall hate you, by Heavens !   120
Love. [*Kissing her.*]   In matters of love, a woman's oath is no more to be minded than a man's.
Ber.   Um—

Enter WORTHY.

Wor. [*Aside.*]   Ha ! what's here ? my old mistress, and so close, i' faith !   I would not spoil her sport for the universe.   [*Exit.*
Ber.   O Ged !—Now do I pray to Heaven,—[*Exit* LOVELESS *running*] with all my heart and soul, that the devil in hell may take me, if ever—I was better pleased in my life !—This man has bewitched me, that's certain.— [*Sighing.*] Well, I am condemned ; but, thanks to Heaven, I feel myself each moment more and more prepared for my execution.   Nay, to that degree, I don't perceive I have the least fear of dying.   No, I find, let the executioner be but a man, and there's nothing will suffer with more resolution than a woman.   Well, I never had but one intrigue yet—but I confess I long to have another.   Pray Heaven it end as the first did though, that we may both grow weary at a time ; for 'tis a melancholy thing for lovers to outlive one another.   140

Re-enter WORTHY.

Wor. [*Aside.*]   This discovery's a lucky one, I hope to make a happy use on't.   That gentlewoman there is no fool ; so I shall be able to make her understand her interest.—[*Aloud.*]   Your servant, madam ; I need not ask you how you do, you have got so good a colour.

Ber.   No better than I used to have, I suppose.

Wor.   A little more blood in your cheeks.

Ber.   The weather's hot.

Wor.   If it were not, a woman may have a colour.

Ber.   What do you mean by that?   150

Wor.   Nothing.

Ber.   Why do you smile then?

Wor.   Because the weather's hot.

Ber.   You'll never leave roguing, I see that.

Wor.   [*Putting his finger to his nose.*]   You'll never leave —I see that.

Ber.   Well, I can't imagine what you drive at.   Pray tell me what you mean?

Wor.   Do you tell me ; it's the same thing.

Ber.   I can't.   160

Wor.   Guess !

Ber.   I shall guess wrong.

Wor.   Indeed you won't.

Ber.   Psha ! either tell, or let it alone.

Wor.   Nay, rather than let it alone, I will tell.   But first I must put you in mind, that after what has passed 'twixt you and I, very few things ought to be secrets between us.

Ber.   Why, what secrets do we hide?   I know of none.

Wor.   Yes, there are two ; one I have hid from you, and t'other you would hide from me.   You are fond of Loveless, which I have discovered ; and I am fond of his wife —

Ber.   Which I have discovered.   174

Wor.   Very well, now I confess your discovery to be true : what do you say to mine?

Ber. Why, I confess—I would swear 'twere false, if I thought you were fool enough to believe me.

Wor. Now I am almost in love with you again. Nay, I don't know but I might be quite so, had I made one short campaign with Amanda. Therefore, if you find 'twould tickle your vanity to bring me down once more to your lure, e'en help me quickly to dispatch her business, that I may have nothing else to do, but to apply myself to yours.   185

Ber. Do you then think, sir, I am old enough to be a bawd ?

Wor. No, but I think you are wise enough to—

Ber. To do what ?

Wor. To hoodwink Amanda with a gallant, that she mayn't see who is her husband's mistress.

Ber. [*Aside.*] He has reason : the hint's a good one.

Wor. Well, madam, what think you on't.

Ber. I think you are so much a deeper politician in these affairs than I am, that I ought to have a very great regard to your advice.   196

Wor. Then give me leave to put you in mind, that the most easy, safe, and pleasant situation for your own amour, is the house in which you now are; provided you keep Amanda from any sort of suspicion. That the way to do that, is to engage her in an intrigue of her own, making yourself her confidant. And the way to bring her to intrigue, is to make her jealous of her husband in a wrong place; which the more you foment, the less you'll be suspected. This is my scheme, in short; which if you follow as you should do, my dear Berinthia, we may all four pass the winter very pleasantly.   207

Ber. Well, I could be glad to have nobody's sins to answer for but my own. But where there is a necessity—

Wor. Right: as you say, where there is a necessity, a Christian is bound to help his neighbour. So, good Berinthia, lose no time, but let us begin the dance as fast as we can.

Ber. Not till the fiddles are in tune, pray sir. Your lady's strings will be very apt to fly, I can tell you that, if they are wound up too hastily. But if you'll have patience to screw 'em to their pitch by degrees, I don't doubt but she may endure to be played upon.

Wor. Ay, and will make admirable music too, or I'm mistaken. But have you had no private closet discourse with her yet about males and females, and so forth, which may give you hopes in her constitution? for I know her morals are the devil against us.   222

Ber. I have had so much discourse with her, that I believe, were she once cured of her fondness to her husband, the fortress of her virtue would not be so impregnable as she fancies.

Wor. What! she runs, I'll warrant you, into that common mistake of fond wives, who conclude themselves virtuous, because they can refuse a man they don't like, when they have got one they do.

Ber. True ; and therefore I think 'tis a presumptuous thing in a woman to assume the name of virtuous, till she has heartily hated her husband, and been soundly in love with somebody else. Whom, if she has withstood,—then —much good may it do her.   235

Wor. Well, so much for her virtue. Now, one word of her inclinations, and every one to their post. What opinion do you find she has of me?

Ber. What you could wish; she thinks you handsome and discreet.

Wor. Good; that's thinking half-seas over. One tide more brings us into port.

Ber. Perhaps it may, though still remember, there's a difficult bar to pass.

Wor. I know there is, but I don't question I shall get well over it, by the help of such a pilot.

Ber. You may depend upon your pilot, she'll do the best she can ; so weigh anchor and begone as soon as you please.

Wor. I'm under sail already.   Adieu !   250

Ber. *Bon voyage !*—[*Exit* WORTHY.]   So, here's fine work ! What a business have I undertaken ! I'm a very pretty gentlewoman truly ! But there was no avoiding it : he'd have ruined me, if I had refused him. Besides, faith, I begin to fancy there may be as much pleasure in carrying on another body's intrigue as one's own. This at least is certain, it exercises almost all the entertaining faculties of a woman : for there's employment for hypocrisy, invention, deceit, flattery, mischief, and lying.

Enter AMANDA, *her* Woman *following her.*

Wom. If you please, madam, only to say, whether you'll have me buy 'em or not.   261

Aman. Yes, no, go fiddle ! I care not what you do. Prithee leave me.

Wom. I have done.   [*Exit.*

Ber. What in the name of Jove's the matter with you ?

Aman. The matter, Berinthia ! I'm almost mad, I'm plagued to death.

Ber. Who is it that plagues you ?

Aman. Who do you think should plague a wife, but her husband ? 270

Ber. O ho, is it come to that ? We shall have you wish yourself a widow by and by.

Aman. Would I were anything but what I am ! A base ungrateful man, after what I have done for him, to use me thus !

Ber. What, he has been ogling now, I'll warrant you ?

Aman. . Yes, he has been ogling.

Ber. And so you are jealous ? is that all ?

Aman. That all ! is jealousy then nothing ?

Ber. It should be nothing, if I were in your case. 280

Aman. Why, what would you do ?

Ber. I'd cure myself.

Aman. How ?

Ber. Let blood in the fond vein : care as little for my husband as he did for me. .

Aman. That would not stop his course.

Ber. Nor nothing else, when the wind's in the warm corner. Look you, Amanda, you may build castles in the air, and fume, and fret, and grow thin and lean, and pale and ugly, if you please. But I tell you, no man worth having is true to his wife, or can be true to his wife, or ever was, or ever will be so. 292

Aman. Do you then really think he's false to me ? for I did but suspect him.

Ber. Think so ! I know he's so.

Aman. Is it possible ? Pray tell me what you know.

Ber. Don't press me then to name names, for that I have sworn I won't do.

Aman.   Well, I won't ; but let me know all you can without perjury.   300

Ber.   I'll let you know enough to prevent any wise woman's dying of the pip ; and I hope you'll pluck up your spirits, and show upon occasion you can be as good a wife as the best of 'em.

Aman.   Well, what a woman can do I'll endeavour.

Ber.   Oh, a woman can do a great deal, if once she sets her mind to it.   Therefore pray don't stand trifling any longer, and teasing yourself with this and that, and your love and your virtue, and I know not what : but resolve to hold up your head, get a-tiptoe, and look over 'em all ; for to my certain knowledge your husband is a pickeering* elsewhere.   312

Aman.   You are sure on't ?

Ber.   Positively ; he fell in love at the play.

Aman.   Right, the very same.   Do you know the ugly thing ?

Ber.   Yes, I know her well enough ; but she's not such an ugly thing neither.

Aman.   Is she very handsome ?

Ber.   Truly I think so.

Aman.   Hey ho !

Ber.   What do you sigh for now ?

Aman.   Oh, my heart !   323

Ber. [*Aside.*]   Only the pangs of nature ; she's in labour of her love ; Heaven send her a quick delivery, I'm sure she has a good midwife.

---

* To pickeer is "to rob or pillage ; from the Italian.   Not much in use."—*Nares.*

Aman. I'm very ill, I must go to my chamber. Dear
Berinthia, don't leave me a moment.

Ber. No, don't fear.—[*Aside.*] I'll see you safe brought
to bed, I'll warrant you.

[*Exeunt,* AMANDA *leaning upon* BERINTHIA.

SCENE III.—Sir TUNBELLY CLUMSEY'S *Country-House.*

Enter Young FASHION *and* LORY.

Fash. So, here's our inheritance, Lory, if we can but get
into possession. But methinks the seat of our family looks
like Noah's ark, as if the chief part on't were designed for
the fowls of the air, and the beasts of the field.

Lory. Pray, sir, don't let your head run upon the orders
of building here; get but the heiress, let the devil take the
house.

Fash. Get but the house, let the devil take the heiress,
I say; at least if she be as old Coupler describes her. But
come, we have no time to squander. Knock at the door.—
[LORY *knocks two or three times.*] What the devil, have they
got no ears in this house? Knock harder.   12

Lory. Egad, sir, this will prove some enchanted castle;
we shall have the giant come out by and by with his club,
and beat our brains out.   [*Knocks again.*

Fash. Hush! they come.

Servant. [*Within.*] Who is there?

Lory. Open the door and see. Is that your country
breeding?

Ser. Ay, but two words to a bargain.—Tummas, is the
blunderbuss primed?

Fash. Oons, give 'em good words, Lory; we shall be shot here a fortune-catching.

Lory. Egad, sir, I think y'are in the right on't.—Ho ! Mr. What-d'ye-call-um.   25

[Servant *appears at the window with a blunderbuss.*

Ser. Weall, naw what's yare business ?

Fash. Nothing, sir, but to wait upon sir Tunbelly, with your leave.

Ser. To weat upon sir Tunbelly ! Why, you'll find that's just as sir Tunbelly pleases.

Fash. But will you do me the favour, sir, to know whether sir Tunbelly pleases or not ?

Ser. Why, look you, do you see, with good words much may be done.—Ralph, go thy weas, and ask sir Tunbelly if he pleases to be waited upon. And dost hear ? call to nurse that she may lock up Miss Hoyden before the geat's open.   37

Fash. D'ye hear that, Lory ?

Lory. Ay, sir, I'm afraid we shall find a difficult job on't. Pray Heaven that old rogue Coupler han't sent us to fetch milk out of the gunroom.

Fash. I'll warrant thee all will go well. See, the door opens.

Enter Sir TUNBELLY, *with his* Servants *armed with guns, clubs, pitchforks, scythes, &c.*

Lory. [*Running behind his master.*] O Lord ! O Lord ! O Lord ! we are both dead men !

Fash. Take heed, fool ! thy fear will ruin us.

Lory. My fear, sir ! 'sdeath, sir, I fear nothing.—[*Aside.*] Would I were well up to the chin in a horsepond !

Sir Tun. Who is it here has any business with me?   49

Fash. Sir, 'tis I, if your name be sir Tunbelly Clumsey.

Sir Tun. Sir, my name is sir Tunbelly Clumsey, whether you have any business with me or not. So you see I am not ashamed of my name—nor my face neither.

Fash. Sir, you have no cause, that I know of.

Sir Tun. Sir, if you have no cause neither, I desire to know who you are; for till I know your name, I shall not ask you to come into my house; and when I know your name—'tis six to four I don't ask you neither.   61

Fash. [*Giving him a letter.*]   Sir, I hope you'll find this letter an authentic passport.

Sir Tun. Cod's my life! I ask your lordship's pardon ten thousand times.—[*To a* Servant.]   Here, run in a-doors quickly. Get a Scotch-coal fire in the great parlour; set all the Turkey-work chairs in their places; get the great brass candlesticks out, and be sure stick the sockets full of laurel, run!—[*Exit* Servant.]   My lord, I ask your lordship's pardon.—[*To other* Servants.]   And do you hear, run away to nurse, bid her let Miss Hoyden loose again, and if it was not shifting day, let her put on a clean tucker, quick!— [*Exeunt* Servants *confusedly.*]   I hope your honour will excuse the disorder of my family; we are not used to receive men of your lordship's great quality every day. Pray where are your coaches and servants, my lord?   77

Fash. Sir, that I might give you and your fair daughter a proof how impatient I am to be nearer akin to you, I left

my equipage to follow me, and came away post with only one
servant.

Sir Tun. Your lordship does me too much honour. It
was exposing your person to too much fatigue and danger, I
protest it was. But my daughter shall endeavour to make
you what amends she can ; and though I say it that should
not say it—Hoyden has charms.

Fash. Sir, I am not a stranger to them, though I am to
her. Common fame has done her justice. 88

Sir Tun. My lord, I am common fame's very grateful
humble servant. My lord —my girl's young, Hoyden is
young, my lord ; but this I must say for her, what she wants
in art, she has by nature ; what she wants in experience, she
has in breeding ; and what's wanting in her age, is made
good in her constitution. So pray, my lord, walk in : pray,
my lord, walk in.

Fash. Sir, I wait upon you.   [*Exeunt.*

———

SCENE IV.—*A Room in the same.*

Miss HOYDEN *discovered alone.*

Hoyd. Sure never nobody was used as I am. I know
well enough what other girls do, for all they think to make
a fool of me. It's well I have a husband coming, or, ecod,
I'd marry the baker, I would so ! Nobody can knock at the
gate, but presently I must be locked up ; and here's the
young greyhound bitch can run loose about the house all
day long, she can ; 'tis very well.

Nurse. [*Without, opening the door.*] Miss Hoyden !
miss ! miss ! miss ! Miss Hoyden !   9

Enter Nurse.

Hoyd. Well, what do you make such a noise for, ha? what do you din a body's ears for? Can't one be at quiet for you?

Nurse. What do I din your ears for! Here's one come will din your ears for you.

Hoyd. What care I who's come? I care not a fig who comes, nor who goes, as long as I must be locked up like the ale-cellar.

Nurse. That, miss, is for fear you should be drank before you are ripe.

Hoyd. Oh, don't you trouble your head about that; I'm as ripe as you, though not so mellow.   20

Nurse. Very well; now have I a good mind to lock you up again, and not let you see my lord to-night.

Hoyd. My lord! why, is my husband come?

Nurse. Yes, marry is he, and a goodly person too.

Hoyd. [*Hugging* Nurse.] O my dear nurse! forgive me this once, and I'll never misuse you again; no, if I do, you shall give me three thumps on the back, and a great pinch by the cheek.

Nurse. Ah, the poor thing, see how it melts. It's as full of good-nature as an egg's full of meat.   30

Hoyd. But, my dear nurse, don't lie now; is he come by your troth?

Nurse. Yes, by my truly, is he.

Hoyd. O Lord! I'll go put on my laced smock, though I'm whipped till the blood run down my heels for't.

[*Exit running.*

Nurse. Eh—the Lord succour thee! How thou art delighted!   [*Exit after her*

G

SCENE V.—*Another Room in the same.*

Enter Sir TUNBELLY *and* Young FASHION. *A* Servant
with wine.

Sir Tun. My lord, I am proud of the honour to see your
lordship within my doors ; and I humbly crave leave to bid
you welcome in a cup of sack wine.

Fash. Sir, to your daughter's health.   [*Drinks.*

Sir Tun. Ah, poor girl, she'll be scared out of her wits
on her wedding-night; for, honestly speaking, she does not
know a man from a woman but by his beard and his
breeches.

Fash. Sir, I don't doubt but she has a virtuous education, which with the rest of her merit makes me long to see
her mine. I wish you would dispense with the canonical
hour, and let it be this very night.   12

Sir Tun. Oh, not so soon neither I that's shooting my
girl before you bid her stand. No, give her fair warning, we'll sign and seal to-night, if you please ; and this day
seven-night—let the jade look to her quarters.

Fash. This day se'nnight I—why, what, do you take me
for a ghost, sir ? 'Slife, sir, I'm made of flesh and blood,
and bones and sinews, and can no more live a week without
your daughter—[*Aside.*] than I can live a month with her.

Sir Tun. Oh, I'll warrant you, my hero ; young men
are hot, I know, but they don't boil over at that rate,
neither. Besides, my wench's wedding-gown is not come
home yet.   24

Fash. Oh, no matter, sir, I'll take her in her shift.—
[*Aside.*] A pox of this old fellow I he'll delay the business
till my damned star finds me out and discovers me.—

[*Aloud.*]   Pray, sir, let it be done without ceremony, 'twill save money.

Sir Tun.   Money!—save money when Hoyden's to be married! Udswoons, I'll give my wench a wedding-dinner, though I go to grass with the king of Assyria for't; and such a dinner it shall be, as is not to be cooked in the poaching of an egg.   Therefore, my noble lord, have a little patience, we'll go and look over our deeds and settlements immediately; and as for your bride, though you may be sharp-set before she's quite ready, I'll engage for my girl she stays your stomach at last.   [*Exeunt.*

ACT IV.

SCENE I.—*A Room in* Sir TUNBELLY CLUMSEY'S *Country-House.*

Enter Miss HOYDEN *and* Nurse.

Nurse. Well, miss, how do you like your husband that is to be ?

Hoyd. O Lord, nurse! I'm so overjoyed I can scarce contain myself.

Nurse. Oh, but you must have a care of being too fond; for men now-a-days hate a woman that loves 'em.

Hoyd. Love him ! why, do you think I love him, nurse? ecod, I would not care if he were hanged, so I were but once married to him !—No—that which pleases me, is to think what work I'll make when I get to London ; for when I am a wife and a lady both, nurse, ecod, I'll flaunt it with the best of 'em.   12

Nurse. Look, look, if his honour be not coming again to you ! Now, if I were sure you would behave yourself handsomely, and not disgrace me that have brought you up, I'd leave you alone together.

Hoyd. That's my best nurse, do as you would be done by ; trust us together this once, and if I don't show my breeding from the head to the foot of me, may I be twice married, and die a maid.

Nurse. Well, this once I'll venture you ; but if you dis-
parage me—   22

Hoyd. Never fear, I'll show him my parts, I'll warrant
him.—[*Exit* Nurse.] These old women are so wise when
they get a poor girl in their clutches ! but ere it be long, I
shall know what's what, as well as the best of 'em.

Enter Young Fashion.

Fash. Your servant, madam ; I'm glad to find you alone,
for I have something of importance to speak to you about.

Hoyd. Sir (my lord, I meant), you may speak to me
about what you please, I shall give you a civil answer.

Fash. You give me so obliging a one, it encourages me
to tell you in few words what I think both for your interest
and mine. Your father, I suppose you know, has resolved
to make me happy in being your husband, and I hope I
may depend upon your consent, to perform what he
desires.   36

Hoyd. Sir, I never disobey my father in anything but
eating of green gooseberries.

Fash. So good a daughter must needs make an admirable
wife ; I am therefore impatient till you are mine, and hope
you will so far consider the violence of my love, that you
won't have the cruelty to defer my happiness so long as
your father designs it.

Hoyd. Pray, my lord, how long is that ?

Fash. Madam, a thousand year—a whole week.

Hoyd. A week !—why, I shall be an old woman by that
time.

Fash. And I an old man, which you'll find a greater
misfortune than t'other.   49

Hoyd. Why, I thought 'twas to be to-morrow morning, as soon as I was up; I'm sure nurse told me so.

Fash. And it shall be to-morrow morning still, if you'll consent.

Hoyd. If I'll consent! Why, I thought I was to obey you as my husband.

Fash. That's when we are married; till then, I am to obey you.

Hoyd. Why then, if we are to take it by turns, it's the same thing; I'll obey you now, and when we are married, you shall obey me.   60

Fash. With all my heart; but I doubt we must get nurse on our side, or we shall hardly prevail with the chaplain.

Hoyd. No more we shan't indeed, for he loves her better than he loves his pulpit, and would always be a preaching to her by his good will.

Fash. Why then, my dear little bedfellow, if you'll call her hither, we'll try to persuade her presently.

Hoyd. O Lord, I can tell you a way how to persuade her to anything.   70

Fash. How's that?

Hoyd. Why, tell her she's a wholesome comely woman —and give her half-a-crown.

Fash. Nay, if that will do, she shall have half a score of 'em.

Hoyd. O gemini! for half that, she'd marry you her-self. I'll run and call her.   [*Exit.*

Fash. So, matters go swimmingly. This is a rare girl, i' faith; I shall have a fine time on't with her at London. I'm much mistaken if she don't prove a March hare all the

year round. What a scampering chase will she make on't,
when she finds the whole kennel of beaux at her tail! Hey
to the park, and the play, and the church, and the devil;
she'll show 'em sport, I'll warrant 'em. But no matter, she
brings an estate will afford me a separate maintenance.   85

Re-enter Miss HOYDEN *and* Nurse.

How do you do, good mistress nurse? I desired your
young lady would give me leave to see you, that I might
thank you for your extraordinary care and conduct in her
education; pray accept of this small acknowledgment for
it at present, and depend upon my farther kindness, when I
shall be that happy thing her husband.

Nurse. [*Aside.*] Gold by makings!—[*Aloud.*] Your
honour's goodness is too great; alas! all I can boast of is,
I gave her pure good milk, and so your honour would have
said, an you had seen how the poor thing sucked it.—Eh,
God's blessing on the sweet face on't! how it used to hang
at this poor teat, and suck and squeeze, and kick and
sprawl it would, till the belly on't was so full, it would drop
off like a leach.   99

Hoyd. [*Aside to* Nurse *angrily.*] Pray one word with
you. Prithee nurse, don't stand ripping up old stories, to
make one ashamed before one's love. Do you think such a
fine proper gentleman as he is cares for a fiddlecome tale of a
draggle-tailed girl? If you have a mind to make him have
a good opinion of a woman, don't tell him what one did
then, tell him what one can do now.—[*To* Young
FASHION.] I hope your honour will excuse my mis-
manners to whisper before you; it was only to give some
orders about the family.   109

Fash. O everything, madam, is to give way to business !
Besides, good housewifery is a very commendable quality
in a young lady.

Hoyd. Pray, sir, are the young ladies good housewives
at London town ? Do they darn their own linen ?

Fash. O no, they study how to spend money, not to
save it.

Hoyd. Ecod, I don't know but that may be better sport
than t'other ; ha, nurse ?

Fash. Well, you shall have your choice when you come
there.   120

Hoyd. Shall I ?—then by my troth I'll get there as fast
as I can.— [*To* Nurse.] His honour desires you'll be so
kind as to let us be married to-morrow.

Nurse. To-morrow, my dear madam ?

Fash. Yes, to-morrow, sweet nurse, privately ; young
folks, you know, are impatient, and Sir Tunbelly would
make us stay a week for a wedding dinner. Now all things
being signed and sealed, and agreed, I fancy there could be
no great harm in practising a scene or two of matrimony in
private, if it were only to give us the better assurance when
we come to play it in public.   131

Nurse. Nay, I must confess stolen pleasures are sweet ;
but if you should be married now, what will you do when
sir Tunbelly calls for you to be wed ?

Hoyd. Why then we'll be married again.

Nurse. What, twice, my child ?

Hoyd. Ecod, I don't care how often I'm married, not I.

Fash. Pray, nurse, don't you be against your young
lady's good, for by this means she'll have the pleasure of
two wedding-days.   140

Hoyd. [*To* Nurse *softly.*] And of two wedding-nights too, nurse.

Nurse. Well, I'm such a tender-hearted fool, I find I can refuse nothing; so you shall e'en follow your own inventions.

Hoyd. Shall I ?—[*Aside.*] O Lord, I could leap over the moon !

Fash. Dear nurse, this goodness of yours shan't go unrewarded ; but now you must employ your power with Mr. Bull the chaplain, that he may do us his friendly office too, and then we shall all be happy : do you think you can prevail with him ?   152

Nurse. Prevail with him !—or he shall never prevail with me, I can tell him that.

Hoyd. My lord, she has had him upon the hip this seven year.

Fash. I'm glad to hear it ; however, to strengthen your interest with him, you may let him know I have several fat livings in my gift, and that the first that falls shall be in your disposal.

Nurse. Nay, then I'll make him marry more folks than one, I'll promise him.   162

Hoyd. Faith do, nurse, make him marry you too, I'm sure he'll do't for a fat living : for he loves eating more than he loves his Bible ; and I have often heard him say, a fat living was the best meat in the world.

Nurse. Ay, and I'll make him commend the sauce too, or I'll bring his gown to a cassock, I will so.

Fash. Well, nurse, whilst you go and settle matters with him, then your lady and I will go take a walk in the garden.

Nurse. I'll do your honour's business in the catching up of a garter.   [*Exit.*

Fash. [*Giving her his hand.*]   Come, madam, dare you venture yourself alone with me ?

Hoyd.   O dear, yes, sir, I don't think you'll do anything to me I need be afraid on.   [*Exeunt.*

SCENE II.—LOVELESS's *Lodgings.*

Enter AMANDA *and* BERINTHIA.

A SONG.

I.

I smile at Love and all its arts,
    The charming Cynthia cried :
Take heed, for Love has piercing darts,
    A wounded swain replied.
Once free and blest as you are now,
    I trifled with his charms,
I pointed at his little bow,
    And sported with his arms :
Till urg'd too far, Revenge ! he cries,
    A fatal shaft he drew,
It took its passage through your eyes,
    And to my heart it flew.

II.

To tear it thence I tried in vain,
    To strive, I quickly found,
Was only to increase the pain,
    And to enlarge the wound.
Ah ! much too well, I fear, you know
    What pain I'm to endure,
Since what your eyes alone could do,
    Your heart alone can cure.
And that (grant Heaven I may mistake !)
    I doubt is doom'd to bear
A burden for another's sake,
    Who ill rewards its care.

Aman. Well, now, Berinthia, I'm at leisure to hear what 'twas you had to say to me.

Ber. What I had to say was only to echo the sighs and groans of a dying lover.

Aman. Phu ! will you never learn to talk in earnest of anything ?

Ber. Why this shall be in earnest, if you please : for my part, I only tell you matter of fact, you may take it which way you like best; but if you'll follow the women of the town, you'll take it both ways; for when a man offers himself to one of them, first she takes him in jest, and then she takes him in earnest.   12

Aman. I'm sure there's so much jest and earnest in what you say to me, I scarce know how to take it; but I think you have bewitched me, for I don't find it possible to be angry with you, say what you will.

Ber. I'm very glad to hear it, for I have no mind to quarrel with you, for more reasons than I'll brag of; but quarrel or not, smile or frown, I must tell you what I have suffered upon your account.

Aman. Upon my account !

Ber. Yes, upon yours ; I have been forced to sit still and hear you commended for two hours together, without one compliment to myself ; now don't you think a woman had a blessed time of that ?   25

Aman. Alas ! I should have been unconcerned at it ; I never knew where the pleasure lay of being praised by the men. But pray who was this that commended me so ?

Ber. One you have a mortal aversion to, Mr. Worthy ; he used you like a text, he took you all to pieces, but spoke so learnedly upon every point, one might see the

spirit of the church was in him.   If you are a woman, you'd
have been in an ecstasy to have heard how feelingly he
handled your hair, your eyes, your nose, your mouth, your
teeth, your tongue, your chin, your neck, and so forth.
Thus he preached for an hour, but when he came to use an
application, he observed that all these without a gallant were
nothing.—Now consider of what has been said, and Heaven
give you grace to put it in practice.   39

Aman.   Alas ! Berinthia, did I incline to a gallant (which
you know I do not), do you think a man so nice as he
could have the least concern for such a plain unpolished
thing as I am ? it is impossible !

Ber.   Now have you a great mind to put me upon
commending you.

Aman.   Indeed that was not my design.

Ber.   Nay, if it were, it's all one, for I won't do't, I'll
leave that to your looking-glass.   But to show you I have
some good nature left, I'll commend him, and may be that
may do as well.   50

Aman.   You have a great mind to persuade me I am in
love with him.

Ber.   I have a great mind to persuade you, you don't
know what you are in love with.

Aman.   I am sure I am not in love with him, nor never
shall be, so let that pass.   But you were saying something
you would commend him for.

Ber.   Oh ! you'd be glad to hear a good character of him,
however.

Aman.   Psha !   60

Ber.   Psha !—Well, 'tis a foolish undertaking for women
in these kind of matters to pretend to deceive one

another.—Have not I been bred a woman as well as you?

Aman. What then?

Ber. Why, then I understand my trade so well, that whenever I am told of a man I like, I cry, Psha! But that I may spare you the pains of putting me a second time in mind to commend him, I'll proceed, and give you this account of him. That though 'tis possible he may have had women with as good faces as your ladyship's, (no discredit to it neither,) yet you must know your cautious behaviour, with that reserve in your humour, has given him his death's wound; he mortally hates a coquette. He says 'tis impossible to love where we cannot esteem; and that no woman can be esteemed by a man who has sense, if she makes herself cheap in the eye of a fool; that pride to a woman is as necessary as humility to a divine; and that far-fetched and dear-bought, is meat for gentlemen as well as for ladies; —in short, that every woman who has beauty may set a price upon herself, and that by under-selling the market, they ruin the trade. This is his doctrine, how do you like it?

Aman. So well, that since I never intend to have a gallant for myself, if I were to recommend one to a friend, he should be the man.   85

Enter WORTHY.

Bless me! he's here, pray Heaven he did not hear me.

Ber. If he did, it won't hurt your reputation; your thoughts are as safe in his heart as in your own.

Wor. I venture in at an unseasonable time of night, ladies; I hope, if I'm troublesome, you'll use the same freedom in turning me out again.

Aman. I believe it can't be late, for Mr. Loveless is not come home yet, and he usually keeps good hours.

Wor. Madam, I'm afraid he'll transgress a little to-night ; for he told me about half an hour ago, he was going to sup with some company he doubted would keep him out till three or four o'clock in the morning, and desired I would let my servant acquaint you with it, that you might not expect him : but my fellow's a blunderhead ; so lest he should make some mistake, I thought it my duty to deliver the message myself.   101

Aman. I'm very sorry he should give you that trouble, sir : but—

Ber. But since he has, will you give me leave, madam, to keep him to play at ombre with us ?

Aman. Cousin, you know you command my house.

Wor. [*To* BERINTHIA.] And, madam, you know you command me, though I'm a very wretched gamester.

Ber. Oh ! you play well enough to lose your money, and that's all the ladies require ; so without any more ceremony, let us go into the next room and call for the cards.

Aman. With all my heart.

[*Exit* WORTHY, *leading* AMANDA.

Ber. Well, how this business will end Heaven knows ; but she seems to me to be in as fair a way—as a boy is to be a rogue, when he's put clerk to an attorney.   [*Exit.*

SCENE III.—BERINTHIA'S *Chamber.*

Enter LOVELESS *cautiously in the dark.*

Love. So, thus far all's well. I'm got into her bed-chamber, and I think nobody has perceived me steal into

the house ; my wife don't expect me home till four
o'clock ; so, if Berinthia comes to bed by eleven, I shall
have a chase of five hours.   Let me see, where shall
I hide myself?   Under her bed?   No ; we shall have
her maid searching there for something or other ; her
closet's a better place, and I have a master-key will open
it.   I'll e'en in there, and attack her just when she
comes to her prayers, that's the most likely to prove her
critical minute, for then the devil will be there to
assist me.   12

[*He opens the closet, goes in, and shuts the door after him.*

Enter BERINTHIA, *with a candle in her hand.*

Ber.   Well, sure I am the best-natured woman in the
world, I that love cards so well (there is but one thing upon
earth I love better), have pretended letters to write, to give
my friends a *tête-à-tête :* however, I'm innocent, for picquet
is the game I set 'em to : at her own peril be it, if she
ventures to play with him at any other.   But now what
shall I do with myself?   I don't know how in the world to
pass my time ; would Loveless were here to *badiner* a little !
Well, he's a charming fellow ; I don't wonder his wife's so
fond of him.   What if I should sit down and think of him
till I fall asleep, and dream of the Lord knows what?   Oh,
but then if I should dream we were married, I should be
frightened out of my wits !—[*Seeing a book.*]   What's this
book?   I think I had best go read.   O splenetic ! it's
a sermon.   Well, I'll go into my closet, and read the
Plotting Sisters.—[*She opens the closet, sees* LOVELESS, *and
shrieks out.*]   O Lord, a ghost ! a ghost ! a ghost ! a
ghost !   30

Re-enter LOVELESS, *running to her.*

Love.   Peace, my dear, it's no ghost; take it in your arms, you'll find 'tis worth a hundred of 'em.

Ber.   Run in again; here's somebody coming.

[LOVELESS *retires as before.*

Enter Maid.

Maid.   O Lord, madam! what's the matter?

Ber.   O Heavens! I'm almost frighted out of my wits; I thought verily I had seen a ghost, and 'twas nothing but the white curtain, with a black hood pinned up against it: you may begone again; I am the fearfullest fool!

[*Exit* Maid.

Re-enter LOVELESS.

Love.   Is the coast clear?

Ber.   The coast clear! I suppose you are clear, you'd never play such a trick as this else.   41

Love.   I'm very well pleased with my trick thus far, and shall be so till I have played it out, if it ben't your fault. Where's my wife?

Ber.   At cards.

Love.   With whom?

Ber.   With Worthy.

Love.   Then we are safe enough.

Ber.   Are you so? Some husbands would be of another mind, if he were at cards with their wives.   50

Love.   And they'd be in the right on't, too: but I dare trust mine.—Besides, I know he's in love in another place, and he's not one of those who court half-a-dozen at a time.

Ber. Nay, the truth on't is, you'd pity him if you saw how uneasy he is at being engaged with us; but 'twas my malice, I fancied he was to meet his mistress somewhere else, so did it to have the pleasure of seeing him fret.

Love. What says Amanda to my staying abroad so late?

Ber. Why, she's as much out of humour as he; I believe they wish one another at the devil.   61

Love. Then I'm afraid they'll quarrel at play, and soon throw up the cards.—[*Offering to pull her into the closet.*] Therefore, my dear, charming angel, let us make a good use of our time.

Ber. Heavens! what do you mean?

Love. Pray what do you think I mean?

Ber. I don't know.

Love. I'll show you.

Ber. You may as well tell me.   70

Love. No, that would make you blush worse than t'other.

Ber. Why, do you intend to make me blush?

Love. Faith I can't tell that; but if I do, it shall be in the dark.   [*Pulling her.*

Ber. O Heavens! I would not be in the dark with you for all the world!

Love. I'll try that.   [*Puts out the candles.*

Ber. O Lord! are you mad? What shall I do for light?   · 80

Love. You'll do as well without it.

Ber. Why, one can't find a chair to sit down.

Love. Come into the closet, madam, there's moonshine upon the couch.

Ber. Nay, never pull, for I will not go.

H

Love.   Then you must be carried.

> [*Takes her in his arms.*

Ber.   [*Very softly.*]   Help! help! I'm ravished! ruined!
undone!   O Lord, I shall never be able to bear it.

> [*Exit* LOVELESS *carrying* BERINTHIA.

SCENE IV.—*A Room in* Sir TUNBELLY CLUMSEY'S
House.

Enter Miss HOYDEN, Nurse, Young FASHION, *and* BULL.

Fash.   This quick dispatch of yours, Mr. Bull, I take so
kindly, it shall give you a claim to my favour as long as I
live, I do assure you.

Hoyd.   And to mine, too, I promise you.

Bull.   I most humbly thank your honours; and I hope,
since it has been my lot to join you in the holy bands of
wedlock, you will so well cultivate the soil, which I have
craved a blessing on, that your children may swarm about
you like bees about a honeycomb.   9

Hoyd.   Ecod, with all my heart; the more the merrier, I
say; ha, nurse?

Enter LORY; *he takes his master hastily aside.*

Lory.   One word with you, for Heaven's sake!

Fash.   What the devil's the matter?

Lory.   Sir, your fortune's ruined; and I don't think
your life's worth a quarter of an hour's purchase.   Yonder's
your brother arrived with two coaches and six horses,
twenty footmen and pages, a coat worth four-score pound,
and a periwig down to his knees: so judge what will
become of your lady's heart.

Fash. Death and furies! 'tis impossible! 20

Lory. Fiends and spectres! sir, 'tis true.

Fash. Is he in the house yet?

Lory. No, they are capitulating with him at the gate. The porter tells him he's come to run away with Miss Hoyden, and has cocked the blunderbuss at him; your brother swears Gad damme, they are a parcel of clawns, and he has a good mind to break off the match; but they have given the word for sir Tunbelly, so I doubt all will come out presently. Pray, sir, resolve what you'll do this moment, for egad they'll maul you. 30

Fash. Stay a little.—[*To* Miss HOYDEN.] My dear, here's a troublesome business my man tells me of, but don't be frightened, we shall be too hard for the rogue. Here's an impudent fellow at the gate (not knowing I was come hither *incognito*) has taken my name upon him, in hopes to run away with you.

Hoyd. O the brazen-faced varlet, it's well we are married, or maybe we might never a been so.

Fash. [*Aside.*] Egad, like enough!—[*Aloud.*] Prithee, dear doctor, run to sir Tunbelly, and stop him from going to the gate before I speak with him. 41

Bull. I fly, my good lord. [*Exit.*

Nurse. An't please your honour, my lady and I had best lock ourselves up till the danger be over.

Fash. Ay, by all means.

Hoyd. Not so fast, I won't be locked up any more. I'm married.

Fash. Yes, pray, my dear, do, till we have seized this rascal.

Hoyd. Nay, if you pray me, I'll do anything.

[*Exeunt* Miss HOYDEN *and* Nurse

Fash. Oh! here's sir Tunbelly coming.—Hark you, sirrah, things are better than you imagine; the wedding's over.   52

Lory. The devil it is, sir !

Fash. Not a word, all's safe : but sir Tunbelly don't know it, nor must not yet ; so I am resolved to brazen the business out, and have the pleasure of turning the impostor upon his lordship, which I believe may easily be done.

Enter Sir TUNBELLY, BULL, *and* Servants, *armed.*

Fash. Did you ever hear, sir, of so impudent an undertaking ?   60

Sir Tun. Never, by the mass! But we'll tickle him, I'll warrant him.

Fash. They tell me, sir, he has a great many people with him disguised like servants.

Sir Tun. Ay, ay, rogues enough ; but I'll soon raise the posse upon 'em.

Fash. Sir, if you'll take my advice, we'll go a shorter way to work. I find whoever this spark is, he knows nothing of my being privately here ; so if you pretend to receive him civilly, he'll enter without suspicion ; and as soon as he is within the gate, we'll whip up the drawbridge upon his back, let fly the blunderbuss to disperse his crew, and so commit him to jail.   73

Sir Tun. Egad, your lordship is an ingenious person, and a very great general; but shall we kill any of 'em or not?

Fash. No, no ; fire over their heads only to fright 'em ; I'll warrant the regiment scours when the colonel's a prisoner.

Sir Tun. Then come along, my boys, and let your courage be great—for your danger is but small.

[*Exeunt.*

SCENE V.—*The Gate before* Sir Tunbelly Clumsey's *House.*

Enter Lord Foppington, *with* La Vérole *and* Servants.

Lord Fop. A pax of these bumpkinly people! will they open the gate, or do they desire I should grow at their moat-side like a willow?—[*To the* Porter.] Hey, fellow—prithee do me the favour, in as few words as thou canst find to express thyself, to tell me whether thy master will admit me or not, that I may turn about my coach, and be gone.

Porter. Here's my master himself now at hand, he's of age, he'll give you his answer.   9

Enter Sir Tunbelly *and his* Servants.

Sir Tun. My most noble lord, I crave your pardon for making your honour wait so long; but my orders to my servants have been to admit nobody without my knowledge, for fear of some attempt upon my daughter, the times being full of plots and roguery.

Lord Fop. Much caution, I must confess, is a sign of great wisdom : but, stap my vitals, I have got a cold enough to destroy a porter !—He, hem—

Sir Tun. I am very sorry for't, indeed, my lord; but if your lordship please to walk in, we'll help you to some brown sugar-candy. My lord, I'll show you the way.   21

Lord Fop.   Sir, I follow you with pleasure.

[*Exit with* Sir TUNBELLY CLUMSEY. *As* Lord
FOPPINGTON'S Servants *go to follow him in,*
they clap the door against LA VÉROLE.

Servants. [*Within.*]   Nay, hold you me there, sir.

La Vér.   *Jernie die, qu'est-ce que veut dire ça ?*

Sir Tun. [*Within.*]   Fire, porter.

Porter. [*Fires.*]   Have among ye, my masters.

La Vér.   *Ah, je suis mort !*—

[*The* Servants *all run off.*

Porter.   Not one soldier left, by the mass !

SCENE VI.—*A Hall in the same.*

Enter Sir TUNBELLY CLUMSEY, BULL, Constable, Clerk,
and Servants, *with* Lord FOPPINGTON, *disarmed.*

Sir Tun.   Come, bring him along, bring him along !

Lord Fop.   What the pax do you mean, gentlemen !   Is
it fair-time, that you are all drunk before dinner ?

Sir Tun.   Drunk, sirrah !—Here's an impudent rogue
for you !—Drunk or sober, bully, I'm a justice of the peace,
and know how to deal with strollers.

Lord Fop.   Strollers !

Sir Tun.   Ay, strollers.   Come, give an account of
yourself; what's your name, where do you live ? do you
pay scot and lot ? are you a Williamite, or a Jacobite ?
Come.   11

Lord Fop.   And why dost thou ask me so many impertinent questions ?

Sir Tun. Because I'll make you answer 'em before I have done with you, you rascal you !

Lord Fop. Before Gad, all the answer I can make thee to 'em, is, that thou art a very extraordinary old fellow, stap my vitals !

Sir Tun. Nay, if you are for joking with deputy lieuten-ants, we'st know how to deal with you.—[*To* Clerk.] Here, draw a warrant for him immediately.   21

Lord Fop. A warrant !—What the devil is't thou wouldst be at, old gentleman ?

Sir Tun. I would be at you, sirrah (if my hands were not tied as a magistrate), and with these two double fists beat your teeth down your throat, you dog you !

Lord Fop. And why wouldst thou spoil my face at that rate ?

Sir Tun. For your design to rob me of my daughter, villain.   31

Lord Fop. Rab thee of thy daughter !—Now do I begin to believe I am a-bed and asleep, and that all this is but a dream.—If it be, 'twill be an agreeable surprise enough to waken by and by ; and instead of the impertinent company of a nasty country justice, find myself perhaps in the arms of a woman of quality.—[*To* Sir TUNBELLY.] Prithee, old father, wilt thou give me leave to ask thee one question ?

Sir Tun. I can't tell whether I will or not, till I know what it is.   40

Lord Fop. Why, then it is, whether thou didst not write to my lord Foppington to come down and marry thy daughter ?

Sir Tun. Yes, marry did I ; and my lord Foppington

is come down, and shall marry my daughter before she's a day older.

Lord Fop. Now give me thy hand, dear dad ; I thought we should understand one another at last.

Sir Tun. This fellow's mad.—Here, bind him hand and foot.   [*They bind him down.*

Lord Fop. Nay, prithee, knight, leave fooling; thy jest begins to grow dull.   52

Sir Tun. Bind him, I say, he's mad.—Bread and water, a dark room, and a whip may bring him to his senses again.

Lord Fop. [*Aside.*] Egad ! if I don't waken quickly, by all I can see, this is like to prove one of the most impertinent dreams that ever I dreamt in my life.

Enter Miss HOYDEN *and* Nurse.

Hoyd. [*Going up to him.*] Is this he that would have run away with me ? Fo ! how he stinks of sweets !—Pray, father, let him be dragged through the horse-pond.

Lord Fop. [*Aside.*] This must be my wife by her natural inclination to her husband.   63

Hoyd. Pray, father, what do you intend to do with him ? hang him ?

Sir Tun. That at least, child.

Nurse. Ay, and it's e'en too good for him too.

Lord Fop. [*Aside.*] *Madame la gouvernante*, I presume. Hitherto this appears to me to be one of the most extraordinary families that ever man of quality matched into.   71

Sir Tun. What's become of my lord, daughter ?

Hoyd. He's just coming, sir.

Lord Fop. [*Aside.*] My lord! what does he mean by that now?

Enter Young Fashion *and* Lory.

[*Seeing him.*] Stap my vitals, Tam! now the dream's out.

Fash. Is this the fellow, sir, that designed to trick me of your daughter?

Sir Tun. This is he, my lord; how do you like him? Is not he a pretty fellow to get a fortune?   80

Fash. I find by his dress he thought your daughter might be taken with a beau.

Hoyd. O gemini! Is this a beau? let me see him again.—Ha! I find a beau's not such an ugly thing neither.

Fash. [*Aside.*] Egad, she'll be in love with him presently; I'll e'en have him sent away to jail.—[*To* Lord Foppington.] Sir, though your undertaking shows you are a person of no extraordinary modesty, I suppose you han't confidence enough to expect much favour from me?   90

Lord Fop. Strike me dumb, Tam, thou art a very impudent fellow!

Nurse. Look, if the varlet has not the frontery to call his lordship plain Thomas!

Bull. The business is, he would feign himself mad, to avoid going to jail.

Lord Fop. [*Aside.*] That must be the chaplain, by his unfolding of mysteries.

Sir Tun. Come, is the warrant writ?

Clerk. Yes, sir.   100

Sir Tun. Give me the pen, I'll sign it.—So now, constable, away with him.

Lord Fop. Hold one moment,—pray, gentlemen. My lord Foppington, shall I beg one word with your lordship?

Nurse. O ho, it's my lord with him now! See how afflictions will humble folks.

Hoyd. Pray, my lord, don't let him whisper too close, lest he bite your ear off.

Lord Fop. I am not altogether so hungry as your lady-ship is pleased to imagine.—[*Aside to* Young FASHION.] Look you, Tam, I am sensible I have not been so kind to you as I ought, but I hope you'll forget what's passed, and accept of the five thousand pounds I offer ; thou mayst live in extreme splendour with it, stap my vitals !   114

Fash. It's a much easier matter to prevent a disease than to cure it ; a quarter of that sum would have secured your mistress ; twice as much won't redeem her.

[*Leaving him.*

Sir Tun. Well, what says he ?

Fash. Only the rascal offered me a bribe to let him go.

Sir Tun. Ay, he shall go, with a pox to him !—Lead on, constable.

Lord Fop. One word more, and I have done.

Sir Tun. Before Gad ! thou art an impudent fellow, to trouble the court at this rate after thou art condemned ; but speak once for all.   125

Lord Fop. Why then, once for all ; I have at last luckily called to mind that there is a gentleman of this country, who I believe cannot live far from this place, if he were here, would satisfy you, I am Navelty, baron of Foppington, with five thousand pounds a year, and that fellow there, a rascal not worth a groat.

Sir Tun. Very well ; now, who is this honest gentleman

you are so well acquainted with?—[*To* Young FASHION.]
Come, sir, we shall hamper him.

Lord Fop. 'Tis sir John Friendly.   135

Sir Tun. So; he lives within half a mile, and came
down into the country but last night; this bold-faced
fellow thought he had been at London still, and so quoted
him; now we shall display him in his colours: I'll send for
sir John immediately.—[*To a* Servant.] Here, fellow, away
presently, and desire my neighbour he'll do me the favour
to step over, upon an extraordinary occasion.—[*Exit* Servant.]
And in the meanwhile you had best secure this sharper in the
gate-house.

Constable. An't please your worship, he may chance to
give us the slip thence. If I were worthy to advise, I think
the dog-kennel's a surer place.   147

Sir Tun. With all my heart; anywhere.

Lord Fop. Nay, for Heaven's sake, sir! do me the favour
to put me in a clean room, that I mayn't daub my clothes.

Sir Tun. O, when you have married my daughter, her
estate will afford you new ones.—Away with him!

Lord Fop. A dirty country justice is a barbarous magistrate, stap my vitals!

[*Exit* Constable *with* Lord FOPPINGTON.

Fash. [*Aside.*] Egad, I must prevent this knight's coming,
or the house will grow soon too hot to hold me.—[*To* Sir
TUNBELLY.] Sir, I fancy 'tis not worth while to trouble sir
John upon this impertinent fellow's desire: I'll send and
call the messenger back.   159

Sir Tun. Nay, with all my heart; for, to be sure, he
thought he was far enough off, or the rogue would never
have named him.

Ser.   Sir, I met sir John just lighting at the gate; he's
come to wait upon you.

Sir Tun.   Nay, then, it happens as one could wish.

Fash. [*Aside.*] The devil it does!—Lory, you see how
things are, here will be a discovery presently, and we shall
have our brains beat out; for my brother will be sure to
swear he don't know me: therefore, run into the stable,
take the two first horses you can light on, I'll slip out at the
back door, and we'll away immediately.   171

Lory.   What, and leave your lady, sir?

Fash.   There's no danger in that as long as I have taken
possession; I shall know how to treat with 'em well enough,
if once I am out of their reach.   Away! I'll steal after thee.

　　　[*Exit* LORY; *his master follows him out at*
　　　　　one door, as Sir JOHN FRIENDLY *enters*
　　　　　at t'other.

Enter Sir JOHN FRIENDLY.

Sir Tun.   Sir John, you are the welcomest man alive;
I had just sent a messenger to desire you'd step over, upon
a very extraordinary occasion.   We are all in arms here.

Sir John.   How so?   179

Sir Tun.   Why, you must know, a finical sort of a tawdry
fellow here (I don't know who the devil he is, not I) hearing,
I suppose, that the match was concluded between my lord
Foppington and my girl Hoyden, comes impudently to the
gate, with a whole pack of rogues in liveries, and would have
passed upon me for his lordship: but what does I? I comes
up to him boldly at the head of his guards, takes him by the
throat, strikes up his heels, binds him hand and foot,

dispatches a warrant, and commits him prisoner to the dog-kennel.   189

Sir John. So ; but how do you know but this was my lord? for I was told he set out from London the day before me, with a very fine retinue, and intended to come directly hither.

Sir Tun. Why, now to show you how many lies people raise in that damned town, he came two nights ago post, with only one servant, and is now in the house with me. But you don't know the cream of the jest yet ; this same rogue (that lies yonder neck and heels among the hounds), thinking you were out of the country, quotes you for his acquaintance, and said if you were here, you'd justify him to be lord Foppington, and I know not what.   191

Sir John. Pray will you let me see him ?

Sir Tun. Ay, that you shall presently.—[*To a* Servant.] Here, fetch the prisoner.   [*Exit* Servant.

Sir John. I wish there ben't some mistake in the business.—Where's my lord ? I know him very well.

Sir Tun. He was here just now.—[*To* Bull.] See for him, doctor, tell him sir John is here to wait upon him.

[*Exit* Bull.

Sir John. I hope, sir Tunbelly, the young lady is not married yet.   200

Sir Tun. No, things won't be ready this week. But why do you say you hope she is not married?

Sir John. Some foolish fancies only, perhaps I'm mistaken.

Re-enter Bull.

Bull. Sir, his lordship is just rid out to take the air.

Sir Tun. To take the air ! Is that his London breeding, to go take the air when gentlemen come to visit him ?

Sir John. 'Tis possible he might want it, he might not be well, some sudden qualm perhaps.

Re-enter Constable, &c., *with* Lord FOPPINGTON.

Lord Fop. Stap my vitals, I'll have satisfaction !   210

Sir John. [*Running to him.*] My dear lord Foppington !

Lord Fop. Dear Friendly, thou art come in the critical minute, strike me dumb !

Sir John. Why, I little thought I should have found you in fetters.

Lord Fop. Why, truly the world must do me the justice to confess, I do use to appear a little more *dégagé :* but this old gentleman, not liking the freedom of my air, has been pleased to skewer down my arms like a rabbit.   220

Sir Tun. Is it then possible that this should be the true lord Foppington at last ?

Lord Fop. Why, what do you see in his face to make you doubt of it ? Sir, without presuming to have any extraordinary opinion of my figure, give me leave to tell you, if you had seen as many lords as I have done, you would not think it impossible a person of a worse *taille* than mine might be a modern man of quality.

Sir Tun. Unbind him, slaves !—My lord, I'm struck dumb, I can only beg pardon by signs ; but if a sacrifice will appease you, you shall have it.—Here, pursue this Tartar, bring him back.—Away, I say !—A dog ! Oons, I'll cut off his ears and his tail, I'll draw out all his teeth, pull his skin over his head—and—and what shall I do more ?   234

Sir John. He does indeed deserve to be made an example of.

Lord Fop. He does deserve to be *chartre*,* stap my vitals !

Sir Tun. May I then hope I have your honour's pardon ?

Lord Fop. Sir, we courtiers do nothing without a bribe : that fair young lady might do miracles.

Sir Tun. Hoyden ! come hither, Hoyden.

Lord Fop. Hoyden is her name, sir ?

Sir Tun. Yes, my lord.   245

Lord Fop. The prettiest name for a song I ever heard.

Sir Tun. My lord—here's my girl, she's yours, she has a wholesome body, and a virtuous mind ; she's a woman complete, both in flesh and in spirit ; she has a bag of milled crowns, as scarce as they are, and fifteen hundred a year stitched fast to her tail : so, go thy ways, Hoyden.

Lord Fop. Sir, I do receive her like a gentleman.

Sir Tun. Then I'm a happy man, I bless Heaven, and if your lordship will give me leave, I will, like a good Christian at Christmas, be very drunk by way of thanksgiving. Come, my noble peer, I believe dinner's ready ; if your honour pleases to follow me, I'll lead you on to the attack of a venison-pasty.   [*Exit.*

Lord Fop. Sir, I wait upon you.—Will your ladyship do me the favour of your little finger, madam ?   261

Hoyd. My lord, I'll follow you presently, I have a little business with my nurse.

---

* *I.e., mis en chartre,* sent to jail.

Lord Fop. Your ladyship's most humble servant.—Come, sir John ; the ladies have *des affaires.*

[*Exit with* Sir JOHN FRIENDLY.

Hoyd. So, nurse, we are finely brought to bed ! what shall we do now ?

Nurse. Ah, dear miss, we are all undone ! Mr. Bull, you were used to help a woman to a remedy.   [*Crying.*

Bull. Alack-a-day ! but it's past my skill now, I can do nothing.   271

Nurse. Who would have thought that ever your invention should have been drained so dry ?

Hoyd. Well, I have often thought old folks fools, and now I'm sure they are so ; I have found a way myself to secure us all.

Nurse. Dear lady, what's that ?

Hoyd. Why, if you two will be sure to hold your tongues, and not say a word of what's past, I'll e'en marry this lord too.   280

Nurse. What ! two husbands, my dear ?

Hoyd. Why, you have had three, good nurse, you may hold your tongue.

Nurse. Ay, but not altogether, sweet child.

Hoyd. Psha ! if you had, you'd ne'er a thought much on't.

Nurse. Oh, but 'tis a sin, sweeting !

Bull. Nay, that's my business to speak to, nurse.—I do confess, to take two husbands for the satisfaction of the flesh, is to commit the sin of exorbitancy ; but to do it for the peace of the spirit, is no more than to be drunk by way of physic. Besides, to prevent a parent's wrath, is to avoid the sin of disobedience ; for when the parent's angry, the child is froward. So that upon the whole matter, I do think, though miss should marry again, she may be saved.

Hoyd. Ecod, and I will marry again then! and so there's an end of the story.   [*Exeunt.*

ACT V.

SCENE I.—*London.*—COUPLER'S *Lodgings.*

Enter COUPLER, Young FASHION, *and* LORY.

Coup. Well, and so sir John coming in—

Fash. And so sir John coming in, I thought it might be manners in me to go out, which I did, and getting on horseback as fast as I could, rid away as if the devil had been at the rear of me. What has happened since, Heaven knows.

Coup. Egad, sirrah, I know as well as Heaven.

Fash. What do you know?

Coup. That you are a cuckold.

Fash. The devil I am! By who?   10

Coup. By your brother.

Fash. My brother! which way?

Coup. The old way; he has lain with your wife.

Fash. Hell and furies! what dost thou mean?

Coup. I mean plainly; I speak no parable.

Fash. Plainly! thou dost not speak common sense, I cannot understand one word thou sayest.

Coup. You will do soon, youngster. In short, you left your wife a widow, and she married again.

Fash. It's a lie.   20

Coup. Ecod, if I were a young fellow, I'd break your head, sirrah.

Fash. Dear dad, don't be angry, for I'm as mad as Tom of Bedlam.

Coup. When I had fitted you with a wife, you should have kept her.

Fash. But is it possible the young strumpet could play me such a trick?

Coup. A young strumpet, sir, can play twenty tricks.

Fash. But prithee instruct me a little farther; whence comes thy intelligence?   31

Coup. From your brother, in this letter; there, you may read it.

Fash. [*Reads.*]

DEAR COUPLER,—[*Pulling off his hat.*] *I have only time to tell thee in three lines, or thereabouts, that here has been the devil. That rascal Tam, having stole the letter thou hadst formerly writ for me to bring to sir Tunbelly, formed a damnable design upon my mistress, and was in a fair way of success when I arrived. But after having suffered some indignities (in which I have all daubed my embroidered coat), I put him to flight. I sent out a party of horse after him, in hopes to have made him my prisoner, which if I had done, I would have qualified him for the seraglio, stap my vitals!*   44

The danger I have thus narrowly 'scaped has made me fortify myself against farther attempts, by entering immediately into an association with the young lady, by which we engage to stand by one another as long as we both shall live.

In short, the papers are sealed, and the contract is signed, so the business of the lawyer is achevé; but I defer the divine

*part of the thing till I arrive at London, not being willing
to consummate in any other bed but my own.*

    Postscript.

    *'Tis possible I may be in tawn as soon as this letter,
far I find the lady is so violently in love with me, I have
determined to make her happy with all the dispatch that is
practicable, without disardering my coach-harses.*

So, here's rare work, i'faith !   59

    Lory.   Egad, Miss Hoyden has laid about her bravely !

    Coup.   I think my country-girl has played her part as
well as if she had been born and bred in St. James's parish.

    Fash.   That rogue the chaplain !

    Lory.   And then that jade the nurse, sir !

    Fash.   And then that drunken sot Lory, sir ! that could
not keep himself sober to be a witness to the marriage.

    Lory.   Sir—with respect—I know very few drunken sots
that do keep themselves sober.

    Fash.   Hold your prating, sirrah, or I'll break your
head !—Dear Coupler, what's to be done ?   70

    Coup.   Nothing's to be done till the bride and bride-
groom come to town.

    Fash.   Bride and bridegroom ! death and furies ! I
can't bear that thou shouldst call 'em so.

    Coup.   Why, what shall I call 'em, dog and cat ?

    Fash.   Not for the world, that sounds more like man
and wife than t'other.

    Coup.   Well, if you'll hear of 'em in no language, we'll
leave 'em for the nurse and the chaplain.

    Fash.   The devil and the witch !   80

    Coup.   When they come to town—

Lory. We shall have stormy weather.

Coup. Will you hold your tongues, gentlemen, or not ?

Lory. Mum !

Coup. I say when they come, we must find what stuff they are made of, whether the churchman be chiefly composed of the flesh, or the spirit; I presume the former. For as chaplains now go, 'tis probable he eats three pound of beef to the reading of one chapter.—This gives him carnal desires, he wants money, preferment, wine, a whore; therefore we must invite him to supper, give him fat capons, sack and sugar, a purse of gold, and a plump sister. Let this be done, and I'll warrant thee, my boy, he speaks truth like an oracle.   94

Fash. Thou art a profound statesman I allow it; but how shall we gain the nurse ?

Coup. Oh! never fear the nurse, if once you have got the priest; for the devil always rides the hag. Well, there's nothing more to be said of the matter at this time, that I know of; so let us go and inquire if there's any news of our people yet, perhaps they may be come. But let me tell you one thing by the way, sirrah, I doubt you have been an idle fellow; if thou hadst behaved thyself as thou shouldst have done, the girl would never have left thee.   [*Exeunt.*

SCENE II.—Berinthia's *Apartment.*
Enter her Maid, *passing the stage, followed by* Worthy.

Wor. Hem, Mrs. Abigail! is your mistress to be spoken with ?

Abig. By you, sir, I believe she may.

Wor. Why 'tis by me I would have her spoken with.

Abig. I'll acquaint her, sir.· [*Exit.*

Wor. One lift more I must persuade her to give me, and then I'm mounted. Well, a young bawd and a handsome one for my money ; 'tis they do the execution ; I'll never go to an old one, but when I have occasion for a witch. Lewdness looks heavenly to a woman, when an angel appears in its cause ; but when a hag is advocate, she thinks it comes from the devil. An old woman has something so terrible in her looks, that whilst she is persuading your mistress to forget she has a soul, she stares hell and damnation full in her face.   15

Enter BERINTHIA.

Ber. Well, sir, what news bring you ?

Wor. No news, madam ; there's a woman going to cuckold her husband.

Ber. Amanda ?

Wor. I hope so.

Ber. Speed her well !

Wor. Ay, but there must be more than a God-speed, or your charity won't be worth a farthing.

Ber. Why, han't I done enough already ?

Wor. Not quite.   25

Ber. What's the matter ?

Wor. The lady has a scruple still, which you must remove.

Ber. What's that ?

Wor. Her virtue—she says.

Ber. And do you believe her ?

Wor. No, but I believe it's what she takes for her virtue ; it's some relics of lawful love. She is not yet fully satisfied her husband has got another mistress ; which unless I can convince her of, I have opened the trenches in vain; for the breach must be wider, before I dare storm the town.   36

Ber. And so I'm to be your engineer?

Wor. I'm sure you know best how to manage the battery.

Ber. What think you of springing a mine? I have a thought just now come into my head, how to blow her up at once.

Wor. That would be a thought indeed.

Ber. Faith, I'll do't; and thus the execution of it shall be. We are all invited to my lord Foppington's to-night to supper; he's come to town with his bride, and makes a ball, with an entertainment of music. Now, you must know, my undoer here, Loveless, says he must needs meet me about some private business (I don't know what 'tis) before we go to the company. To which end he has told his wife one lie, and I have told her another. But to make her amends, I'll go immediately, and tell her a solemn truth.   52

Wor. What's that?

Ber. Why, I'll tell her, that to my certain knowledge her husband has a rendezvous with his mistress this after- noon; and that if she'll give me her word she'll be satisfied with the discovery, without making any violent inquiry after the woman, I'll direct her to a place where she shall see 'em meet. Now, friend, this I fancy may help you to a critical minute. For home she must go again to dress. You (with your good breeding) come to wait upon us to the ball, find her all alone, her spirit inflamed against her husband for his treason, and her flesh in a heat from some contemplations upon the treachery, her blood on a fire, her

conscience in ice ; a lover to draw, and the devil to drive.—
Ah, poor Amanda !   66

Wor. [*Kneeling.*] Thou angel of light, let me fall down
and adore thee !

Ber. Thou minister of darkness, get up again, for I hate
to see the devil at his devotions.

Wor. Well, my incomparable Berinthia, how shall I
requite you ?

Ber. Oh, ne'er trouble yourself about that : virtue is its
own reward. There's a pleasure in doing good, which sufficiently pays itself. Adieu !   75

Wor. Farewell, thou best of women !

           [*Exeunt several ways.*

     Enter AMANDA *meeting* BERINTHIA.

Aman. Who was that went from you ?

Ber. A friend of yours.

Aman. What does he want ?

Ber. Something you might spare him, and be ne'er the
poorer.

Aman. I can spare him nothing but my friendship ; my
love already's all disposed of : though, I confess, to one
ungrateful to my bounty.   84

Ber. Why, there's the mystery ! You have been so
bountiful, you have cloyed him. Fond wives do by their
husbands, as barren wives do by their lapdogs ; cram 'em
with sweetmeats till they spoil their stomachs.

Aman. Alas ! had you but seen how passionately fond
he has been since our last reconciliation, you would have
thought it were impossible he ever should have breathed an
hour without me.

Ber. Ay, but there you thought wrong again, Amanda; you should consider, that in matters of love men's eyes are always bigger than their bellies. They have violent appetites, 'tis true, but they have soon dined.   96

Aman. Well; there's nothing upon earth astonishes me more than men's inconstancy.

Ber. Now there's nothing upon earth astonishes me less, when I consider what they and we are composed of: for nature has made them children, and us babies. Now, Amanda, how we used our babies you may remember. We were mad to have 'em as soon as we saw 'em; kissed 'em to pieces as soon as we got 'em; then pulled off their clothes, saw 'em naked, and so threw 'em away.   105

Aman. But do you think all men are of this temper?

Ber. All but one.

Aman. Who's that?

Ber. Worthy.

Aman. Why, he's weary of his wife too, you see.

Ber. Ay, that's no proof.

Aman. What can be a greater?

Ber. Being weary of his mistress.

Aman. Don't you think 'twere possible he might give you that too?   115

Ber. Perhaps he might, if he were my gallant; not if he were yours.

Aman. Why do you think he should be more constant to me, than he would to you? I'm sure I'm not so handsome.

Ber. Kissing goes by favour; he likes you best.

Aman. Suppose he does: that's no demonstration he would be constant to me.   123

Ber. No, that I'll grant you: but there are other reasons to expect it. For you must know after all, Amanda, the inconstancy we commonly see in men of brains, does not so much proceed from the uncertainty of their temper, as from the misfortunes of their love. A man sees perhaps a hundred women he likes well enough for an intrigue, and away ; but possibly, through the whole course of his life, does not find above one who is exactly what he could wish her: now her, 'tis a thousand to one, he never gets. Either she is not to be had at all (though that seldom happens, you'll say), or he wants those opportunities that are necessary to gain her ; either she likes somebody else much better than him, or uses him like a dog, because he likes nobody so well as her. Still something or other Fate claps in the way between them and the woman they are capable of being fond of: and this makes them wander about from mistress to mistress, like a pilgrim from town to town, who every night must have a fresh lodging, and's in haste to be gone in the morning.   142

Aman. 'Tis possible there may be something in what you say ; but what do you infer from it as to the man we were talking of ?

Ber. Why, I infer, that you being the woman in the world the most to his humour, 'tis not likely he would quit you for one that is less.

Aman. That is not to be depended upon, for you see Mr. Loveless does so.   150

Ber. What does Mr. Loveless do ?

Aman. Why, he runs after something for variety, I'm sure he does not like so well as he does me.

Ber. That's more than you know, madam.

Aman. No, I'm sure on't. I'm not very vain, Berinthia, and yet I'd lay my life, if I could look into his heart, he thinks I deserve to be preferred to a thousand of her.

Ber. Don't be too positive in that neither; a million to one but she has the same opinion of you. What would you give to see her?   161

Aman. Hang her, dirty trull!—Though I really believe she's so ugly she'd cure me of my jealousy.

Ber. All the men of sense about town say she's handsome.

Aman. They are as often out in those things as any people.

Ber. Then I'll give you farther proof—all the women about town say she's a fool. Now I hope you're convinced?

Aman. Whate'er she be, I'm satisfied he does not like her well enough to bestow anything more than a little outward gallantry upon her.   171

Ber. Outward gallantry!—[*Aside.*] I can't bear this.—[*Aloud.*] Don't you think she's a woman to be fobbed off so. Come, I'm too much your friend to suffer you should be thus grossly imposed upon by a man who does not deserve the least part about you, unless he knew how to set a greater value upon it. Therefore, in one word, to my certain knowledge, he is to meet her now, within a quarter of an hour, somewhere about that Babylon of wickedness, Whitehall. And if you'll give me your word that you'll be content with seeing her masked in his hand, without pulling her headclothes off, I'll step immediately to the person from whom I have my intelligence, and send you word whereabouts you may stand to see 'em meet. My friend and I'll watch 'em from another place, and dodge 'em to their private lodging ; but don't you offer to follow 'em, lest you do it awkwardly, and spoil all.   I'll come home to you again as soon as I have earthed 'em, and give you an account in what corner of the house the scene of their lewdness lies.   190

Aman.   If you can do this, Berinthia, he's a villain.

Ber.   I can't help that ; men will be so.

Aman.   Well, I'll follow your directions, for I shall never rest till I know the worst of this matter.

Ber.   Pray, go immediately and get yourself ready then. Put on some of your woman's clothes, a great scarf and a mask, and you shall presently receive orders.—[*Calls.*] Here, who's there ? get me a chair quickly.

Enter Servant.

Ser.   There are chairs at the door, madam.

Ber.   'Tis well ; I'm coming.   [*Exit* Servant.

Aman.   But pray, Berinthia, before you go, tell me how I may know this filthy thing, if she should be so forward (as I suppose she will) to come to the rendezvous first ; for methinks I would fain view her a little.   204

Ber.   Why, she's about my height ; and very well shaped.

Aman.   I thought she had been a little crooked ?

Ber.   O no, she's as straight as I am.   But we lose time ; come away.   [*Exeunt.*

SCENE III.—Young FASHION's *Lodgings.*

Enter Young FASHION, *meeting* LORY.

Fash.   Well, will the doctor come ?

Lory.   Sir, I sent a porter to him as you ordered me.

He found him with a pipe of tobacco and a great tankard of ale, which he said he would dispatch while I could tell three, and be here.

Fash. He does not suspect 'twas I that sent for him.

Lory. Not a jot, sir; he divines as little for himself as he does for other folks.

Fash. Will he bring nurse with him?

Lory. Yes.   10

Fash. That's well; where's Coupler?

Lory. He's half-way up the stairs taking breath; he must play his bellows a little, before he can get to the top.

Enter COUPLER.

Fash. Oh, here he is.—Well, Old Phthisic, the doctor's coming.

Coup. Would the pox had the doctor!—I'm quite out of wind.—[*To* LORY.] Set me a chair, sirrah. Ah!—[*Sits down.*]—[*To* Young FASHION.] Why the plague canst not thou lodge upon the ground-floor?   20

Fash. Because I love to lie as near heaven as I can.

Coup. Prithee, let heaven alone; ne'er affect tending that way; thy centre's downwards.

Fash. That's impossible! I have too much ill-luck in this world to be damned in the next.

Coup. Thou art out in thy logic. Thy major is true, but thy minor is false; for thou art the luckiest fellow in the universe.

Fash. Make out that.

Coup. I'll do't: last night the devil ran away with the parson of Fatgoose living.   31

Fash. If he had run away with the parish too, what's that to me?

Coup. I'll tell thee what it's to thee.—This living is worth five hundred pounds a-year, and the presentation of it is thine, if thou canst prove thyself a lawful husband to Miss Hoyden.

Fash. Sayest thou so, my protector? Then, egad, I shall have a brace of evidences here presently.

Coup. The nurse and the doctor? 40

Fash. The same. The devil himself won't have interest enough to make 'em withstand it.

Coup. That we shall see presently.—Here they come.

Enter Nurse *and* BULL ; *they start back, seeing* Young FASHION.

Nurse. Ah, goodness, Roger, we are betrayed!

Fash. [*Laying hold on 'em.*] Nay, nay, ne'er flinch for the matter, for I have you safe.—Come, to your trials immediately; I have no time to give you copies of your indictment. There sits your judge.

Both. [*Kneeling.*] Pray, sir, have compassion on us.

Nurse. I hope, sir, my years will move your pity; I am an aged woman. 51

Coup. That is a moving argument indeed.

Bull. I hope, sir, my character will be considered; I am Heaven's ambassador.

Coup. Are not you a rogue of sanctity?

Bull. Sir (with respect to my function), I do wear a gown.

Coup. Did not you marry this vigorous young fellow to a plump young buxom wench?

Nurse. [*Aside to* BULL.] Don't confess, Roger, unless you are hard put to it indeed. 61

Coup. Come, out with't !—Now is he chewing the cud of his roguery, and grinding a lie between his teeth.

Bull. Sir,—I cannot positively say—I say, sir,—positively I cannot say—

Coup. Come, no equivocations, no Roman turns upon us. Consider thou standest upon Protestant ground, which will slip from under thee like a Tyburn cart; for in this country we have always ten hangmen for one Jesuit.

Bull. [*To* Young FASHION.] Pray, sir, then will you but permit me to speak one word in private with nurse. 71

Fash. Thou art always for doing something in private with nurse.

Coup. But pray let his betters be served before him for once : I would do something in private with her myself.— Lory, take care of this reverend gownman in the next room a little.—Retire, priest.—[*Exit* LORY *with* BULL.] Now, virgin, I must put the matter home to you a little : do you think it might not be possible to make you speak truth?

Nurse. Alas, sir ! I don't know what you mean by truth. 81

Coup. Nay, 'tis possible thou mayest be a stranger to it.

Fash. Come, nurse, you and I were better friends when we saw one another last ; and I still believe you are a very good woman in the bottom. I did deceive you and your young lady, 'tis true, but I always designed to make a very good husband to her, and to be a very good friend to you. And 'tis possible, in the end, she might have found herself happier, and you richer, than ever my brother will make you. 90

Nurse. Brother! why is your worship then his lordship's brother?

Fash. I am; which you should have known, if I durst have stayed to have told you; but I was forced to take horse a little in haste, you know.

Nurse. You were indeed, sir : poor young man, how he was bound to scour for't! Now won't your worship be angry, if I confess the truth to you?—When I found you were a cheat (with respect be it spoken), I verily believed miss had got some pitiful skip-jack * varlet or other to her husband, or I had ne'er let her think of marrying again. 101

Coup. But where was your conscience all this while, woman? Did not that stare in your face with huge saucer-eyes, and a great horn upon the forehead? Did not you think you should be damned for such a sin?—Ha?

Fash. Well said, divinity! press that home upon her.

Nurse. Why, in good truly, sir, I had some fearful thoughts on't, and could never be brought to consent, till Mr. Bull said it was a peckadilla, and he'd secure my soul for a tithe-pig. 110

Fash. There was a rogue for you !

Coup. And he shall thrive accordingly; he shall have a good living.—Come, honest nurse, I see you have butter in your compound ; you can melt. Some compassion you can have of this handsome young fellow.

Nurse. I have, indeed, sir.

Fash. Why then, I'll tell you what you shall do for me. You know what a warm living here is fallen; and that it

---

* The name of skip-jack was properly applied to "youths who ride horses up and down for the sight of purchasers."—NARES.

must be in the disposal of him who has the disposal of miss.
Now if you and the doctor will agree to prove my marriage,
I'll present him to it, upon condition he makes you his
bride.   122

Nurse. Naw the blessing of the Lord follow your good
worship both by night and by day!—Let him be fetched in
by the ears; I'll soon bring his nose to the grindstone.

Coup. [*Aside.*] Well said, old white-leather!—[*Aloud.*]
Hey, bring in the prisoner there!

Re-enter LORY *with* BULL.

Coup.   Come, advance, holy man.   Here's your duck
does not think fit to retire with you into the chancel at this
time; but she has a proposal to make to you in the face of
the congregation.—Come, nurse, speak for yourself, you are
of age.   132

Nurse.   Roger, are not you a wicked man, Roger, to set
your strength against a weak woman, and persuade her it
was no sin to conceal miss's nuptials?   My conscience flies
in my face for it, thou priest of Baal! and I find by woful
experience, thy absolution is not worth an old cassock;
therefore I am resolved to confess the truth to the whole
world, though I die a beggar for it.   But his worship overflows with his mercy and his bounty; he is not only pleased
to forgive us our sins, but designs thou sha't squat thee
down in Fatgoose living; and which is more than all, has
prevailed with me to become the wife of thy bosom.   143

Fash.   All this I intend for you, doctor.   What you are to
do for me I need not tell you.

Bull.   Your worship's goodness is unspeakable.   Yet
there is one thing seems a point of conscience; and

K

conscience is a tender babe. If I should bind myself, for the sake of this living, to marry nurse, and maintain her afterwards, I doubt it might be looked on as a kind of simony.   151

Coup. [*Rising up.*] If it were sacrilege, the living's worth it : therefore no more words, good doctor ; but with the parish— [*Giving* Nurse *to him.*] here—take the parsonage-house. 'Tis true, 'tis a little out of repair ; some dilapidations there are to be made good ; the windows are broke, the wainscot is warped, the ceilings are peeled, and the walls are cracked ; but a little glazing, painting, whitewash, and plaster, will make it last thy time.

Bull. Well, sir, if it must be so, I shan't contend. What Providence orders, I submit to.   161

Nurse. And so do I, with all humility.

Coup. Why, that now was spoke like good people. Come, my turtle-doves, let us go help this poor pigeon to his wandering mate again ; and after institution and induction, you shall all go a-cooing together.   [*Exeunt.*

SCENE IV.—Loveless's *Lodgings.*

Enter AMANDA *in a scarf, &c., as just returned, her* Woman *following her.*

Aman. Prithee what care I who has been here ?

Wom. Madam, 'twas my lady Bridle and my lady Tiptoe.

Aman. My lady Fiddle and my lady Faddle ! What dost stand troubling me with the visits of a parcel of impertinent women ? When they are well seamed with the

small-pox, they won't be so fond of showing their faces.—
There are more coquettes about this town—
     Wom. Madam, I suppose they only came to return your
ladyship's visit, according to the custom of the world.   10
     Aman. Would the world were on fire, and you in the
middle on't! Begone! leave me!—[*Exit* Woman.]   At
last I am convinced. My eyes are testimonies of his false-
hood. The base, ungrateful, perjured villain !—
Good gods ! what slippery stuff are men compos'd of !
Sure the account of their creation's false,
And 'twas the woman's rib that they were form'd of.
But why am I thus angry?
This poor relapse should only move my scorn.
'Tis true,   20
The roving flights of his unfinish'd youth
Had strong excuses* from the plea of nature ;
Reason had thrown the reins loose on his neck,
And slipp'd him to unlimited desire.
If therefore he went wrong, he had a claim
To my forgiveness, and I did him right.
But since the years of manhood rein him in,
And reason, well digested into thought,
Has pointed out the course he ought to run ;
If now he strays,   30
'Twould be as weak and mean in me to pardon,
As it has been in him t' offend. But hold :
'Tis an ill cause indeed, where nothing's to be said for't.

---

     * The old editions read "excuse." I have followed Leigh Hunt,
whose substitution of the plural for the singular saves the metre, without altering the sense.

My beauty possibly is in the wane ;
Perhaps sixteen has greater charms for him :
Yes, there's the secret.   But let him know,
My quiver's not entirely emptied yet,
I still have darts, and I can shoot 'em too ;
They're not so blunt, but they can enter still :
The want's not in my power, but in my will.   40
Virtue's his friend ; or, through another's heart,
I yet could find the way to make his smart.

                         [*Going off, she meets* WORTHY.

Ha ! he here !
Protect me, Heaven ! for this looks ominous.

                   Enter WORTHY.

    Wor.   You seem disorder'd, madam ;
I hope there's no misfortune happen'd to you ?
    Aman.   None that will long disorder me, I hope.
    Wor.   Whate'er it be disturbs you, I would to Heaven
'Twere in my power to bear the pain,
Till I were able to remove the cause.   50
    Aman.   I hope ere long it will remove itself.
At least, I have given it warning to be gone.
    Wor.   Would I durst ask, where 'tis the thorn torments
            you !
Forgive me, if I grow inquisitive ;
'Tis only with desire to give you ease.
    Aman.   Alas ! 'tis in a tender part.
It can't be drawn without a world of pain :
Yet out it must ;
For it begins to fester in my heart.
    Wor.   If 'tis the sting of unrequited love,   6

Remove it instantly :
I have a balm will quickly heal the wound.
    Aman. You'll find the undertaking difficult :
The surgeon, who already has attempted it,
Has much tormented me.
    Wor. I'll aid him with a gentler hand,
—If you will give me leave.
    Aman. How soft soe'er the hand may be,
There still is terror in the operation.
    Wor. Some few preparatives would make it easy,   70
Could I persuade you to apply 'em.
Make home reflections, madam, on your slighted love :
Weigh well the strength and beauty of your charms :
Rouse up that spirit women ought to bear,
And slight your god, if he neglects his angel.
With arms of ice receive his cold embraces,
And keep your fire for those who come in flames.
Behold a burning lover at your feet,
His fever raging in his veins !
See how he trembles, how he pants !   80
See how he glows, how he consumes !
Extend the arms of mercy to his aid ;
His zeal may give him title to your pity,
Although his merit cannot claim your love.
    Aman. Of all my feeble sex, sure I must be the weakest,
Should I again presume to think on love. [*Sighing.*]
Alas ! my heart has been too roughly treated.
    Wor. 'Twill find the greater bliss in softer usage.
    Aman. But where's that usage to be found ?
    Wor.   'Tis here,
Within this faithful breast ; which if you doubt,   90

I'll rip it up before your eyes ;
Lay all its secrets open to your view ;
And then, you'll see 'twas sound.

Aman. With just such honest words as these, the worst
of men deceived me.

Wor. He therefore merits all revenge can do ;
His fault is such,
The extent and stretch of vengeance cannot reach it.
Oh ! make me but your instrument of justice ;
You'll find me execute it with such zeal,   100
As shall convince you I abhor the crime.

Aman. The rigour of an executioner
Has more the face of cruelty than justice :
And he who puts the cord about the wretch's neck,
Is seldom known to exceed him in his morals.

Wor. What proof then can I give you of my truth ?

Aman. There is on earth but one.

Wor. And is that in my power ?

Aman.   It is :
And one that would so thoroughly convince me,
I should be apt to rate your heart so high,   110
I possibly might purchase't with a part of mine.

Wor. Then Heaven, thou art my friend, and I am blest ;
For if 'tis in my power, my will I'm sure
Will reach it. No matter what the terms
May be, when such a recompense is offer'd.
Oh ! tell me quickly what this proof must be !
What is it will convince you of my love ?

Aman. I shall believe you love me as you ought,
If from this moment you forbear to ask
Whatever is unfit for me to grant.—   120

You pause upon it, sir.—I doubt, on such hard terms,
A woman's heart is scarcely worth the having.
   Wor. A heart, like yours, on any terms is worth it ;
'Twas not on that I paus'd.   But I was thinking
                   [*Drawing nearer to her.*
Whether some things there may not be,
Which women cannot grant without a blush,
And yet which men may take without offence.
                       [*Taking her hand.*
Your hand, I fancy, may be of the number :
Oh, pardon me ! if I commit a rape   [*Kissing it eagerly.*
Upon't ; * and thus devour it with my kisses.   130
   Aman. O Heavens ! let me go.
   Wor. Never, whilst I have strength to hold you
        here.
          [*Forcing her to sit down on a couch.*
My life, my soul, my goddess—Oh, forgive me !
   Aman. Oh whither am I going ? Help, Heaven, or I
        am lost.
   Wor. Stand neuter, gods, this once, I do invoke
        you.
   Aman. Then save me, virtue, and the glory's thine.
   Wor. Nay, never strive.
   Aman.   I will, and conquer too.
My forces rally bravely to my aid,   [*Breaking from him.*
And thus I gain the day.
   Wor. Then mine as bravely double their attack ;   140
                    [*Seizing her again.*

---

* " Upon it," in the early editions, in which much of this scene is printed as prose. Nevertheless, it is written in metre, and I have ventured, in this instance, to follow Leigh Hunt in printing the whole scene uniformly as verse.

And thus I wrest it from you.   Nay, struggle not;
For all's in vain : or death or victory ;
I am determined.

Aman.   And so am I :   [*Rushing from him.*
Now keep your distance, or we part for ever.

Wor. [*Offering again.*]   For Heaven's sake !—

Aman. [*Going.*]   Nay then, farewell !

Wor.   Oh stay ! and see the magic force of love.
                    [*Kneeling, and holding by her clothes.*
Behold this raging lion at your feet,
Struck dead with fear, and tame as charms can make
      him.
What must I do to be forgiven by you?   150

Aman.   Repent, and never more offend.

Wor.   Repentance for past crimes is just and easy ;
But sin no more's a task too hard for mortals.

Aman.   Yet those who hope for heaven
Must use their best endeavours to perform it.

Wor.   Endeavours we may use, but flesh and blood are
      got
In t'other scale ; and they are ponderous things.

Aman.   Whate'er they are, there is a weight in resolu-
      tion
Sufficient for their balance.   The soul, I do confess,
Is usually so careless of its charge,   160
So soft, and so indulgent to desire,
It leaves the reins in the wild hand of nature,
Who like a Phaeton, drives the fiery chariot,
And sets the world on flame.
Yet still the sovereignty is in the mind,
Whene'er it pleases to exert its force.

Perhaps you may not think it worth your while
To take such mighty pains for my esteem ;
But that I leave to you.
You see the price I set upon my heart ;   170
Perhaps 'tis dear : but, spite of all your art,
You'll find on cheaper terms we ne'er shall part.*

[*Exit.*

Wor.   Sure there's divinity about her !
And sh'as dispens'd some portion on't to me.
For what but now was the wild flame of love,
Or (to dissect that specious term) the vile,
The gross desires of flesh and blood,
Is in a moment turned to adoration.
The coarser appetite of nature's gone, and 'tis,
Methinks, the food of angels I require.   180
How long this influence may last, Heaven knows ;
But in this moment of my purity,
I could on her own terms accept her heart.
Yes, lovely woman !   I can accept it.
For now 'tis doubly worth my care.
Your charms are much increas'd, since thus adorn'd.
When truth's extorted from us, then we own
The robe of virtue is a graceful habit.
Could women but our secret counsels scan,
Could they but reach the deep reserves of man,   190
They'd wear it on, that that of love might last ;
For when they throw off one, we soon the other cast.
Their sympathy is such—
The fate of one, the other scarce can fly ;
They live together, and together die.   [*Exit.*

---

* Bargain ; agree.

SCENE V.—*A Room in* Lord FOPPINGTON'S *House.*

Enter Miss HOYDEN *and* Nurse.

Hoyd. But is it sure and certain, say you, he's my lord's own brother?

Nurse. As sure as he's your lawful husband.

Hoyd. Ecod, if I had known that in time, I don't know but I might have kept him : for, between you and I, nurse, he'd have made a husband worth two of this I have. But which do you think you should fancy most, nurse?

Nurse. Why, truly, in my poor fancy, madam, your first husband is the prettier gentleman.

Hoyd. I don't like my lord's shapes, nurse.   10

Nurse. Why, in good truly, as a body may say, he is but a slam.

Hoyd. What do you think now he puts me in mind of? Don't you remember a long, loose, shambling sort of a horse my father called Washy?

Nurse. As like as two twin-brothers !

Hoyd. Ecod, I have thought so a hundred times : faith, I'm tired of him.

Nurse. Indeed, madam, I think you had e'en as good stand to your first bargain.   20

Hoyd. Oh, but, nurse, we han't considered the main thing yet. If I leave my lord, I must leave my lady too ; and when I rattle about the streets in my coach, they'll only say, There goes mistress—mistress—mistress what? What's this man's name I have married, nurse?

Nurse. 'Squire Fashion.

Hoyd. 'Squire Fashion is it ?—Well, 'Squire, that's better

than nothing. Do you think one could not get him made a
knight, nurse?

Nurse. I don't know but one might, madam, when the
king's in a good humour.   31

Hoyd. Ecod, that would do rarely. For then he'd be as
good a man as my father, you know.

Nurse. By'r Lady, and that's as good as the best of 'em.

Hoyd. So 'tis, faith ; for then I shall be my lady, and
your ladyship at every word, and that's all I have to care for.
Ha, nurse, but hark you me; one thing more, and then I
have done. I'm afraid, if I change my husband again, I
shan't have so much money to throw about, nurse.   39

Nurse. Oh, enough's as good as a feast. Besides,
madam, one don't know but as much may fall to your share
with the younger brother as with the elder. For though
these lords have a power of wealth indeed, yet, as I
have heard say, they give it all to their sluts and their
trulls, who joggle it about in their coaches, with a murrain
to 'em ! whilst poor madam sits sighing, and wishing, and
knotting, and crying, and has not a spare half-crown to buy
her a *Practice of Piety.**   48

Hoyd. Oh, but for that don't deceive yourself, nurse. For
this I must say for my lord, and a— [*Snapping her fingers*]
for him ; he's as free as an open house at Christmas. For
this very morning he told me I should have two hundred a
year to buy pins. Now, nurse, if he gives me two hundred
a year to buy pins, what do you think he'll give me to buy
fine petticoats?

---

* A manual of devotion.

Nurse. Ah, my dearest, he deceives thee faully, and he's no better than a rogue for his pains! These Londoners have got a gibberidge with 'em would confound a gipsy. That which they call pin-money is to buy their wives everything in the 'varsal world, down to their very shoe-ties. Nay, I have heard folks say, that some ladies, if they will have gallants, as they call 'em, are forced to find them out of their pin-money too.   63

Hoyd. Has he served me so, say ye?—Then I'll be his wife no longer, so that's fixed. Look, here he comes, with all the fine folk at's heels. Ecod, nurse, these London ladies will laugh till they crack again, to see me slip my collar, and run away from my husband. But, d'ye hear? Pray, take care of one thing : when the business comes to break out, be sure you get between me and my father, for you know his tricks ; he'll knock me down.

Nurse. I'll mind him, ne'er fear, madam.   72

Enter Lord FOPPINGTON, LOVELESS, WORTHY, AMANDA,
and BERINTHIA.

Lord Fop. Ladies and gentlemen, you are all welcome. —Loveless, that's my wife; prithee do me the favour to salute her; and dost hear,—[*Aside to him*] if thau hast a mind to try thy fartune, to be revenged of me, I won't take it ill, stap my vitals !

Love. You need not fear, sir ; I'm too fond of my own wife to have the least inclination to yours.

[*All salute* Miss HOYDEN.

Lord Fop. [*Aside.*] I'd give a thousand paund he would make love to her, that he may see she has sense enough to prefer me to him, though his own wife

has not.—[*Viewing him.*]   He's a very beastly fellow, in
my opinion.   84

Hoyd. [*Aside.*]   What a power of fine men there are in
this London!   He that kissed me first is a goodly gentleman, I promise you.   Sure those wives have a rare time on't
that live here always.

Enter Sir TUNBELLY CLUMSEY, *with* Musicians,
Dancers, &c.

Sir Tun. Come, come in, good people, come in!   Come,
tune your fiddles, tune your fiddles!—[*To the hautboys.*]
Bagpipes, make ready there.   Come, strike up.   [*Sings.*
        For this is Hoyden's wedding-day,
        And therefore we keep holiday,
              And come to be merry.
Ha! there's my wench, i'faith.   Touch and take, I'll warrant
her; she'll breed like a tame rabbit.   96

Hoyd. [*Aside.*]   Ecod, I think my father's gotten drunk
before supper.

Sir Tun. [*To* LOVELESS *and* WORTHY.]   Gentlemen,
you are welcome.—[*Saluting* AMANDA *and* BERINTHIA.]
Ladies, by your leave.—[*Aside.*]   Ha! they bill like turtles.
Udsookers, they set my old blood a-fire; I shall cuckold
somebody before morning.

Lord Fop. [*To* Sir TUNBELLY.]   Sir, you being master
of the entertainment, will you desire the company to sit?

Sir Tun. Oons, sir, I'm the happiest man on this side
the Ganges!

Lord Fop. [*Aside.*]   This is a mighty unaccountable
old fellow.—[*To* Sir TUNBELLY.]   I said, sir, it would be convenient to ask the company to sit.   110

Sir Tun. Sit?—with all my heart.—Come, take your places, ladies; take your places, gentlemen.—Come, sit down, sit down; a pox of ceremony! take your places.

[*They sit, and the masque begins.*

Dialogue between CUPID *and* HYMEN.

Cup. Thou bane to my empire, thou spring of contest, Thou source of all discord, thou period to rest, Instruct me, what wretches in bondage can see, That the aim of their life is still pointed to thee.

Hym. Instruct me, thou little, impertinent god, From whence all thy subjects have taken the mode To grow fond of a change, to whatever it be,   120 And I'll tell thee why those would be bound who are free.

Chorus.

For change, we're for change, to whatever it be, We are neither contented with freedom nor thee.
            Constancy's an empty sound,
            Heaven, and earth, and all go round,
            All the works of Nature move,
            And the joys of life and love
            Are in variety.

Cup. Were love the reward of a painstaking life, Had a husband the art to be fond of his wife,   130 Were virtue so plenty, a wife could afford, These very hard times, to be true to her lord, Some specious account might be given of those Who are tied by the tail, to be led by the nose.

But since 'tis the fate of a man and his wife,
To consume all their days in contention and strife ;
Since, whatever the bounty of Heaven may create her,
He's morally sure he shall heartily hate her,
I think 'twere much wiser to ramble at large,
And the volleys of love on the herd to discharge.   140

Hym.   Some colour of reason thy counsel might bear,
Could a man have no more than his wife to his share :
Or were I a monarch so cruelly just,
To oblige a poor wife to be true to her trust ;
But I have not pretended, for many years past,
By marrying of people, to make 'em grow chaste.

I therefore advise thee to let me go on,
Thou'lt find I'm the strength and support of thy throne ;
For hadst thou but eyes, thou wouldst quickly perceive it,
            How smoothly the dart   150
            Slips into the heart
            Of a woman that's wed ;
            Whilst the shivering maid
Stands trembling, and wishing, but dare not receive it.

Chorus.

For change, we're for change, to whatever it be,
We are neither contented with freedom nor thee.
            Constancy's an empty sound,
            Heaven, and earth, and all go round,
            All the works of Nature move,
            And the joys of life and love   160
                  Are in variety.

                              [*End of the masque.*

Sir Tun. So ; very fine, very fine, i'faith ! this is something like a wedding. Now, if supper were but ready, I'd
say a short grace ; and if I had such a bedfellow as Hoyden
to-night—I'd say as short prayers.

Enter Young FASHION, COUPLER, *and* BULL.

How now !—what have we got here? a ghost? Nay, it
must be so, for his flesh and blood could never have
dared to appear before me.—[*To* Young FASHION.] Ah,
rogue !

Lord Fop. Stap my vitals, Tam again?   170

Sir Tun. My lord, will you cut his throat? or shall I ?

Lord Fop. Leave him to me, sir, if you please.—Prithee,
Tam, be so ingenuous now as to tell me what thy business is
here ?

Fash. 'Tis with your bride.

Lord Fop. Thau art the impudentest fellow that Nature
has yet spawned into the warld, strike me speechless !

Fash. Why, you know my modesty would have starved
me ; I sent it a-begging to you, and you would not give it a
groat.   180

Lord Fop. And dost thau expect by an excess of
assurance to extart a maintenance fram me ?

Fash. [*Taking* Miss HOYDEN *by the hand.*] I do intend
to extort your mistress from you, and that I hope will prove
one.

Lord Fop. I ever thaught Newgate or Bedlam would be
his fartune, and naw his fate's decided.—Prithee, Loveless,
dost know of ever a mad doctor hard by ?

Fash. There's one at your elbow will cure you presently.
—[*To* BULL.] Prithee, doctor, take him in hand quickly. 190

Lord Fop. Shall I beg the favour of you, sir, to pull your fingers out of my wife's hand ?

Fash. His wife ! Look you there; now I hope you are all satisfied he's mad.

Lord Fop. Naw is it nat passible far me to penetrate what species of fally it is thau art driving at !

Sir Tun. Here, here, here, let me beat out his brains, and that will decide all.

Lord Fop. No ; pray, sir, hold, we'll destray him presently accarding to law.   200

Fash. [*To* BULL.] Nay, then advance, doctor : come, you are a man of conscience, answer boldly to the questions I shall ask. Did not you marry me to this young lady before ever that gentleman there saw her face ?

Bull. Since the truth must out—I did.

Fash. Nurse, sweet nurse, were not you a witness to it ?

Nurse. Since my conscience bids me speak—I was.

Fash. [*To* Miss HOYDEN.] Madam, am not I your lawful husband ?

Hoyd. Truly I can't tell, but you married me first.   210

Fash. Now I hope you are all satisfied ?

Sir Tun. [*Offering to strike him, is held by* LOVELESS *and* WORTHY.] Oons and thunder, you lie !

Lord Fop. Pray, sir, be calm ; the battle is in disarder, but requires more canduct than courage to rally our forces. —Pray, dactor, one word with you.—[*Aside to* BULL.] Look you, sir, though I will not presume to calculate your notions of damnation fram the description you give us of hell, yet since there is at least a passibility you may have a pitchfark thrust in your backside, methinks it should not be worth your while to risk your saul in the next warld, for the

L

sake of a beggarly yaunger brather, who is nat able to make your bady happy in this. 222

Bull. Alas! my lord, I have no worldly ends; I speak the truth, Heaven knows.

Lord Fop. Nay, prithee, never engage Heaven in the matter, for by all I can see, 'tis like to prove a business for the devil.

Fash. Come, pray, sir, all above-board; no corrupting of e vidences, if you please. This young lady is my lawful wife, and I'll justify it in all the courts of England; so your lord-ship (who always had a passion for variety) may go seek a n ew mistress if you think fit. 232

Lord Fop. I am struck dumb with his impudence, and cannot pasitively tell whether ever I shall speak again or nat.

Sir Tun. Then let me come and examine the business a little, I'll jerk the truth out of 'em presently. Here, give me my dog-whip.

Fash. Look you, old gentleman, 'tis in vain to make a noise; if you grow mutinous, I have some friends within call, have swords by their sides above four foot long; there-fore be calm, hear the evidence patiently, and when the jury have given their verdict, pass sentence according to law. Here's honest Coupler shall be foreman, and ask as many questions as he pleases. 245

Coup. All I have to ask is, whether nurse persists in her evidence? The parson, I dare swear, will never flinch from his.

Nurse. [*To* Sir TUNBELLY, *kneeling.*] I hope in Heaven y our worship will pardon me: I have served you long and faithfully, but in this thing I was overreached; your worship, however, was deceived as well as I, and if the wedding-dinner had been ready, you had put madam to bed to him with your own hands.

Sir Tun. But how durst you do this, without acquainting of me?   256

Nurse. Alas! if your worship had seen how the poor thing begged, and prayed, and clung, and twined about me, like ivy to an old wall, you would say, I who had suckled it and swaddled it, and nursed it both wet and dry, must have had a heart of adamant to refuse it.

Sir Tun. Very well!

Fash. Foreman, I expect your verdict.

Coup. Ladies and gentlemen, what's your opinions?

All. A clear case! a clear case!

Coup. Then, my young folks, I wish you joy.

Sir Tun. [*To* Young FASHION.] Come hither, stripling; if it be true then, that thou hast married my daughter, prithee tell me who thou art?   269

Fash. Sir, the best of my condition is, I am your son-in-law; and the worst of it is, I am brother to that noble peer there.

Sir Tun. Art thou brother to that noble peer?—Why, then, that noble peer, and thee, and thy wife, and the nurse, and the priest—may all go and be damned together! [*Exit.*

Lord Fop. [*Aside.*] Now, for my part, I think the wisest thing a man can do with an aching heart is to put on a serene countenance; for a philosophical air is the most becoming thing in the world to the face of a person of quality. I will therefore bear my disgrace like a great man, and let the people see I am above an affront.—[*Aloud.*] Dear Tam, since things are thus fallen aut, prithee give me leave to wish thee jay; I do it *de bòn cœur*, strike me dumb! You have married a woman beautiful in her person, charming in her airs, prudent in her canduct, canstant in her inclinations, and of a nice marality, split my windpipe!   286

Fash. Your lordship may keep up your spirits with your grimace if you please; I shall support mine with this lady, and two thousand pound a-year.—[*Taking* Miss HOYDEN'S *hand.*]

Come, madam :—
We once again, you see, are man and wife,
And now, perhaps, the bargain's struck for life.
If I mistake, and we should part again,
At least you see you may have choice of men :
Nay, should the war at length such havoc make,
That lovers should grow scarce, yet for your sake,
Kind Heaven always will preserve a beau :
　　　　　　　　　　[*Pointing to* Lord FOPPINGTON.
You'll find his lordship ready to come to.

Lord Fop. Her ladyship shall stap my vitals, if I do.
　　　　　　　　　　　　[*Exeunt omnes.*

EPILOGUE.

Gentlemen and Ladies,
THESE people have regal'd you here to-day
(In my opinion) with a saucy play ;
In which the author does presume to show,
That coxcomb, *ab origine*—was beau.
Truly, I think the thing of so much weight,
That if some sharp chastisement ben't his fate,
Gad's curse ! it may in time destroy the state.
I hold no one its friend, I must confess,
Who would discauntenance your men of dress.   10
Far, give me leave t' abserve, good clothes are things
Have ever been of great support to kings ;
All treasons come from slovens, it is nat
Within the reach of gentle beaux to plat ;
They have no gall, no spleen, no teeth, no stings,
Of all Gad's creatures, the most harmless things.
Through all recard, no prince was ever slain
By one who had a feather in his brain.
They're men of too refin'd an education,
To squabble with a court—for a vile dirty nation.   20
I'm very pasitive you never saw
A through republican a finish'd beau.
Nor, truly, shall you very often see
A Jacobite much better dress'd than he.

In shart, through all the courts that I have been in,
Your men of mischief—still are in faul linen.
Did ever one yet dance the Tyburn jig,*
With a free air, or a well-pawder'd wig?
Did ever highwayman yet bid you stand,
With a sweet bawdy snuff-bax† in his hand? 30
Ar do you ever find they ask your purse
As men of breeding do?—Ladies, Gad's curse!
This author is a dag, and 'tis not fit
You should allow him ev'n one grain of wit:
To which, that his pretence may ne'er be nam'd,
My humble motion is,—he may be damn'd.

---

* *I.e.*, ascend the gallows.
† *I.e.*, a snuff-box with a bawdy picture on the lid.

ÆSOP.

Æsop was produced at Drury Lane about the middle of January, 1697, and published anonymously, in 4to, the same month.

The title-page of the first edition reads as follows: *Æsop, a Comedy. As it is acted at the Theatre-Royal in Drury-lane. London, Printed for Thomas Bennet at the Half-Moon in St. Paul's Church-Yard, 1697.*

Æsop is a very free translation, with frequent and important variations, of a French comedy called *Les Fables d'Ésope*, by Boursault, a dramatist of some celebrity, who was born in 1638, and died in 1701.* The French play, which is in five acts, and in verse, was first performed at Paris in the year 1690.

In this, as in his other translations, Vanbrugh has consulted at once the bent of his own genius and the taste of his audience, in forsaking the characteristic sentiment of French serious comedy, and treating the whole subject in a livelier, but at the same time coarser, vein. He naturally appears at his best in the purely comic scenes: in the

---

* Boursault " est un de ces auteurs dramatiques qui, au dix-septième siècle, eurent de la vogue à défaut de gloire, et dont quelques productions sont encore estimées aujourd'hui."—*Nouvelle Biographie Générale.*

conversations of Æsop with the neighbours, and especially in the fables, he has vastly improved upon Boursault, who is comparatively heavy in scenes of this description. On the other hand, the story of Euphrosine and Agenor (Vanbrugh's Euphronia and Oronces) is told by Boursault in language simpler and more touching than that of the English poet, who, in discarding the sentimentality, has lost something of the humanity of the original play. A single sentence will aptly illustrate the difference in sentiment between the French and English authors. When Agenor is told that his mistress is married, instead of raving like Oronces (Act II.) he exclaims :

> "Ah madame,
> Avez-vous pu trahir une si belle flâme ?"

The scene between Æsop and the country gentleman, Polidorus Hogstye, in the fourth act, belongs to Vanbrugh alone. He has, however, omitted one of the prettiest scenes in Boursault's comedy—the last of the third act, between Æsop and two children ; of which the sentiment was, I suppose, too innocent to be tolerated by an English audience of that time.

Vanbrugh claims the fifth act as his own : it is nearly so, the beginning of it alone presenting some resemblance to the French. With Boursault, it is true, Æsop unites the lovers at last, but the details of the French piece differ entirely from those of the English. The French Æsop recites the fable of the man with two wives, who pulled out all his hair between them. This story so powerfully affects Léarque, that he at once accepts Agenor as his son-in-law, and all ends happily. Goldsmith narrates an incident in the life of Beau Nash, from which he supposes Vanbrugh to have borrowed the catastrophe of *Æsop*. Nash, in the early part of his life, under circumstances similar to those in the play, resigned the mistress of his affections to a favoured rival; generously settling a fortune upon the lady, and inducing her reluctant father to give his consent to the match. It is possible that Vanbrugh was acquainted with this story, which, however, does not bear a much closer resemblance to the catastrophe of his play than to that of Boursault's.

The second part of *Æsop*, a fragment, which, of course, was never put upon the stage, is the original production of Vanbrugh, and was published, for the first time, with the second edition of the play, 4to, 1697. The first scene, it will be noticed, contains a highly coloured representation of the quarrel between the patentee of Drury Lane and his actors.

PREFACE.

To speak for a play, if it can't speak for itself, is vain; and if it can, 'tis needless. For one of these reasons (I can't yet tell which, for 'tis now but the second day of acting) I resolve to say nothing for Æsop, though I know he'd be glad of help; for let the best happen that can, his journey's up hill, with a dead English weight at the tail of him.

At Paris, indeed, he scrambled up something faster (for 'twas up hill there too) than I'm afraid he will do here: the French having more mercury in their heads, and less beef and pudding in their bellies. Our solidity may set hard, what their folly makes easy; for fools I own they are, you know we have found 'em so in the conduct of the war: I wish we may do so in the management of the peace;* but that's neither Æsop's business nor mine.

This play, gentlemen (or one not much unlike it), was writ in French about six years since by one Monsieur Boursault; 'twas played at Paris by the French comedians, and this was its fate:

---

* This was written in January, 1697. In the following September the war between the King of France and the Allies was concluded, after long negotiations, by the Peace of Ryswick, on terms disadvantageous to France. By this treaty Louis XIV. agreed to withdraw his support from the Stuarts, and recognized William III. as King of England.

The first day it appeared, 'twas routed;—people seldom being fond of what they don't understand, their own sweet persons excepted. The second (by the help of some bold knight-errants) it rallied; the third it advanced; the fourth it gave a vigorous attack; and the fifth put all the feathers in town to the scamper, pursuing 'em on to the fourteenth, and then they cried out quarter.

'Tis not reasonable to expect Æsop should gain so great a victory here, since 'tis possible by fooling with his sword I may have turned the edge on't. For I confess in the translation I have not at all stuck to the original. Nay, I have gone farther: I have wholly added the fifth Act, and crowded a country gentleman into the fourth, for which I ask Monsieur Boursault's pardon with all my heart, but doubt I never shall obtain it, for bringing him into such company. Though after all, had I been so complaisant to have waited on his play word for word, 'tis possible even that might not have ensured the success of it: for though it swam in France, it might have sunk in England. Their country abounds in cork, ours in lead.

DRAMATIS PERSONÆ.

MEN.

Æsop	Mr. *Cibber.*
Learchus, Governor of *Cyzicus*	Mr. *Dogget.*
Oronces, in love with *Euphronia*	Mr. *Harland.*

WOMEN.

Euphronia, Daughter to *Learchus,* in love with *Oronces*	Mrs. *Temple.*
Doris, her Nurse	Mrs. *Verbruggen.*

People who come to *Æsop,* upon several occasions, independent one of another.

Two Country Tradesmen	{ Mr. *Pinkethman* * and Mr. *Smeton.*
Roger, a Country Bumpkin	Mr. *Haynes.*†
Quaint, a Herald	Mr. *Pinkethman.*
Fruitful,‡ an Innkeeper	Mr. *Smeton.*
A Country Gentleman	Mr. *Pinkethman.*

A Priest, Musicians, &c.

Hortensia, an affected Learned Lady	Mrs. *Kent.*
Aminta, a Lewd Mother	Mrs. *Willis.*
Forgewill, a Scrivener's Widow	Mrs. *Finch.*
Fruitful, ‡ Wife to the Innkeeper	Mrs. *Powell.*

[SCENE.—CYZICUS : in *Learchus's* House.]

---

* Pinkethman, or Penkethman, was one of the young actors of the Theatre Royal, who began to grow into esteem after the secession of Betterton and the leading members of the company, in 1695. Cibber tells us that he "had certainly, from Nature, a great deal of comic Power about him; but his Judgment was by no means equal to it; for he would make frequent Deviations into the Whimsies of an *Harlequin.*" "He seems to have been a vast favourite with the Gallery" (Genest), and retired from the stage about 1723.

† The part of Roger, in *Æsop,* was one which, in the judgment of Anthony Aston, no one ever played like Joe Haynes. According to the same authority, Haynes was more remarkable for the pranks he played, and for his prologues and epilogues, than for his acting. The title of "Count Haynes," by which he was known, he bestowed upon himself during his travels in France, and ran heavily into debt on the strength of it. His pranks are recorded in an amusing little book, entitled the *Life of the late famous Comedian, Jo. Hayns,* London, 1701.

‡ The first edition has "Breedwell," instead of "Fruitful," as the name of the innkeeper and his wife, in the list of *Dramatis Personæ.* In the play itself, however, the name "Fruitful" is given, as here.

PROLOGUE.

GALLANTS ! we never yet produc'd a play
With greater fears than this we act to-day
Barren of all the graces of the stage,
Barren of all that entertains this age ;
No hero, no romance, no plot, no show,
No rape, no bawdy, no intrigue, no beau :
There's nothing in't with which we use to please ye ;
With downright dull instruction we're to tease ye :
The stage turns pulpit, and the world's so fickle,
The playhouse in a whim turns conventicle.   10
But preaching here must prove a hungry trade,
The patentees will find so, I'm afraid :
For though with heavenly zeal you all abound,
As by your lives and morals may be found ;
Though every female here o'erflows with grace,
And chaste Diana's written in her face ;
Though maids renounce the sweets of fornication,
And one lewd wife's not left in all the nation ;
Though men grow true, and the foul fiend defy ;
Though tradesmen cheat no more, nor lawyers lie ;   20
Though not one spot be found on Levi's tribe,
Nor one soft courtier that will touch a bribe ;
Yet in the midst of such religious days
Sermons have never borne the price of plays.

ÆSOP.

A COMEDY.

ACT I.

SCENE.—*A Room in* LEARCHUS'S *House.*

Enter LEARCHUS, EUPHRONIA, *and* DORIS.

Lear. At length I am blessed with the sight of the
world's wonder, the delight of mankind, the incomparable
Æsop. You had time to observe him last night, daughter,
as he sat at supper with me. Tell me how you like him,
child ; is he not a charming person ?

Euph. Charming !

Lear. What sayest thou to him, Doris ? Thou art a
good judge, a wench of a nice palate.

Dor. You would not have me flatter, sir ?

Lear. No, speak thy thoughts boldly.   10

Dor. Boldly, you say ?

Lear. Boldly, I say.

Dor. Why then, sir, my opinion of the gentleman is,
that he's uglier than an old beau.

Lear. How, Impudence ?

Dor. Nay, if you are angry, sir, second thoughts are
best ; he's as proper as a pikeman, holds up his head like a

dancing-master, has the shape of a barb, the face of an angel, the voice of a cherubin, the smell of a civet-cat—

Lear. In short, thou art fool enough not to be pleased with him.   21

Dor. Excuse me for that, sir; I have wit enough to make myself merry with him.

Lear. If his body's deformed, his soul is beautiful: would to kind Heaven, as he is, my daughter could but find the means to please him !

Euph. To what end, dear father ?

Lear. That he might be your husband, dear daughter.

Euph. My husband ! Shield me, kind Heaven !

Dor. Psha ! he has a mind to make us laugh, that's all.

Lear. Æsop, then, is not worth her care, in thy opinion ?   32

Dor. Why truly, sir, I'm always for making suitable matches, and don't much approve of breeding monsters. I would have nothing marry a baboon but what has been got by a monkey.

Lear. How darest thou liken so incomparable a man to so contemptible a beast ?

Dor. Ah, the inconstancy of this world ! Out of sight, out of mind. Your little monkey is scarce cold in his grave, and you have already forgot what you used so much to admire. Do but call him to remembrance, sir, in his red coat, new gloves, little hat, and clean linen ; then discharge your conscience, utter the truth from your heart, and tell us whether he was not the prettier gentleman of the two.—By my virginity, sir (though that's but a slippery oath, you'll say), had they made love to me together, Æsop should have worn the willow.   48

M

Lear. Since nothing but an animal will please thee, 'tis pity my monkey had not that virginity thou hast sworn by. But I, whom wisdom charms, even in the homeliest dress, can never think the much deserving Æsop unworthy of my daughter.

Dor. Now, in the name of wonder, what is't you so admire in him ?

Lear. Hark, and thou shalt know ; but you, Euphronia, be you more especially attentive.

'Tis true, he's plain ; but that, my girl,'s a trifle.
All manly beauty's seated in the soul ;
And that of Æsop, envy's self must own,   60
Outshines whate'er the world has yet produc'd.
Crœsus, the prosperous favourite of Heaven,
Crœsus, the happiest potentate on earth,
Whose treasure (though immense) is the least part
Of what he holds from Providence's care,
Leans on his shoulder as his grand support ;
Admires his wisdom, dotes upon his truth,
And makes him pilot to imperial sway.
But in this elevated post of power,
What's his employ? where does he point his thoughts ?   70
To live in splendour, luxury, and ease,
Do endless mischiefs, by neglecting good,
And build his family on others' ruins?
No :
He serves the prince, and serves the people too ;
Is useful to the rich, and helps the poor ;
There's nothing stands neglected, but himself.
With constant pain, and yet with constant joy,
From place to place, throughout the realm he goes,

With useful lessons, form'd to every rank :   80
The people learn obedience from his tongue,
The magistrate is guided in command,
The prince is minded of a father's care ;
The subject's taught the duty of a child.
And as 'tis dangerous to be bold with truth,
He often calls for fable to his aid,
Where under abject names of beasts and birds,
Virtue shines out, and vice is cloth'd in shame :
And thus by inoffensive wisdom's force
He conquers folly, wheresoe'er he moves.   90
This is his portrait.

    Dor.   A very good picture of a very ill face.

    Lear.   Well, daughter ; what, not a word ?   Is it possible
anything that I am father of can be untouched with so much
merit ?

    Euph.   My duty may make all things possible : but
Æsop is so ugly, sir.   97

    Lear.   His soul has so much beauty in't, your reason
ought to blind your eyes.   Besides, my interest is concerned ;
his power alarms me.   I know throughout the kingdom he's
the scourge of evil magistrates ; turns out governors, when
they turn tyrants ; breaks officers for false musters ;
excludes judges from giving sentence, when they have been
absent during the trial ; hangs lawyers when they take fees
on both sides ; forbids physicians to take money of those
they don't cure.   'Tis true, my innocence ought to banish
my fears : but my government, child, is too delicious a
morsel not to set many a frail mouth a-watering.   Who
knows what accusations envy may produce ?   But all would
be secure, if thou couldst touch the heart of Æsop.   Let me

blow up thy ambition, girl; the fire of that will make thy
eyes sparkle at him.—[*She sighs.*] What's that sigh for now,
ha?—A young husband, by my conscience! Ah, daughter,
hadst thou a young husband, he'd make thee sigh indeed.
I'll tell thee what he's composed of. He has a wig full of
pulvilio*, a pocket full of dice, a heart full of treason, a
mouth full of lies, a belly full of drink, a carcass full of
plasters, a tail full of pox, and a head full of—nothing.
There's his picture.; wear it at thy heart if thou canst. But
here comes one of greater worth. 120

Enter ÆSOP.

Lear. Good   morning   to   my   noble   lord!   your
excellency—

Æsop. Softly, good governor: I'm a poor wanderer
from place to place, too weak to train the weight of
grandeur with me! The name of excellency's not for me.

Lear. My noble lord, 'tis due to your employ; your
predecessors all—

Æsop. My predecessors all deserved it, sir; they were
great men in wisdom, birth, and service: whilst I, a poor,
unknown, decrepit wretch, mounted aloft for Fortune's
pastime, expect each moment to conclude the farce, by
sinking to the mud, from whence I sprung. 132

Lear. Great Crœsus' gratitude will still support you;
his coffers all are open to your will, your future fortune's
wholly in your power.

Æsop. But 'tis a power that I shall ne'er employ.

Lear. Why so, my lord?

---

* Sweet-scented powder.

Æsop. I'll tell you, sir.

A hungry goat, who had not eat
Some nights and days—(for want of meat)   140
Was kindly brought at last,
By Providence's care,
To better cheer,
After a more than penitential fast.

He found a barn well stor'd with grain ;
To enter in requir'd some pain,
But a delicious bait
Makes the way easy, though the pass is strait.

Our guest observing various meats,
He puts on a good modish face,   150
He takes his place,
He ne'er says grace,
But where he likes, he there falls to and eats.

At length with jaded teeth and jaws,
He made a pause,
And finding still some room,
Fell to as he had done before ;
For time to come laid in his store ;
And when his guts could hold no more,
He thought of going home.   160

But here he met the glutton's curse ;
He found his belly grown so great,
'Twas vain to think of a retreat,
Till he had render'd all he'd eat,
And well he far'd no worse.

To the application, governor.

Lear. 'Tis easy to be made, my lord.

Æsop. I'm glad on't. Truth can never be too clear.

[*Seeing* EUPHRONIA.

Is this young damsel your fair daughter, sir?

Lear. 'Tis my daughter, my good lord. Fair too, if
she appears such in the eyes of the unerring Æsop.   171

Æsop. [*Going up to salute her.*] I never saw so beautiful a creature.

Lear. [*Aside.*] Now's the time; kiss, soft girl, and fire
him.

Æsop. [*Gazing at her.*] How partial's nature 'twixt her
form and mine!

Lear. [*Aside.*] Look, look, look, how he gazes at her!—
Cupid's hard at work, I see that already. Slap; there he
hits him!—If the wench would but do her part.—But see,
see, how the perverse young baggage stands biting her
thumbs, and won't give him one kind glance!—Ah, the
sullen jade! Had it been a handsome strong dog of five-
and-twenty, she'd have fallen a coquetting on't, with every
inch about her. But maybe it's I that spoil sport, I'll make
a pretence to leave 'em together.—[*Aloud.*] Will your
lordship please to drink any coffee this morning?   187

Æsop. With all my heart, governor.

Lear. Your lordship will give me leave to go and order
it myself; for unless I am by, 'tis never perfect.

Æsop. Provided you leave me this fair maid in hostage
for your return, I consent.

Lear. My good lord does my daughter too much
honour.—[*Aside, going off.*] Ah, that the wench would but
do her part!—[*Turning back to* EUPHRONIA, *aside.*] Hark
you, hussy! You can give yourself airs sometimes, you

know you can. Do you remember what work you made
with yourself at church t'other day? Play your tricks over
again once more for my pleasure, and let me have a good
account of this statesman, or, d'ye hear?—you shall die a
maid ; go chew upon that ; go.   [*Exit.*

Æsop. Here I am left, fair damsel, too much exposed
to your charms not to fall your victim.   203

Euph. Your fall will then be due to your own weakness,
sir ; for Heaven's my witness, I neither endeavour nor wish
to wound you.

Æsop. I understand you, lady; your heart's already
disposed of, 'tis seldom otherwise at your age.

Euph. My heart disposed of!   209

Dor. Nay, never mince the matter, madam. The
gentleman looks like a civil gentleman, e'en confess
the truth to him. He has a good interest with your father,
and no doubt will employ it to break the heathenish match
he proposes to you.—[*To* ÆSOP.] Yes, sir, my young lady
has been in love these two years, and that with as pretty a
fellow as ever entered a virgin's heart ; tall, straight, young,
vigorous, good clothes, long periwig, clean linen ; in brief,
he has everything that's necessary to set a young lady
a-longing, and to stay it when he has done. But her father,
whose ambition makes him turn fool in his old age, comes
with a back stroke upon us, and spoils all our sport.
Would you believe it, sir? he has proposed to her to-day
the most confounded ugly fellow. Look, if the very
thoughts of him don't set the poor thing a-crying. And you,
sir, have so much power with the old gentleman, that one
word from you would set us all right again. If he will have
her a wife, in the name of Venus let him provide her a

handsome husband, and not throw her into the paws of a thing that nature in a merry humour has made half man, half monkey.   230

Æsop. Pray what's this monster's name, lady?

Euph. No matter for his name, sir; my father will know who you mean at first word.

Æsop. But you should not always choose by the outside alone; believe me, fair damsel, a fine periwig keeps many a fool's head from the weather. Have a care of your young gallant.

Dor. There's no danger, I have examined him; his inside's as good as his out: I say he has wit, and I think I know.   240

Euph. Nay, she says true; he's even a miracle of wit and beauty: did you but see him, you'd be yourself my rival.

Æsop. Then you are resolved against the monster.

Dor. Fy, sir, fy! I wonder you'll put her in mind of that foul frightful thing. We shall have her dream of nothing all night but bats and owls, and toads and hedgehogs, and then we shall have such a squeaking and squalling with her, the whole house will be in an uproar. Therefore, pray, sir, name him no more, but use your interest with her father that she may never hear of him again.   250

Æsop. But if I should be so generous to save you from the old gallant, what shall I say for your young one?

Euph. Oh, sir, you may venture to enlarge upon his perfections; you need not fear saying too much in his praise.

Dor. And pray, sir, be as copious upon the defects of t'other; you need not fear outrunning the text there neither, say the worst you can.

Euph. You may say the first is .the most graceful man that Asia ever brought forth.   260

Dor. And you may say the latter is the most deformed monster that copulation ever produced.

Euph. Tell him that Oronces (for that's his dear name) has all the virtues that compose a perfect hero.

Dor. And tell him that Pigmy has all the vices that go to equip an attorney.

Euph. That to one, I could be true to the last moment of my life.

Dor. That for t'other, she'd cuckold him the very day of her marriage.—This, sir, in few words, is the theme you are desired to preach upon.   271

Æsop. I never yet had one that furnished me more matter.

Enter Servant.

Ser. My lord, there's a lady below desires to speak with your honour.

Æsop. What lady?

Ser. It's my lady—my lady.—[*To* DORIS.] The lady there, the wise lady, the great scholar, that nobody can understand.

Dor. O ho, is it she? pray let's withdraw, and oblige her, madam; she's ready to swoon at the insipid sight of one of her own sex.   282

Euph. You'll excuse us, sir, we leave you to wiser company.   [*Exeunt* EUPHRONIA *and* DORIS.

Enter HORTENSIA.

Hort. The Déesse who from Atropos's breast preserves

the names of heroes and their actions, proclaims your fame throughout this mighty orb, and—

Æsop. [*Aside.*] Shield me, my stars ! what have you sent me here?—[*Aloud.*] For pity's sake, good lady, be more human : my capacity is too heavy to mount to your style : if you would have me know what you mean, please to come down to my understanding. 292

Hort. I've something in my nature soars too high
For vulgar flight, I own ;
But Æsop's sphere must needs be within call ;
Æsop and I may sure converse together.
I know he's modest, but I likewise know
His intellects are categorical.

Æsop. Now, by my faith, lady, I don't know what *intellect* is ; and methinks *categorical* sounds as if you called me names. Pray speak that you may be understood ; language was designed for it, indeed it was. 303

Hort. Of vulgar things, in vulgar phrase we talk ;
But when of Æsop we must speak,
The theme's too lofty for an humble style :
Æsop is sure no common character.

Æsop. No, truly ; I am something particular. Yet, if I am not mistaken, what I have extraordinary about me may be described in very homely language. Here was a young gentlewoman but just now pencilled me out to a hair, I thought ; and yet, I vow to Gad, the learned'st word I heard her make use of, was monster. 313

Hort. That was a woman, sir, a very woman ;
Her cogitations all were on the outward man.
But I strike deeper, 'tis the mind I view.

The soul's the worthy object of my care ;
The soul, that sample of divinity,
That glorious ray of heavenly light. The soul,
That awful throne of thought, that sacred seat
Of contemplation. The soul, that noble source
Of wisdom, that fountain of comfort, that spring of joy,
That happy token of eternal life :   323
The soul, that—

Æsop. Pray, lady, are you married ?

Hort. Why that question, sir ?

Æsop. Only that I might wait upon your husband to wish him joy.

Hort. When people of my composition would marry, they first find something of their own species to join with ; I never could resolve to take a thing of common fabric to my bed, lest when his brutish inclinations prompt him, he should make me mother to a form like his own.   334

Æsop. Methinks a lady so extremely nice should be much at a loss who to converse with.

Hort. Sir, I keep my chamber, and converse with myself ; 'tis better being alone, than to misally one's conversation. Men are scandalous, and women are insipid : discourse without figure makes me sick at my soul. Oh the charms of a metaphor ! What harmony there is in words of erudition ! The music of 'em is inimaginable.

Æsop. Will you hear a fable, lady ?   344

Hort. Willingly, sir ; the apologue pleases me when the application of it is just.

Æsop. It is, I'll answer for't.

Once on a time, a nightingale
  To changes prone;
Unconstant, fickle, whimsical,
  (A female one)
Who sung like others of her kind,
Hearing a well-taught linnet's airs,
Had other matters in her mind;
To imitate him she prepares.   355
Her fancy straight was on the wing:
  " I fly," quoth she,
  " As well as he;
  I don't know why
  I should not try
As well as he to sing."
From that day forth she chang'd her note,
She spoil'd her voice, she strain'd her throat;
She did, as learned women do,
  Till everything   365
  That heard her sing,
Would run away from her—as I from you.
                    [Exit, running.

Hort. How grossly does this poor world suffer itself to be
imposed upon!—Æsop, a man of sense!—Ha! ha! ha! ha!
ha! Alas, poor wretch! I should not have known him but
by his deformity; his soul's as nauseous to my understand-
ing, as his odious body to my sense of feeling. Well;
'Mongst all the wits that are allow'd to shine,
Methinks there's nothing yet approaches mine:
Sure I was sent the homely age t'adorn;   375
What star, I know not, rul'd when I was born;
But everything besides myself's my scorn.   *[Exit.*

ACT II.

SCENE.—*A Room in* LEARCHUS'S *House.*

Enter EUPHRONIA *and* DORIS.

Dor. What in the name of Jove's the matter with you?
Speak, for Heaven's sake !

Euph. Oh ! what shall I do ? Doris, I'm undone.

Dor. What, ravished?

Euph. No, ten times worse ! ten times worse ! Unlace
me, or I shall swoon.

Dor. Unlace you ! why, you are not thereabouts, I
hope.

Euph. No, no ; worse still ; worse than all that.

Dor. Nay, then it's bad indeed.—[DORIS *unlaces her.*]
There, how d'ye do now?   11

Euph. So ; it's going over.

Dor. Courage ; pluck up your spirits ! Well, now what's
the matter ?

Euph. The matter ! thou sha't hear. Know that—that
cheat—Æsop—

Dor. Like enough ; speak ! What has he done ? that
ugly ill-boding Cyclops.

Euph. Why, instead of keeping his promise, and speaking for Oronces, he has not said one word but what has been
for himself. And by my father's order, before to-morrow
noon he's to marry me.   22

Dor. He marry you !

Euph. Am I in the wrong to be in this despair ? Tell me, Doris, if I am to blame?

Dor. To blame! no, by my troth. That ugly, old, treacherous piece of vermin! that melancholy mixture of impotence and desire! does his mouth stand to a young partridge? Ah, the old goat! And your father? He downright dotes at last then ? 30

Euph. Ah, Doris; what a husband does he give me! and what a lover does he rob me of! Thou know'st 'em both ; think of Oronces, and think of Æsop.

Dor. [*Spitting.*] A foul monster! And yet, now I think on't, I'm almost as angry at t'other too. Methinks he makes but a slow voyage on't for a man in love : 'tis now above two months since he went to Lesbos, to pack up the old bones of his dead father ; sure he might have made a little more haste.

Enter ORONCES.

Euph. Oh ! my heart; what do I see ? 40

Dor. Talk of the devil, and he's at your elbow.

Oron. My dear soul !

[EUPHRONIA *runs, and leaps about his neck.*

Euph. Why would you stay so long from me ?

Oron. 'Twas not my fault indeed ; the winds—

Dor. The winds! Will the winds blow you your mistress again? We have had winds too, and waves into the bargain, storms and tempests, sea monsters, and the devil an' all. She struggled as long as she could, but a woman can do no more than she can do ; when her breath was gone, down she sunk. 50

Oron. What's the meaning of all this?

Dor. Meaning! There's meaning and mumping too: your mistress is married, that's all.

Oron. Death and furies!

Euph. [*Clinging about him.*] Don't you frighten him too much, neither, Doris.—No, my dear, I'm not yet executed, though I'm condemned.

Oron. Condemned! to what? Speak! quick!

Dor. To be married.

Oron. Married! When? how? where? to what? to whom?   61

Dor. Æsop! Æsop! Æsop! Æsop! Æsop!

Oron. Fiends and spectres! What! that piece of deformity! that monster! that crump!

Dor. The same, sir, the same.—I find he knows him.— You might have come home sooner.

Oron. Dear Euphronia, ease me from my pain.
Swear that you neither have nor will consent.
I know this comes from your ambitious father;
But you're too generous, too true to leave me: 70
Millions of kingdoms ne'er would shake my faith,
And I believe your constancy as firm.

Euph. You do me justice, you shall find you do: for racks and tortures, crowns and sceptres joined, shall neither fright me from my truth, nor tempt me to be false. On this you may depend.   76

Dor. Would to the Lord you would find some other place to make your fine speeches in! Don't you know that our dear friend Æsop's coming to receive his visits here? In this great downy chair your pretty little husband-elect is to sit and hear all the complaints in the town: one of wisdom's chief recompenses being to be constantly troubled with the business of fools.—Pray, madam, will you take the gentleman by the hand, and lead him into your chamber; and when you are there, don't lie whining, and crying, and sighing, and wishing.—[*Aside.*] If he had not been more modest than wise, he might have set such a mark upon the goods before now, that ne'er a merchant of 'em all would have bought 'em out of his hands. But young fellows are always in the wrong : either so impudent they are nauseous, or so modest they are useless.—[*Aloud.*] Go, pray get you gone together.   92

Euph. But if my father catch us, we are ruined.

Dor. By my conscience, this love will make us all turn fools ! Before your father can open the door, can't he slip down the back-stairs ? I'm sure he may, if you don't hold him; but that's the old trade. Ah—well, get you gone, however.—Hark ! I hear the old baboon cough; away !— [*Exeunt* ORONCES *and* EUPHRONIA *running.*] Here he comes, with his ugly beak before him ! Ah—a luscious bedfellow, by my troth !   101

Enter LEARCHUS *and* ÆSOP.

Lear. Well, Doris, what news from my daughter ? Is she prudent ?

Dor. Yes, very prudent.

Lear. What says she ? what does she do ?

Dor. Do !—what should she do ? Tears her cornet ;* bites her thumbs ; throws her fan in the fire ; thinks it's dark

---

* A woman's cap : from the French *cornette*, "*sorte de coiffure de femme en déshabillé.*"—Littré.

night at noon-day; dreams of monsters and hobgoblins;
raves in her sleep of forced marriage and cuckoldom; cries
Avaunt Deformity! then wakens of a sudden, with fifty
arguments at her fingers' ends, to prove the lawfulness of
rebellion in a child, when a parent turns tyrant.   112

Lear. Very fine! but all this shan't serve her turn.—I
have said the word, and will be obeyed.—My lord does her
honour.

Dor. [*Aside.*] Yes, and that's all he can do to her.—
[*To* LEARCHUS.] But I can't blame the gentleman, after
all; he loves my mistress because she's handsome, and she
hates him because he's ugly. I never saw two people more
in the right in my life.—[*To* ÆSOP.] You'll pardon me, sir,
I'm somewhat free.   121

Æsop. Why, a ceremony would but take up time.—But,
governor, methinks I have an admirable advocate about
your daughter.

Lear. Out of the room, Impudence! Begone, I say!

Dor. So I will; but you'll be as much in the wrong
when I'm gone as when I'm here: and your conscience, I
hope, will talk as pertly to you as I can do.

Æsop. If she treats me thus before my face, I may conclude I'm finely handled behind my back.   130

Dor. I say the truth here; and I can say no worse anywhere.   [*Exit.*

Lear. I hope your lordship won't be concerned at what
this prattling wench bleats out; my daughter will be
governed, she's bred up to obedience. There may be some
small difficulty in weaning her from her young lover; but
twon't be the first time she has been weaned from a breast,
my lord.

N

Æsop. Does she love him fondly, sir ?

Lear. Foolishly, my lord. 140

Æsop. And he her ?

Lear. The same.

Æsop. Is he young ?

Lear. Yes, and vigorous.

Æsop. Rich ?

Lear. So, so.

Æsop. Well-born ?

Lear. He has good blood in his veins.

Æsop. Has he wit ?

Lear. He had, before he was in love. 150

Æsop. And handsome with all this ?

Lear. Or else we should not have half so much trouble with him.

Æsop. Why do you then make her quit him for me ? All the world knows I am neither young, noble, nor rich ; and as for my beauty—Look you, governor, I'm honest : but when children cry, they tell 'em, Æsop's a-coming. Pray, sir, what is it makes you so earnest to force your daughter ? 159

Lear. Am I then to count for nothing the favour you are in at court ? Father-in-law to the great Æsop, what may I not aspire to ? My foolish daughter, perhaps, mayn't be so well pleased with't, but we wise parents usually weigh our children's happiness in the scale of our own inclinations.

Æsop. Well, governor, let it be your care, then, to make her consent.

Lear. This moment, my lord, I reduce her either to obedience, or to dust and ashes. [*Exit.*

Æsop. Adieu !—[*Calls to a* Servant.] Now let in the
people who come for audience.   171
[ÆSOP *sits in his chair, reading of papers.*

Enter two ordinary Tradesmen.

1st Tra. There he is, neighbour, do but look at him.

2nd Tra. Ay, one may know him ; he's well marked.
But, dost hear me ? what title must we give him ? for if we
fail in that point, d'ye see me, we shall never get our
business done. Courtiers love titles almost as well as they
do money, and that's a bold word now.

1st Tra. Why, I think we had best call him his
Grandeur.

2nd Tra. That will do ; thou hast hit on't. Hold still,
let me speak.—May it please your grandeur—   181

Æsop. There I interrupt you, friend ; I have a weak
body that will ne'er be able to bear that title.

2nd Tra. D'ye hear that, neighbour ? what shall we
call him now ?

1st Tra. Why, call him,—call him—his Excellency ;
try what that will do.

2nd Tra. May it please your excellency—

Æsop. Excellency's a long word ; it takes up too much
time in business. Tell me what you'd have in few words.

2nd Tra. Neighbour, this man will never give ten
thousand pounds to be made a lord. But what shall I say
to him now ? He puts me quite out of my play.   193

1st Tra. Why, e'en talk to him as we do to one
another.

2nd Tra. Shall I ? why, so I will then.—Hem !
Neighbour ; we want a new governor, neighbour.

N 2

Æsop.   A new governor, friend ?

2nd Tra.   Ay, friend.

Æsop.   Why, what's the matter with your old one?   200

2nd Tra.   What's the matter ?   Why, he grows rich ; that's the matter : and he that's rich can't be innocent; that's all.

Æsop.   Does he use any of you harshly ? or punish you without a fault?

2nd Tra.   No, but he grows as rich as a miser ; his purse is so crammed, it's ready to burst again.

Æsop.   When 'tis full 'twill hold no more.   A new governor will have an empty one.

2nd Tra.   'Fore Gad, neighbour, the little gentleman's in the right on't !   211

1st Tra.   Why, truly I don't know but he may.   For now it comes in my head, it cost me more money to fat my hog, than to keep him fat when he was so.   Prithee, tell him we'll e'en keep our old governor.

2nd Tra.   I'll do't.—Why, look you, sir, d'ye see me ? having seriously considered of the matter, my neighbour Hobson, and I here, we are content to jog on a little longer with him we have : but if you'd do us another courtesy, you might.   220

Æsop.   What's that, friend?

2nd Tra.   Why, that's this : our king Crœsus is a very good prince, as a man may say:—but—a—but—taxes are high, an't please you ; and—a—poor men want money, d'ye see me.   It's very hard, as we think, that the poor should work to maintain the rich.   If there were no taxes, we should do pretty well.

1st Tra.   Taxes indeed are very burthensome.

Æsop.   I'll tell you a story, countrymen.

Once on a time, the hands and feet,   230
As mutineers, grew mighty great ;*
They met, caball'd, and talk'd of treason,
They swore by Jove they knew no reason
The belly should have all the meat ;
It was a damn'd notorious cheat ;
They did the work, and—death and hell, they'd eat !

The belly, who ador'd good cheer,
Had like t' have died away for fear :
Quoth he, " Good folks, you little know
What 'tis you are about to do ;   240
If I am starv'd, what will become of you ? "

   " We neither know nor care," cried they ;
" But this we will be bold to say,
We'll see you damn'd
Before we'll work,
And you receive the pay."

With that the hands to pocket went,
Full wristband deep ;
The legs and feet fell fast asleep :
Their liberty they had redeem'd,   250
And all except the belly seem'd
Extremely well content.

But mark what follow'd : 'twas not long
Before the right became the wrong ;
The mutineers were grown so weak,

---

* *I.e.*, intimate ; familiar.

They found 'twas more than time to squeak :
They call for work, but 'twas too late.
The stomach (like an aged maid,
Shrunk up for want of human aid,)
The common debt of nature paid,   260
And with its destiny entrain'd their fate.

What think you of this story, friends, ha? Come, you
look like wise men; I'm sure you understand what's for
your good.   In giving part of what you have, you secure all
the rest.   If the king had no money, there could be no
army; and if there were no army, your enemies would be
amongst you.   One day's pillage would be worse than
twenty years' taxes.   What say you? is't not so?

2nd Tra.   By my troth, I think he's in the right on't
again !   Who'd think that little humpback of his should
have so much brains in't, neighbour?   271

Æsop.   Well, honest men, is there anything else that I
can serve you in ?

1st Tra.   D'ye hear that, Humphry?—Why, that was
civil now.   But courtiers seldom want good-breeding; let's
give the devil his due.—Why, to tell you the truth, honest
gentleman, we had a whole budget full of grievances to complain of.   But I think—a—ha, neighbour?—we had e'en
as good let 'em alone.   279

2nd Tra.   Why, good feath, I think so too, for by all I
can see, we are like to make no great hond on't.   Besides,
between thee and me, I begin to daubt, whether aur grievances do us such a plaguy deal of mischief as we fancy.

1st Tra.   Or put case they did, Humphry; I'se afraid he
that goes to a courtier, in hope to get fairly rid of 'em, may

be said (in aur country dialect) to take the wrong sow by
the ear.—But here's neighbour Roger, he's a wit, let's leave
him to him.   [*Exeunt.*

Enter ROGER, *a country bumpkin ; looks seriously upon
ÆSOP ; then bursts out a-laughing.*

Rog. Ha! ha! ha! ha! ha! Did ever mon behold the
like? ha! ha! ha! ha! ha!   290
Æsop. Hast thou any business with me, friend?
Rog. Yes, by my troth, have I ; but if Roger were to be
hanged up for't, look you now, he could not hold laughing.
What I have in my mind, out it comes : but bar that, I'se
an honest lad as well as another.
Æsop. My time's dearer to me than yours, friend.
Have you anything to say to me?
Rog. Gadswookers, do people use to ask for folks when
they have nothing to say to 'em? I'se tell you my
business.   300
Æsop. Let's hear it.
Rog. I have, as you see, a little wit.
Æsop. True.
Rog. I live in a village hard by, and I'se the best man
in it, though I say it, that should not say it. I have good
drink in my cellar, and good corn in my barn ; I have cows
and oxen, hogs and sheep, cocks and hens, and geese and
turkeys ; but the truth will out, and so out let it. I'se e'en
tired of being called plain Roger. I has a leathern purse ;
and in that purse there's many a fair half-crown, with the
king's sweet face upon it, God bless him ; and with this
money I have a mind to bind myself prentice to a courtier.
It's a good trade, as I have heard say ; there's money

stirring : let a lad be but diligent, and do what he's bid, he
shall be let into the secret, and share part of the profits.   I
have not lived to these years for nothing : those that will
swim must go into deep water.   I'se get our wife Joan to be
the queen's chambermaid ; and then—crack says me I !
and forget all my acquaintance.   But to come to the
business.   You who are the king's great favourite, I desire
you'll be pleased to sell me some of your friendship, that I
may get a court-place.   Come, you shall choose me one
yourself ; you look like a shrewd man ; by the mass you do !

Æsop.   I choose thee a place !   324

Rog.   Yes : I would willingly have it such a sort of a
pleace as would cost little, and bring in a great deal ; in a
.word, much profit, and nothing to do.

Æsop.   But you must name what post you think would
suit your humour.

Rog.   Why, I'se pratty indifferent as to that : secretary of
state, or butler ; twenty shillings more, twenty shillings less,
is not the thing I stand upon.   I'se no haggler, gadswookers ;
and he that says I am—'zbud he lies !   There's my humour
now.   334

Æsop.   But hark you, friend, you say you are well as
you are ; why then do you desire to change?

Rog.   Why, what a question now is there, for a man of
your parts !   I'm well, d'ye see me ; and what of all that ?
I desire to be better.   There's an answer for you.—[*Aside.*]
Let Roger alone with him.

Æsop.   Very well : this is reasoning ; and I love a man
should reason with me.   But let us inquire a little whether
your reasons are good or not.   You say at home you want
for nothing.   344

Rog. Nothing, 'for George.

Æsop. You have good drink?

Rog. 'Zbud the best i'th' parish !   [*Singing.*

    And dawn it merrily goes, my lad,

    And dawn it merrily goes !

Æsop. You eat heartily ?

Rog. I have a noble stomach.

Æsop. You sleep well?

Rog. Just as I drink, till I can sleep no longer.

Æsop. You have some honest neighbours ?   354

Rog. Honest ! 'Zbud we are all so, the tawn raund, we
live like breether; when one can sarve another, he does it
with all his heart and guts; when we have anything that's
good, we eat it together; holidays and Sundays we play at
nine-pins, tumble upon the grass with wholesome young
maids, laugh till we split, daunce till we are weary, eat till
we burst, drink till we are sleepy, then swap into bed, and
snore till we rise to breakfast.

Æsop. And all this thou wouldst leave to go to court !
I'll tell thee what once happened.   364

A mouse, who long had liv'd at court,

(Yet ne'er the better Christian for't)

Walking one day to see some country sport,

He met a home-bred village-mouse,

Who with an awkward speech and bow,

That savour'd much of cart and plough,

Made a shift, I know not how,

T'invite him to his house.

Quoth he, " My lord, I doubt you'll find

Our country fare of homely kind,   374

But by my troth, you're welcome to't,
Y'ave that, and bread, and cheese to boot : "
And so they sat and din'd.

    Rog. Very well.

    Æsop. The courtier could have eat, at least,
As much as any household priest,
But thought himself oblig'd in feeding
To show the difference of town-breeding ;
He pick'd, and cull'd, and turn'd the meat,
He champ'd and chew'd and could not eat :   384
No toothless woman at fourscore
Was ever seen to mumble more.
He made a thousand ugly faces,
Which (as sometimes in ladies' cases)
Were all design'd for airs and graces.

    Rog. Ha! ha!

    Æsop. At last he from the table rose,
He pick'd his teeth, and blow'd his nose,
And with an easy negligence,
As though he lately came from France,   394
He made a careless sliding bow ;
" 'Fore Gad," quoth he, " I don't know how
I shall return your friendly treat ;
But if you'll take a bit of meat
In town with me,
You there shall see
How we poor courtiers eat."

    Rog. Tit for tat ; that was friendly.

    Æsop. There needed no more invitation
To e'er a country squire i'th' nation :   404
Exactly to the time he came,

Punctual as woman when she meets
A man between a pair of sheets,
As good a stomach, and as little shame.
    Rog. Ho! ho! ho! ho! ho!
    Æsop. To say the truth, he found good cheer,
With wine, instead of ale and beer :
But just as they sat down to eat,
Comes bouncing in a hungry cat.
    Rog. O Lord! O Lord! O Lord!   414
    Æsop. The nimble courtier skipp'd from table,
The squire leap'd too, as he was able :
It can't be said that they were beat,
It was no more than a retreat ;
Which, when an army, not to fight
By day-light, runs away by night,
Was ever judg'd a great and glorious feat.
    Rog. Ever! ever! ever!
    Æsop. The cat retir'd, our guests return,
The danger past becomes their scorn,   424
They fall to eating as before ;—
The butler rumbles at the door.
    Rog. Good Lord!
    Æsop. To boot and saddle again they sound.
    Rog. Ta ra ! tan tan ta ra ! ra ra tan ta ra !
    Æsop. They frown, as they would stand their ground,
But (like some of our friends) they found
'Twas safer much to scour.
    Rog. Tantive! Tantive! Tantive! &c.
    Æsop. At length the squire, who hated arms,   434
Was so perplex'd with these alarms,
He rose up in a kind of heat :

" Udzwooks ! " quoth he, "with all your meat,
I will maintain a dish of pease,
A radish, and a slice of cheese,
With a good dessert of ease,
Is much a better treat.
However ;
Since every man should have his due,
I own, sir, I'm oblig'd to you　　　　　　　　　　　444
For your intentions at your board ;
But pox upon your courtly crew ! "

　　Rog. Amen ! I pray the Lord.

　　Ha ! ha ! ha ! ha ! ha ! Now the de'il cuckold me if this story be not worth a sermon.—Give me your hond, sir.—If it had na' been for your friendly advice, I was going to be fool enough to be secretary of state.

　　Æsop. Well, go thy ways home, and be wiser for the future.　　　　　　　　　　　453

　　Rog. And so I will : for that same mause, your friend, was a witty person, gadsbudlikins ! and so our wife Joan shall know : for between you and I, 'tis she has put me upon going to court. Sir, she has been so praud, so saucy, so rampant, ever since I brought her home a laced pinner, and a pink-colour pair of shoe-strings, from Tickledawne Fair, the parson o'th' parish can't rule her ; and that you'll say's much. But so much for that. Naw, I thank you for your good caunsel, honest little gentleman ; and to show you that I'se not ungrateful—give me your hond once more—if you'll take the pains but to walk dawn to our town—a word in your ear—I'st send you so drunk whome again, you shall remember friendly Roger as long as you have breath in your body.　　　　　*[Exit.* 467

Æsop. Farewell ! what I both envy and despise :
Thy happiness and ignorance provoke me.
How noble were the thing call'd knowledge,
Did it but lead us to a bliss like thine !
But there's a secret curse in wisdom's train,
Which on its pleasures stamps perpetual pain,
And makes the wise man loser by his gain.*   [*Exit.*

---

* The first edition reads :—" And makes the wise man lose, by what
he gains."

ACT III.

SCENE.—*A Room in* LEARCHUS'S *House.*

Enter ÆSOP.

Æsop.   Who waits there?

Enter Servant.

If there be anybody that has business with me, let 'em in.

Serv.   Yes, sir.   [*Exit.*

Enter QUAINT, *who stands at a distance, making a great many fawning bows.*

Æsop.   Well, friend, who are you?

Quaint.   My name's Quaint, sir, the profoundest of all your honour's humble servants.

Æsop.   And what may your business be with me, sir?

Quaint.   My business, sir, with every man, is first of all to do him service.

Æsop.   And your next is, I suppose, to be paid for't twice as much as 'tis worth.   11

Quaint.   Your honour's most obedient, humble servant.

Æsop.   Well, sir, but upon what account am I going to be obliged to you?

Quaint.   Sir, I'm a genealogist.

Æsop.   A genealogist!

Quaint.   At your service, sir.

Æsop.   So, sir.   18

Quaint. Sir, I am informed from common fame, as well as from some little private familiar intelligence, that your wisdom is entering into treaty with the *primum mobile* of good and evil, a fine lady. I have travelled, sir; I have read, sir; I have considered, sir; and I find, sir, that the nature of a fine lady is to be—a fine lady, sir; a fine lady's a fine lady, sir, all the world over; she loves a fine house, fine furniture, fine coaches, fine liveries, fine petticoats, fine smocks; and if she stops there—she's a fine lady indeed, sir. But to come to my point. It being the Lydian custom, that the fair bride should be presented on her wedding-day with something that may signify the merit and the worth of her dread lord and master, I thought the noble Æsop's pedigree might be the welcomest gift that he could offer. If his honour be of the same opinion—I'll speak a bold word; there's ne'er a herald in all Asia shall put better blood in his veins, than—sir, your humble servant, Jacob Quaint.   36

Æsop. Dost thou then know my father, friend? for I protest to thee I am a stranger to him.

Quaint. Your father, sir, ha! ha! I know every man's father, sir, and every man's grandfather, and every man's great-grandfather. Why, sir, I'm a herald by nature; my mother was a Welshwoman.

Æsop. A Welshwoman! Prithee of what country's that?   44

Quaint. That, sir, is a country in the world's backside, where every man is born a gentleman, and a genealogist. Sir, I could tell my mother's pedigree before I could speak plain; which, to show you the depth of my art, and the strength of my memory, I'll trundle you down in an instant.

—Noah had three sons, Shem, Ham, and Japhet ; Shem—

Æsop.   Hold, I conjure thee, in the name of all thy ancestors !

Quaint.   Sir, I could take it higher, but I begin at Noah for brevity's sake.   54

Æsop.   No more on't, I entreat thee.

Quaint.   Your honour's impatient, perhaps, to hear your own descent.   A word to the wise is enough.   Hem, hem : Solomon, the wise king of Judea—

Æsop.   Hold once more !

Quaint.   Ha ! ha ! your honour's modest, but—Solomon, the wise king of Judea—

Æsop.   Was my ancestor, was he not ?

Quaint.   He was, my lord, which no one sure can doubt, who observes how much of prince there hangs about you. 64

Æsop.   What ! is't in my mien ?

Quaint.   You have something—wondrous noble in your air.

Æsop.   Personable too ?   View me well.

Quaint.   N—not tall ; but majestic.

Æsop.   My shape ?

Quaint.   A world of symmetry in it.

Æsop.   The lump upon my back ?

Quaint.   N—not regular ; but agreeable.   73

Æsop.   Now by my honesty thou art a villain, herald. But flattery's a thrust I never fail to parry.   'Tis a pass thou shouldst reserve for young fencers ; with feints like those they're to be hit : I do not doubt but thou hast found it so ; hast not ?

Quaint.   I must confess, sir, I have sometimes made 'em bleed by't.   But I hope your honour will please to excuse me, since, to speak the truth, I get my bread by't, and maintain my wife and children : and industry, you know, sir, is a commendable thing. Besides, sir, I have debated the business a little with my conscience ; for I'm like the rest of my neighbours, I'd willingly get money, and be saved too, if the thing may be done upon any reasonable terms: and so, sir, I say, to quiet my conscience, I have found out at last that flattery is a duty.   88

Æsop. A duty !

Quaint. Ay, sir, a duty : for the duty of all men is to make one another pass their time as pleasantly as they can. Now, sir, here's a young lord, who has a great deal of land, a great deal of title, a great deal of meat, a great deal of noise, a great many servants, and a great many diseases. I find him very dull, very restless, tired with ease, cloyed with plenty, a burden to himself, and a plague to his family. I begin to flatter : he springs off of the couch ; turns himself round in the glass ; finds all I say true ; cuts a caper a yard high ; his blood trickles round in his veins; his heart's as light as his heels ; and before I leave him—his purse is as empty as his head. So we both are content; for we part much happier than we met.   102

Æsop. Admirable rogue ! what dost thou think of murder and of rape ? Are not they duties too ?
Wer't not for such vile fawning things as thou art,
Young nobles would not long be what they are :
They'd grow asham'd of luxury and ease,
And rouse up the old spirit of their fathers ;
Leave the pursuit of a poor frighten'd hare,
And make their foes to tremble in her stead ;   110
Furnish their heads with sciences and arts,

O

And fill their hearts with honour, truth, and friendship;
Be generous to some, and just to all;
Drive home their creditors with bags of gold,
Instead of chasing 'em with swords and staves;
Be faithful to their king and country both,
And stab the offerer of a bribe from either;
Blush even at a wandering thought of vice,
And boldly own they durst be friends to virtue;
Tremble at nothing but the frowns of Heaven,   120
And be no more asham'd of Him that made 'em.

Quaint. [*Aside.*] If I stand to hear this crump preach a
little longer, I shall be fool enough perhaps to be bubbled
out of my livelihood, and so lose a bird in the hand for
two in the bush.—[*Aloud.*] Sir, since I have not been able
to bring you to a good opinion of yourself, 'tis very probable
I shall scarce prevail with you to have one of me. But if
you please to do me the favour to forget me, I shall ever
acknowledge myself—sir, your most obedient, faithful,
humble servant.   [*Going.* 130

Æsop. Hold; if I let thee go, and give thee nothing,
thou'lt be apt to grumble at me; and therefore—Who waits
there?

Enter Servant.

Quaint. [*Aside.*] I don't like his looks, by Gad!
Æsop. I'll present thee with a token of my love.
Quaint. A—another time, sir, will do as well.
Æsop. No; I love to be out of debt, though 'tis being
out of the fashion.—[*To* Servant.] So, d'ye hear? give
this honest gentleman half a score good strokes on the back
with a cudgel.   140

Quaint. By no means in the world, sir.

Æsop. Indeed, sir, you shall take 'em.

Quaint. Sir, I don't merit half your bounty.

Æsop. O 'tis but a trifle !

Quaint. Your generosity makes me blush.

                [*Looking about to make his escape.*

Æsop. That's your modesty, sir.

Quaint. Sir, you are pleased to compliment. But a —twenty pedigrees for a clear coast !

           [*Running off,* the Servant *after him.*

Æsop. Wait upon him downstairs, fellow.—I'd do't myself, were I but nimble enough ; but he makes haste to avoid ceremony.   151

Enter Servant.

Ser. Sir, here's a lady in great haste, desires to speak with you.

Æsop. Let her come in.   [*Exit* Servant.

Enter AMINTA, *weeping.*

Amin. O sir, if you don't help me, I'm undone !

Æsop. What, what's the matter, lady ?

Amin. My daughter, sir, my daughter's run away with a filthy fellow.

Æsop. A slippery trick indeed !

Amin. For Heaven's sake, sir, send immediately to pursue 'em, and seize 'em. But 'tis in vain, 'twill be too late, 'twill be too late ! I'll warrant at this very moment they are got together in a room with a couch in't. All's gone, all's gone ! though 'twere made of gold 'tis lost. Oh, my honour ! my honour ! A forward girl she was always ; I saw it in her eyes the very day of her birth.   166

O 2

Æsop. That indeed was early; but how do you know she's gone with a fellow?

Amin. I have e'en her own insolent handwriting for't, sir; take but the pains to read what a letter she has left me.

Æsop. [*Reads.*] *I love, and am beloved, and that's the reason I run away.*—Short, but significant !—*I'm sure there's nobody knows better than your ladyship what allowances are to be made to flesh and blood; I therefore hope this from your justice, that what you have done three times yourself, you'll pardon once in your daughter.*—The dickens !   177

Amin. Now, sir, what do you think of the business?

Æsop. Why truly, lady, I think it one of the most natural businesses I have met with a great while. I'll tell you a story.

> A crab-fish once her daughter told
> (In terms that savour'd much of scold),
> She could not bear to see her go,
> Sidle, sidle, to and fro;
> " The devil's in the wench ! " quoth she,
> " When so much money has been paid,
> To polish you like me ;
> It makes me almost mad to see
> Y'are still so awkward an ungainly jade."   190
>   Her daughter smil'd, and look'd askew,
> She answer'd (for to give her her due)
> Pertly, as most folks' daughters do :
> " Madam, your ladyship," quoth she,
> " Is pleas'd to blame in me
> What, on inquiry, you may find,

Admits a passable excuse,
From a proverb much in use ;
That 'cat will after kind.' "

Amin. Sir, I took you to be a man better bred, than to
liken a lady to a crab-fish.   201

Æsop. What I want in good-breeding, lady, I have in
truth and honesty : as what you have wanted in virtue, you
have had in a good face.

Amin. Have had, sir ! what I have had, I have still ; and
shall have a great while, I hope. I'm no grandmother, sir.

Æsop. But in a fair way for't, madam.

Amin. Thanks to my daughter's forwardness then, not
my years. I'd have you to know, sir, I have never a
wrinkle in my face. A young pert slut ! Who'd think she
should know so much at her age ?   211

Æsop. Good masters make quick scholars, lady ; she has
learned her exercise from you.

Amin. But where's the remedy, sir ?

Æsop. In trying if a good example will reclaim her,
as an ill one has debauched her. Live private, and avoid
scandal.

Amin. Never speak it ; I can no more retire, than I can
go to church twice of a Sunday.

Æsop. What ! your youthful blood boils in your veins,
I'll warrant.   221

Amin. I have warmth enough to endure the air, old
gentleman. I need not shut myself up in a house these
twenty years.

Æsop. [*Aside.*] She takes a long lease of lewdness :
she'll be an admirable tenant to lust.

Amin. [*Walking hastily to and fro.*] People think when a woman is turned forty, she's old enough to turn out of the world ; but I say, when a woman is turned forty, she's old enough to have more wit. The most can be said is, her face is the worse for wearing : I'll answer for all the rest of her fabric. The men would be to be pitied, by my troth would they, if we should quit the stage, and leave 'em nothing but a parcel of young pert sluts, that neither know how to speak sense nor keep themselves clean. But don't let 'em fear, we an't going yet.—[ÆSOP *stares upon her, and as she turns from him runs off the stage.*] How now ! What, left alone ! An unmannerly piece of deformity ! Methinks he might have had sense enough to have made love to me. But I have found men strangely dull for these last ten or twelve years. Sure they'll mend in time, or the world won't be worth living in.   242

> For let philosophers say all they can,
> The source of woman's joys is plac'd in man.
>
> [*Exit.*

Enter LEARCHUS *and* EUPHRONIA, DORIS *following at a distance.*

Lear. [*To* EUPHRONIA.] I must tell you, mistress, I'm too mild with you ; parents should never entreat their children, nor will I hereafter. Therefore, in a word, let Oronces be loved, let Æsop be hated ; let one be a peacock, let t'other be a bat : I'm father, you are daughter ; I command, and you shall obey.   250

Euph. I never yet did otherwise ; nor shall I now, sir ; but pray let reason guide you.

Lear. So it does : but 'tis my own, not yours, hussy.

Dor. Ah !—Well, I'll say no more ; but were I in her place, by the mass, I'd have a tug for't !

Lear. Demon, born to distract me ! Whence art thou, in the name of fire and brimstone ? Have not I satisfied thee ? have not I paid thee what's thy due ? and have not I turned thee out of doors, with orders never more to stride my threshold, ha ? Answer, abominable spirit ! what is't that makes thee haunt me ?   261

Dor. A foolish passion, to do you good in spite of your teeth : pox on me for my zeal ! I say.

Lear. And pox on thee, and thy zeal too ! I say.

Dor. Now if it were not for her sake more than for yours, I'd leave all to your own management, to be revenged of you. But rather than I'll see that sweet thing sacrificed— I'll play the devil in your house.

Lear. Patience, I summon thee to my aid !   269

Dor. Passion, I defy thee ! to the last drop of my blood I'll maintain my ground. What have you to charge me with ? speak. I love your child better than you do, and you can't bear that, ha ? is't not so ? Nay, it's well y'are ashamed on't ; there's some sign of grace still. Look you, sir, in few words, you'll make me mad ; and 'twere enough to make anybody mad (who has brains enough to be so) to see so much virtue shipwrecked at the very port. The world never saw a virgin better qualified ; so witty, so discreet, so modest, so chaste ; in a word, I brought her up myself, and 'twould be the death of me to see so virtuous a maid become a lewd wife ; which is the usual effect of parents' pride and covetousness.   282

Lear. How, strumpet ! would anything be able to debauch my daughter ?

Dor. Your daughter? yes, your daughter, and myself into the bargain: a woman's but a woman; and I'll lay a hundred pound on nature's side. Come, sir, few words dispatch business. Let who will be the wife of Æsop, she's a fool, or he's a cuckold. But you'll never have a true notion of this matter till you suppose yourself in your daughter's place. As thus:—You are a pretty, soft, warm, wishing young lady: I'm a straight, proper, handsome, vigorous, young fellow. You have a peevish, positive, covetous, old father, and he forces you to marry a little, lean, crooked, dry, sapless husband. This husband's gone abroad, you are left at home. I make you a visit; find you all alone; the servant pulls to the door; the devil comes in at the window. I begin to wheedle, you begin to melt; you like my person, and therefore believe all I say; so first I make you an atheist, and then I make you a whore. Thus the world goes, sir.　　　　　　　　　　301

Lear. Pernicious pestilence! Has thy eternal tongue run down its larum yet?

Dor. Yes.

Lear. Then get out of my house, Abomination!

Dor. I'll not stir a foot.

Lear. Who waits there? Bring me my great stick.

Dor. Bring you a stick! bring you a head-piece; that you'd call for, if you knew your own wants.

Lear. Death and furies, the devil, and so forth; I shall run distracted!　　　　　　　　　　311

Euph. Pray, sir, don't be so angry at her. I'm sure she means well, though she may have an odd way of expressing herself.

Lear. What, you like her meaning? who doubts it, off-

spring of Venus! But I'll make you stay your stomach with
meat of my choosing, you liquorish young baggage you!
In a word, Æsop's the man; and to-morrow he shall be
your lord and master. But since he can't be satisfied unless
he has your heart, as well as all the rest of your trumpery,
let me see you receive him in such a manner that he may
think himself your choice as well as mine; 'twill make him
esteem your judgment: for we usually guess at other
people's understandings, by their approving our actions, and
liking our faces. See, here the great man comes!—[*To*
DORIS.] Follow me, Insolence! and leave 'em to express
their passion to each other.—[*To* EUPHRONIA.] Remember
my last word to you is, obey.   328

Dor. [*Aside to* EUPHRONIA.] And remember my last
advice to you is, rebel.

                    [*Exit* LEARCHUS. DORIS *following him.*
Euph. Alas! I'm good-natured; the last thing that's
said to me usually leaves the deepest impression.

Enter ÆSOP; *they stand some time without speaking.*

Æsop. They say, that lovers, for want of words, have eyes
to speak with. I'm afraid you do not understand the
language of mine, since yours, I find, will make no answer
to 'em. But I must tell you, lady, there is a numerous train
of youthful virgins, that are endowed with wealth and beauty
too, who yet have thought it worth their pains and care to
point their darts at Æsop's homely breast; whilst you so
much contemn what they pursue, that a young senseless fop's
preferred before me.   341

Euph. Did you but know that fop you dare to term so,
his very looks would fright you into nothing.

Æsop. A very bauble !

Euph. How !

Æsop. A butterfly !

Euph. I can't bear it !

Æsop. A parroquet, can prattle and look gaudy.

Euph. It may be so ; but let me paint him and you in your proper colours, I'll do it exactly, and you shall judge which I ought to choose. 351

Æsop. No, hold ! I'm naturally not over-curious ; besides, 'tis pride makes people have their pictures drawn.

Euph. Upon my word, sir, you may have yours taken a hundred times before anybody will believe 'tis done upon that account.

Æsop. [*Aside.*] How severe she is upon me !—[*Aloud.*] You are resolved then to persist, and be fond of your feather ; sigh for a periwig, and die for a cravat-string ?

Euph. Methinks, sir, you might treat with more respect what I've thought fit to own I value ; your affronts to him are doubly such to me. If you continue your provoking language, you must expect my tongue will sally too ; and if you are as wise as some would make you, you can't but know I should have theme enough. 365

Æsop. But is it possible you can love so much as you pretend ?

Euph. Why do you question it ?

Æsop. Because nobody loves so much as they pretend. But hark you, young lady ! marriage is to last a long, long time ; and where one couple bless the sacred knot, a train of wretches curse the institution. You are in an age where hearts are young and tender, a pleasing object gets admittance soon. But since to marriage there's annexed this

dreadful word, *For Ever*, the following example ought to
move you :   376

A peacock once of splendid show,
Gay, gaudy, foppish, vain—a beau,
Attack'd a fond young pheasant's heart
With such success,
He pleas'd her, though he made her smart ;
He pierc'd her with so much address,
She smil'd the moment that he fix'd his dart.
    A cuckoo in a neighbouring tree,
Rich, honest, ugly, old—like me,
Lov'd her as he lov'd his life :
No pamper'd priest e'er studied more
To make a virtuous nun a whore,
Than he to get her for his wife.
But all his offers still were vain,   390
His limbs were weak, his face was plain ;
Beauty, youth, and vigour weigh'd
With the warm desiring maid :
No bird, she cried, would serve her turn,
But what could quench as well as burn,
She'd have a young gallant ; so one she had.
But ere a month was come and gone,
The bride began to change her tone,
She found a young gallant was an inconstant one.
She wander'd to a neighbouring grove,   400
Where after musing long on love,
She told her confidant she found,
When for one's life one must be bound,
(Though youth indeed was a delicious bait,)

An aged husband, rich, though plain,
Would give a slavish wife less pain ;   :
And what was more, was sooner slain,
Which was a thing of weight.   408

Behold, young lady, here, the cuckoo of the fable. I am deformed, 'tis true, yet I have found the means to make a figure amongst men, that well has recompensed the wrongs of Nature. My rival's beauty promises you much ; perhaps my homely form might yield you more ; at least consider on't, 'tis worth your thought.

Euph. I must confess, my fortune would be greater ;
But what's a fortune to a heart like mine ?
'Tis true, I'm but a young philosopher,
Yet in that little space my glass has run,
I've spent some time in search of happiness :
The fond pursuit I soon observ'd of riches,   420
Inclin'd me to inquire into their worth ;
I found their value was not in themselves,
But in their power to grant what we could ask.
I then proceeded to my own desires,
To know what state of life would suit with them :
I found 'em moderate in their demands ;
They neither ask'd for title, state, or power ;
They slighted the aspiring post of envy :
'Tis true, they trembled at the name contempt ;
A general esteem was all they wish'd ;   430
And that I did not doubt might be obtain'd,
If, furnish'd but with virtue and good-nature,
My fortune prov'd sufficient to afford me
Conveniences of life, and independence.

This, sir, was the result of my inquiry ;
And by this scheme of happiness I build,
When I prefer the man I love to you.

Æsop. How wise, how witty, and how cleanly, young
women grow, as soon as ever they are in love !

Euph. How foppish, how impertinent, and how nauseous
are old men, when they pretend to be so too !   441

Æsop. How pert is youth !

Euph. How dull is age !

Æsop. Why so sharp, young lady ?

Euph. Why so blunt, old gentleman ?

Æsop. 'Tis enough ; I'll to your father, I know how to
deal with him, though I don't know how to deal with you.
Before to-morrow noon, damsel, wife shall be written on
your brow.   [*Exit.*

Euph. Then before to-morrow night, statesman,
husband shall be stamped upon your forehead.   [*Exit.*

ACT IV.

SCENE.—*A Room in* LEARCHUS'S *House.*

Enter ORONCES *and* DORIS.

Dor. Patience, I beseech you.

Oron. Patience! What, and see that lovely creature thrown into the arms of that pedantic monster: 'sdeath, I'd rather see the world reduced to atoms, mankind turned into crawfish, and myself an old woman!

Dor. So you think an old woman a very unfortunate thing, I find; but you are mistaken, sir; she may plague other folks, but she's as entertaining to herself as any one part of the creation.

Oron. [*Walking to and fro.*] She's the devil!—and I'm one of the damned, I think! But I'll make somebody howl for't, I will so.   12

Dor. You'll e'en do as all the young fellows in the town do, spoil your own sport: ah!—had young men's shoulders but old courtiers' heads upon 'em, what a delicious time would they have on't! For shame be wise; for your mistress' sake at least use some caution.

Oron. For her sake I'll respect, even like a deity, her father. He shall strike me, he shall tread upon me, and find me humbler even than a crawling worm, for I'll not turn again; but for Æsop, that unfinished lump, that chaos

of humanity, I'll use him,—nay, expect it, for I'll do't—the
first moment that I see him, I'll—   23

Dor. Not challenge him, I hope.—'Twould be a pretty
sight truly, to see Æsop drawn up in battalia: fie, for
shame! be wise once in your life; think of gaining time,
by putting off the marriage for a day or two, and not of
waging war with Pigmy. Yonder's the old gentleman walking by himself in the gallery; go and wheedle him, you
know his weak side; he's good-natured in the bottom. Stir
up his old fatherly bowels a little, I'll warrant you'll move
him at last: go, get you gone, and play your part dis-
creetly.   33

Oron. Well, I'll try; but if words won't do with one,
blows shall with t'other; by Heavens they shall.   [*Exit.*

Dor. Nay, I reckon we shall have rare work on't by and
by. Shield us, kind Heaven! what things are men in love!
Now they are stocks and stones; then they are fire and
quicksilver; first whining and crying, then swearing and
damning; this moment they are in love, and next moment
they are out of love. Ah! could we but live without 'em—
but it's in vain to think on't.   [*Exit.* 42

Enter ÆSOP at one side of the stage, Mrs. FORGEWILL *at
t'other.*

Mrs. Forge. Sir, I am your most devoted servant.
What I say is no compliment, I do assure you.

Æsop. Madam, as far as you are really mine, I believe
I may venture to assure you I am yours.

Mrs. Forge. I suppose, sir, you know that I'm a widow?

Æsop. Madam, I don't so much as know you are a
woman.

Mrs. Forge. O surprising! why, I thought the whole town had known it. Sir, I have been a widow this twelve-month.

52

Æsop. If a body may guess at your heart by your petticoat, lady, you don't design to be so a twelvemonth more.

Mrs. Forge. O bless me! not a twelvemonth? why, my husband has left me four squalling brats. Besides, sir, I'm undone.

Æsop. You seem as cheerful an undone lady as I have met with.

Mrs. Forge. Alas, sir, I have too great a spirit ever to let afflictions spoil my face. Sir, I'll tell you my condition; and that will lead me to my business with you. Sir, my husband was a scrivener.

Æsop. The deuce he was! I thought he had been a count at least.

66

Mrs. Forge. Sir, 'tis not the first time I have been taken for a countess; my mother used to say, as I lay in my cradle, I had the air of a woman of quality; and, truly, I have always lived like such. My husband, indeed, had something sneaking in him, (as most husbands have, you know, sir,) but from the moment I set foot in his house, bless me, what a change was there! His pewter was turned into silver, his goloshoes into a glass coach, and his little travelling mare into a pair of Flanders horses. Instead of a greasy cookmaid, to wait at table, I had four tall footmen in clean linen; all things became new and fashionable, and nothing looked awkward in my family. My furniture was the wonder of my neighbourhood, and my clothes the admiration of the whole town; I had a necklace that was envied by the queen, and a pair of pendants that set a duchess a-crying. In a word, I saw nothing I liked but I bought it; and my husband, good man, durst ne'er refuse paying for't. Thus I lived, and I flourished, till he sickened and died; but, ere he was cold in his grave, his creditors plundered my house. But what pity it was to see fellows with dirty shoes come into my best rooms, and touch my hangings with their filthy fingers! You won't blame me, sir, if, with all my courage, I weep at this sensible part of my misfortune.   90

Æsop. A very sad story, truly!

Mrs. Forge. But now, sir, to my business. Having been informed this morning that the king has appointed a great sum of money for the marriage of young women who have lived well and are fallen to decay, I am come to acquaint you I have two strapping daughters just fit for the matter; and to desire you'll help 'em to portions out of the king's bounty, that they mayn't whine and pine, and be eaten up with the green-sickness, as half the young women in the town are, or would be, if there were not more helps for a disease than one. This, sir, is my business.   101

Æsop. And this, madam, is my answer:

A crawling toad, all speckled o'er,
Vain, gaudy, painted, patch'd—a whore,
Seeing a well-fed ox hard by,
Regards him with an envious eye,
And (as the poets tell)
"Ye gods, I cannot bear't!" quoth she,
"I'll burst, or be as big as he!"
And so began to swell.   110

P

Her friends and kindred round her came,
They show'd her she was much to blame,
The thing was out of reach.
She told 'em they were busy folk,
And when her husband would have spoke,
She bid him kiss her br—h.
With that they all e'en gave her o'er,
And she persisted as before,
Till, with a deal of strife,
She swell'd at last so much her spleen,   120
She burst like one that we have seen,
Who was a scrivener's wife.

This, widow, I take to be your case, and that of a great
many others ; for this is an age where most people get falls
by clambering too high, to reach at what they should not
do. The shoemaker's wife reduces her husband to a
cobbler, by endeavouring to be as spruce as the tailor's ;
the tailor's brings hers to a botcher, by going as fine as the
mercer's ; the mercer's lowers hers to a foreman, by perking
up to the merchant's ; the merchant's wears hers to a
broker, by strutting up to quality ; and quality bring theirs
to nothing, by striving to outdo one another. If women
were humbler, men would be honester. Pride brings want,
want makes rogues, rogues come to be hanged, and the
devil alone's the gainer. Go your ways home, woman, and,
as your husband maintained you by his pen, maintain yourself by your needle ; put your great girls to service,
employment will keep 'em honest ; much work, and plain
diet, will cure the green-sickness as well as a husband. 139

Mrs. Forge. Why, you pitiful pigmy, preaching, canting,

pickthank! you little, sorry, crooked, dry, withered eunuch! do you know that—

Æsop. I know that I am so deformed you han't wit enough to describe me; but I have this good quality, that a foolish woman can never make me angry.

Mrs. Forge. Can't she so! I'll try that, I will.

[*She falls upon him, holds his hands, and boxes his ears.*

Æsop. Help! help! help!

Enter Servants. *She runs off, they after her.*

Nay, e'en let her go—let her go—don't bring her back again. I'm for making a bridge of gold—for my enemy to retreat upon.—I'm quite out of breath.—A terrible woman, I protest!   151

Enter a Country Gentleman *drunk, in a hunting dress, with a* Huntsman, Groom, Falconer, *and other* Servants; *one leading a couple of hounds, another greyhounds, a third a spaniel, a fourth a gun upon his shoulder, the* Falconer *a hawk upon his fist, &c.**

Gent. Haux! Haux! Haux! Haux! Haux! Joular, there, boy! Joular! Joular! Tinker! Pedlar! Miss! Miss! Miss! Miss! Miss!—Blood and oons!—Oh, there he is; that must be he, I have seen his picture.—[*Reeling up to* ÆSOP.] Sir—if your name's Æsop—I'm your humble servant.

Æsop. Sir, my name is Æsop, at your service.

Gent. Why then, sir—compliments being passed on

---

* The following scene belongs to Vanbrugh alone.

both sides, with your leave—we'll proceed to business.—
Sir, I am by profession—a gentleman of—three thousand
pounds a year—sir. I keep a good pack of hounds, and a
good stable of horses.—[*To his* Groom.] How many
horses have I, sirrah?—Sir, this is my groom.   164
                    [*Presenting him to* ÆSOP.

Groom. Your worship has six coach-horses (cut and long-
tail), two runners, half-a-dozen hunters, four breeding mares,
and two blind stallions, besides pads, routs, and dog-
horses.

Gent. Look you there, sir, I scorn to tell a lie. He
that questions my honour—he's a son of a whore. But to
business.—Having heard, sir, that you were come to this
town, I have taken the pains to come hither too, though I
had a great deal of business upon my hands, for I had
appointed three justices of the peace to hunt with 'em this
morning—and be drunk with 'em in the afternoon. But
the main chance must be looked to—and that's this—I
desire, sir, you'll tell the king from me—I don't like these
taxes—in one word as well as in twenty—I don't like these
taxes.

Æsop. Pray, sir, how high may you be taxed?   180

Gent. How high may I be taxed, sir?—Why, I may be
taxed, sir,—four shillings in the pound, sir; one-half I pay
in money—and t'other half I pay in perjury, sir.—Hey,
Joular! Joular! Joular! haux! haux! haux! haux! haux!
whoo! hoo!—Here's the best hound-bitch in Europe, zoons
is she. And I had rather kiss her than kiss my wife—rot
me if I had not. But, sir, I don't like these taxes.

Æsop. Why, how would you have the war carried on?

Gent. War carried on, sir?—Why, I had rather have no

war carried on at all, sir, than pay taxes.   I don't desire to
be ruined, sir.   191
Æsop. Why, you say you have three thousand pounds
a year.

Gent. And so I have, sir.—Lettacre !—Sir, this is my
steward.—How much land have I, Lettacre ?

Lettacre. Your worship has three thousand paunds
a year, as good lond as any's i' th' caunty; and two thausand
paunds worth of wood to cut dawn at your worship's
pleasure, and put the money in your pocket.

Gent. Look you there, sir, what have you to say to
that ?   201

Æsop. I have to say, sir, that you may pay your taxes in
money, instead of perjury, and still have a better revenue
than I'm afraid you deserve.   What service do you do your
king, sir ?

Gent. None at all, sir : I'm above it.

Æsop. What service may you do your country, pray ?

Gent. I'm justice of the peace—and captain of the
militia.

Æsop. Of what use are you to your kindred ?   210

Gent. I'm the head of the family, and have all the
estate.

Æsop. What good do you do your neighbours ?

Gent. I give 'em their bellies full of beef every time
they come to see me ; and make 'em so drunk, they spew it
up again before they go away.

Æsop. How do you use your tenants ?

Gent. Why, I screw up their rents till they break and
run away; and if I catch 'em again, I let 'em rot in a
jail.   220

Æsop. How do you treat your wife?

Gent. I treat her all day with ill-nature and tobacco, and all night with snoring and a dirty shirt.

Æsop. How do you breed your children?

Gent. I breed my eldest son—a fool; my youngest breed themselves; and my daughters—have no breeding at all.

Æsop. 'Tis very well, sir: I shall be sure to speak to the king of you; or if you think fit to remonstrate to him, by way of petition or address, how reasonable it may be to let men of your importance go scot-free, in the time of a necessary war, I'll deliver it in council, and speak to it as I ought.   233

Gent. Why, sir, I don't disapprove your advice; but my clerk is not here, and I can't spell well.

Æsop. You may get it writ at your leisure, and send it to me. But because you are not much used to draw up addresses perhaps, I'll tell you in general what kind of one this ought to be.

May it please your Majesty—You'll excuse me if I don't know your name and title.

Gent. Sir, Polidorus Hogstye, of Beast-Hall, in Swine-county.   243

Æsop. Very well.

May it please your Majesty:

   Polidorus Hogstye, of Beast-Hall, in Swine-county, most humbly represents, that he hates to pay taxes, the dreadful consequences of 'em being inevitably these, that he must retrench two dishes in ten, where not above six of 'em are designed for gluttony:

Four bottles out of twenty; where not above fifteen of 'em
are for drunkenness: 252

Six horses out of thirty; of which not above twenty are
kept for state:

And four servants out of a score; where one half do nothing
but make work for t'other.

To this deplorable condition must your important subject be
reduced, or forced to cut down his timber, which he would
willingly preserve against an ill run at dice.

And as to the necessity of the war for the security of the
kingdom, he neither knows nor cares whether it be necessary
or not.   262

He concludes with his prayers for your majesty's life, upon
condition you will protect him and his fox-hounds at Beast-
Hall without e'er a penny of money.

This, sir, I suppose, is much what you would be at?

Gent. Exactly, sir; I'll be sure to have one drawn up to
the selfsame purpose; and next fox-hunting, I'll engage half
the company shall set their hands to't. Sir, I am your—
most devoted servant; and if you please to let me see you
at Beast-Hall, here's my huntsman, Houndsfoot, will show
you a fox shall lead you through so many hedges and briars,
you shall have no more clothes on your back in half an
hour's time—than you had—in the womb of your mother.—
Haux! haux! haux! &c.   275

[*Exit shouting, followed by his attendants.*

Æsop. O tempora! O mores!

Enter Mr. FRUITFUL *and his wife.*

Mr. Fruit. Heavens preserve the noble Æsop; grant him long life and happy days !

Mrs. Fruit. And send him a fruitful wife, with a hopeful issue !

Æsop. And what is it I'm to do for you, good people, to make you amends for all these friendly wishes ? 282

Mr. Fruit. Sir, here's myself and my wife—

Mrs. Fruit. Sir, here's I and my husband—[*To her husband.*] Let me speak in my turn, goodman Forward.— [*To* ÆSOP.] Sir, here's I and my husband, I say, think we have as good pretensions to the king's favour as ever a lord in the land.

Æsop. If you have no better than some lords in the land, I hope you won't expect much for your service.

Mr. Fruit. An't please you, you shall be judge yourself. 292

Mrs. Fruit. That's as he gives sentence, Mr. Littlewit; who gave you power to come to a reference ? If he does not do us right, the king himself shall ; what's to be done here ! —[*To* ÆSOP.] Sir, I'm forced to correct my husband a little ; poor man, he is not used to court-business; but to give him his due, he's ready enough at some things. Sir, I have had twenty fine children by him ; fifteen of 'em are alive, and alive like to be ; five tall daughters are wedded and bedded, and ten proper sons serve their king and their country. 302

Æsop. A goodly company, upon my word !

Mrs. Fruit. Would all men take as much pains for the peopling the kingdom, we might tuck up our aprons, and cry a fig for our enemies! but we have such a parcel of drones amongst us.—Hold up your head, husband.—He's a little out of countenance, sir, because I chid him; but the man's a very good man at the bottom. But to come to my business, sir; I hope his majesty will think it reasonable to allow me something for the service I have done him; 'tis pity but labour should be encouraged, especially when what one has done, one has done't with a good-will.   313

Æsop. What profession are you of, good people?

Mrs. Fruit. My husband's an innkeeper, sir; he bears the name, but I govern the house.

Æsop. And what posts are your sons in, in the service?

Mrs. Fruit. Sir, there are four monks.

Mr. Fruit. Three attorneys.

Mrs. Fruit. Two scriveners.

Mr. Fruit. And an exciseman.

Æsop. The deuce o' the service! why, I thought they had been all in the army.   323

Mrs. Fruit. Not one, sir.

Æsop. No, so it seems, by my troth! Ten sons that serve their country, quotha! monks, attorneys, scriveners, and excisemen, serve their country with a vengeance. You deserve to be rewarded, truly; you deserve to be hanged, you wicked people you! Get you gone out of my sight: I never was so angry in my life.   [*Exit.*

Mr. Fruit. So; who's in the right now, you or I? I told you what would come on't; you must be always a-breeding, and breeding, and the king would take care of 'em, and the queen would take care of 'em: and always some pretence or other there was. But now we have got a great kennel of whelps, and the devil will take care of 'em, for aught I see.   For your sons are all rogues, and your daughters are all whores; you know they are.   338

Mrs. Fruit. What, you are a grudging of your pains now, you lazy, sluggish, phlegmatic drone! You have a mind to die of a lethargy, have you? but I'll raise your spirits for you, I will so.   Get you gone home, go; go home, you idle sot you!   I'll raise your spirits for you!*

[*Exit, pushing him before her.*

Re-enter ÆSOP.

Æsop.   Monks, attorneys, scriveners, and excisemen!

Enter ORONCES.

Oron.   O here he is.—Sir, I have been searching you, to say two words to you.

Æsop.   And now you have found me, sir, what are they?

Oron.   They are, sir—that my name's Oronces: you comprehend me.

Æsop.   I comprehend your name.   350

Oron.   And not my business?

Æsop.   Not I, by my troth.

Oron.   Then I shall endeavour to teach it you, Monsieur Æsop.

Æsop.   And I to learn it, Monsieur Oronces.

Oron.   Know, sir—that I admire Euphronia.

Æsop.   Know, sir—that you are in the right on't.

Oron.   But I pretend, sir, that nobody else shall admire her.

---

* In this capital scene Vanbrugh has greatly improved upon his original.   In the French play, one Furet, a bailiff, comes to Æsop, to boast of his large family and demand the king's bounty; but there is no Madame Furet.

Æsop.   Then I pretend, sir, she won't admire you.   360
Oron.   Why so, sir ?
Æsop.   Because, sir—
Oron.   What, sir ?
Æsop.   She's a woman, sir.
Oron.   What then, sir ?
Æsop.   Why then, sir, she desires to be admired by every man she meets.
Oron.   Sir, you are too familiar.
Æsop.   Sir, you are too haughty; I must soften that harsh tone of yours : it don't become you, sir ; it makes a gentleman appear a porter, sir ; and that you may know the use of good language, I'll tell you what once happened.

Once on a time—   373
Oron.   I'll have none of your old wives' fables, sir, I have no time to lose; therefore, in a word—
Æsop.   In a word, be mild : for nothing else will do you service. Good manners and soft words have brought many a difficult thing to pass.   Therefore hear me patiently.

A cook one day, who had been drinking,
(Only as many times, you know,
You spruce, young, witty beaux will do,
T'avoid the dreadful pain of thinking,)
Had orders sent him to behead
A goose, like any chaplain fed.   385
He took such pains to set his knife right,
'Thad done one good t'have lost one's life by't.
But many men have many minds,
There's various tastes in various kinds ;

A swan (who by mistake he seiz'd)
With wretched life was better pleas'd :
For as he went to give the blow,
In tuneful notes she let him know,
She neither was a goose, nor wish'd
To make her exit so.   395
  The cook (who thought of naught but blood,
Except it were the grease,
For that you know's his fees)
To hear her sing, in great amazement stood.
" Cods-fish !" quoth he, " 'twas well you spoke,
For I was just upon the stroke :
Your feathers have so much of goose,
A drunken cook could do no less
Than think you one ; that you'll confess :
But y'have a voice so soft, so sweet,   405
That rather than you shall be eat,
The house shall starve for want of meat : "
And so he turn'd her loose.

Now, sir, what say you ? Will you be the swan or the
goose ?
 Oron. The choice can't sure be difficult to make ;
I hope you will excuse my youthful heat,
Young men and lovers have a claim to pardon :
But since the faults of age have no such plea,
I hope you'll be more cautious of offending.   415
The flame that warms Euphronia's heart and mine
Has long, alas ! been kindled in our breasts :
Even years are pass'd since our two souls were wed,
'Twould be adultery but to wish to part 'em.

And would a lump of clay alone content you,
A mistress cold and senseless in your arms,
Without the least remains or signs of life,
Except her sighs, to mourn her absent lover?
Whilst you should press her in your eager arms,
With fond desire and ecstasy of love,   425
Would it not pierce you to the very soul,
To see her tears run trickling down her cheeks,
And know their fountain meant 'em all to me?
Could you bear this?
Yet thus the gods revenge themselves on those
Who stop the happy course of mutual love.
If you must be unfortunate one way,
Choose that where justice may support your grief,
And shun the weighty curse of injur'd lovers.

Æsop. Why, this is pleading like a swan indeed!   435
Were anything at stake but my Euphronia—

Oron. Your Euphronia, sir !—

Æsop.   The goose—take heed—
Were anything, I say, at stake but her,
Your plea would be too strong to be refus'd.
But our debate's about a lady, sir,
That's young, that's beautiful, that's made for love.
—So am not I, you'll say? But you're mistaken, sir;
I'm made to love, though not to be belov'd.
I have a heart like yours; I've folly too: 445
I've every instrument of love like others.

Oron. But, sir, you have not been so long a lover;
Your passion's young and tender,
'Tis easy for you to become its master;
Whilst I should strive in vain: mine's old and fix'd.

Æsop. The older 'tis, the easier to be governed. Were mine of as long a standing, 'twere possible I might get the better on't. Old passions are like old men ; weak, and soon jostled into the channel. 454

Oron. Yet age sometimes is strong, even to the verge of life.

Æsop. Ay, but there our comparison don't hold.

Oron. You are too merry to be much in love.

Æsop. And you too sad to be so long.

Oron. My grief may end my days, so quench my flame, But nothing else can e'er extinguish it.

Æsop. Don't be discouraged, sir ; I have seen many a man outlive his passion twenty years.

Oron. But I have sworn to die Euphronia's slave.

Æsop. A decayed face always absolves a lover's oath.

Oron. Lovers whose oaths are made to faces then ! But 'tis Euphronia's soul that I adore, Which never can decay. 467

Æsop. I would fain see a young fellow in love with a soul of threescore.

Oron. Quit but Euphronia to me, and you shall ; At least if Heaven's bounty will afford us But years enough to prove my constancy, And this is all I ask the gods and you. [*Exit.*

Æsop. A good pretence, however, to beg a long life. How grossly do the inclinations of the flesh impose upon the simplicity of the spirit! Had this young fellow but studied anatomy, he'd have found the source of his passion lay far from his mistress's soul. Alas ! alas ! had women no more charms in their bodies than what they have in their minds, we should see more wise men in the world, much fewer lovers and poets. [*Exit.*

ACT V.

SCENE.—*A Room in* LEARCHUS'S *House.*

Enter EUPHRONIA *and* DORIS.

Euph. Heavens, what is't you make me do, Doris? Apply myself to the man I loathe; beg favours from him I hate; seek a reprieve from him I abhor? 'Tis low, 'tis mean, 'tis base in me.

Dor. Why, you hate the devil as much as you do Æsop (or within a small matter), and should you think it a scandal to pray him to let you alone a day or two, if he were a-going to run away with you; ha?

Euph. I don't know what I think, nor what I say, nor what I do: but sure thou'rt not my friend, thus to advise me.   11

Dor. I advise? I advise nothing; e'en follow your own way; marry him, and make much of him. I have a mind to see some of his breed; if you like it, I like it. He shan't breed out of me only; that's all I have to take care of.

Euph. Prithee don't distract me.

Dor. Why, to-morrow's the day, fixed and firm, you know it. Much meat, little order, great many relations, few friends, horse-play, noise, and bawdy stories; all's ready for a complete wedding.   20

Euph. Oh! what shall I do?

Dor. Nay, I know this makes you tremble; and yet your tender conscience scruples to drop one hypocritical curtsy, and say, Pray, Mr. Æsop, be so kind to defer it a few days longer.

Euph. Thou know'st I cannot dissemble.

Dor. I know you can dissemble well enough when you should not do't. Do you remember how you used to plague your poor Oronces; make him believe you loathed him, when you could have kissed the ground he went on; affront him in all public places; ridicule him in all company; abuse him wherever you went; and when you had reduced him within ambs-ace of hanging or drowning, then come home with tears in your eyes, and cry, Now, Doris, let's go lock ourselves up, and talk of my dear Oronces.—Is not this true ?   36

Euph. Yes, yes, yes. But, prithee, have some compassion on me. Come, I'll do anything thou biddest me.— What shall I say to this monster ? tell me, and I'll obey thee.

Dor. Nay, then there's some hopes of you.—Why, you must tell him—'Tis natural to you to dislike folks at first sight : that since you have considered him better, you find your aversion abated : that though perhaps it may be a hard matter for you ever to think him a beau, you don't despair in time of finding out his *je-ne-sais-quoi*. And that on t'other side, though you have hitherto thought (as most young women do) that nothing could remove your first affection, yet you have very great hopes in the natural inconstancy of your sex. Tell him, 'tis not impossible, a change may happen, provided he gives you time : but that if he goes to force you, there's another piece of nature peculiar to woman, which may chance to spoil all, and that's contradiction. Ring that argument well in his ears : he's a philosopher, he knows it has weight in't. In short, wheedle, whine, flatter, lie, weep, spare nothing ; it's a moist age, women have tears enough ; and when you have melted him down, and gained more time, we'll employ it in closet-debates how to cheat him to the end of the chapter. 59

Euph. But you don't consider, Doris, that by this means I engage myself to him ; and can't afterwards with honour retreat.

Dor. Madam, I know the world.—Honour's a jest, when jilting's useful. Besides, he that would have you break your oath with Oronces, can never have the impudence to blame you for cracking your word with himself. But who knows what may happen between the cup and the lip ? Let either of the old gentlemen die, and we ride triumphant. Would I could but see the statesman sick a little, I'd recommend a doctor to him, a cousin of mine, a man of conscience, a wise physician ; tip but the wink, he understands you. 71

Euph. Thou wicked wench, wouldst poison him ?

Dor. I don't know what I would do. I think, I study, I invent, and somehow I will get rid of him. I do more for you, I'm sure, than you and your knight-errant do together for yourselves.

Euph. Alas ! both he and I do all we can ; thou know'st we do.

Dor. Nay, I know y'are willing enough to get together ; but y'are a couple of helpless things, Heaven knows. 80

Euph. Our stars, thou seest, are bent to opposition.

Dor. Stars !—I'd fain see the stars hinder me from running away with a man I liked.

Euph. Ay, but thou know'st, should I disoblige my father, he'd give my portion to my younger sister.

Dor. Ay, there the shoe pinches, there's the love of the age ! Ah !—to what an ebb of passion are lovers sunk in these days ! Give me a woman that runs away with a man when his whole estate's packed up in his snapsack : that tucks up her coats to her knees ; and through thick and through thin, from quarters to camp, trudges heartily on, with a child at her back, another in her arms, and a brace in her belly : there's flame with a witness, where this is the effects on't. But we must have love in a featherbed : forsooth, a coach and six horses, clean linen, and a caudle ! Fie, for shame !—O ho, here comes our man ! Now show yourself a woman, if you are one. 97

Enter ÆSOP.

Æsop. I'm told, fair virgin, you desire to speak with me. Lovers are apt to flatter themselves : I take your message for a favour. I hope 'twas meant so.

Euph. Favours from women are so cheap of late, men may expect 'em truly without vanity.

Æsop. If the women are so liberal, I think the men are generous too on their side. 'Tis a well-bred age, thank Heaven ; and a deal of civility there passes between the two sexes.—What service is't that I can do you, lady ?

Euph. Sir, I have a small favour to entreat you. 107

Æsop. What is't ? I don't believe I shall refuse you.

Euph. What if you should promise me you won't ?

Æsop. Why then I should make a divorce between my good-breeding and my sense, which ought to be as sacred a knot as that of wedlock.

Euph. Dare you not trust then, sir, the thing you love?

Æsop. Not when the thing I love don't love me: never !

Dor. Trust is sometimes the way to be beloved.

Æsop. Ay, but 'tis oftener the way to be cheated.

Euph. Pray promise me you'll grant my suit.

Dor. 'Tis a reasonable one, I give you my word for't.

Æsop. If it be so, I do promise to grant it. 120

Dor. That's still leaving yourself judge.

Æsop. Why, who's more concerned in the trial?

Dor. But nobody ought to be judge in their own cause.

Æsop. Yet he that is so, is sure to have no wrong done him.

Dor. But if he does wrong to others, that's worse.

Æsop. Worse for them, but not for him.

Dor. True politician, by my troth !

Æsop. Men must be so, when they have to do with sharpers. 130

. *Euph.* If I should tell you then, there were a possibility I might be brought to love you, you'd scarce believe me?

Æsop. I should hope as a lover, and suspect as a statesman.

Dor. [*Aside.*] Love and wisdom ! There's the passion of the age again.

Euph. You have lived long, sir, and observed much: did you never see Time produce strange changes?

Æsop. Amongst women, I must confess I have.

Euph. Why, I'm a woman, sir. 140

Æsop. Why, truly, that gives me some hopes.

Euph. I'll increase 'em, sir ; I have already been in love two years.

Dor. And time, you know, wears all things to tatters.

Æsop. Well observed.

Euph. What if you should allow me some, to try what I can do ?

Æsop. Why, truly, I would have patience a day or two, if there were as much probability of my being your new gallant, as perhaps there may be of your changing your old one.   151

Dor. She shall give you fair play for't, sir; opportunity and leave to prattle, and that's what carries most women in our days. Nay, she shall do more for you. You shall play with her fan ; squeeze her little finger; buckle her shoe ; read a romance to her in the arbour; and saunter in the woods on a moonshiny night. If this don't melt her, she's no woman, or you no man.

Æsop. I'm not a man to melt a woman that way : I know myself, and know what they require. 'Tis through a woman's eye you pierce her heart. And I've no darts can make their entrance there.   162

Dor. You are a great statesman, sir ; but I find you know little of our matters. A woman's heart's to be entered forty ways. Every sense she has about her keeps a door to it. With a smock-face, and a feather, you get in at her eyes. With powerful nonsense, in soft words, you creep in at her ears. An essenced peruke, and a sweet handkerchief, lets you in at her nose. With a treat, and a boxful of sweetmeats, you slip in at her mouth : and if you would enter by her sense of feeling, 'tis as beaten a road as the rest. What think you now, sir? There are more ways to the wood than one, you see.   173

Æsop. Why, y'are an admirable pilot : I don't doubt but

you have steered many a ship safe to harbour. But I'm an old stubborn seaman; I must sail by my own compass still.

Euph. And, by your obstinacy, lose your vessel.

Æsop. No : I'm just entering into port ; we'll be married to-morrow.

Euph. For Heaven's sake, defer it some days longer! I cannot love you yet, indeed I cannot.   182

Æsop. Nor never will, I dare swear.

Euph. Why then will you marry me ?

Æsop. Because I love you.

Euph. If you loved me, you would never make me miserable.

Æsop. Not if I loved you for your sake ; but I love you for my own.

Dor. [*Aside.*] There's an old rogue for you.

Euph. [*Weeping.*] Is there no way left ? Must I be wretched ?   192

Æsop. 'Tis but resolving to be pleased. You can't imagine the strength of resolution. I have seen a woman resolve to be in the wrong all the days of her life ; and by the help of her resolution, she has kept her word to a tittle.

Euph. Methinks the subject we're upon should be of weight enough to make you serious.

Æsop. Right. To-morrow morning pray be ready, you'll find me so : I'm serious. Now I hope you are pleased.   201

[*Turning away from her.*

Euph. Break heart ! for if thou hold'st, I'm miserable.

[*Going off weeping, and leaning upon* DORIS.

Dor. [*To* ÆSOP.] Now may the extravagance of a lewd

wife, with the insolence of a virtuous one, join hand in hand
to bring thy grey hairs to the grave.

[*Exeunt* EUPHRONIA *and* DORIS.

Æsop. My old friend wishes me well to the last, I see.

Enter LEARCHUS *hastily, followed by* ORONCES.

Oron. Pray hear me, sir.

Lear. 'Tis in vain: I'm resolved, I tell thee.—Most
noble Æsop, since you are pleased to accept of my poor
offspring for your consort, be so charitable to my old age,
to deliver me from the impertinence of youth, by making
her your wife this instant; for there's a plot against my life;
they have resolved to tease me to death to-night, that they
may break the match to-morrow morning. Marry her this
instant, I entreat you.   215

Æsop. This instant, say you?

Lear. This instant; this very instant.

Æsop. 'Tis enough; get all things ready; I'll be with
you in a moment.   [*Exit.*

Lear. Now, what say you, Mr. Flamefire? I shall have
the whip-hand of you presently.

Oron. Defer it but till to-morrow, sir.

Lear. That you may run away with her to-night, ha?—
Sir, your most obedient humble servant.—Hey, who waits
there? Call my daughter to me: quick.—I'll give her
her dispatches presently.   226

Enter EUPHRONIA.

Euph. D'ye call, sir?

Lear. Yes, I do, minx. Go shift yourself, and put on
your best clothes. You are to be married.

Euph. Married, sir!

Lear. Yes, married, madam ; and that this instant too.

Euph. Dear sir !

Lear. Not a word: obedience and a clean smock. Dispatch ! [*Exit* EUPHRONIA *weeping.*] [LEARCHUS *going off, turns to* ORONCES.] Sir, your most obedient humble servant. 236

Oron. Yet hear what I've to say.

Lear. And what have you to say, sir ?

Oron. Alas ! I know not what I have to say !

Lear. Very like so.—That's a sure sign he's in love now.

Oron. Have you no bowels ?

Lear. Ha ! ha ! bowels in a parent ! Here's a young fellow for you !—Hark thee, stripling ; being in a very merry humour, I don't care if I discover some paternal secrets to thee. Know then ; that how humorsome, how whimsical soever we may appear, there's one fixed principle that runs through almost the whole race of us ; and that's to please ourselves. Why dost think I got my daughter ? Why, there was something in't that pleased me. Why dost think I marry my daughter ? Why, to please myself still. And what is't that pleases me ? Why, my interest ; what dost think it should be ? If Æsop's my son-in-law, he'll make me a lord : if thou art my son-in-law—thou'lt make me a grandfather. Now I having more mind to be a lord than a grandfather, give my daughter to him, and not to thee. 256

Oron. Then shall her happiness weigh nothing with you ?

Lear. Not this. If it did, I'd give her to thee, and not to him.

Oron. Do you think forced marriage the way to keep women virtuous ?

Lear. No ; nor I don't care whether women are virtuous or not.

Oron. You know your daughter loves me.

Lear. I do so.

Oron. What if the children that Æsop may happen to father, should chance to be begot by me ?

Lear. Why, then Æsop would be the cuckold, not I.

Oron. Is that all you care?

Lear. Yes : I speak as a father.   270

Oron. What think you of your child's concern in t'other world ?

Lear. Why, I think it my child's concern ; not mine. I speak as a father.

Oron. Do you remember you once gave me your consent to wed your daughter ?

Lear. I did.

Oron. Why did you so ?

Lear. Because you were the best match that offered at that time. I did like a father.   280

Oron. Why then, sir, I'll do like a lover. I'll make you keep your word, or cut your throat.

Lear. Who waits there, ha ?

Enter Servants.

Seize me that bully there. Carry him to prison, and keep him safe.   [*They seize him.*

Oron. Why, you won't use me thus?

Lear. Yes, but I will though.—Away with him !—Sir, your most humble servant. I wish you a good night's rest; and as far as a merry dream goes, my daughter's at your service.   290

Oron. Death and furies !

[*Exeunt* Servants *with* ORONCES.

Lear. [*Singing.*]

Dol, de tol dol, dol dol, de tol dol:
*Lilly Burleighre's lodged in a bough.**

Enter a Troop of Musicians, Dancers, *&c.*

Lear. How now ! what have we got here ?

Mus. Sir, we are a troop of trifling fellows, fiddlers and dancers, come to celebrate the wedding of your fair daughter, if your honour pleases to give us leave.

Lear. With all my heart. But who do you take me for, sir ; ha ?

Mus. I take your honour for our noble governor of Cyzicus.   301

Lear. Governor of Cyzicus ! Governor of a cheese-cake ! I'm father-in-law to the great Æsop, sirrah.—[*All bow to him.*]—[*Aside.*] I shall be a great man.—[*Aloud.*] Come, tune your fiddles : shake your legs ; get all things ready.

---

* The famous ballad of *Lilliburlero*, attributed, on rather weak grounds, to Lord Wharton, is said to have played no inconsiderable part in the Revolution of 1688. " A foolish ballad was made at that time, treating the Papists, and chiefly the Irish, in a very ridiculous manner, which had a burden said to be Irish words, ' Lero, lero, liliburlero,' that made an impression on the army (King William's) that cannot be imagined by those that saw it not. The whole army, and at last the people, both in city and country, were singing it perpetually. And perhaps never had so slight a thing so great an effect."—*Burnet,* quoted in Percy's *Reliques,* where the ballad may be read. Percy's version, however, contains not the lines sung by Learchus : possibly different versions were extant. The old tune of *Lilliburlero* will always be remembered for the sake of my Uncle Toby.

My son-in-law will be here presently.—I shall be a great man. [*Exit.*

1st Mus. A great marriage, brother. What dost think will be the end on't? 309

2nd Mus. Why, I believe we shall see three turns upon't. This old fellow here will turn fool; his daughter will turn strumpet; and his son-in-law will turn 'em both out of doors. But that's nothing to thee nor me, as long as we are paid for our fiddling. So tune away, gentlemen.

1st Mus. D'ye hear, trumpets? When the bride appears, salute her with a melancholy waft. 'Twill suit her humour; for I guess she mayn't be over well pleased. 319

Enter LEARCHUS *with several* Friends, *and a* Priest.

Lear. Gentlemen and friends, y'are all welcome. I have sent to as many of you as our short time would give me leave, to desire you would be witnesses of the honour the great Æsop designs ourself and family.—Hey; who attends there?

Enter Servant.

Go, let my daughter know I wait for her.—[*Exit* Servant.] 'Tis a vast honour that is done me, gentlemen.

Gent. It is indeed, my lord.

Lear. [*Aside.*] Look you there: if they don't call me my lord already.—I shall be a great man. 329

Re-enter EUPHRONIA *weeping, and leaning upon* DORIS, *both in deep mourning.*

Lear. How now ! what's here ? all in deep mourning !—
Here's a provoking baggage for you !

> [*The trumpets sound a melancholy air till* ÆSOP
> *appears ; and then the violins and hautboys*
> *strike up a Lancashire hornpipe.*

Enter ÆSOP *in a gay foppish dress, long peruke, &c., a gaudy*
equipage of Pages *and* Footmen, *all enter in an airy,*
brisk manner.

Æsop. [*In an affected tone to* EUPHRONIA.] Gad take
my soul, mame, I hope I shall please you now !—Gentlemen all, I'm your humble servant. I'm going to be a very
happy man, you see.—[*To* EUPHRONIA.] When the heat
of the ceremony's over, if your ladyship pleases, mame, I'll
wait upon you to take the air in the Park. Hey, page ; let
there be a coach and six horses ready instantly.—[*Observing*
her dress.] I vow to Gad, mame, I was so taken up with
my good fortune, I did not observe the extreme fancy of
your ladyship's wedding clothes !—Infinitely pretty, as I
hope to be saved ! a world of variety, and not at all
gaudy !—[*To* LEARCHUS.] My dear father-in-law, embrace
me.   344

Lear. Your lordship does me too much honour.—
[*Aside.*] I shall be a great man.

Æsop. Come, gentlemen, are all things ready ? Where's
the priest ?

Priest. Here, my noble lord.

Æsop. Most reverend, will you please to say grace that
I may fall to ; for I'm very hungry, and here's very good
meat.—But where's my rival all this while ? The least we
can do, is to invite him to the wedding.   353

Lear. My lord, he's in prison.

Æsop. In prison ! how so ?

Lear. He would have murdered me.

Æsop. A bloody fellow ! But let's see him, however. Send for him quickly. Ha, governor—that handsome daughter of yours, I will so mumble her !—

Lear. I shall be a great man.   360

Enter ORONCES, *pinioned and guarded.*

Æsop. O ho, here's my rival ! Then we have all we want. Advance, sir, if you please. I desire you'll do me the favour to be a witness to my marriage, lest one of these days you should take a fancy to dispute my wife with me.

Oron. Do you then send for me to insult me? 'Tis base in you.

Æsop. I have no time now to throw away upon points of generosity ; I have hotter work upon my hands.—Come, priest, advance.   370

Lear. Pray hold him fast there ; he has the devil and all of mischief in's eye.

Æsop. [*To* EUPHRONIA.] Will your ladyship please, mame, to give me your fair hand—Heyday !

[*She refuses her hand.*

Lear. I'll give it you, my noble lord, if she won't.— [*Aside.*] A stubborn, self-willed, stiff-necked strumpet !

[LEARCHUS *holds out her hand to* ÆSOP, *who takes it ;* ORONCES *stands on* ÆSOP'S *left hand, and the* Priest *before 'em.*

Æsop. Let my rival stand next me : of all men I'd have him be satisfied.

Oron.   Barbarous inhuman monster !

Æsop.   Now, priest, do thy office.   380

> [*Flourish with the trumpets.*

Priest.   Since the eternal laws of fate decree,

That he, thy husband ; she, thy wife should be,

May Heaven take you to its care.

May Jupiter look kindly down,

Place on your heads contentment's crown ;

And may his godhead never frown

Upon this happy pair.

> [*Flourish again of trumpets. As the* Priest *pro-*
> *nounces the last line,* ÆSOP *joins* ORONCES *and*
> EUPHRONIA'S *hands.*

Oron.   O happy change !   Blessings on blessings wait on
the generous Æsop.

Æsop.   Happy, thrice happy may you ever be.   390

And if you think there's something due to me,

Pay it in mutual love and constancy.

Euph. [*To* ÆSOP.]   You'll pardon me, most generous
man,

If in the present transports of my soul,

Which you yourself have by your bounty caus'd,

My willing tongue is tied from uttering

The thoughts that flow from a most grateful heart.

Æsop.   For what I've done I merit little thanks,

Since what I've done, my duty bound me to.

I would your father had acquitted his :   400

But he who's such a tyrant o'er his children,

To sacrifice their peace to his ambition,

Is fit to govern nothing but himself.

And therefore, sir, at my return to court,   [*To* LEARCHUS.

I shall take care this city may be sway'd
By more humanity than dwells in you.

Lear. [*Aside.*] I shall be a great man.

Euph. [*To* ÆSOP.] Had I not reason, from your constant
goodness,
To judge your bounty, sir, is infinite,
I should not dare to sue for farther favours.   410
But pardon me, if imitating Heaven and you,
I easily forgive my aged father,
And beg that Æsop would forgive him too.

[*Kneeling to him.*

Æsop. The injury he would have done to you, was great
indeed: but 'twas a blessing he designed for me; if
therefore you can pardon him, I may.—[*To* LEARCHUS.]
Your injured daughter, sir, has on her knees entreated
for her cruel, barbarous father; and by her goodness has
obtained her suit. If in the remnant of your days, you can
find out some way to recompense her, do it, that men and
gods may pardon you, as she and I have done.—But let me
see, I have one quarrel still to make up. Where's my old
friend Doris?   423

Dor. She's here, sir, at your service; and as much your
friend as ever: true to her principles, and firm to her
mistress. But she has a much better opinion of you now
than she had half an hour ago.

Æsop. She has reason: for my soul appeared then as
deformed as my body. But I hope now, one may so far
mediate for t'other, that provided I don't make love, the
women won't quarrel with me; for they are worse enemies
even than they are friends.—Come, gentlemen, I'll humour
my dress a little longer, and share with you in the diver-

sions these boon companions have prepared us.   Let's take
our places, and see how they can divert us.   435

> [ÆSOP *leads the* Bride *to her place. All being
> seated, there's a short concert of hautboys,
> trumpets, &c. After which a dance between
> an* Old Man *and a* Young Woman, *who shuns
> him still as he comes near her. At last he
> stops, and begins this dialogue; which they
> sing together.*

Old Man.

Why so cold, and why so coy?
What I want in youth and fire,
I have in love and in desire :
To my arms, my love, my joy !
Why so cold, and why so coy?

Woman.

'Tis sympathy perhaps with you ;
You are cold, and I'm so too.

Old Man.

My years alone have froze my blood ;
Youthful heat in female charms,
Glowing in my aged arms,   445
Would melt it down once more into a flood.

Woman.

Women, alas, like flints, ne'er burn alone ;
To make a virgin know

There's fire within the stone,
Some manly steel must boldly strike the blow.

Old Man.

Assist me only with your charms,
You'll find I'm man, and still am bold ;
You'll find I still can strike, though old :
I only want your aid to raise my arm.

Enter a Youth, *who seizes on the* Young Woman.

Youth.

Who talks of charms, who talks of aid ?   455
I bring an arm
That wants no charm,
To rouse the fire that's in a flinty maid.
Retire, old age !

Woman.

—Winter, begone !
Behold, the youthful spring comes gaily on.
Here, here's a torch to light a virgin's fire.
To my arms, my love, my joy !
When women have what they desire,
They're neither cold nor coy.   465

[*She takes him in her arms. The song and dance
ended, ÆSOP takes* EUPHRONIA *and* ORONCES
by the hands, leading them forwards.

Æsop. By this time, my young eager couple, 'tis
probable you would be glad to be alone; perhaps you'll
have a mind to go to bed even without your supper ; for

brides and bridegrooms eat little on their wedding-night.
But since, if matrimony were worn as it ought to be, it
would perhaps sit easier about us than usually it does, I'll
give you one word of counsel, and so I shall release you.

When one is out of humour, let the other be dumb.

Let your diversions be such as both may have a share in
'em.   475

Never let familiarity exclude respect.

Be clean in your clothes, but nicely so in your persons.
Eat at one table, lie in one room, but sleep in two beds :
I'll tell the ladies why.—   [*Turning to the boxes.*

In the sprightly month of May,
When males and females sport and play,
And kiss and toy away the day ;
An eager sparrow, and his mate,
Chirping on a tree were sate
Full of love—and full of prate.   485
They talk'd of nothing but their fires,
Of raging heats, and strong desires,
Of eternal constancy ;
How true and faithful they would be ;
Of this and that, and endless joys,
And a thousand more such toys.
The only thing they apprehended,
Was that their lives would be so short,
They could not finish half their sport
Before their days were ended.   495
But as from bough to bough they rove,
    They chanc'd at last,
    In furious haste,

R

On a twig with birdlime spread,
(Want of a more downy bed)
To act a scene of love.
Fatal it prov'd to both their fires.
For though at length they broke away,
And balk'd the schoolboy of his prey,
Which made him weep the livelong day,   505
The bridegroom, in the hasty strife,
Was stuck so fast to his dear wife,
That though he us'd his utmost art,
He quickly found it was in vain,
To put himself to farther pain,
They never more must part.
A gloomy shade o'ercast his brow;
He found himself—I know not how:
He look'd—as husbands often do.
Where'er he mov'd, he felt her still,   515
She kiss'd him oft against his will:
Abroad, at home, at bed and board,
With favours she o'erwhelm'd her lord.
Oft he turn'd his head away,
And seldom had a word to say,
Which absolutely spoil'd her play,
For she was better stor'd.
Howe'er, at length her stock was spent,
(For female fires sometimes may be
Subject to mortality;)   525
So back to back they sit and sullenly repent.
But the mute scene was quickly ended:
The lady, for her share, pretended
The want of love lay at his door;

For her part, she had still in store
Enough for him, and twenty more,
Which could not be contended.
He answer'd her in homely words,
(For sparrows are but ill-bred birds,)
That he already had enjoy'd   535
So much, that truly he was cloy'd.
Which so provok'd her spleen,
That after some good hearty prayers,
A jostle, and some spiteful tears,
They fell together by the ears,
And ne'er were fond again.   [*Exeunt omnes.*

PART II.

SCENE I.

Enter Players.

Æsop.   Well, good people, who are all you ?

All.   Sir, we are players.

Æsop.   Players! what players?

Play.   Why, sir, we are stage-players, that's our calling : though we play upon other things too ; some of us play upon the fiddle ; some play upon the flute; we play upon one another ; we play upon the town ; and we play upon the patentees.*

---

* The whole of this scene relates to the quarrel between the patentees of the Theatre Royal and the actors, already referred to (see *ante*, p. 155). Charles II. issued letters patent to Thomas Killigrew and Sir William Davenant separately, granting to these gentlemen, their heirs, &c., the monopoly of theatrical representations in London.   In 1682, Killigrew and Davenant being dead, and the affairs of both theatres in a very languishing condition, the patents were united, and the companies amalgamated : they remained as one company at Drury Lane until 1695, when the disgust between the leading actors and the managing patentee, Rich, who had purchased a share in the patent some years previously, resulted in the withdrawal of the better part of the company from the Theatre Royal, and their establishment, by royal licence, as a separate company, under Betterton's management, in a new theatre in Lincoln's Inn Fields. This disagreement between the patentees and the actors was due to more

Æsop. Patentees! prithee, what are they? 9

Play. Why, they are, sir—sir, they are—ecod, I don't know what they are!—fish or flesh—masters or servants—sometimes one—sometimes t'other, I think—just as we are in the mood.

Æsop. Why, I thought they had a lawful authority over you.

Play. Lawful authority, sir!—sir, we are freeborn Englishmen, we care not for law nor authority neither, when we are out of humour.

Æsop. But I think they pretended at least to an authority over you; pray upon what foundation was it built? 21

Play. Upon a rotten one—if you'll believe us. Sir, I'll tell you what these projectors did: they embarked twenty thousand pound upon a leaky vessel.—She was built at Whitehall; I think they called her—·the Patent—ay, the

---

than one cause; but what brought matters to a head was the attempt of the patentees to balance the falling-off in the receipts of the theatre by reducing the salaries of the principal actors. " To bring this about with a better Grace," writes Cibber, " they, under Pretence of bringing younger Actors forwards, order'd several of *Betterton's* and Mrs. *Barry's* chief Parts to be given to young *Powel* and Mrs. *Bracegirdle.*" But the scheme did not succeed. Although "the giddy head of Powel" was not averse to competition with Betterton, Mrs. Bracegirdle, more wisely, declined to attempt any of Mrs. Barry's parts; while Mrs. Barry showed her resentment of such treatment by actively co-operating with Betterton in opposition to the patentees. To this incident, as I take it, Vanbrugh alludes in the words "a rock that lay hid under a petticoat," in the above scene. It must be noted that Vanbrugh writes here as a strong partisan of the patentees, who had produced two of his plays, and one of whom (Sir Thomas Skipwith) was his particular friend. His account of the affair is a mere caricature.

Patent : her keel was made of a broad seal—and the king
gave 'em a white staff for their mainmast. She was a pretty
tight frigate to look upon, indeed : they spared nothing to
set her off; they gilded her, and painted her, and rigged
and gunned her ; and so sent her a-privateering. But the
first storm that blew, down went the mast! ashore went the
ship !—Crack ! says the keel :—Mercy ! cried the pilot;
but the wind was so high, his prayers could not be heard—
so they split upon a rock—that lay hid under a petticoat.

Æsop. A very sad story, this : but what became of the
ship's company? 36

Play. Why, sir, your humble servants here, who were
the officers, and the best of the sailors (little Ben* amongst
the rest), seized on a small bark that lay to our hand, and
away we put to sea again. To say the truth, we were better
manned than rigged, and ammunition was plaguy scarce
amongst us. However, a-cruising we went, and some petty
small prizes we have made; but the blessing of heaven not
being among us—or how the devil 'tis, I can't tell ; but we
are not rich. 45

Æsop. Well, but what became of the rest of the crew?

Play. Why, sir, as for the scoundrels, they, poor dogs,
stuck by the wreck. The captain gave them bread and
cheese, and good words. He told them if they would
patch her up, and venture t'other cruise, he'd prefer 'em
all ; so to work they went, and to sea they got her.

Æsop. I hope he kept his word with 'em.

Play. That he did ; he made the boatswain's mate

---

* "Little Ben" is, of course, Betterton, the leader of the seceding
actors.

lieutenant; he made the cook doctor; he was forced to be
purser, and pilot, and gunner himself; and the swabber
took orders to be chaplain.*　　　　　　　　　　　56

Æsop. But with such unskilful officers, I'm afraid,
they'll hardly keep above water long.

Play. Why, truly, sir, we care not how soon they are
under: but cursed folks thrive, I think. I know nothing
else that makes 'em swim. I'm sure, by the rules of
navigation, they ought to have overset long since; for they
carry a great deal of sail, and have very little ballast.

Æsop. I'm afraid you ruin one another. I fancy if you
were all in a ship together again, you'd have less work and
more profit.　　　　　　　　　　　　　　　　66

Play. Ah, sir—we are resolved we'll never sail under
captain Patentee again.

Æsop. Prithee, why so?

Play. Sir, he has used us like dogs.

Wom. And bitches too, sir.

Æsop. I'm sorry to hear that; pray how was't he
treated you?

Play. Sir, 'tis impossible to tell; he used us like the
English at Amboyna.†　　　　　　　　　　　　75

---

* After the secession of Betterton and his party, the patentees found
themselves obliged, in order to make sure of a company, to increase
the salaries of those actors who remained. "*Powel* and *Verbruggen*,
who had then but forty Shillings a Week, were now raised each of them
to four Pounds, and others in Proportion."—*Cibber.*

† Amboyna is one of the Molucca, or Spice Islands. In the 16th
century it belonged to the Portuguese, from whom it was taken by the
Dutch about the beginning of the 17th century. The English East
India Company, the rival of the Dutch merchants in the spice trade,
some years later formed a settlement and established a factory on the

Æsop. But I would know some particulars; tell me what 'twas he did to you.

Play. What he did, sir!—why, he did in the first place, sir—in the first place, sir, he did—ecod, I don't know what he did.—Can you tell, wife?

Wom. Yes, marry can I; and a burning shame it was too.

Play. Oh, I remember now, sir, he would not give us plums enough in our pudding.

Æsop. That indeed was very hard; but did he give you as many as he promised you? 86

Play. Yes, and more; but what of all that? we had not as many as we had a mind to.

1st Wom. Sir, my husband tells you truth.

Æsop. I believe he may. But what other wrongs did he do you?

1st Wom. Why, sir, he did not treat me with respect; 'twas not one day in three he would so much as bid me good-morrow.

2nd Wom. Sir, he invited me to dinner, and never drank my health. 96

---

island; and the jealousy thus excited gave rise to continual disturbances. In 1619 a treaty was signed in London, by which matters were supposed to be accommodated between the Company and the Dutch. But the contention still went on, and at length, in February, 1623, Captain Towerson and nine other Englishmen, with nine Japanese and a Portuguese sailor, were seized on the island, upon a charge of conspiring to expel the Dutch; condemned, tortured (it is said), and executed. No satisfaction was obtained for this outrage, until, in 1654, Cromwell obliged the States of Holland to pay a considerable sum to the representatives of the murdered Englishmen. The "massacre of Amboyna" forms the subject of a very poor tragedy by Dryden.

1st Wom. Then he cocked his hat at Mrs. Pert.

2nd Wom. Yes, and told Mrs. Slippery he had as good a face as she had.

Æsop. Why, these were insufferable abuses !

2nd Play. Then, sir, I did but come to him one day, and tell him I wanted fifty pound, and what do you think he did by me, sir?—sir, he turned round upon his heel like a top—

1st Play. But that was nothing to the affront he put upon me, sir. I came to him, and in very civil words, as I thought, desired him to double my pay : sir, would you believe it ? he had the barbarity to ask me if I intended to double my work ; and because I told him no, sir—he did use me—good Lord, how he did use me !   109

Æsop. Prithee how ?

1st Play. Why, he walked off, and answered me never a word.

Æsop. How had you patience?

1st Play. Sir, I had not patience. I sent him a challenge ; and what do you think his answer was ?—he sent me word I was a scoundrel son of a whore, and he would only fight me by proxy !

Æsop. Very fine !   118

1st Play. At this rate, sir, were we poor dogs used—till one frosty morning down he comes amongst us—and very roundly tells us—that for the future, no purchase no pay. They that would not work should not eat.—Sir, we at first asked him coolly and civilly, Why? His answer was, because the town wanted diversion, and he wanted money. —Our reply to this, sir, was very short ; but I think to the purpose.

Æsop. What was it ?

1st Play. It was, sir, that so we wallowed in plenty and ease—the town and he might be damned! This, sir, is the true history of separation—and we hope you'll stand our friend.

Æsop. I'll tell you what, sirs— 131

I once a pack of beagles knew
That much resembled—I know who;
With a good huntsman at their tail,
In full command,
With whip in hand,
They'd run apace
The cheerful chace,
And of their game were seldom known to fail.
But, being at length their chance to find 140
A huntsman of a gentler kind,
They soon perceiv'd the rein was slack,
The word went quickly through the pack—
They one and all cried " Liberty !
This happy moment we are free.
We'll range the woods,
Like nymphs and gods,
And spend our mouths in praise of mutiny."
With that old Jowler trots away,
And Bowman singles out his prey ; 150
Thunder bellow'd through the wood,
And swore he'd burst his guts with blood.
Venus tripp'd it o'er the plain,
With boundless hopes of boundless gain.
Juno, she slipp'd down the hedge,
But left her sacred word for pledge,
That all she pick'd up by the by

Should to the public treasury.
And well they might rely upon her ;
For Juno was a bitch of honour.   160
In short, they all had hopes to see
A heavenly crop of mutiny,
And so to reaping fell :
But in a little time they found,
It was the devil had till'd the ground,
And brought the seed from hell.
The pack divided, nothing throve :
Discord seiz'd the throne of love.
Want and misery all endure,
All take pains, and all grow poor.   170
When they had toil'd the livelong day,
And came at night to view their prey,
Oft, alas ! so ill they'd sped,
That half went supperless to bed.
At length, they all in council sate,
Where at a very fair debate,
It was agreed at last,
That slavery with ease and plenty,
When hounds were something turn'd of twenty,
Was much a better fate,   180
Than 'twas to work and fast.

1st Play. Well, sir—and what did they do then ?
Æsop. Why, they all went home to their kennel again.
If you think they did wisely, you'll do well to follow their
example.   [*Exit.*
1st Play. Well, beagles, what think you of the little
gentleman's advice ?

2nd Wom. I think he's a little ugly philosopher, and talks like a fool.   189

1st Play. Ah, why, there's it now! If he had been a tall, handsome blockhead, he had talked like a wise man.

2nd Wom. Why, do you think, Mr. Jowler, that we'll ever join again?

1st Play. I do think, sweet Mrs. Juno, that if we do not join again, you must be a little freer of your carcass than you are, or you must bring down your pride to a serge petticoat.

1st Wom. And do you think, sir, after the affronts I have received, the patent and I can ever be friends?

1st Play. I do think, madam, that if my interest had not been more affronted than your face, the patent and you had never been foes.   201

1st Wom. And so, sir, then you have serious thoughts of a reconciliation?

1st Play. Madam, I do believe I may.

1st Wom. Why then, sir, give me leave to tell you, that —make it my interest, and I'll have serious thoughts on't too.

2nd Wom. Nay, if you are thereabouts, I desire to come into the treaty.

3rd Play. And I.

4th Play. And I.   210

2nd Play. And I. No separate peace; none of your Turin play,* I beseech you.

---

* In 1696, Victor Amadeus II., Duke of Savoy, one of the allied powers at war with France, was induced by the threats and promises of Louis XIV. to break his engagements, and to conclude a separate peace with France. The treaty of peace was signed first, privately, at Loretto, and afterwards, publicly, at Turin, August 29, 1696.

1st Play. Why then, since you are all so christianly disposed, I think we had best adjourn immediately to our council-chamber ; choose some potent prince for mediator and guarantee; fix upon the place of treaty, dispatch our plenipos, and whip up the peace like an oyster. For under the rose, my confederates, here is such a damned discount upon our bills, I'm afraid, if we stand it out another campaign, we must live upon slender subsistence. * [*Exeunt.*

SCENE II.

Enter a Country Gentleman, *who walks to and fro, looking angrily upon* ÆSOP.

Æsop. Have you any business with me, sir ?

Gent. I can't tell whether I have or not.

Æsop. You seem disturbed, sir.

Gent. I'm always so at the sight of a courtier.

Æsop. Pray what may it be that gives you so great an antipathy to 'em ?

Gent. My profession.

Æsop. What's that ?

Gent. Honesty.   9

Æsop. 'Tis an honest profession. I hope, sir, for the general good of mankind, you are in some public employment.

---

* The re-union of the theatrical companies, here suggested, was, at the time, only a devout imagination of Vanbrugh's. It came to pass, however, at a later date (1708), when the Haymarket Theatre was given over to opera, and the actors from thence rejoined the company at Drury Lane.

Gent. So I am, sir ;—no thanks to the court.

Æsop. You are then, I suppose, employed by—

Gent. My country.

Æsop. Who have made you—

Gent. A senator.

Æsop. Sir, I reverence you.　　　　　　　　　　*[Bowing.*

Gent. Sir, you may reverence as low as you please; but I shall spare none of you. Sir, I am entrusted by my country with above ten thousand of their grievances, and in order to redress 'em, my design is to hang ten thousand courtiers.　　　　　　　　　　　　　　　　　22

Æsop. Why, 'tis making short work, I must confess. But are you sure, sir, that would do't ?

Gent. Sure !—ay, sure.

Æsop. How do you know ?

Gent. Why, the whole country says so, and I at the head of 'em. Now let me see who dares say the contrary.

Æsop. Not I, truly. But, sir, if you won't take it ill, I'll ask you a question or two.　　　　　　　　　　　　30

Gent. Sir, I shall take ill what I please; and if you, or e'er a courtier of you all, pretend the contrary, I say it's a breach of privilege. Now put your question, if you think fit.

Æsop. Why then, sir, with all due regard to your character, and your privilege too, I would be glad to know what you chiefly complain of?

Gent. Why, sir, I do chiefly complain, that we have— a great many ships, and very little trade; a great many tenants, and very little money; a great many soldiers, and very little fighting; a great many gazettes, and little good news ; a great many statesmen, and very little wisdom; a great many parsons, and not an ounce of religion.　　42

Æsop. Why truly, sir, I do confess these are grievances very well worth your redressing. I perceive you are truly sensible of our diseases, but I'm afraid you are a little out in the cure.

Gent. Sir, I perceive you take me for a country physician : but you shall find, sir, that a country doctor is able to deal with a court quack ; and to show you that I do understand something of the state of the body politic, I will tell you, sir, that I have heard a wise man say, the court is the stomach of the nation, in which, if the business be not thoroughly digested, the whole carcass will be in disorder. Now, sir, I do find by the latitude of the members, and the vapours that fly into the head, that this same stomach is full of indigestions, which must be removed. And therefore, sir, I am come post to town with my head full of *crocus metallorum*, and design to give the court a vomit. 58

Æsop. Sir, the physic you mention, though necessary sometimes, is of too violent a nature to be used without a great deal of caution. I'm afraid you are a little too rash in your prescriptions. Is it not possible you may be mistaken in the cause of the distemper ?

Gent. Sir, I do not think it possible I should be mistaken in anything.

Æsop. Pray, sir, have you been long a senator ?

Gent. No, sir.

Æsop. Have you been much about town ?

Gent. No, sir. 69

Æsop. Have you conversed much with men of business ?

Gent. No, sir.

Æsop. Have you made any serious inquiry into the present disorders of the nation ?

Gent.   No, sir.

Æsop.   Have you ever heard what the men now employed in business have to say for themselves?

Gent.   No, sir.

Æsop.   How then do you know they deserve to be punished for the present disorders in your affairs?

Gent.   I'll tell you how I know.   80

Æsop.   I would be glad to hear.

Gent.   Why, I know by this—I know it, I say, by this—that I'm sure on't.—And to give you demonstration that I'm sure on't, there's not one man in a good post in the nation—but I'd give my vote to hang him.   Now I hope you are convinced.

Æsop.   As for example: the first minister of state, why would you hang him?

Gent.   Because he gives bad counsel.

Æsop.   How do you know?   90

Gent.   Why, they say so.

Æsop.   And who would you put in his room?

Gent.   One that would give better.

Æsop.   Who's that?

Gent.   Myself.

Æsop.   The secretary of state, why would you hang him?

Gent.   Because he has not good intelligence.

Æsop.   How do you know?

Gent.   I have heard so.   100

Æsop.   And who would you put in his place?

Gent.   My father.

Æsop.   The treasurer, why would you hang him?

Gent.   Because he does not understand his business.

Æsop. How do you know?

Gent. I dreamt so.

Æsop. And who would you have succeed him?

Gent. My uncle.

Æsop. The admiral, why would you hang him?

Gent. Because he has not destroyed the enemies.   110

Æsop. How do you know he could do it?

Gent. Why, I believe so.

Æsop. And who would you have command in his stead?

Gent. My brother.

Æsop. And the general, why would you hang him?

Gent. Because he took ne'er a town last campaign.

Æsop. And how do you know 'twas in his power?

Gent. Why, I don't care a souse whether it was in's power or not. But I have a son at home, a brave chopping lad; he has been captain in the militia this twelve months, and I'd be glad to see him in his place. What do you stare for, sir; ha? Egad, I tell you he'd scour all to the devil. He's none of your fencers, none of your sa-sa men. Numphs is downright, that's his play. You may see his courage in his face : he has a pair of cheeks like two bladders, a nose as flat as your hand, and a forehead like a bull.   126

Æsop. In short, sir, I find if you and your family were provided for, things would soon grow better than they do.

Gent. And so they would, sir. Clap me at the head of the state, and Numphs at the head of the army; he with his club-musket, and I with my club-headpiece, we'd soon put an end to your business.

Æsop. I believe you would indeed. And therefore since I happen to be acquainted with your extraordinary abilities, I am resolved to give the king an account of you,

S

and employ my interest with him, that you and your son
may have the posts you desire. 137

Gent. Will you, by the Lord?—Give me your fist,
sir—the only honest courtier that ever I met with in my life.

Æsop. But, sir, when I have done you this mighty piece
of service, I shall have a small request to beg of you, which
I hope you won't refuse me.

Gent. What's that?

Æsop. Why, 'tis in behalf of the two officers who are to
be displaced to make room for you and your son.

Gent. The secretary and the general? 146

Æsop. The same. 'Tis pity they should be quite out of
business; I must therefore desire you'll let me recommend
one of 'em to you for your bailiff, and t'other for your
huntsman.

Gent. My bailiff and my huntsman!—Sir, that's not to
be granted.

Æsop. Pray, why?

Gent. Why?—because one would ruin my land, and
t'other would spoil my fox-hounds. 155

Æsop. Why do you think so?

Gent. Why do I think so?—These courtiers will ask the
strangest questions!—Why, sir, do you think that men bred
up to the state and the army, can understand the business
of ploughing and hunting?

Æsop. I did not know but they might.

Gent. How could you think so?

Æsop. Because I see men bred up to ploughing and
hunting, understand the business of the state and the army.

Gent. I'm shot—I han't one word to say for myself—
I never was so caught in my life. 166

Æsop. I perceive, sir, by your looks, what I have said
has made some impression upon you ; and would perhaps
do more if you would give it leave.—[*Taking his hand.*]
Come, sir, though I am a stranger to you, I can be your
friend ; my favour at court does not hinder me from being
a lover of my country. 'Tis my nature, as well as principles,
to be pleased with the prosperity of mankind. I wish all
things happy, and my study is to make 'em so. The dis-
tempers of the government (which I own are great) have
employed the stretch of my understanding, and the deepest
of my thoughts, to penetrate the cause, and to find out the
remedy. But, alas ! all the product of my study is this :—
that I find there is too near a resemblance between the
diseases of the state and those of the body, for the most
expert minister to become a greater master in one than the
college is in t'other : and how far their skill extends you
may see by this lump upon my back. Allowances in all
professions there must be, since 'tis weak man that is the
weak professor. Believe me, senator, for I have seen the
proof on't ; the longest beard amongst us is a fool. Could
you but stand behind the curtain, and there observe the
secret springs of state, you'd see in all the good or evil that
attends it, ten ounces of chance for one grain either of
wisdom or roguery.   190
You'd see, perhaps, a venerable statesman
Sit fast asleep in a great downy chair ;
Whilst in that soft vacation of his thought,
Blind chance (or what at least we blindly call so)
Shall so dispose a thousand secret wheels,
That when he wakes, he needs but write his name,
To publish to the world some bless'd event,

S 2

For which his statue shall be rais'd in brass.
Perhaps a moment thence you shall behold him
Torturing his brain ; his thoughts all stretch'd upon 200
The rack for public service : the livelong night,
When all the world's at rest,
Consum'd in care, and watching for their safety,
When by a whirlwind in his fate,
In spite of him some mischief shall befall 'em,
For which a furious sentence straight shall pass,
And they shall vote him to the scaffold.
Even thus uncertain are rewards and punishments ;
And even thus little do the people know
When 'tis the statesman merits one or t'other. 210

Gent. Now do I believe I am beginning to be a wise man ; for I never till now perceived I was a fool. But do you then really believe, sir, our men in business do the best they can ?

Æsop. Many of 'em do : some perhaps do not. But this you may depend upon ; he that is out of business is the worst judge in the world of him that is in : first, because he seldom knows anything of the matter : and, secondly, because he always desires to get his place.

Gent. And so, sir, you turn the tables upon the plaintiff, and lay the fool and knave at his door. 221

Æsop. If I do him wrong, I'm sorry for't. Let him examine himself, he'll find whether I do or not. [*Exit.*

Gent. Examine !—I think I have had enough of that already. There's nothing left, that I know of, but to give sentence : and truly I think there's no great difficulty in that. A very pretty fellow I am indeed ! Here am I come bellowing and roaring, two hundred miles post, to find myself

an ass; when with one quarter of an hour's consideration
I might have made the self-same discovery, without going
over my threshold. Well! if ever they send me on their
errand to reform the state again, I'll be damned. But this
I'll do: I'll go home and reform my family if I can: them
I'm sure I know. There's my father's a peevish old coxcomb: there's my uncle's a drunken old sot: there's my
brother's a cowardly bully: son Numphs is a lubberly
whelp: I've a great ramping daughter, that stares like a
heifer; and a wife that's a slatternly sow.   [*Exit.*

SCENE III.

Enter a young, gay, airy Beau, *who stands smiling
contemptibly upon* ÆSOP.

Æsop. Well, sir, what are you?

Beau. A fool.

Æsop. That's impossible;—for if thou wert, thou'dst
think thyself a wise man.

Beau. So I do.—This is my own opinion—the t'other's
my neighbours'.   [*Walking airily about.*

Æsop. [*Gazing after him.*] Have you any business with
me, sir?

Beau. Sir, I have business with nobody; pleasure's my
study.   10

Æsop. [*Aside.*] An odd fellow this!—[*Aloud.*] Pray,
sir, who are you?

Beau. I can't tell.

Æsop. Do you know who I am?

Beau. No, sir : I'm a favourite at court, and I neither know myself nor anybody else.

Æsop. Are you in any employment ?

Beau. Yes.

Æsop. What is it ?

Beau. I don't know the name on't. 20

Æsop. You know the business on't, I hope ?

Beau. That I do—the business of it is—to—put in a deputy, and receive the money.

Æsop. Pray what may be your name ?

Beau. Empty.

Æsop. Where do you live?

Beau. In the side-box.

Æsop. What do you do there ?

Beau. I ogle the ladies.

Æsop. To what purpose ? 30

Beau. To no purpose.

Æsop. Why then do you do it ?

Beau. Because they like it, and I like it.

Æsop. Wherein consists the pleasure ?

Beau. In playing the fool.

Æsop. Pray, sir, what age are you ?

Beau. Five-and-twenty, my body; my head's about fifteen.

Æsop. Is your father living ?

Beau. Dead, thank God.

Æsop. Has he been long so ? 40

Beau. Positively yes.

Æsop. Where were you brought up ?

Beau. At school.

Æsop. What school ?

Beau. The school of Venus.

Æsop. Were you ever at the university ?

Beau. Yes.

Æsop. What study did you follow there ?

Beau. My bedmaker.

Æsop. How long did you stay?   50

Beau. Till I had lost my maidenhead.

Æsop. Why did you come away ?

Beau. Because I was expelled.

Æsop. Where did you go then?

Beau. To court.

Æsop. Who took care of your education there ?

Beau. A whore and a dancing-master.

Æsop. What did you gain by them ?

Beau. A minuet and the pox.

Æsop. Have you an estate ?   60

Beau. I had.

Æsop. What's become on't ?

Beau. Spent.

Æsop. In what ?

Beau. In a twelvemonth.

Æsop. But how ?

Beau. Why, in dressing, drinking, whoring, claps, dice, and scriveners. What do you think of me now, old gentleman ?

Æsop. Pray what do you think of yourself?

Beau. I don't think at all: I know how to bestow my time better.   71

Æsop. Are you married?

Beau. No—have you ever a daughter to bestow upon me?

Æsop. She would be well bestowed !

Beau. Why, I'm a strong young dog, you old put, you: she may be worse coupled.

Æsop. Have you then a mind to a wife, sir ?

Beau. Yaw, myn Heer.

Æsop. What would you do with her ?

Beau. Why, I'd take care of her affairs, rid her of all her troubles, her maidenhead, and her portion. 81

Æsop. And pray what sort of wife would you be willing to throw yourself away upon ?

Beau. Why, upon one that has youth, beauty, quality, virtue, wit, and money.

Æsop. And how may you be qualified yourself, to back you in your pretensions to such a one ?

Beau. Why, I am qualified with—a periwig—a snuff-box —a feather—a smooth face—a fool's head—and a patch.

Æsop. But one question more : what settlements can you make ? 91

Beau. Settlements ?—why, if she be a very great heiress indeed, I believe I may settle—myself upon her for life, and my pox upon her children for ever.

Æsop. 'Tis enough ; you may expect I'll serve you, if it lies in my way. But I would not have you rely too much upon your success, because people sometimes are mistaken ; as for example—

> An ape there was of nimble parts,
> A great intruder into hearts,   100
> As brisk, and gay, and full of air,
> As you, or I, or any here ;
> Rich in his dress, of splendid show,
> And with a head like any beau.
> Eternal mirth was in his face ;
> Where'er he went,

He was content,
So Fortune had but kindly sent
Some ladies—and a looking-glass.
Encouragement they always gave him,   110
Encouragement to play the fool ;
For soon they found it was a tool,
Would hardly be so much in love,
But that the mumbling of a glove,
Or tearing of a fan, would save him.

These bounties he accepts as proof
Of feats done by his wit and youth,
He gives their freedom gone for ever ;
Concludes each female heart undone,
Except that very happy one,   120
To which he'd please to do the favour.
In short, so smooth his matters went,
He guess'd, where'er his thoughts were bent,
The lady he must carry.
So put on a fine new cravat,
He comb'd his wig, he cock'd his hat,
And gave it out he'd marry.
But here, alas ! he found to's cost,
He had reckon'd long without his host :
For wheresoe'er he made th' attack,   130
Poor pug with shame was beaten back.

The first fair she he had in chace, ·
Was a young cat, extremely rich,
Her mother was a noted witch ;
So had the daughter proved but civil,

He had been related to the devil.
But when he came
To urge his flame,
She scratch'd him o'er the face.

With that he went among the bitches,   140
Such as had beauty, wit, and riches,
And swore Miss Maulkin, to her cost,
Should quickly see what she had lost :
But the poor unlucky swain
Miss'd his shepherdess again ;
His fate was to miscarry.
It was his destiny to find,
That cats and dogs are of a mind,
When monkeys come to marry.   149

Beau. 'Tis very well ;—'tis very well, old spark ; I say
'tis very well.   Because I han't a pair of plod shoes, and a
dirty shirt, you think a woman won't venture upon me for a
husband.   Why, now to show you, old father, how little you
philosophers know of the ladies—I'll tell you an adventure
of a friend of mine.

A band, a bob-wig, and a feather,
Attack'd a lady's heart together :
The band in a most learned plea,
Made up of deep philosophy,
Told her, if she would please to wed   160
A reverend beard, and take, instead
Of vigorous youth,
Old solemn truth,
With books and morals, into bed,
How happy she would be.

The bob he talk'd of management,
What wondrous blessings Heaven sent
On care, and pains, and industry ;
And truly he must be so free,
To own he thought your airy beaux,   170
With powder'd wigs and dancing shoes,
Were good for nothing (mend his soul!)
But prate, and talk, and play the fool.

He said 'twas wealth gave joy and mirth,
And that to be the dearest wife
Of one who labour'd all his life,
To make a mine of gold his own,
And not spend sixpence when he'd done,
Was heaven upon earth.

When these two blades had done, d'ye see,   180
The feather (as it might be me)
Steps out, sir, from behind the screen,
With such an air, and such a mien,—
Look you, old gentleman, in short,
He quickly spoil'd the stateman's sport.

It prov'd such sunshine weather,
That you must know, at the first beck
The lady leap'd about his neck,
And off they went together.

There's a tale for your tale, old dad ; and so—*serviteur*.
                                                    [*Exit.*

THE PROVOK'D WIFE.

The Provok'd Wife was produced by Betterton's company, at the theatre in Lincoln's Inn Fields, about the end of April, or beginning of May, 1697; and published in 4to, without the author's name, on the 11th of May of the same year. The title-page of the original edition reads as follows: "*The Provok'd Wife: a Comedy, As it is Acted at the New Theatre in Little Lincolns-Inn-Fields. By the Author of a new Comedy call'd the Relapse, or Virtue in Danger. London. Printed by J. O. for R. Wellington, at the Lute in St. Paul's Church Yard, and Sam. Briscoe in Covent-Garden* 1697."

Genest, and other writers, following Cibber, have supposed that this play was produced before *Æsop*. The true dates, however, are established by the advertisements of the two plays, which I have already quoted from the *London Gazette* and the *Post Man*. Further confirmation (were it needed) of the priority of *Æsop* is supplied by the prologue to *The Provok'd Wife*, wherein mention is made of *three* plays by the author, *The Provok'd Wife* being, of course, the latest. The prologue contains a line which reads like a prognostic of Collier's onslaught:—"Kind Heaven! inspire some venom'd priest to write." From the epilogue, "by another hand," we learn that Vanbrugh made over to the company his right, as author, to the profits of the third and sixth nights' performances.

The scenes which were afterwards substituted for those, in the fourth act, in which Sir John Brute appeared disguised as a parson, were written by Vanbrugh, according to Cibber, for a revival of the play in 1725; but according to Genest, for the performances at the Haymarket theatre in January, 1706. They appear to have been printed, for the first time, in a 12mo edition of the play, published at Dublin in 1743; where they are given, not in the form of an appendix, but in the place of the original scenes, which are omitted. In the title-page of this edition it is expressly asserted that the new scene (strictly, scenes) was "never before printed"; nor is it contained in any earlier edition of the play which I have seen. The full text of the title-page is as follows: "*The Provok'd Wife: a Comedy. In which is inserted, an Original Scene, never before printed. Written by Sir John Vanbrugh. Dublin: Printed by S. Powell, for George Risk, at Shakespear's-Head in Dame's-street, near the Horse-guard,* MDCCXLIII."

In the present volume, the additional scenes are printed as an appendix to the play.

DRAMATIS PERSONÆ.

MEN.

Constant	...Mr. *Verbruggen.*
Heartfree	... Mr. *Hudson.*
Sir *John Brute*	... Mr. *Betterton.*
Treble, a Singing Master	... Mr. *Bowman.*
Rasor, Valet de Chambre to Sir *John Brute* ...	.. Mr. *Bowen.*
Justice of the Peace	... Mr. *Bright.*

Lord *Rake,*
Colonel *Bully,* } Companions to Sir *John Brute.*

Constable and Watch.

WOMEN.

Lady *Brute*	... Mrs. *Barry.**
Belinda, her Niece	Mrs. *Bracegirdle.*†
Lady *Fancyful*	... Mrs. *Bowman.*‡
Mademoiselle	... Mrs. *Willis.*

Cornet and *Pipe,* Servants to Lady *Fancyful.*
Lovewell, Woman to Lady *Brute.*

[SCENE.—LONDON.]

---

* Elizabeth Barry was but fifteen years old when she first appeared on the stage, in 1673. From an unpromising beginning she made such advance, that before the end of the century she was "in possession of almost all the chief parts in tragedy." She "created" Otway's Monimia and Belvidera, Southern's Isabella, Congreve's Zara, &c. Cibber speaks of her dignified presence, her majestic mien, her full clear voice, and her unrivalled power of exciting pity in the audience. She died Nov. 7, 1713, and was buried in Acton Churchyard.

† Anne Bracegirdle also made an early appearance on the stage, playing the page's part in Otway's *Orphan* at the age of six years. Her friendship with Congreve, in whose plays she was always the leading actress, is well known. She was "the *Cara*, the Darling of the Theatre. . . . . It was even a Fashion among the Gay and Young, to have a Taste or *Tendre* for Mrs. *Bracegirdle*" (Cibber). She seems to have been as modest and well-conducted as she was charming, for Gildon's malicious attacks upon her reputation may be safely disregarded. She retired from he stage about 1707, and died Sept., 1748.

‡ Mrs. Bowman was the daughter of an intimate friend of Betterton's, who dying in poverty, Betterton took the girl under his protection, and brought her up. She became an actress of considerable repute, and married John Bowman, the singer and actor, whose name also appears above.

T

PROLOGUE.

SINCE 'tis the intent and business of the stage,
To copy out the follies of the age ;
To hold to every man a faithful glass,
And show him of what species he's an ass :
I hope the next that teaches in the school,
Will show our author he's a scribbling fool.
And, that the satire may be sure to bite,
Kind Heaven ! inspire some venom'd priest to write,
And grant some ugly lady may indite !
For I would have him lash'd, by heavens I would !   10
Till his presumption swam away in blood.
Three plays at once proclaims a face of brass,
No matter what they are ; that's not the case ;
To write three plays, e'en that's to be an ass.
But what I least forgive, he knows it too,
For to his cost he lately has known you. *
Experience shows, to many a writer's smart,
You hold a court where mercy ne'er had part ;
So much of the old serpent's sting you have,
You love to damn, as Heaven delights to save.   20
In foreign parts, let a bold volunteer,
For public good, upon the stage appear,
He meets ten thousand smiles to dissipate his fear.

---

* An allusion, as I take it, to the partial failure of *Æsop*.

All tickle on the adventuring young beginner,
And only scourge the incorrigible sinner;
They touch indeed his faults, but with a hand
So gentle, that his merit still may stand :
Kindly they buoy the follies of his pen,
That he may shun 'em when he writes again.
But 'tis not so in this good-natur'd town ;
All's one, an ox, a poet, or a crown ;
Old England's play was always knocking down.

THE PROVOK'D WIFE.

A COMEDY.

ACT I.

SCENE I.—*A Room in* Sir JOHN BRUTE'S *House.*

Enter Sir JOHN BRUTE.

Sir John. What cloying meat is love—when matrimony's the sauce to it! Two years' marriage has debauched my five senses. Everything I see, everything I hear, everything I feel, everything I smell, and everything I taste—methinks has wife in't. No boy was ever so weary of his tutor, no girl of her bib, no nun of doing penance, nor old maid of being chaste, as I am of being married. Sure, there's a secret curse entailed upon the very name of wife. My lady is a young lady, a fine lady, a witty lady, a virtuous lady— and yet I hate her. There is but one thing on earth I loathe beyond her: that's fighting. Would my courage come up but to a fourth part of my ill-nature, I'd stand buff to her relations, and thrust her out of doors. But marriage has sunk me down to such an ebb of resolution, I dare not draw my sword, though even to get rid of my wife. But here she comes   16

Enter Lady BRUTE.

Lady Brute. Do you dine at home to-day, sir John?

Sir John. Why, do you expect I should tell you what I don't know myself?

Lady Brute. I thought there was no harm in asking you.

Sir John. If thinking wrong were an excuse for impertinence, women might be justified in most things they say or do.

Lady Brute. I'm sorry I've said anything to displease you.   26

Sir John. Sorrow for things past is of as little importance to me, as my dining at home or abroad ought to be to you.

Lady Brute. My inquiry was only that I might have provided what you liked.

Sir John. Six to four you had been in the wrong there again; for what I liked yesterday I don't like to-day, and what I like to-day, 'tis odds I mayn't like to-morrow.

Lady Brute. But if I had asked you what you liked?

Sir John. Why, then, there would be more asking about it than the thing is worth.   37

Lady Brute. I wish I did but know how I might please you.

Sir John. Ay, but that sort of knowledge is not a wife's talent.

Lady Brute. Whate'er my talent is, I'm sure my will has ever been to make you easy.

Sir John. If women were to have their wills, the world would be finely governed.   45

Lady Brute. What reason have I given you to use me as you do of late? It once was otherwise : you married me for love.

Sir John. And you me for money. So you have your reward, and I have mine.

Lady Brute. What is it that disturbs you.

Sir John. A parson.

Lady Brute. Why, what has he done to you?   53

Sir John. He has married me.   [*Exit.*

Lady Brute. The devil's in the fellow, I think!—I was told before I married him that thus 'twould be : but I thought I had charms enough to govern him; and that where there was an estate, a woman must needs be happy; so my vanity has deceived me, and my ambition has made me uneasy. But there's some comfort still; if one would be revenged of him, these are good times; a woman may have a gallant, and a separate maintenance too.—The surly puppy!—Yet he's a fool for't; for hitherto he has been no monster : but who knows how far he may provoke me? I never loved him, yet I have been ever true to him; and that, in spite of all the attacks of art and nature upon a poor weak woman's heart, in favour of a tempting lover. Methinks so noble a defence as I have made should be rewarded with a better usage.—Or who can tell—perhaps a good part of what I suffer from my husband may be a judgment upon me for my cruelty to my lover.—Lord, with what pleasure could I indulge that thought, were there but a possibility of finding arguments to make it good!—And how do I know but there may?—Let me see.—What opposes?—My matrimonial vow?—Why, what did I vow? I think I promised to be true to my husband.

Well; and he promised to be kind to me. But he han't
kept his word.—Why, then, I'm absolved from mine.—Ay,
that seems clear to me. The argument's good between the
king and the people, why not between the husband and the
wife? Oh, but that condition was not expressed.—No
matter, 'twas understood. Well, by all I see, if I argue the
matter a little longer with myself, I shan't find so many
bugbears in the way as I thought I should. Lord, what fine
notions of virtue do we women take up upon the credit of
old foolish philosophers! Virtue's its own reward, virtue's
this, virtue's that;—virtue's an ass, and a gallant's worth
forty on't.   88

Enter Belinda.

Lady Brute. Good-morrow, dear cousin!

Bel. Good-morrow, madam; you look pleased this
morning.

Lady Brute. I am so.

Bel. With what, pray?

Lady Brute. With my husband.

Bel. Drown husbands! for yours is a provoking fellow.
As he went out just now, I prayed him to tell me what time
of day 'twas; and he asked me if I took him for the church-
clock, that was obliged to tell all the parish.   98

Lady Brute. He has been saying some good obliging
things to me too. In short, Belinda, he has used me so
barbarously of late, that I could almost resolve to play the
downright wife—and cuckold him.

Bel. That would be downright, indeed.

Lady Brute. Why, after all, there's more to be said for't
than you'd imagine, child. I know, according to the strict

statute law of religion, I should do wrong; but if there were a Court of Chancery in Heaven, I'm sure I should cast him.

Bel. If there were a House of Lords you might.

Lady Brute. In either I should infallibly carry my cause. Why, he is the first aggressor, not I. 110

Bel. Ay, but you know, we must return good for evil.

Lady Brute. That may be a mistake in the translation.— Prithee, be of my opinion, Belinda; for I'm positive I'm in the right; and if you'll keep up the prerogative of a woman, you'll likewise be positive you are in the right, whenever you do anything you have a mind to. But I shall play the fool and jest on, till I make you begin to think I'm in earnest.

Bel. I shan't take the liberty, madam, to think of anything that you desire to keep a secret from me. 120

Lady Brute. Alas, my dear! I have no secrets. My heart could never yet confine my tongue.

Bel. Your eyes, you mean; for I am sure I have seen them gadding, when your tongue has been locked up safe enough.

Lady Brute. My eyes gadding! prithee after who, child?

Bel. Why, after one that thinks you hate him as much as I know you love him.

Lady Brute. Constant, you mean.

Bell. I do so. 130

Lady Brute. Lord, what should put such a thing into your head?

Bel. That which puts things into most people's heads— observation.

Lady Brute. Why, what have you observed, in the name of wonder?

Bel. I have observed you blush when you meet him, force yourself away from him, and then be out of humour with everything about you. In a word, never was poor creature so spurred on by desire, and so reined in with fear!

Lady Brute. How strong is fancy!   141

Bel. How weak is woman!

Lady Brute. Prithee, niece, have a better opinion of your aunt's inclinations.

Bel. Dear aunt, have a better opinion of your niece's understanding.

Lady Brute. You'll make me angry.

Bel. You'll make me laugh.

Lady Brute. Then you are resolved to persist?

Bel. Positively.   150

Lady Brute. And all I can say—

Bel. Will signify nothing.

Lady Brute. Though I should swear 'twere false—

Bel. I should think it true.

Lady Brute. Then let us both forgive—[*Kissing her*] for we have both offended: I in making a secret, you in discovering it.

Bel. Good-nature may do much: but you have more reason to forgive one, than I have to pardon t'other.   159

Lady Brute. 'Tis true, Belinda, you have given me so many proofs of your friendship, that my reserve has been indeed a crime. But that you may more easily forgive me, remember, child, that when our nature prompts us to a thing our honour and religion have forbid us, we would (were't possible) conceal, even from the soul itself, the knowledge of the body's weakness.

Bel. Well, I hope, to make your friend amends, you'll

hide nothing from her for the future, though the body should
still grow weaker and weaker.   169

Lady Brute.   No, from this moment I have no more
reserve; and for a proof of my repentance, I own, Belinda,
I'm in danger.   Merit and wit assault me from without;
nature and love solicit me within; my husband's barbarous
usage piques me to revenge; and Satan, catching at the fair
occasion, throws in my way that vengeance which, of all vengeance, pleases women best.

Bel.   'Tis well Constant don't know the weakness of the
fortifications; for, o' my conscience, he'd soon come on to
the assault !   .   179

Lady Brute.   Ay, and I'm afraid carry the town too.
But whatever you may have observed, I have dissembled so
well as to keep him ignorant.   So you see I'm no coquette,
Belinda : and if you'll follow my advice, you'll never be one
neither.   'Tis true, coquetry is one of the main ingredients
in the natural composition of a woman; and I, as well as
others, could be well enough pleased to see a crowd of young
fellows ogling, and glancing, and watching all occasions to do
forty foolish officious things.   Nay, should some of 'em push
on, even to hanging or drowning, why, faith, if I should let
pure woman alone, I should e'en be but too well pleased
with't.   191

Bel.   I'll swear 'twould tickle me strangely.

Lady Brute.   But after all, 'tis a vicious practice in us to
give the least encouragement but where we design to come to
a conclusion.   For 'tis an unreasonable thing to engage a
man in a disease which we beforehand resolve we never will
apply a cure to.

Bel.   'Tis true; but then a woman must abandon one of

the supreme blessings of her life. For I am fully convinced
no man has half that pleasure in possessing a mistress as a
woman has in jilting a gallant.   201

Lady Brute. The happiest woman then on earth must
be our neighbour.

Bel. O the impertinent composition ! She has vanity
and affectation enough to make her a ridiculous original, in
spite of all that art and nature ever furnished to any of her
sex before her.

Lady Brute. She concludes all men her captives ; and
whatever course they take, it serves to confirm her in that
opinion.   210

Bel. If they shun her, she thinks 'tis modesty, and
takes it for a proof of their passion.

Lady Brute. And if they are rude to her, 'tis conduct,
and done to prevent town-talk.

Bel. When her folly makes 'em laugh, she thinks they
are pleased with her wit.

Lady Brute. And when her impertinence makes 'em
dull, concludes they are jealous of her favours.

Bel. All their actions and their words, she takes for
granted, aim at her.   220

Lady Brute. And pities all other women because she
thinks they envy her.

Bel. Pray, out of pity to ourselves, let us find a better
subject, for I am weary of this. Do you think your
husband inclined to jealousy ?

Lady Brute. Oh, no ; he does not love me well enough
for that. Lord, how wrong men's maxims are ! They are
seldom jealous of their wives, unless they are very fond of
'em ; whereas they ought to consider the women's inclina-

tions, for there depends their fate. Well, men may talk; but they are not so wise as we, that's certain.   231

Bel. At least in our affairs.

Lady Brute. Nay, I believe we should outdo 'em in the business of the state too; for methinks they do and undo, and make but bad work on't.

Bel. Why then don't we get into the intrigues of government as well as they?

Lady Brute. Because we have intrigues of our own that make us more sport, child. And so let's in, and consider of 'em.   [*Exeunt.*

———

SCENE II.—*A Dressing Room.*

Enter Lady FANCYFUL, MADEMOISELLE, *and* CORNET.

Lady Fan. How do I look this morning?

Cor. Your ladyship looks very ill, truly.

Lady Fan. Lard, how ill-natured thou art, Cornet, to tell me so, though the thing should be true. Don't you know that I have humility enough to be but too easily out of conceit with myself. Hold the glass; I dare swear that will have more manners than you have.—Mademoiselle, let me have your opinion too.

Mad. My opinion pe, matam, dat your ladyship never look so well in your life.   10

Lady Fan. Well, the French are the prettiest obliging people; they say the most acceptable, well-mannered things, —and never flatter.

Mad. Your ladyship say great justice inteed.

Lady Fan. Nay, everything's just in my house but Cornet. The very looking-glass gives her the *démenti*. But I'm almost afraid it flatters me, it makes me look ·so very engaging.   [*Looking affectedly in the glass.*

Mad. Inteed, matam, your face pe handsomer den all de looking-glass in tee world, croyez-moi !   20

Lady Fan. But is it possible my eyes can be so languishing—and so very full of fire ?

Mad. Matam, if de glass was burning-glass, I believe your eyes set de fire in de house.

Lady Fan. You may take that night-gown, Mademoiselle. —Get out of the room, Cornet! I can't endure you.— [*Exit* CORNET.] This wench, methinks, does look so unsufferably ugly.

Mad. Every ting look ugly, matam, dat stand by your latiship.   30

Lady Fan. No really, Mademoiselle, methinks you look mighty pretty.

Mad. Ah, matam, de moon have no éclat, ven de sun appear.

Lady Fan. O pretty expression ! Have you ever been in love, Mademoiselle ?

Mad. Oui, matam.   [*Sighing.*

Lady Fan. And were you beloved again ?

Mad. No, matam.   [*Sighing.*   39

Lady Fan. O ye gods! what an unfortunate creature should I be in such a case! But nature has made me nice for my own defence : I'm nice, strangely nice, Mademoiselle. I believe were the merit of whole mankind bestowed upon one single person, I should still think the fellow wanted something to make it worth my while to take notice of him.

And yet I could love ; nay, fondly love, were it possible to
have a thing made on purpose for me : for I'm not cruel,
Mademoiselle ; I'm only nice.   48

Mad. Ah, matam, I wish I was fine gentleman for your
sake. I do all de ting in de world to get leetle way into
your heart. I make song, I make verse, I give you de
serenade, I give great many present to Mademoiselle ; I no
eat, I no sleep, I be lean, I be mad, I hang myself, I drown
myself. Ah, ma chère dame, que je vous aimerais !

                                        [*Embracing her.*

Lady Fan. Well, the French have strange obliging
ways with 'em ; you may take those two pair of gloves,
Mademoiselle.

Mad. Me humbly tanke my sweet lady.   58

Enter CORNET.

Cor. Madam, here's a letter for your ladyship by the
penny-post.   [*Exit*

Lady Fan. Some new conquest, I'll warrant you. For
without vanity, I looked extremely clear last night, when I
went to the Park.—O agreeable ! Here's a new song made
of me : and ready set too. O thou welcome thing !—
[*Kissing it.*] Call Pipe hither, she shall sing it instantly.

Enter PIPE.

Here, sing me this new song, Pipe.   66

SONG.

I.

Fly, fly, you happy shepherds, fly !
Avoid Philira's charms ;
The rigour of her heart denies
The heaven that's in her arms.

Ne'er hope to gaze, and then retire,
    Nor yielding, to be blest :
Nature, who form'd her eyes of fire,
    Of ice compos'd her breast.

II.

Yet, lovely maid, this once believe   75
    A slave whose zeal you move ;
The gods, alas, your youth deceive,
    Their heaven consists in love.
In spite of all the thanks you owe,
    You may reproach 'em this,
That where they did their form bestow,
    They have denied their bliss.

[*Exit* PIPE.

Lady Fan. Well, there may be faults, Mademoiselle, but the design is so very obliging, 'twould be a matchless ingratitude in me to discover 'em.   85

Mad. Ma foi, matam, I tink de gentleman's song tell you de trute : if you never love, you never be happy.—Ah, que j'aime l'amour moi !

Re-enter CORNET, *with another letter.**

Cor. Madam, here's another letter for your ladyship.

[*Exit.*

Lady Fan. 'Tis thus I am importuned every morning, Mademoiselle. Pray how do the French ladies when they are thus accablées ?

Mad. Matam, dey never complain. Au contraire, when one Frense laty have got hundred lover—den she do all she can—to get hundred more.   95

Lady Fan. Well, strike me dead, I think they have le

---

* The early editions read, " *Enter* Servant *with another letter.*"

goût bon ! For 'tis an unutterable pleasure to be adored by all the men, and envied by all the women.—Yet I'll swear I'm concerned at the torture I give 'em. Lard, why was I formed to make the whole creation uneasy ! But let me read my letter.—[*Reads.*] *If you have a mind to hear of your faults, instead of being praised for your virtues, take the pains to walk in the Green-walk in St. James's with your woman an hour hence. You'll there meet one who hates you for some things, as he could love you for others, and therefore is willing to endeavour your reformation. If you come to the place I mention, you'll know who I am ; if you don't, you never shall : so take your choice.*—This is strangely familiar, Mademoiselle ; now have I a provoking fancy to know who this impudent fellow is.   110

Mad. Den take your scarf and your mask, and go to de rendezvous. De Frense laty do justement comme ça.

Lady Fan. Rendezvous ! What, rendezvous with a man, Mademoiselle !

Mad. Eh, pourquoi non ?

Lady Fan. What, and a man perhaps I never saw in my life !

Mad. Tant mieux : c'est donc quelque chose de nouveau.

Lady Fan. Why, how do I know what designs he may have ? He may intend to ravish me, for aught I know. 121

Mad. Ravish !—bagatelle. I would fain see one impudent rogue ravish Mademoiselle ; oui, je le voudrais.

Lady Fan. Oh, but my reputation, Mademoiselle, my reputation ; ah, ma chère réputation !

Mad. Matam, quand on l'a une fois perdue, on n'en est plus embarrassée.

Lady Fan. Fi, Mademoiselle, fi ! Reputation is a jewel.

Mad. Qui coûte bien cher, matam.

Lady Fan. Why, sure you would not sacrifice your honour to your pleasure ? 131

Mad. Je suis philosophe.

Lady Fan. Bless me, how you talk ! Why, what if honour be a burden, Mademoiselle, must it not be borne?

Mad. Chacun à sa façon. Quand quelque chose m'incommode moi, je m'en défais, vite.

Lady Fan. Get you gone, you little naughty French-woman you ! I vow and swear I must turn you out of doors, if you talk thus.

Mad. Turn me out of doors !—turn yourself out of doors, and go see what de gentleman have to say to you.— Tenez.—Voilà [*Giving her her things hastily*] votre écharpe, voilà votre coiffe, voilà votre masque, voilà tout.—[*Calling within.*] Hé, Mercure, coquin ! call one chair for matam, and one oder for me : va-t'en vite.—[*Turning to her lady, and helping her on hastily with her things.*] Allons, matam ; dépêchez-vous donc. Mon Dieu, quels scrupules ! 147

Lady Fan. Well, for once, Mademoiselle, I'll follow your advice, out of the intemperate desire I have to know who this ill-bred fellow is. But I have too much délicatesse to make a practice on't.

Mad. Belle chose vraiment que la délicatesse, lorsqu'il s'agit de se divertir !—Ah, ça—Vous voilà équipée ; partons.—Hé bien !—qu'avez vous donc ?

Lady Fan. J'ai peur.

Mad. Je n'en ai point moi.

Lady Fan. I dare not go.

Mad. Démeurez donc.

U

Lady Fan.   Je suis poltronne.

Mad.   Tant pis pour vous.   160

Lady Fan.   Curiosity's a wicked devil.

Mad.   C'est une charmante sainte.

Lady Fan.   It ruined our first parents.

Mad.   Elle a bien diverti leurs enfans.

Lady Fan.   L'honneur est contre.

Mad.   Le plaisir est pour.

Lady Fan.   Must I then go?

Mad.   Must you go!—must you eat, must you drink, must you sleep, must you live? De nature bid you do one, de nature bid you do toder.—Vous me ferez enrager!

Lady Fan.   But when reason corrects nature, Mademoiselle?   172

Mad.   Elle est donc bien insolente, c'est sa sœur aînée.

Lady Fan.   Do you then prefer your nature to your reason, Mademoiselle?

Mad.   Oui dà.

Lady Fan.   Pourquoi?

Mad.   Because my nature make me merry, my reason make me mad.

Lady Fan.   Ah la méchante Française!

Mad.   Ah la belle Anglaise!

                              [*Exit, forcing her* Lady *off.*

ACT II.

SCENE I.—*St. James's Park.*

Enter Lady Fancyful *and* Mademoiselle.

Lady Fan. Well, I vow, Mademoiselle, I'm strangely impatient to know who this confident fellow is.

Enter Heartfree.

Look, there's Heartfree. But sure it can't be him; he's a professed woman-hater. Yet who knows what my wicked eyes may have done?

Mad. Il nous approche, madame.

Lady Fan. Yes, 'tis he: now will he be most intolerably cavalier, though he should be in love with me.

Heart. Madam, I'm your humble servant; I perceive you have more humility and good-nature than I thought you had.   11

Lady Fan. What you attribute to humility and good-nature, sir, may perhaps be only due to curiosity. I had a mind to know who 'twas had ill-manners enough to write that letter.   [*Throwing him his letter.*

Heart. Well, and now I hope you are satisfied.

Lady Fan. I am so, sir; good b'w'y t'ye.

Heart. Nay, hold there; though you have done your business, I han't done mine: by your ladyship's leave, we must have one moment's prattle together. Have you a mind to be the prettiest woman about town, or not? How she stares upon me! What! this passes for an impertinent question with you now, because you think you are so already. 24

Lady Fan. Pray, sir, let me ask you a question in my turn : by what right do you pretend to examine me?

Heart. By the same right that the strong govern the weak, because I have you in my power; for you cannot get so quickly to your coach but I shall have time enough to make you hear everything I have to say to you.

Lady Fan. These are strange liberties you take, Mr. Heartfree !

Heart. They are so, madam, but there's no help for it ; for know, that I have a design upon you. 34

Lady Fan. Upon me, sir !

Heart. Yes; and one that will turn to your glory, and my comfort, if you will but be a little wiser than you use to be.

Lady Fan. Very well, sir.

Heart. Let me see—your vanity, madam, I take to be about some eight degrees higher than any woman's in the town, let t'other be who she will; and my indifference is naturally about the same pitch. Now could you find the way to turn this indifference into fire and flames, methinks your vanity ought to be satisfied; and this, perhaps, you might bring about upon pretty reasonable terms. 45

Lady Fan. And pray at what rate would this indifference be bought off, if one should have so depraved an appetite to desire it ?

Heart. Why, madam, to drive a quaker's bargain, and make but one word with you, if I do part with it—you must lay me down—your affectation.

Lady Fan. My affectation, sir !

Heart. Why, I ask you nothing but what you may very well spare.

Lady Fan. You grow rude, sir !—Come, Mademoiselle, 'tis high time to be gone.   56

Mad. Allons, allons, allons !

Heart. [*Stopping 'em.*] Nay, you may as well stand still; for hear me you shall, walk which way you please.

Lady Fan. What mean you, sir?

Heart. I mean to tell you, that you are the most ungrateful woman upon earth.

Lady Fan. Ungrateful ! To who ?

Heart. To nature.

Lady Fan. Why, what has nature done for me ?   65

Heart. What you have undone by art. It made you handsome ; it gave you beauty to a miracle, a shape without a fault, wit enough to make 'em relish, and so turned you loose to your own discretion ; which has made such work with you, that you are become the pity of our sex, and the jest of your own. There is not a feature in your face but you have found the way to teach it some affected convulsion ; your feet, your hands, your very fingers' ends, are directed never to move without some ridiculous air or other ; and your language is a suitable trumpet, to draw people's eyes upon the raree-show.   76

Mad. [*Aside.*] Est-ce qu'on fait l'amour en Angleterre comme ça ?

Lady Fan. [*Aside.*] Now could I cry for madness, but that I know he'd laugh at me for it.

Heart. Now do you hate me for telling you the truth, but that's because you don't believe it is so ; for were you

once convinced of that, you'd reform for your own sake.
But 'tis as hard to persuade a woman to quit anything that
makes her ridiculous, as 'tis to prevail with a poet to see a
fault in his own play.   86

Lady Fan. Every circumstance of nice breeding must
needs appear ridiculous to one who has so natural an antipathy to good manners.

Heart. But suppose I could find the means to convince
you, that the whole world is of my opinion, and that those
who flatter and commend you, do it to no other intent, but
to make you persevere in your folly, that they may continue
in their mirth.

Lady Fan. Sir, though you and all that world you talk of
should be so impertinently officious as to think to persuade
me I don't know how to behave myself, I should still have
charity enough for my own understanding, to believe myself
in the right, and all you in the wrong.

Mad. Le voilà mort !   100

[*Exeunt* Lady FANCYFUL *and* MADEMOISELLE.

Heart. [*Gazing after her.*] There her single clapper
has published the sense of the whole sex. Well, this once I
have endeavoured to wash the blackamoor white ; but
henceforward I'll sooner undertake to teach sincerity to a
courtier, generosity to an usurer, honesty to a lawyer, nay,
humility to a divine, than discretion to a woman I see has
once set her heart upon playing the fool.

Enter CONSTANT.

Morrow, Constant.

Const. Good morrow, Jack : what are you doing here
this morning ?   110

Heart. Doing! guess, if thou canst.—Why, I have been endeavouring to persuade my lady Fancyful that she's the foolishest woman about town.

Const. A pretty endeavour truly!

Heart. I have told her in as plain English as I could speak, both what the town says of her, and what I think of her. In short, I have used her as an absolute king would do Magna Charta.

Const. And how does she take it?

Heart. As children do pills; bite 'em, but can't swallow 'em.   121

Const. But, prithee, what has put it into your head, of all mankind, to turn reformer?

Heart. Why, one thing was, the morning hung upon my hands, I did not know what to do with myself; and another was, that as little as I care for women, I could not see with patience one that Heaven had taken such wondrous pains about, be so very industrious to make herself the Jack-pudding of the creation.   129

Const. Well, now could I almost wish to see my cruel mistress make the self-same use of what Heaven has done for her, that so I might be cured of a disease that makes me so very uneasy; for love, love is the devil, Heartfree.

Heart. And why do you let the devil govern you?

Const. Because I have more flesh and blood than grace and self-denial. My dear, dear mistress!—'Sdeath! that so genteel a woman should be a saint, when religion's out of fashion!

Heart. Nay, she's much in the wrong truly; but who knows how far time and good example may prevail?   140

Const. Oh! they have played their parts in vain already.

'Tis now two years since that damned fellow her husband invited me to his wedding : and there was the first time I saw that charming woman, whom I have loved ever since, more than e'er a martyr did his soul ; but she's cold, my friend, still cold as the northern star.

Heart. So are all women by nature, which makes 'em so willing to be warmed.

Const. Oh, don't profane the sex ! Prithee think 'em all angels for her sake, for she's virtuous even to a fault.   150

Heart. A lover's head is a good accountable thing truly ! He adores his mistress for being virtuous, and yet is very angry with her because she won't be lewd.

Const. Well, the only relief I expect in my misery is to see thee some day or other as deeply engaged as myself, which will force me to be merry in the midst of all my misfortunes.

Heart. That day will never come, be assured, Ned. Not but that I can pass a night with a woman, and for the time, perhaps, make myself as good sport as you can do. Nay, I can court a woman too, call her nymph, angel, goddess, what you please : but here's the difference 'twixt you and I ; I persuade a woman she's an angel, and she persuades you she's one. Prithee let me tell you how I avoid falling in love ; that which serves me for prevention, may chance to serve you for a cure.   166

Const. Well, use the ladies moderately then, and I'll hear you.

Heart. That using 'em moderately undoes us all ; but I'll use 'em justly, and that you ought to be satisfied with. I always consider a woman, not as the tailor, the shoemaker, the tire-woman, the sempstress, and (which is more than all

that) the poet makes her ; but I consider her as pure nature
has contrived her, and that more strictly than I should have
done our old grandmother Eve, had I seen her naked in the
garden ; for I consider her turned inside out.   Her heart
well-examined, I find there pride, vanity, covetousness,
indiscretion, but above all things, malice ; plots eternally
a-forging to destroy one another's reputations, and as
honestly to charge the levity of men's tongues with the
scandal; hourly debates how to make poor gentlemen in
love with 'em, with no other intent but to use 'em like dogs
when they have done ; a constant desire of doing more
mischief, and an everlasting war waged against truth and
good-nature.   185

Const.   Very well, sir ; an admirable composition truly !

Heart.   Then for her outside, I consider it merely as an
outside ; she has a thin tiffany covering, over just such stuff
as you and I are made on.   As for her motion, her mien,
her airs, and all those tricks, I know they affect you mightily.
If you should see your mistress at a coronation, dragging her
peacock's train, with all her state and insolence about her,
'twould strike you with all the awful thoughts that heaven
itself could pretend to from you ; whereas I turn the whole
matter into a jest, and suppose her strutting in the self-same
stately manner, with nothing on but her stays, and her under
scanty quilted petticoat.   197

Const.   Hold thy profane tongue ! for I'll hear no
more.

Heart.   What ! you'll love on then ?

Const.   Yes, to eternity.

Heart.   Yet you have no hopes at all.

Const.   None.

Heart. Nay, the resolution may be discreet enough; perhaps you have found out some new philosophy, that love's like virtue, its own reward : so you and your mistress will be as well content at a distance, as others that have less learning are in coming together.   208

Const. No; but if she should prove kind at last, my dear Heartfree.   [*Embracing him.*

Heart. Nay, prithee, don't take me for your mistress, for lovers are very troublesome.

Const. Well, who knows what time may do?

Heart. And just now he was sure time could do nothing.

Const. Yet not one kind glance in two years is somewhat strange.

Heart. Not strange at all; she don't like you, that's all the business.

Const. Prithee, don't distract me.   220

Heart. Nay, you are a good handsome young fellow, she might use you better.   Come, will you go see her?   Perhaps she may have changed her mind; there's some hopes as long as she's a woman.

Const. Oh, 'tis in vain to visit her ! Sometimes to get a sight of her I visit that beast her husband ; but she certainly finds some pretence to quit the room as soon as I enter.

Heart. It's much she don't tell him you have made love to her too, for that's another good-natured thing usual amongst women, in which they have several ends.   Sometimes 'tis to recommend their virtue, that they may be lewd with the greater security.   Sometimes 'tis to make their husbands fight, in hopes they may be killed when their affairs require it should be so : but most commonly 'tis to engage

two men in a quarrel, that they may have the credit of being
fought for ; and if the lover's killed in the business, they cry,
Poor fellow, he had ill luck !—and so they go to cards. 237

Const. Thy injuries to women are not to be forgiven.
Look to't, if ever thou dost fall into their hands—

Heart. They can't use me worse than they do you, that
speak well of 'em.—O ho ! here comes the knight.

Enter Sir John Brute.

Your humble servant, Sir John.

Sir John. Servant, sir.

Heart. How does all your family ?

Sir John. Pox o' my family !

Const. How does your lady ? I han't seen her abroad
a good while.

Sir John. Do ! I don't know how she does, not I ; she
was well enough yesterday : I han't been at home to-night.

Const. What, were you out of town ? 250

Sir John. Out of town ! no, I was drinking.

Const. You are a true Englishman ; don't know your
own happiness. If I were married to such a woman, I
would not be from her a night for all the wine in France.

Sir John. Not from her ! Oons ; what a time should
a man have of that !

Heart. Why, there's no division, I hope ?

Sir John. No ; but there's a conjunction, and that's
worse ; a pox o' the parson !—Why the plague don't you
two marry ? I fancy I look like the devil to you. 260

Heart. Why, you don't think you have horns, do you ?

Sir John. No, I believe my wife's religion will keep her
honest.

Heart. And what will make her keep her religion?

Sir John. Persecution ; and therefore she shall have it.

Heart. Have a care, knight ; women are tender things.

Sir John. And yet, methinks, 'tis a hard matter to break their hearts.

Const. Fie ! fie ! you have one of the best wives in the world, and yet you seem the most uneasy husband.

Sir John. Best wives !—the woman's well enough, she has no vice that I know of, but she's a wife, and—damn a wife ! If I were married to a hogshead of claret, matrimony would make me hate it.   274

Heart. Why did you marry, then ? you were old enough to know your own mind.

Sir John. Why did I marry ! I married because I had a mind to lie with her, and she would not let me.

Heart. Why did you not ravish her?

Sir John. Yes ! and so have hedged myself into forty quarrels with her relations, besides buying my pardon. But more than all that, you must know, I was afraid of being damned in those days ; for I kept sneaking cowardly company, fellows that went to church, said grace to their meat, and had not the least tincture of quality about 'em.

Heart. But I think you are got into a better gang now.   287

Sir John. Zoons, sir, my lord Rake and I are hand and glove, I believe we may get our bones broke together to-night ; have you a mind to share a frolic ?

Const. Not I, truly ; my talent lies to softer exercises.

Sir John. What, a down-bed and a strumpet? A pox of venery ! I say. Will you come and drink with me this afternoon ?

Const. I can't drink to-day, but we'll come and sit an hour with you if you will.

Sir John. Phu! pox, sit an hour! Why can't you drink?

Const. Because I'm to see my mistress.

Sir John. Who's that?

Const. Why, do you use to tell?   300

Sir John. Yes.

Const. So won't I.

Sir John. Why?

Const. Because 'tis a secret.

Sir John. Would my wife knew it, 'twould be no secret long.

Const. Why, do you think she can't keep a secret?

Sir John. No more than she can keep Lent.

Heart. Prithee, tell it her to try, Constant.   309

Sir John. No, prithee, don't, that I mayn't be plagued with it.

Const. I'll hold you a guinea you don't make her tell it you.

Sir John. I'll hold you a guinea I do.

Const. Which way?

Sir John. Why, I'll beg her not to tell it me.

Heart. Nay, if anything does it, that will.

Const. But do you think, sir—   318

Sir John. Oons, sir, I think a woman and a secret are the two impertinentest themes in the universe! Therefore, pray let's hear no more of my wife nor your mistress. Damn 'em both with all my heart, and everything else that daggles a petticoat, except four generous whores, with Betty Sands at the head of 'em, who are drunk with my lord Rake and I ten times in a fortnight.   [*Exit.*

Const. Here's a dainty fellow for you! and the veriest
coward too. But his usage of his wife makes me ready to
stab the villain.   328

Heart. Lovers are short-sighted: all their senses run
into that of feeling. This proceeding of his is the only
thing on earth can make your fortune. If anything can
prevail with her to accept of a gallant, 'tis his ill-usage of
her ; for women will do more for revenge than they'll do for
the gospel. Prithee take heart, I have great hopes for you ;
and since I can't bring you quite off of her, I'll endeavour
to bring you quite on ; for a whining lover is the damn'dest
companion upon earth.

Const. My dear friend, flatter me a little more with these
hopes ; for whilst they prevail, I have heaven within me, and
could melt with joy.

Heart. Pray, no melting yet : let things go farther
first. This afternoon perhaps we shall make some advance.
In the meanwhile, let's go dine at Locket's, and let hope
get you a stomach.   [*Exeunt.*

SCENE II.—*A Room in* Lady FANCYFUL'S *House.*

Enter Lady FANCYFUL *and* MADEMOISELLE.

Lady Fan. Did you ever see anything so importune,
Mademoiselle?

Mad. Inteed, matam, to say de trute, he want leetel
good-breeding.

Lady Fan. Good-breeding! he wants to be caned,
Mademoiselle : an insolent fellow ! And yet let me expose
my weakness, 'tis the only man on earth I could resolve to

dispense my favours on, were he but a fine gentlemen. Well, did men but know how deep an impression a fine gentleman makes in a lady's heart, they would reduce all their studies to that of good-breeding alone.   11

Enter Cornet.

Cor. Madam, here's Mr. Treble. He has brought home the verses your ladyship made, and gave him to set.

Lady Fan. O let him come in by all means.—[*Exit* Cornet.] Now, Mademoiselle, am I going to be unspeakably happy.

Enter Treble *and* Pipe.

So, Mr. Treble, you have set my little dialogue?

Treb. Yes, madam, and I hope your ladyship will be pleased with it.

Lady Fan. Oh, no doubt on't; for really, Mr. Treble, you set all things to a wonder. But your music is in particular heavenly when you have my words to clothe in't.

Treb. Your words themselves, madam, have so much music in 'em, they inspire me.   24

Lady Fan. Nay, now you make me blush, Mr. Treble; but pray let's hear what you have done.

Treb. You shall, madam.

A Song *to be sung between a Man and a Woman.*

> *M.*   Ah! lovely nymph, the world's on fire :
>   Veil, veil those cruel eyes !
> *W.*   The world may then in flames expire,
>   And boast that so it dies.
>
> *M.*   But when all mortals are destroy'd,
>   Who then shall sing your praise ?
> *W.*   Those who are fit to be employ'd :
>   The gods shall altars raise.   35

Treb.   How does your ladyship like it, madam ?

Lady Fan.   Rapture, rapture, Mr. Treble, I'm all rapture ! O wit and art, what power you have, when joined ! I must needs tell you the birth of this little dialogue, Mr. Treble. Its father was a dream, and its mother was the moon.   I dreamt that by an unanimous vote I was chosen queen of that pale world : and that the first time I appeared upon my throne—all my subjects fell in love with me. Just then I waked, and seeing pen, ink, and paper lie idle upon the table, I slid into my morning-gown, and writ this impromptu.   46

Treb.   So I guess the dialogue, madam, is supposed to be between your majesty and your first minister of state.

Lady Fan.   Just.   He as minister advises me to trouble my head about the welfare of my subjects ; which I as sovereign find a very impertinent proposal.   But is the town so dull, Mr. Treble, it affords us never another new song ?

Treb.   Madam, I have one in my pocket, came out but yesterday, if your ladyship pleases to let Mrs. Pipe sing it.   56

Lady Fan.   By all means.--Here, Pipe, make what music you can of this song, here.

SONG.

I.

Not an angel dwells above
Half so fair as her I love,
   Heaven knows how she'll receive me :
If she smiles, I'm blest indeed ;
If she frowns, I'm quickly freed ;
   Heaven knows she ne'er can grieve me.

II.

None can love her more than I,   65
Yet she ne'er shall make me die,
    If my flame can never warm her ;
Lasting beauty I'll adore,
I shall never love her more,
Cruelty will so deform her.

Lady Fan. Very well.—This is Heartfree's poetry,
without question.

Treb. Won't your ladyship please to sing yourself this
morning ?

Lady Fan. O Lord, Mr. Treble, my cold is still so
barbarous to refuse me that pleasure. He,—he,—hem.

                                              [*Coughs.*

Treb. I'm very sorry for it, madam. Methinks all mankind should turn physicians for the cure on't.   78

Lady Fan. Why truly, to give mankind their due, there's
few that know me, but have offered their remedy.

Treb. They have reason, madam ; for I know nobody
sings so near a cherubin as your ladyship.

Lady Fan. What I do, I owe chiefly to your skill and
care, Mr. Treble. People do flatter me, indeed, that I have
a voice, and a *je-ne-sais-quoi* in the conduct of it, that will
make music of anything. And truly I begin to believe so,
since what happened t'other night. Would you think it, Mr.
Treble ? walking pretty late in the Park, (for I often walk late
in the Park, Mr. Treble) a whim took me to sing Chevy-
Chase, and would you believe it ? next morning I had three
copies of verses and six billets-doux at my levee upon it.

Treb. And without all dispute you deserved as many
more, madam. Are there any farther commands for your
ladyship's humble servant ?   94

                            x

Lady Fan. Nothing more at this time, Mr. Treble. But I shall expect you here every morning for this month, to sing my little matter there to me. I'll reward you for your pains.

Treb. O Lord, madam !—

Lady Fan. Good morrow, sweet Mr. Treble.

Treb. Your ladyship's most obedient servant.

[*Exit with* PIPE.

Enter Servant.

Serv. Will your ladyship please to dine yet ?

Lady Fan. Yes, let 'em serve.—[*Exit* Servant.] Sure this Heartfree has bewitched me, Mademoiselle. You can't imagine how oddly he mixed himself in my thoughts during my rapture e'en now. I vow 'tis a thousand pities he is not more polished : don't you think so ?   106

Mad. Matam, I tink it so great pity, dat if I was in your ladyship place, I take him home in my house, I lock him up in my closet, and I never let him go till I teach him every-ting dat fine laty expect from fine gentleman.

Lady Fan. Why truly, I believe I should soon subdue his brutality ; for without doubt he has a strange penchant to grow fond of me, in spite of his aversion to the sex, else he would ne'er have taken so much pains about me. Lord, how proud would some poor creatures be of such a conquest ! But I, alas, I don't know how to receive as a favour what I take to be so infinitely my due. But what shall I do to new-mould him, Mademoiselle ? for till then he's my utter aversion.   119

Mad. Matam, you must laugh at him in all de place dat you meet him, and turn into de ridicule all he say and all he do.

Lady Fan. Why truly, satire has ever been of wondrous use to reform ill-manners. Besides, 'tis my particular talent to ridicule folks. I can be severe, strangely severe, when I will, Mademoiselle.—Give me the pen and ink—I find myself whimsical—I'll write to him.—[*Sitting down to write.*] Or I'll let it alone, and be severe upon him that way. —[*Rising up again.*] Yet active severity is better than passive. —[*Sitting down.*] 'Tis as good let alone too; for every lash I give him perhaps he'll take for a favour.—[*Rising.*] Yet 'tis a thousand pities so much satire should be lost.— [*Sitting.*] But if it should have a wrong effect upon him, 'twould distract me.—[*Rising.*] Well, I must write though, after all.—[*Sitting.*] Or I'll let it alone, which is the same thing—   [*Rising.*

Mad. [*Aside.*] La voilà déterminée.   ˋ   [*Exeunt.*

ACT III.

SCENE I.—*A Room in* Sir JOHN BRUTE'S *House.*

Sir JOHN BRUTE, Lady BRUTE, *and* BELINDA *discovered rising from table;* Servant *waiting.*

Sir John. [*To* Servant.] Here, take away the things; I expect company. But first bring me a pipe; I'll smoke.

[Servant *gives* Sir JOHN *a pipe, removes the things, and exit.*

Lady Brute. Lord, sir John, I wonder you won't leave that nasty custom!

Sir John. Prithee don't be impertinent.

Bel. [*Aside to* Lady BRUTE.] I wonder who those are he expects this afternoon?

Lady Brute. I'd give the world to know. Perhaps 'tis Constant; he comes here sometimes; if it does prove him, I'm resolved I'll share the visit.   10

Bel. We'll send for our work and sit here.

Lady Brute. He'll choke us with his tobacco.

Bel. Nothing will choke us when we are doing what we have a mind to.—Lovewell!   [*Calls.*

Enter LOVEWELL.

Love. Madam!

Lady Brute. Here; bring my cousin's work and mine hither.

[*Exit* LOVEWELL, *re-enters with their work, and then retires.*

Sir John. Whu ! Pox ! can't you work somewhere else ?

Lady Brute. We shall be careful not to disturb you, sir.

Bel. Your pipe will make you too thoughtful, uncle, if you were left alone ; our prittle-prattle will cure your spleen.   22

Sir John. Will it so, Mrs. Pert ? Now I believe it will so increase it,—[*Sitting and smoking*] I shall take my own house for a paper-mill.

Lady Brute. [*Aside to* BELINDA.] Don't let's mind him ; let him say what he will.

Sir John. A woman's tongue a cure for the spleen— oons !—[*Aside.*] If a man had got the headache, they'd be for applying the same remedy.

Lady Brute. You have done a great deal, Belinda, since yesterday.   32

Bel. Yes, I have worked very hard; how do you like it ?

Lady Brute. Oh, 'tis the prettiest fringe in the world ! Well, cousin, you have the happiest fancy : prithee advise me about altering my crimson petticoat.

Sir John. A pox o' your petticoat ! Here's such a prating, a man can't digest his own thoughts for you.

Lady Brute. Don't answer him.—Well, what do you advise me ?

Bel. Why, really I would not alter it at all. Methinks 'tis very pretty as it is.   43

Lady Brute. Ay, that's true : but you know one grows weary of the prettiest things in the world, when one has had 'em long.

Sir John. Yes, I have taught her that.

Bel. Shall we provoke him a little ?

Lady Brute. With all my heart.—Belinda, don't you long to be married?

Bel. Why, there are some things in't I could like well enough.

Lady Brute. What do you think you should dislike?

Bel. My husband, a hundred to one else.   54

Lady Brute. O ye wicked wretch! sure you don't speak as you think.

Bel. Yes, I do: especially if he smoked tobacco.

> [*He looks earnestly at 'em.*

Lady Brute. Why, that many times takes off worse smells.

Bel. Then he must smell very ill indeed.

Lady Brute. So some men will, to keep their wives from coming near 'em.

Bel. Then those wives should cuckold 'em at a distance.   64

> [*He rises in a fury, throws his pipe at 'em, and drives 'em out. As they run off,* Constant *and* Heartfree *enter.* Lady Brute *runs against* Constant.

Sir John. Oons, get you gone up stairs, you confederating strumpets you, or I'll cuckold you with a vengeance!

Lady Brute. O Lord, he'll beat us, he'll beat us!— Dear, dear Mr. Constant, save us!   [*Exit with* Belinda.

Sir John. I'll cuckold you, with a pox!

Const. Heavens, sir John! what's the matter?

Sir John. Sure, if woman had been ready created, the devil, instead of being kicked down into hell, had been married.   74

Heart. Why, what new plague have you found now?

Sir John. Why, these two gentlewomen did but hear me say, I expected you here this afternoon; upon which they presently resolved to take up the room, o' purpose to plague me and my friends.

Const. Was that all? Why, we should have been glad of their company.

Sir John. Then I should have been weary of yours : for I can't relish both together. They found fault with my smoking tobacco too ; and said, men stunk. But I have a good mind—to say something.   85

Const. No, nothing against the ladies, pray.

Sir John. Split the ladies ! Come, will you sit down ?— [*To a* Servant.] Give us some wine, fellow.—You won't smoke ?

Const. No, nor drink neither at this time, I must ask your pardon.

Sir John. What, this mistress of yours runs in your head ; I'll warrant it's some such squeamish minx as my wife, that's grown so dainty of late she finds fault even with a dirty shirt.   95

Heart. That a woman may do, and not be very dainty neither.

Sir John. Pox o' the women ! let's drink. Come, you shall take one glass, though I send for a box of lozenges to sweeten your mouth after it.

Const. Nay, if one glass will satisfy you, I'll drink it, without putting you to that expense.

Sir John. Why, that's honest.—Fill some wine, sirrah ! —So, here's to you, gentlemen !—A wife's the devil. To your being both married !   [*They drink.*

Heart. O your most humble servant, sir.   106
Sir John. Well, how do you like my wine?
Const. 'Tis very good indeed.
Heart. 'Tis admirable.
Sir John. Then give us t'other glass.
Const. No, pray excuse us now. We'll come another time, and then we won't spare it.
Sir John. This one glass, and no more. Come, it shall be your mistress's health : and that's a great compliment from me, I assure you.
Const. And 'tis a very obliging one to me : so give us the glasses.   117
Sir John. So : let her live !
                    [*They drink :* Sir JOHN *coughs in the glass.*
Heart. And be kind.
Const. What's the matter ? does it go the wrong way ?
Sir John. If I had love enough to be jealous, I should take this for an ill omen : for I never drank my wife's health in my life, but I puked in the glass.
Const. Oh, she's too virtuous to make a reasonable man jealous.   126
Sir John. Pox of her virtue ! If I could but catch her adulterating, I might be divorced from her by law.
Heart. And so pay her a yearly pension, to be a distinguished cuckold.

Enter Servant.

Serv. Sir, there's my lord Rake, colonel Bully, and some other gentlemen, at the Blue-posts, desire your company.
                    [*Exit.*

Sir John. Cod's so, we are to consult about playing the devil to-night.

Heart. Well, we won't hinder business.

Sir John. Methinks I don't know how to leave you though ; but for once I must make bold. Or look you : maybe the conference mayn't last long ; so if you'll wait here half an hour, or an hour ; if I don't come then—why then—I won't come at all.   140

Heart. [*Aside to* Constant.] A good modest proposition truly !

Const. But let's accept on't, however. Who knows what may happen ?

Heart. Well, sir, to show you how fond we are of your company, we'll expect your return as long as we can.

Sir John. Nay, maybe I mayn't stay at all : but business, you know, must be done. So your servant—or, hark you, if you have a mind to take a frisk with us, I have an interest with my lord, I can easily introduce you.   150

Const. We are much beholding to you : but for my part, I'm engaged another way.

Sir John. What, to your mistress, I'll warrant ! Prithee leave your nasty punk to entertain herself with her own lewd thoughts, and make one with us to-night.

Const. Sir, 'tis business that is to employ me.

Heart. And me ; and business must be done, you know.

Sir John. Ay, women's business, though the world were consumed for't.   [*Exit.*

Const. Farewell, beast !—And now, my dear friend, would my mistress be but as complaisant as some men's wives, who think it a piece of good-breeding to receive the visits of their husband's friends in his absence !   163

Heart. Why, for your sake I could forgive her, though she should be so complaisant to receive something else in his absence. But what way shall we invent to see her?

Const. O ne'er hope it: invention will prove as vain as wishes.

Re-enter Lady BRUTE *and* BELINDA.

Heart. [*Aside to* CONSTANT.] What do you think now, friend?

Const. I think I shall swoon.

Heart. I'll speak first then, whilst you fetch breath.

Lady Brute. We think ourselves obliged, gentlemen, to come and return you thanks for your knight-errantry. We were just upon being devoured by the fiery dragon.   175

Bel. Did not his fumes almost knock you down, gentlemen?

Heart. Truly, ladies, we did undergo some hardships; and should have done more, if some greater heroes than ourselves hard by had not diverted him.

Const. Though I'm glad of the service you are pleased to say we have done you, yet I'm sorry we could do it no other way than by making ourselves privy to what you would perhaps have kept a secret.

Lady Brute. For sir John's part, I suppose he designed it no secret, since he made so much noise: and, for myself, truly I am not much concerned, since 'tis fallen only into this gentleman's hands and yours; who, I have many reasons to believe, will neither interpret nor report anything to my disadvantage.   190

Const. Your good opinion, madam, was what I feared I never could have merited.

Lady Brute. Your fears were vain then, sir ; for I am just to everybody.

Heart. Prithee, Constant, what is't you do to get the ladies' good opinions, for I'm a novice at it ?

Bel. Sir, will you give me leave to instruct you ?

Heart. Yes, that I will, with all my soul, madam.

Bel. Why then, you must never be slovenly, never be out of humour ; fare well, and cry roast-meat ; smoke tobacco, nor drink but when you are a-dry.   201

Heart. That's hard.

Const. Nay, if you take his bottle from him, you break his heart, madam.

Bel. Why, is it possible the gentleman can love drinking ?

Heart. Only by way of antidote.

Bel. Against what, pray ?

Heart. Against love, madam.

Lady Brute. Are you afraid of being in love, sir?   210

Heart. I should, if there were any danger of it.

Lady Brute. Pray, why so ?

Heart. Because I always had an aversion to being used like a dog.

Bel. Why, truly, men in love are seldom used better.

Lady Brute. But was you never in love, sir?

Heart. No, I thank Heaven, madam.

Bel. Pray where got you your learning, then ?

Heart. From other people's expense.

Bel. That's being a spunger, sir, which is scarce honest. If you'd buy some experience with your own money, as 'twould be fairlier got, so 'twould stick longer by you.   223

Enter Footman.

Foot. Madam, here's my lady Fancyful, to wait upon your ladyship. [*Exit.*

Lady Brute. Shield me, kind Heaven! What an inundation of impertinence is here coming upon us!

Enter Lady FANCYFUL, *who runs first to* Lady BRUTE, *then to* BELINDA, *kissing 'em.*

Lady Fan. My dear lady Brute! and sweet Belinda! methinks 'tis an age since I saw you.

Lady Brute. Yet 'tis but three days; sure you have passed your time very ill, it seems so long to you.

Lady Fan. Why really, to confess the truth to you, I am so everlastingly fatigued with the addresses of unfortunate gentlemen, that were it not for the extravagancy of the example, I should e'en tear out these wicked eyes with my own fingers, to make both myself and mankind easy.—What think you on't, Mr. Heartfree, for I take you to be my faithful adviser? . 238

Heart. Why truly, madam,—I think—every project that is for the good of mankind ought to be encouraged.

Lady Fan. Then I have your consent, sir—

Heart. To do whatever you please, madam.

Lady Fan. You had a much more limited complaisance this morning, sir.—Would you believe it, ladies? the gentleman has been so exceeding generous, to tell me of above fifty faults in less time than it was well possible for me to commit two of 'em.

Const. Why truly, madam, my friend there is apt to be something familiar with the ladies. 249

Lady Fan. He is, indeed, sir; but he's wondrous charitable

with it. He has had the goodness to design a reformation, even down to my fingers'-ends.—'Twas thus, I think,
sir, you'd have had 'em stand ?—[*Opening her fingers in an
awkward manner.*] My eyes too he did not like.—How
was't you would have directed 'em ?—Thus, I think.—
[*Staring at him.*] Then there was something amiss in my
gait too ! I don't know well how 'twas, but, as I take it, he
would have had me walk like him.—Pray, sir, do me the
favour to take a turn or two about the room, that the company
may see you.—He's sullen, ladies, and won't. But, to
make short, and give you as true an idea as I can of the
matter, I think 'twas much about this figure in general he
would have moulded me to : but I was an obstinate woman,
and could not resolve to make myself mistress of his
heart by growing as awkward as his fancy.   265

> [*She walks awkwardly about, staring and looking
> ungainly ; then changes on a sudden to the
> extremity of her usual affectation.*

Heart. Just thus women do, when they think we are in
love with 'em, or when they are so with us.

> [*Here* Constant *and* Lady Brute *talk together apart.*

Lady Fan. 'Twould, however, be less vanity for me to
conclude the former than you the latter, sir.

Heart. Madam, all I shall presume to conclude is, that
if I were in love, you'd find the means to make me soon
weary on't.

Lady Fan. Not by over-fondness, upon my word, sir.—
But pray let's stop here ; for you are so much governed by
instinct, I know you'll grow brutish at last.   275

Bel. [*Aside.*] Now I'm sure she's fond of him ; I'll try
to make her jealous.—[*Aloud.*] Well, for my part, I should

be glad to find somebody would be so free with me, that I might know my faults, and mend 'em.

Lady Fan.   Then pray let me recommend this gentleman to you : I have known him some time, and will be surety for him, that upon a very limited encouragement on your side, you shall find an extended impudence on his.

Heart.   I thank you, madam, for your recommendation : but hating idleness, I'm unwilling to enter into a place where I believe there would be nothing to do. I was fond of serving your ladyship, because I knew you'd find me constant employment.   288

Lady Fan.   I told you he'd be rude, Belinda.

Bel.   Oh, a little bluntness is a sign of honesty, which makes me always ready to pardon it.—So, sir, if you have no other exceptions to my service, but the fear of being idle in't, you may venture to list yourself: I shall find you work, I warrant you.

Heart.   Upon those terms I engage, madam ; and this (with your leave) I take for earnest.

[*Offering to kiss her hand.*

Bel.   Hold there, sir ! I'm none of your earnest-givers : but if I'm well served, I give good wages, and pay punctually.   299

[Heartfree *and* Belinda *seem to continue talking familiarly.*]

Lady Fan.   [*Aside.*]   I don't like this jesting between 'em.—Methinks the fool begins to look as if he were in earnest—but then he must be a fool indeed !—Lard, what a difference there is between me and her !—[*Looking at* Belinda *scornfully.*]   How I should despise such a thing, if I were a man !—What a nose she has ! what a chin ! what a neck !—Then, her eyes !—and the worst kissing lips in the universe !—No, no, he can never like her, that's positive.— Yet I can't suffer 'em together any longer.—[*Aloud.*] Mr. Heartfree, do you know that you and I must have no quarrel for all this ?—I can't forbear being a little severe now and then : but women, you know, may be allowed anything.

Heart. Up to a certain age, madam.   312

Lady Fan. Which I'm not yet past, I hope.

Heart. [*Aside.*] Nor never will, I dare swear.

Lady Fan. [*To* Lady Brute.] Come, madam, will your ladyship be witness to our reconciliation ?

Lady Brute. You agree then at last.

Heart. [*Slightingly.*] We forgive.

Lady Fan. [*Aside.*] That was a cold, ill-natured reply.

Lady Brute. Then there's no challenges sent between you ?   321

Heart. Not from me, I promise !—[*Aside to* Constant.] But that's more than I'll do for her, for I know she can as well be damned as forbear writing to me.

Const. That I believe. But I think we had best be going, lest she should suspect something, and be malicious.

Heart. With all my heart.

Const. Ladies, we are your humble servants. I see sir John is quite engaged, 'twould be in vain to expect him.— Come, Heartfree.   [*Exit.*

Heart. Ladies, your servant.—[*To* Belinda.] I hope, madam, you won't forget our bargain; I'm to say what I please to you.   333

Bel. Liberty of speech entire, sir. [*Exit* Heartfree.

Lady Fan. [*Aside.*] Very pretty truly !—But how the blockhead went out! languishing at her; and not a look toward me!—Well, churchmen may talk, but miracles are not ceased. For 'tis more than natural, such a rude fellow as he, and such a little impertinent as she, should be capable of making a woman of my sphere uneasy. But I can bear her sight no longer—methinks she's grown ten times uglier than Cornet. I must go home, and study revenge.— [*To* Lady Brute.] Madam, your humble servant; I must take my leave. 344

Lady Brute. What, going already, madam?

Lady Fan. I must beg you'll excuse me this once; for really I have eighteen visits to return this afternoon. So you see I am importuned by the women as well as the men.

Bel. [*Aside.*] And she's quits with 'em both.

Lady Fan. [*Going.*] Nay, you shan't go one step out of the room.

Lady Brute. Indeed I'll wait upon you down.

Lady Fan. No, sweet lady Brute, you know I swoon at ceremony. 354

Lady Brute. Pray, give me leave.

Lady Fan. You know I won't.

Lady Brute. Indeed I must.

Lady Fan. Indeed you shan't.

Lady Brute. Indeed I will.

Lady Fan. Indeed you shan't.

Lady Brute. Indeed I will.

Lady Fan. Indeed you shan't. Indeed, indeed, indeed you shan't. [*Exit running. They follow.*

Re-enter Lady Brute.

Lady Brute. This impertinent woman has put me out of humour for a fortnight.—What an agreeable moment has

her foolish visit interrupted !—Lord, how like a torrent love
flows into the heart, when once the sluice of desire is opened !
Good gods ! what a pleasure there is in doing what we should
not do !   369

Re-enter Constant.

Ha ! here again ?

Const. Though the renewing my visit may seem a little
irregular, I hope I shall obtain your pardon for it, madam,
when you know I only left the room, lest the lady who was
here should have been as malicious in her remarks, as she's
foolish in her conduct.

Lady Brute. He who has discretion enough to be tender
of a woman's reputation, carries a virtue about him may
atone for a great many faults.   378

Const. If it has a title to atone for any, its pretensions
must needs be strongest where the crime is love. I therefore hope I shall be forgiven the attempt I have made upon
your heart, since my enterprise has been a secret to all the
world but yourself.

Lady Brute. Secrecy indeed in sins of this kind is an
argument of weight to lessen the punishment ; but nothing's
a plea for a pardon entire, without a sincere repentance.

Const. If sincerity in repentance consists in sorrow for
offending, no cloister ever enclosed so true a penitent as I
should be. But I hope it cannot be reckoned an offence to
love, where 'tis a duty to adore.   390

Lady Brute. 'Tis an offence, a great one, where it would
rob a woman of all she ought to be adored for, her virtue.

Const. Virtue !—Virtue, alas, is no more like the thing
that's called so, than 'tis like vice itself. Virtue consists in

Y

goodness, honour, gratitude, sincerity, and pity; and not in peevish, snarling, strait-laced chastity. True virtue, where-soe'er it moves, still carries an intrinsic worth about it, and is in every place, and in each sex, of equal value. So is not continence, you see: that phantom of honour, which men in every age have so contemned, they have thrown it amongst the women to scrabble for.   401

Lady Brute. If it be a thing of so very little value, why do you so earnestly recommend it to your wives and daughters?

Const. We recommend it to our wives, madam, because we would keep 'em to ourselves; and to our daughters, because we would dispose of 'em to others.

Lady Brute. 'Tis then of some importance, it seems, since you can't dispose of 'em without it.

Const. That importance, madam, lies in the humour of the country, not in the nature of the thing.

Lady Brute. How do you prove that, sir?   412

Const. From the wisdom of a neighbouring nation in a contrary practice. In monarchies things go by whimsy, but commonwealths weigh all things in the scale of reason.

Lady Brute. I hope we are not so very light a people, to bring up fashions without some ground.

Const. Pray what does your ladyship think of a powdered coat for deep mourning?

Lady Brute. I think, sir, your sophistry has all the effect that you can reasonably expect it should have; it puzzles, but don't convince.

Const. I'm sorry for it.

Lady Brute. I'm sorry to hear you say so.

Const. Pray why?   425

Lady Brute. Because if you expected more from it, you have a worse opinion of my understanding than I desire you should have.

Const. [*Aside.*] I comprehend her : she would have me set a value upon her chastity, that I may think myself the more obliged to her when she makes me a present of it.—[*Aloud.*] I beg you will believe I did but rally, madam ; I know you judge too well of right and wrong to be deceived by arguments like those. I hope you'll have so favourable an opinion of my understanding too, to believe the thing called virtue has worth enough with me to pass for an eternal obligation where'er 'tis sacrificed.   437

Lady Brute. It is, I think, so great a one, as nothing can repay.

Const. Yes ; the making the man you love your everlasting debtor.

Lady Brute. When debtors once have borrowed all we have to lend, they are very apt to grow shy of their creditors company.

Const. That, madam, is only when they are forced to borrow of usurers, and not of a generous friend. Let us choose our creditors, and we are seldom so ungrateful to shun 'em.   448

Lady Brute. What think you of sir John, sir ? I was his free choice.

Const. I think he's married, madam.

Lady Brute. Does marriage then exclude men from your rule of constancy ?

Const. It does. Constancy's a brave, free, haughty, generous agent, that cannot buckle to the chains of wedlock. There's a poor sordid slavery in marriage, that turns the flowing tide of honour, and sinks us to the lowest ebb of infamy. 'Tis a corrupted soil; ill-nature, avarice, sloth, cowardice, and dirt, are all its product.

Lady Brute. Have you no exceptions to this general rule, as well as to t'other ? 461

Const. Yes ; I would (after all) be an exception to it myself, if you were free in power and will to make me so.

Lady Brute. Compliments are well placed, where 'tis impossible to lay hold on 'em.

Const. I would to heaven 'twere possible for you to lay hold on mine, that you might see it is no compliment at all. But since you are already disposed of beyond redemption, to one who does not know the value of the jewel you have put into his hands, I hope you would not think him greatly wronged, though it should sometimes be looked on by a friend, who knows how to esteem it as he ought. 472

Lady Brute. If looking on't alone would serve his turn, the wrong perhaps might not be very great.

Const. Why, what if he should wear it now and then a day, so he gave good security to bring it home again at night ?

Lady Brute. Small security I fancy might serve for that. One might venture to take his word.

Const. Then where's the injury to the owner ?

Lady Brute. 'Tis injury to him if he think it one. For if happiness be seated in the mind, unhappiness must be so too. 483

Const. Here I close with you, madam, and draw my conclusive argument from your own position : if the injury lie in the fancy, there needs nothing but secrecy to prevent the wrong.

Lady Brute. [*Going.*] A surer way to prevent it, is to hear no more arguments in its behalf.

Const. [*Following her.*] But, madam—

Lady Brute. But, sir, 'tis my turn to be discreet now, and not suffer too long a visit.

Const. [*Catching her hand.*] By heaven you shall not stir, till you give me hopes that I shall see you again at some more convenient time and place. 495

Lady Brute. I give you just hopes enough—[*Breaking from him*] to get loose from you: and that's all I can afford you at this time. [*Exit running.*

Const. Now by all that's great and good, she is a charming woman! In what ecstasy of joy she has left me! For she gave me hope; did she not say she gave me hope? —Hope! ay; what hope!—enough to make me let her go! Why that's enough in conscience. Or, no matter how 'twas spoke; hope was the word; it came from her, and it was said to me.

Re-enter Heartfree.

Ha, Heartfree! Thou hast done me noble service in prattling to the young gentlewoman without there; come to my arms, thou venerable bawd, and let me squeeze thee— [*Embracing him eagerly*] as a new pair of stays does a fat country girl, when she's carried to court to stand for a maid of honour. 511

Heart. Why, what the devil's all this rapture for?

Const. Rapture! there's ground for rapture, man; there's hopes, my Heartfree; hopes, my friend!

Heart. Hopes! of what?

Const. Why, hopes that my lady and I together (for

'tis more than one body's work) should make sir John a cuckold.

Heart. Prithee, what did she say to thee?

Const. Say! what did she not say? She said that— says she—she said—zoons, I don't know what she said: but she looked as if she said everything I'd have her; and so if thou'lt go to the tavern, I'll treat thee with anything that gold can buy: I'll give all my silver amongst the drawers, make a bonfire before the door, say the plenipos have signed the peace, * and the Bank of England's grown honest.   [*Exeunt.*

SCENE II.—*The Blue Posts.*

Lord RAKE, Sir JOHN BRUTE, Colonel BULLY, *and others discovered at a table, drinking.* Page *waiting.*

All. Huzza!

Rake. Come, boys, charge again.—So.—Confusion to all order! Here's liberty of conscience!

All. Huzza!

Rake. I'll sing you a song I made this morning to this purpose.

Sir John. 'Tis wicked, I hope.

Bully. Don't my lord tell you he made it?

Sir John. Well then, let's ha't.   9

---

* By May, 1697, when *The Provok'd Wife* was first produced, negotiations for a general peace had been some months in progress. The peace was concluded, at Ryswick, in the following September.

Lord RAKE *sings.*

I.

What a pother of late
Have they kept in the state
About setting our consciences free !
A bottle has more
Dispensations in store,
Than the king and the state can decree.

II.

When my head's full of wine,
I o'erflow with design,
And know no penal laws that can curb me.
Whate'er I devise
Seems good in my eyes,
And religion ne'er dares to disturb me. 21

III.

No saucy remorse
Intrudes in my course,
Nor impertinent notions of evil,
So there's claret in store,
In peace I've my whore,
And in peace I jog on to the deviL

All. So there's claret, &c.

Rake [*repeats*]. And in peace I jog on to the devil.

Well, how do you like it, gentlemen ?

All. O, admirable !

Sir John. I would not give a fig for a song that is not full of sin and impudence. 33

Rake. Then my muse is to your taste.—But drink away ; the night steals upon us ; we shall want time to be lewd in.—Hey, page, sally out, sirrah, and see what's doing in the camp ; we'll beat up their quarters presently.

Page. I'll bring your lordship an exact account. [*Exit.*

Rake. Now let the spirit of clary go round! Fill me a brimmer. Here's to our forlorn hope !—Courage, knight ; victory attends you.

Sir John. And laurels shall crown me ; drink away, and be damned.   43

Rake. Again, boys ; t'other glass, and damn morality.

Sir John. [*Drunk.*] Ay—damn morality !—and damn the watch !—and let the constable be married !

All. Huzza !

Re-enter Page.

Rake. How are the streets inhabited, sirrah ?

Page. My lord, it's Sunday night, they are full of drunken citizens.

Rake. Along then, boys, we shall have a feast.

Bully. Along, noble knight.

Sir John. Ay—along, Bully ; and he that says sir John Brute is not as drunk and as religious as the drunkenest citizen of them all—is a liar, and the son of a whore.

Bully. Why, that was bravely spoke, and like a free-born Englishman.   57

Sir John. What's that to you, sir, whether I am an Englishman or a Frenchman?

Bully. Zoons, you are not angry, sir ?

Sir John. Zoons, I am angry, sir !—for if I'm a free-born Englishman, what have you to do, even to talk of my privileges ?

Rake. Why, prithee, knight, don't quarrel here, leave private animosities to be decided by daylight; let the night be employed against the public enemy.   66

Sir John. My lord, I respect you because you are a man of quality : but I'll make that fellow know, I am within a hair's-breadth as absolute by my privileges, as the king of France is by his prerogative. He by his prerogative takes money where it is not his due ; I by my privilege refuse paying it where I owe it. Liberty and property, and Old England, huzza !

All. Huzza !

[*Exit* Sir JOHN, *reeling, the rest following him.*

SCENE III.—*A Bedchamber.*

Enter Lady BRUTE *and* BELINDA.

Lady Brute. Sure, it's late, Belinda ; I begin to be sleepy.

Bel. Yes, 'tis near twelve. Will you go to bed ?

Lady Brute. To bed, my dear ! and by that time I am fallen into a sweet sleep (or perhaps a sweet dream, which is better and better), sir John will come home roaring drunk, and be overjoyed he finds me in a condition to be disturbed.

Bel. Oh, you need not fear him, he's in for all night. The servants say he's gone to drink with my lord Rake.

Lady Brute. Nay, 'tis not very likely, indeed, such suitable company should part presently. What hogs men turn, Belinda, when they grow weary of women ! 13

Bel. And what owls they are whilst they are fond of 'em !

Lady Brute. But that we may forgive well enough, because they are so upon our accounts.

Bel. We ought to do so indeed, but 'tis a hard matter. For when a man is really in love, he looks so insufferably silly, that though a woman liked him well enough before, she has then much ado to endure the sight of him. And this I take to be the reason why lovers are so generally ill used.

Lady Brute. Well, I own now, I'm well enough pleased to see a man look like an ass for me.   25

Bel. Ay, I'm pleased he should look like an ass too— that is, I am pleased with myself for making him look so.

Lady Brute. Nay, truly, I think if he'd find some other way to express his passion, 'twould be more for his advantage.

Bel. Yes; for then a woman might like his passion, and him too.

Lady Brute. Yet, Belinda, after all, a woman's life would be but a dull business, if 'twere not for men; and men that can look like asses too. We should never blame fate for the shortness of our days; our time would hang wretchedly upon our hands.   37

Bel. Why, truly, they do help us off with a good share on't. For were there no men in the world, o' my conscience, I should be no longer a-dressing than I'm a-saying my prayers; nay, though it were Sunday: for you know one may go to church without stays on.

Lady Brute. But don't you think emulation might do something? For every woman you see desires to be finer than her neighbour.

Bel. That's only that the men may like her better than her neighbour. No; if there were no men, adieu fine petticoats, we should be weary of wearing 'em.   48

Lady Brute. And adieu plays, we should be weary of seeing 'em.

Bel. Adieu Hyde-Park, the dust would choke us.

Lady Brute, Adieu St. James's, walking would tire us.

Bel. Adieu London, the smoke would stifle us.

Lady Brute. And adieu going to church, for religion would ne'er prevail with us.

Both. Ha! ha! ha! ha! ha!

Bel. Our confession is so very hearty, sure we merit absolution.   58

Lady Brute. Not unless we go through with't, and confess all. So, prithee, for the ease of our consciences, let's hide nothing.

Bel. Agreed.

Lady Brute. Why, then, I confess that I love to sit in the fore-front of a box ; for, if one sits behind, there's two acts gone perhaps before one's found out. And when I am there, if I perceive the men whispering and looking upon me, you must know I cannot for my life forbear thinking they talk to my advantage. And that sets a thousand little tickling vanities on foot—   69

Bel. Just my case for all the world ; but go on.

Lady Brute. I watch with impatience for the next jest in the play, that I may laugh and show my white teeth. If the poet has been dull, and the jest be long a-coming, I pretend to whisper one to my friend, and from thence fall into a little small discourse, in which I take occasion to show my face in all humours, brisk, pleased, serious, melancholy, languishing.—Not that what we say to one another causes any of these alterations ; but—   78

Bel. Don't trouble yourself to explain ; for, if I'm not

mistaken, you and I have had some of these necessary dialogues before now, with the same intention.

Lady Brute. Why, I'll swear, Belinda, some people do give strange agreeable airs to their faces in speaking. Tell me true—did you never practise in the glass?

Bel. Why, did you?

Lady Brute. Yes, faith, many a time.　　　　　　86

Bel. And I too, I own it; both how to speak myself, and how to look when others speak. But my glass and I could never yet agree what face I should make when they come blurt out with a nasty thing in a play. For all the men presently look upon the women, that's certain; so, laugh we must not, though our stays burst for't, because that's telling truth, and owning we understand the jest: and to look serious is so dull, when the whole house is a-laughing.　　　　　　95

Lady Brute. Besides, that looking serious does really betray our knowledge in the matter as much as laughing with the company would do: for, if we did not understand the thing, we should naturally do like other people.

Bel. For my part, I always take that occasion to blow my nose.

Lady Brute. You must blow your nose half off then at some plays.

Bel. Why don't some reformer or other beat the poet for't?　　　　　　105

Lady Brute. Because he is not so sure of our private approbation as of our public thanks. Well, sure, there is not upon earth so impertinent a thing as women's modesty.

Bel. Yes; men's *fantasque*, that obliges us to it. If we quit our modesty, they say we lose our charms; and yet they know that very modesty is affectation, and rail at our hypocrisy.

Lady Brute. Thus one would think 'twere a hard matter to please 'em, niece : yet our kind mother nature has given us something that makes amends for all. Let our weakness be what it will, mankind will still be weaker; and whilst there is a world, 'tis woman that will govern it. But, prithee, one word of poor Constant before we go to bed, if it be but to furnish matter for dreams.—I dare swear he's talking of me now, or thinking of me at least, though it be in the middle of his prayers.   121

Bel. So he ought, I think; for you were pleased to make him a good round advance to-day, madam.

Lady Brute. Why, I have e'en plagued him enough to satisfy any reasonable woman. He has besieged me these two years to no purpose.

Bel. And if he besieged you two years more, he'd be well enough paid, so he had the plundering of you at last.

Lady Brute. That may be : but I'm afraid the town won't be able to hold out much longer : for, to confess the truth to you, Belinda, the garrison begins to grow mutinous.   133

Bel. Then the sooner you capitulate the better.

Lady Brute. Yet, methinks, I would fain stay a little longer to see you fixed too, that we might start together, and see who could love longest. What think you, if Heartfree should have a month's mind to you ?

Bel. Why, faith, I could almost be in love with him for despising that foolish, affected lady Fancyful ; but I'm afraid he's too cold ever to warm himself by my fire.

Lady Brute. Then he deserves to be froze to death. Would I were a man for your sake, dear rogue.　　143

[*Kissing her.*

Bel. You'd wish yourself a woman again for your own, or the men are mistaken. But if I could make a conquest of this son of Bacchus, and rival his bottle, what should I do with him? He has no fortune, I can't marry him; and sure you would not have me commit fornication.

Lady Brute. Why, if you did, child, 'twould be but a good friendly part; if 'twere only to keep me in countenance whilst I commit—you know what.

Bel. Well, if I can't resolve to serve you that way, I may perhaps some other as much to your satisfaction. But, pray, how shall we contrive to see these blades again quickly?

Lady Brute. We must e'en have recourse to the old way; make 'em an appointment 'twixt jest and earnest, 'twill look like a frolic, and that you know's a very good thing to save a woman's blushes.　　158

Bel. You advise well; but where shall it be?

Lady Brute. In Spring-Garden.* But they shan't know

---

* The New Spring-Garden, afterwards famous by the name of Vauxhall. It was opened about 1661, and remained a place of popular resort and entertainment for nearly two centuries, being closed in 1859. The old Spring-Garden, at the north-east corner of St. James's Park, was mostly built over at the date of *The Provok'd Wife*. Pepys records a visit to New Spring-Garden, May 28, 1667: "I by water to Foxhall, and there walked in Spring-Garden. A great deal of company, and the weather and garden pleasant: and it is very pleasant and cheap going thither, for a man may go to spend what he will, or nothing, all as one. But to hear the nightingale and other birds, and here fiddles and there a harp, and here a Jew's trump, and here laughing, and there fine people walking, is mighty divertising."

their women till their women pull off their masks; for a
surprise is the most agreeable thing in the world : and I find
myself in a very good humour, ready to do 'em any good
turn I can think on.

Bel. Then pray write 'em the necessary billet without
farther delay.

Lady Brute. Let's go into your chamber, then, and
whilst you say your prayers, I'll do it, child.   [*Exeunt.*

ACT IV.

SCENE I.—*Covent-Garden.*

Enter Lord Rake, Sir John Brute, Colonel Bully, *and others, with swords drawn.*

Rake.   Is the dog dead?

Bully.   No, damn him! I heard him wheeze.

Rake.   How the witch his wife howled!

Bully.   Ay, she'll alarm the watch presently.

Rake.   Appear, knight, then; come, you have a good cause to fight for, there's a man murdered.

Sir John.   Is there! then let his ghost be satisfied, for I'll sacrifice a constable to it presently, and burn his body upon his wooden chair.   9

Enter a Tailor, *with a bundle under his arm.*

Bully.   How now! what have we got here? a thief!

Tailor.   No, an't please you, I'm no thief.

Rake.   That we'll see presently.—Here, let the general examine him.

Sir John.   Ay, ay, let me examine him, and I'll lay a hundred pound I find him guilty in spite of his teeth—for he looks—like a—sneaking rascal.—Come, sirrah, without equivocation or mental reservation, tell me of what opinion you are, and what calling; for by them—I shall guess at your morals.   19

Tail. An't please you, I'm a dissenting journeyman tailor.

Sir John. Then, sirrah, you love lying by your religion, and theft by your trade; and so, that your punishment may be suitable to your crimes,—I'll have you first gagged—and then hanged.

Tail. Pray, good worthy gentlemen, don't abuse me; indeed I'm an honest man, and a good workman, though I say it that should not say it.

Sir John. No words, sirrah, but attend your fate.

Rake. Let me see what's in that bundle.   30

Tail. An't please you, it's the doctor of the parish's gown.

Rake. The doctor's gown!—Hark you, knight, you won't stick at abusing the clergy, will you?

Sir John. No, I'm drunk, and I'll abuse anything—but my wife; and her I name—with reverence.

Rake. Then you shall wear this gown whilst you charge the watch; that though the blows fall upon you, the scandal may light upon the church.

Sir John. A generous design—by all the gods!—give it me.   [*Takes the gown and puts it on.*

Tail. O dear gentlemen, I shall be quite undone, if you take the gown.   43

Sir John. Retire, sirrah: and since you carry off your skin—go home, and be happy.

Tail. [*Pausing.*] I think I had e'en as good follow the gentleman's friendly advice; for if I dispute any longer, who knows but the whim may take him to case me? These courtiers are fuller of tricks than they are of money; they'll sooner cut a man's throat than pay his bill.   [*Exit.*

z

Sir John. So, how d'ye like my shapes now?

Rake. This will do to a miracle; he looks like a bishop going to the holy war.—But to your arms, gentlemen, the enemy appears.   54

Enter Constable *and* Watch.

Watchman. Stand! Who goes there? Come before the constable.

Sir John. The constable's a rascal—and you are the son of a whore!

Watch. A good civil answer for a parson, truly!

Con. Methinks, sir, a man of your coat might set a better example.

Sir John. Sirrah, I'll make you know—there are men of my coat can set as bad examples—as you can do, you dog you!   64

     [Sir JOHN *strikes the* Constable. *They knock him
         down, disarm him, and seize him.* Lord
         RAKE *and the rest run away.*

Con. So, we have secured the parson, however.

Sir John. Blood, and blood—and blood!

Watch. Lord have mercy upon us! how the wicked wretch raves of blood. I'll warrant he has been murdering somebody to-night.

Sir John. Sirrah, there's nothing got by murder but a halter. My talent lies towards drunkenness and simony.

Watch. Why, that now was spoke like a man of parts, neighbours: it's pity he should be so disguised.

Sir John. You lie!—I'm not disguised, for I am drunk barefaced.   75

Watch. Look you there again!—This is a mad parson,

Mr. Constable; I'll lay a pot of ale upon's head, he's a good preacher.

Con. Come, sir, out of respect to your calling, I shan't put you into the round-house; but we must secure you in our drawing-room till morning, that you may do no mischief. So, come along.

Sir John. You may put me where you will, sirrah, now you have overcome me.—But if I can't do mischief, I'll think of mischief—in spite of your teeth, you dog you.

[*Exeunt.*

SCENE II.—*A Bedchamber.*

Enter Heartfree.

Heart. What the plague ails me?—Love? No, I thank you for that, my heart's rock still.—Yet 'tis Belinda that disturbs me; that's positive.—Well, what of all that? Must I love her for being troublesome? at that rate I might love all the women I meet, egad. But hold!—though I don't love her for disturbing me, yet she may disturb me because I love her.—Ay, that may be, faith. I have dreamed of her, that's certain.—Well, so I have of my mother; therefore, what's that to the purpose? Ay, but Belinda runs in my mind waking.—And so does many a damned thing that I don't care a farthing for.—Methinks, though, I would fain be talking to her, and yet I have no business.—Well, am I the first man that has had a mind to do an impertinent thing? 14

Enter Constant.

Const. How now, Heartfree! what makes you up and dressed so soon? I thought none but lovers quarrelled with their beds; I expected to have found you snoring, as I used to do.

Heart. Why, faith, friend, 'tis the care I have of your affairs that makes me so thoughtful; I have been studying all night how to bring your matter about with Belinda.

Const. With Belinda!

Heart. With my lady, I mean:—and faith, I have mighty hopes on't. Sure you must be very well satisfied with her behaviour to you yesterday?   25

Const. So well, that nothing but a lover's fears can make me doubt of success. But what can this sudden change proceed from?

Heart. Why, you saw her husband beat her, did you not?

Const. That's true: a husband is scarce to be borne upon any terms, much less when he fights with his wife. Methinks she should e'en have cuckolded him upon the very spot, to show that after the battle she was master of the field.   35

Heart. A council of war of women would infallibly have advised her to't. But, I confess, so agreeable a woman as Belinda deserves a better usage.

Const. Belinda again!

Heart. My lady, I mean.—What a pox makes me blunder so to-day?—[*Aside.*] A plague of this treacherous tongue!

Const. Prithee look upon me seriously, Heartfree.—

Now answer me directly. Is it my lady or Belinda employs your careful thoughts thus ? 45

Heart. My lady, or Belinda !

Const. In love ! by this light, in love !

Heart. In love !

Const. Nay, ne'er deny it; for thou'lt do it so awkwardly, 'twill but make the jest sit heavier about thee. My dear friend, I give thee much joy.

Heart. Why, prithee, you won't persuade me to it, will you ?

Const. That she's mistress of your tongue, that's plain ; and I know you are so honest a fellow, your tongue and heart always go together. But how—but how the devil,— pha ! ha ! ha ! ha !— 57

Heart. Heyday ! why, sure you don't believe it in earnest ?

Const. Yes, I do, because I see you deny it in jest.

Heart. Nay, but look you, Ned—a—deny in jest—a— gadzooks, you know I say—a—when a man denies a thing in jest—a—

Const. Pha ! ha ! ha ! ha ! ha !

Heart. Nay, then we shall have it. What, because a man stumbles at a word ! Did you never make a blunder ?

Const. Yes, for I am in love, I own it.

Heart. Then so am I. Now laugh till thy soul's glutted with mirth.—[*Embracing him.*] But, dear Constant don't tell the town on't. 70

Const. Nay then, 'twere almost pity to laugh at thee after so honest a confession. But tell us a little, Jack, by what new-invented arms has this mighty stroke been given ?

Heart. E'en by that unaccountable weapon, called

Je-ne-sais-quoi: for everything that can come within the verge of beauty, I have seen it with indifference.

Const. So in few words then; the *Je-ne-sais-quoi* has been too hard for the quilted petticoat.

Heart. Egad, I think the *Je-ne-sais-quoi* is in the quilted petticoat; at least 'tis certain I ne'er think on't without—a —a *Je-ne-sais-quoi* in every part about me.   81

Const. Well, but have all your remedies lost their virtue ? have you turned her inside out yet ?

Heart. I dare not so much as think on't.

Const. But don't the two years' fatigue I have had discourage you ?

Heart. Yes : I dread what I foresee, yet cannot quit the enterprise. Like some soldiers, whose courage dwells more in their honour than their nature; on they go, though the body trembles at what the soul makes it undertake.   91

Const. Nay, if you expect your mistress will use you, as your profanations against her sex deserve, you tremble justly. But how do you intend to proceed, friend ?

Heart. Thou knowest I'm but a novice ; be friendly and advise me.

Const. Why, look you, then; I'd have you—serenade and a—write a song—go to church—look like a fool—be very officious—ogle—write—and lead out : and who knows, but in a year or two's time, you may be—called a troublesome puppy, and sent about your business ?   101

Heart. That's hard.

Const. Yet thus it oft falls out with lovers, sir.

Heart. Pox on me for making one of the number.

Const. Have a care : say no saucy things ; 'twill but

augment your crime; and if your mistress hears on't, increase your punishment.

Heart. Prithee, say something then to encourage me : you know I helped you in your distress.   109

Const. Why, then, to encourage you to perseverance, that you may be thoroughly ill-used for your offences, I'll put you in mind, that even the coyest ladies of 'em all are made up of desires, as well as we ; and though they do hold out a long time, they will capitulate at last.   For that thundering engineer, Nature, does make such havoc in the town, they must surrender at long run, or perish in their own flames.

Enter a Footman.

Foot. Sir, there's a porter without with a letter; he desires to give it into your own hands.

Const. Call him in.   [*Exit* Footman.

Enter Porter.

Const. What, Joe ! is it thee ?   120

Porter. An't please you, sir, I was ordered to deliver this into your hands, by two well-shaped ladies, at the New Exchange.*   I was at your honour's lodgings, and your servants sent me hither.

Const. 'Tis well.   Are you to carry any answer ?

---

* A long, oblong building on the south side of the Strand, nearly opposite Bedford Street : part of the site is now occupied by Coutts's Bank.   The New Exchange was opened in 1609, and became a favourite resort of the beaux and ladies after the Restoration.   "It was erected partly on the plan of the Royal Exchange, with vaults beneath, over which was an open, paved arcade ; and above were walks of shops occupied by perfumers and publishers, milliners and sempstresses."— *Timbs' Curiosities of London.*   It was pulled down in 1737.

Porter. No, my noble master. They gave me my orders, and whip, they were gone, like a maidenhead at fifteen.

Const. Very well; there. [*Gives him money.*

Porter. God bless your honour. [*Exit.*

Const. Now let's see what honest trusty Joe has brought us.—[*Reads.*] *If you and your playfellow can spare time from your business and devotions, don't fail to be at Spring-Garden about eight in the evening. You'll find nothing there but women, so you need bring no other arms than what you usually carry about you.*—So, playfellow : here's something to stay your stomach till your mistress's dish is ready for you.

Heart. Some of our old battered acquaintance. I won't go, not I.   138

Const. Nay, that you can't avoid : there's honour in the case; 'tis a challenge, and I want a second.

Heart. I doubt I shall be but a very useless one to you; for I'm so disheartened by this wound Belinda has given me, I don't think I shall have courage enough to draw my sword.

Const. Oh, if that be all, come along; I'll warrant you find sword enough for such enemies as we have to deal withal.

————

SCENE III.—*The Street before the* Justice's *House.*

Enter Constable *and* Watch, *with* Sir JOHN BRUTE.

Con. Come along, sir; I thought to have let you slip this morning, because you were a minister : but you are as drunk and as abusive as ever. We'll see what the justice of the peace will say to you.

Sir John. And you shall see what I'll say to the justice of the peace, sirrah. [*They knock at the door.*

Enter Servant.

Con. Pray acquaint his worship we have got an unruly parson here. We are unwilling to expose him, but don't know what to do with him.   9

Serv. I'll acquaint my master.   [*Exit.*

Sir John. You—constable—what damned justice is this?

Con. One that will take care of you, I warrant you.

Enter Justice.

Just. Well, Mr. Constable, what's the disorder here?

Con. An't please your worship—

Sir John. Let me speak, and be damned!—I'm a divine, and can unfold mysteries better than you can do.

Just. Sadness, sadness! a minister so overtaken! Pray, sir, give the constable leave to speak, and I'll hear you very patiently; I assure you, sir, I will.   19

Sir John. Sir—you are a very civil magistrate : your most humble servant.

Con. An't please your worship then, he has attempted to beat the watch to-night, and swore—

Sir John. You lie!

Just. Hold, pray, sir, a little.

Sir John. Sir, your very humble servant.

Con. Indeed, sir, he came at us without any provocation called us whores and rogues, and laid us on with a great quarter-staff. He was in my lord Rake's company: they have been playing the devil to-night.   30

Just. Hem—hem—pray, sir—may you be chaplain to my lord?

Sir John. Sir—I presume—I may if I will.

Just. My meaning, sir, is—are you so?

Sir John. Sir—you mean very well.

Just. He—hem—hem—under favour, sir, pray answer me directly.

Sir John. Under favour, sir—do you use to answer directly when you are drunk?

Just. Good lack, good lack! here's nothing to be got from him.—Pray, sir, may I crave your name?   41

Sir John. Sir—my name's—[*He hiccups.*]—Hiccup, sir.

Just. Hiccup! Doctor Hiccup! I have known a great many country parsons of that name, especially down in the Fens.—Pray where do you live, sir?

Sir John. Here——and there, sir.

Just. Why, what a strange man is this!—Where do you preach, sir? have you any cure?

Sir John. Sir—I have—a very good cure—for a clap, at your service.   50

Just. Lord have mercy upon us!

Sir John. [*Aside.*] This fellow does ask so many impertinent questions, I believe, egad, 'tis the justice's wife in the justice's clothes.

Just. Mr. Constable, I vow and protest I don't know what to do with him.

Con. Truly he has been but a troublesome guest to us all night.

Just. I think I had e'en best let him go about his business, for I'm unwilling to expose him.   60

Con. E'en what your worship thinks fit.

Sir John. Sir—not to interrupt Mr. Constable, I have a small favour to ask.

Just. Sir, I open both my ears to you.

Sir John. Sir, your very humble servant. I have a little

urgent business calls upon me ; and therefore I desire the
favour of you to bring matters to a conclusion.

Just.   Sir, if I were sure that business were not to commit
more disorders, I would release you.

Sir John.   None—by my priesthood.   70

Just.   Then, Mr. Constable, you may discharge him.

Sir John.   Sir, your very humble servant.   If you please
to accept of a bottle—

Just.   I thank you kindly, sir ; but I never drink in a
morning.   Good-bye to ye, sir, good-bye to ye.

Sir John.   Good-bye t'ye, good sir.— [*Exit* Justice.]   So
—now, Mr. Constable, shall you and I go pick up a whore
together ?

Con.   No, thank you, sir ; my wife's enough to satisfy any
reasonable man.   80

Sir John.   [*Aside.*]   He ! he ! he ! he ! he !—the fool is
married then.—[*Aloud.*]   Well, you won't go ?

Con.   Not I, truly.

Sir John.   Then I'll go by myself ; and you and your
wife may be damned !   [*Exit.*

Con.   [*Gazing after him.*]   Why, God-a-mercy, parson !
                                                [*Exeunt.*

SCENE IV.—*Spring-Garden.*

CONSTANT *and* HEARTFREE *cross the stage.   As they go off,*
enter Lady FANCYFUL *and* MADEMOISELLE *masked, and*
dogging 'em.

Const.   So : I think we are about the time appointed.
Let us walk up this way.   [*Exit with* HEARTFREE.

Lady Fan. Good! Thus far I have dogged 'em without being discovered. 'Tis infallibly some intrigue that brings them to Spring-Garden. How my poor heart is torn and racked with fear and jealousy! Yet let it be anything but that flirt Belinda, and I'll try to bear it. But if it prove her, all that's woman in me shall be employed to destroy her. [*Exit with* MADEMOISELLE.

Re-enter CONSTANT *and* HEARTFREE. Lady FANCYFUL *and* MADEMOISELLE *still following at a distance.*

Const. I see no females yet that have anything to say to us. I'm afraid we are bantered. 11

Heart. I wish we were; for I'm in no humour to make either them or myself merry.

Const. Nay, I'm sure you'll make them merry enough if I tell 'em why you are dull. But prithee, why so heavy and sad before you begin to be ill used?

Heart. For the same reason, perhaps, that you are so brisk and well pleased; because both pains and pleasures are generally more considerable in prospect than when they come to pass. 20

Enter Lady BRUTE *and* BELINDA, *masked, and poorly dressed.*

Const. How now, who are these? Not our game, I hope.

Heart. If they are, we are e'en well enough served, to come hunting here, when we had so much better game in chase elsewhere.

Lady Fan. [*To* MADEMOISELLE.] So, those are their ladies without doubt. But I'm afraid that doily stuff is not worn for want of better clothes. They are the very shape and size of Belinda and her aunt.

Mad. So day be inteed, matam.

Lady Fan. We'll slip into this close arbour, where we may hear all they say.   31

[*Exeunt* Lady Fancyful *and* Mademoiselle.

Lady Brute. What, are you afraid of us, gentlemen ?

Heart. Why truly, I think we may, if appearance don't lie.

Bel. Do you always find women what they appear to be, sir ?

Heart. No, forsooth ; but I seldom find 'em better than they appear to be.

Bel. Then the outside's best, you think ?

Heart. 'Tis the honestest.   40

Const. Have a care, Heartfree ; you are relapsing again.

Lady Brute. Why, does the gentleman use to rail at women ?

Const. He has done formerly.

Bel. I suppose he had very good cause for't.—They did not use you so well as you thought you deserved, sir.

Lady Brute. They made themselves merry at your expense, sir.

Bel. Laughed when you sighed.   50

Lady Brute. Slept while you were waking.

Bel. Had your porter beat.

Lady Brute. And threw your billets-doux in the fire.

Heart. Heyday ! I shall do more than rail presently.

Bel. Why, you won't beat us, will you ?

Heart. I don't know but I may.

Const. What the devil's coming here ? Sir John in a gown ?—and drunk i'faith.

Enter Sir JOHN BRUTE.

Sir John. What, a pox!—here's Constant, Heartfree—
and two whores, egad!—O you covetous rogues! what, have
you never a spare punk for your friend?—But I'll share with
you.   [*He seizes both the women.*

Heart. Why, what the plague have you been doing,
knight?   64

Sir John. Why, I have been beating the watch, and
scandalising the clergy.

Heart. A very good account, truly!

Sir John. And what do you think I'll do next?

Const. Nay, that no man can guess.

Sir John. Why, if you'll let me sup with you, I'll treat
both your strumpets.

Lady Brute. [*Aside.*] O Lord, we are undone!

Heart. No, we can't sup together, because we have
some affairs elsewhere. But if you'll accept of these two
ladies, we'll be so complaisant to you, to resign our right
in 'em.   76

Bel. [*Aside.*] Lord, what shall we do?

Sir John. Let me see, their clothes are such damned
clothes, they won't pawn for the reckoning.

Heart. Sir John, your servant. Rapture attend you.

Const. Adieu, ladies! make much of the gentleman.

Lady Brute. Why, sure you won't leave us in the hands
of a drunken fellow to abuse us!

Sir John. Who do you call a drunken fellow, you slut
you? I'm a man of quality; the king has made me a knight.

Heart. Ay, ay, you are in good hands. Adieu, adieu!

                                                    [*Runs off.*

Lady Brute. The devil's hands!—Let me go, or I'll—
For Heaven's sake protect us !   88
[*She breaks from him, runs to* Constant, *twitching
off her mask, and clapping it on again.*
Sir John. I'll devil you, you jade you ! I'll demolish
your ugly face !
Const. Hold a little, knight, she swoons.
Sir John. I'll swoon her !
Const. Hey, Heartfree !

Re-enter Heartfree. Belinda *runs to him, and shows
her face.*

Heart. O heavens ! My dear creature, stand there a
little.
Const. [*Aside to* Heartfree.] Pull him off, Jack.
Heart. Hold, mighty man ; look you, sir, we did but
jest with you. These are ladies of our acquaintance, that
we had a mind to frighten a little, but now you must leave
us.   ·   100
Sir John. Oons, I won't leave you, not I !
Heart. Nay, but you must though ; and therefore make
no words on't.
Sir John. Then you are a couple of damned uncivil
fellows : and I hope your punks will give you sauce to your
mutton !   [*Exit.*
Lady Brute. Oh, I shall never come to myself again,
I'm so frightened.
Const. 'Twas a narrow 'scape indeed.
Bel. Women must needs have frolics, you see, whatever
they cost 'em.   111
Heart. This might have proved a dear one though.

Lady Brute. You are the more obliged to us, for the risk we run upon your accounts.

Const. And I hope you'll acknowledge something due to our knight-errantry, ladies. This is a second time we have delivered you.

Lady Brute. 'Tis true; and since we see fate has designed you for our guardians, 'twill make us the more willing to trust ourselves in your hands. But you must not have the worse opinion of us for our innocent frolic.   121

Heart. Ladies, you may command our opinions in everything that is to your advantage.

Bel. Then, sir, I command you to be of opinion, that women are sometimes better than they appear to be.

[Lady BRUTE *and* CONSTANT *talk apart.*

Heart. Madam, you have made a convert of me in everything. I'm grown a fool: I could be fond of a woman.

Bel. I thank you, sir, in the name of the whole sex.

Heart. Which sex nothing but yourself could ever have atoned for.   131

Bel. Now has my vanity a devilish itch to know in what my merit consists.

Heart. In your humility, madam, that keeps you ignorant it consists at all.

Bel. One other compliment with that serious face, and I hate you for ever after.

Heart. Some women love to be abused: is that it you would be at?

Bel. No, not that neither; but I'd have men talk plainly what's fit for women to hear; without putting 'em either to a real or an affected blush.   142

Heart. Why then, in as plain terms as I can find to express myself, I could love you even to—matrimony itself, a-most, egad.

Bel. Just as sir John did her ladyship there. What think you? Don't you believe one month's time might bring you down to the same indifference, only clad in a little better manners, perhaps? Well, you men are unaccountable things, mad till you have your mistresses, and then stark mad till you are rid of 'em again. Tell me, honestly, is not your patience put to a much severer trial after possession than before?   153

Heart. With a great many, I must confess, it is, to our eternal scandal ; but I—dear creature, do but try me.

Bel. That's the surest way, indeed, to know, but not the safest.—[*To* Lady BRUTE.] Madam, are not you for taking a turn in the Great Walk? It's almost dark, nobody will know us.

Lady Brute. Really I find myself something idle, Belinda; besides I dote upon this little odd private corner. But don't let my lazy fancy confine you.

Const. [*Aside.*] So, she would be left alone with me ; that's well.   164

Bel. Well, we'll take our turn, and come to you again.— [*To* HEARTFREE.] Come, sir, shall we go pry into the secrets of the garden? Who knows what discoveries we may make?

Heart. Madam, I'm at your service.

Const. [*Aside to* HEARTFREE.] Don't make too much haste back ; for d'ye hear—I may be busy.

Heart. Enough.   [*Exit with* BELINDA.

Lady Brute. Sure you think me scandalously free, Mr.

Constant. I'm afraid I shall lose your good opinion
of me. 175

Const. My good opinion, madam, is like your cruelty,
never to be removed.

Lady Brute. But if I should remove my cruelty, then
there's an end of your good opinion.

Const. There is not so strict an alliance between 'em
neither. 'Tis certain I should love you then better (if that
be possible) than I do now; and where I love I always
esteem.

Lady Brute. Indeed, I doubt you much. Why, suppose
you had a wife, and she should entertain a gallant? 185

Const. If I gave her just cause, how could I justly
condemn her?

Lady Brute. Ah, but you'd differ widely about just
causes.

Const. But blows can bear no dispute.

Lady Brute. Nor ill manners much, truly.

Const. Then no woman upon earth has so just a cause
as you have.

Lady Brute. Oh, but a faithful wife is a beautiful
character. 195

Const. To a deserving husband I confess it is.

Lady Brute. But can his faults release my duty?

Const. In equity, without doubt. And where laws
dispense with equity, equity should dispense with laws.

Lady Brute. Pray let's leave this dispute; for you men
have as much witchcraft in your arguments as women have
in their eyes.

Const. But whilst you attack me with your charms, 'tis
but reasonable I assault you with mine. 204

Lady Brute. The case is not the same. What mischief we do we can't help, and therefore are to be forgiven.

Const. Beauty soon obtains pardon for the pain that it gives, when it applies the balm of compassion to the wound : but a fine face and a hard heart is almost as bad as an ugly face and a soft one ; both very troublesome to many a poor gentleman

Lady Brute. Yes, and to many a poor gentlewoman too, I can assure you. But pray, which of 'em is it that most afflicts you ?   214

Const. Your glass and conscience will inform you, madam. But for Heaven's sake ! (for now I must be serious) if pity or if gratitude can move you :—[*Taking her hand*] if constancy and truth have power to tempt you : if love, if adoration can affect you, give me at least some hopes that time may do what you perhaps mean never to perform ; 'twill ease my sufferings, though not quench my flame.

Lady Brute. Your sufferings eased, your flame would soon abate : and that I would preserve, not quench it, sir.   224

Const. Would you preserve it, nourish it with favours ; for that's the food it naturally requires.

Lady Brute. Yet on that natural food 'twould surfeit soon, should I resolve to grant all that you would ask.

Const. And in refusing all you starve it. Forgive me, therefore, since my hunger rages, if I at last grow wild, and in my frenzy force at least this from you.—[*Kissing her hand.*] Or if you'd have my flame soar higher still, then grant me this, and this, and this—[*Kissing first her hand, then her neck*],—and thousands more.—[*Aside.*] For now's the time, she melts into compassion.   235

A A 2

Lady Brute. [*Aside.*]   Poor coward virtue, how it shuns the battle.—[*Aloud.*]   O Heavens ! let me go.

Const.   Ay, go, ay : where shall we go, my charming angel ?—Into this private arbour.—Nay, let's lose no time— moments are precious.

Lady Brute.   And lovers wild.   Pray let us stop here; at least for this time.

Const.   'Tis impossible.   He that has power over you can have none over himself.   244

> [*As he is forcing her into the arbour,* Lady FANCY-
> FUL *and* MADEMOISELLE *bolt out upon them,*
> *and run over the stage.*

Lady Brute.   Ah, I'm lost !

Lady Fan.   Fi ! fi ! fi ! fi ! fi !

Mad.   Fi ! fi ! fi ! fi ! fi !

Const.   Death and furies ! who are these ?

Lady Brute.   O Heavens ! I'm out of my wits : if they knew me, I'm ruined.

Const.   Don't be frightened ! ten thousand to one they are strangers to you.

Lady Brute.   Whatever they are, I won't stay here a moment longer.   254

Const.   Whither will you go ?

Lady Brute.   Home, as if the devil were in me.—Lord ! where's this Belinda now ?

Re-enter BELINDA *and* HEARTFREE.

Oh ! it's well you are come : I'm so frightened, my hair stands on end.   Let's begone, for Heaven's sake !

Bel.   Lord ! what's the matter?

Lady Brute.   The devil's the matter, we are discovered.

Here's a couple of women have done the most impertinent
thing !—Away! away ! away ! away! away !   263
               [*Exit running, the others following.*

Re-enter Lady Fancyful *and* Mademoiselle.

Lady Fan. Well, Mademoiselle, 'tis a prodigious thing
how women can suffer filthy fellows to grow so familiar with
'em.

Mad. Ah, matam, il n'y a rien de si naturel.

Lady Fan. Fi ! fi ! fi ! But oh, my heart ! O jealousy !
O torture ! I'm upon the rack. What shall I do ? My
lover's lost, I ne'er shall see him mine.—[*Pausing.*] But I
may be revenged, and that's the same thing. Ah, sweet
revenge ! Thou welcome thought, thou healing balsam to
my wounded soul, be but propitious on this one occasion, I'll
place my heaven in thee for all my life to come.   274

To woman how indulgent nature's kind !
No blast of fortune long disturbs her mind :
Compliance to her fate supports her still ;
If love won't make her happy—mischief will.
               [*Exeunt.*

ACT V.

SCENE I.—*A Room in* Lady FANCYFUL'S *House.*

Enter Lady FANCYFUL *and* MADEMOISELLE.

Lady Fan. Well, Mademoiselle; did you dog the filthy things?

Mad. O que oui, matam.

Lady Fan. And where are they?

Mad. Au logis.

Lady Fan. What, men and all?

Mad. Tous ensemble.

Lady Fan. O confidence! what, carry their fellows to their own house?

Mad. C'est que le mari n'y est pas.   10

Lady Fan. No, so I believe, truly. But he shall be there, and quickly too, if I can find him out. Well, 'tis a prodigious thing, to see when men and women get together, how they fortify one another in their impudence. But if that drunken fool, her husband, be to be found in e'er a tavern in town, I'll send him amongst 'em. I'll spoil their sport!

Mad. En vérité, matam, ce serait dommage.

Lady Fan. 'Tis in vain to oppose it, Mademoiselle; therefore never go about it. For I am the steadiest creature in the world—when I have determined to do mischief. So, come along.   [*Exeunt.*

SCENE II.—*A Room in* Sir John Brute's *House.*

Enter Constant, Heartfree, Lady Brute, Belinda,
   and Lovewell.

Lady Brute. But are you sure you don't mistake,
Lovewell?

Love. Madam, I saw 'em all go into the tavern together,
and my master was so drunk he could scarce stand. [*Exit.*

Lady Brute. Then, gentlemen, I believe we may venture
to let you stay, and play at cards with us an hour or two:
for they'll scarce part till morning.

Bel. I think 'tis a pity they should ever part.

Const. The company that's here, madam.

Lady Brute. Then, sir, the company that's here must
remember to part itself in time.   11

Const. Madam, we don't intend to forfeit your future
favours by indiscreet usage of this. The moment you give
us the signal, we shan't fail to make our retreat.

Lady Brute. Upon those conditions then let us sit down
to cards.

Re-enter Lovewell.

Love. O Lord, madam! here's my master just staggering
in upon you; he has been quarrelsome yonder, and they
have kicked him out of the company.

Lady Brute. Into the closet, gentlemen, for Heaven's
sake! I'll wheedle him to bed, if possible.   21

[Constant *and* Heartfree *run into the closet.*

Enter Sir John Brute, *all dirt and bloody.*

Lady Brute. Ah—ah—he's all over blood!

Sir John. What the plague does the woman—squall for?
Did you never see a man in pickle before?

Lady Brute. Lord, where have you been?

Sir John. I have been at—cuffs.

Lady Brute. I fear that is not all. I hope you are not
wounded.

Sir John. Sound as a roach, wife.

Lady Brute. I'm mighty glad to hear it.   30

Sir John. You know—I think you lie.

Lady Brute. I know you do me wrong to think so, then.
For Heaven's my witness, I had rather see my own blood
trickle down, than yours.

Sir John. Then will I be crucified.

Lady Brute. 'Tis a hard fate I should not be believed.

Sir John. 'Tis a damned atheistical age, wife.

Lady Brute. I am sure I have given you a thousand
tender proofs how great my care is of you. Nay, spite of all
your cruel thoughts, I'll still persist, and at this moment, if
I can, persuade you to lie down, and sleep a little.   41

Sir John. Why—do you think I am drunk—you slut you?

Lady Brute. Heaven forbid I should: but I'm afraid
you are feverish. Pray let me feel your pulse.

Sir John. Stand off, and be damned!

Lady Brute. Why, I see your distemper in your very
eyes. You are all on fire. Pray go to bed; let me entreat
you.

Sir John. Come kiss me, then.

Lady Brute. [*Kissing him.*] There: now go.—[*Aside.*]
He stinks like poison.   51

Sir John. I see it goes damnably against your stomach—
and therefore—kiss me again.

Lady Brute.   Nay, now you fool me.

Sir John.   Do't, I say.

Lady Brute.   [*Aside.*]   Ah, Lord have mercy upon me !
—[*Kisses him.*]   Well ; there : now will you go ?

Sir John.   Now, wife, you shall see my gratitude.   You
give me two kisses—I'll give you—two hundred.

[*Kisses and tumbles her.*

Lady Brute.   O Lord !   Pray, sir John, be quiet.   Heavens,
what a pickle am I in !   61

Bel.   [*Aside.*]   If I were in her pickle, I'd call my gallant
out of the closet, and he should cudgel him soundly.

Sir John.   So, now you being as dirty and as nasty as
myself, we may go pig together.   But first I must have a
cup of your cold-tea, wife.   [*Going to the closet.*

Lady Brute.   [*Aside.*]   Oh, I'm ruined!—[*Aloud.*]   There's
none there, my dear.

Sir John.   I'll warrant you I'll find some, my dear.

Lady Brute.   You can't open the door, the lock's spoiled ;
I have been turning and turning the key this half-hour to no
purpose.   I'll send for the smith to-morrow.   72

Sir John.   There's ne'er a smith in Europe can open a
door with more expedition than I can do.—As for example !
—Pou.—[*He bursts open the door with his foot.*]   How now !
What the devil have we got here ?—Constant !—Heartfree !
—and two whores again, egad !—This is the worst cold-tea—
that ever I met with in my life.—

Re-enter Constant *and* Heartfree.

Lady Brute.   [*Aside.*]   O Lord, what will become of
us ?

Sir John.   Gentlemen—I am your very humble servant—

I give you many thanks—I see you take care of my family—
I shall do all I can to return the obligation.   83

Const. Sir, how oddly soever this business may appear
to you, you would have no cause to be uneasy if you knew
the truth of all things; your lady is the most virtuous
woman in the world, and nothing has passed but an innocent
frolic.

Heart. Nothing else, upon my honour, sir.

Sir John. You are both very civil gentlemen—and my
wife, there, is a very civil gentlewoman; therefore I don't
doubt but many civil things have passed between you.
Your very humble servant!

Lady Brute. [*Aside to* CONSTANT.] Pray be gone: he's
so drunk he can't hurt us to-night, and to-morrow morning
you shall hear from us.   96

Const. [*Aside to* Lady BRUTE.] I'll obey you, madam.
—[*Aloud.*] Sir, when you are cool, you'll understand
reason better. So then I shall take the pains to inform you.
If not—I wear a sword, sir, and so good-bye to you !—Come
along, Heartfree.   [*Exeunt* CONSTANT *and* HEARTFREE.

Sir John. Wear a sword, sir !—And what of all that, sir?
—He comes to my house; eats my meat; lies with my
wife ; dishonours my family ; gets a bastard to inherit my
estate—and when I ask a civil account of all this—Sir, says
he, I wear a sword.—Wear a sword, sir ! Yes, sir, says he,
I wear a sword.—It may be a good answer at cross-
purposes ; but 'tis a damned one to a man in my whimsical
circumstances—Sir, says he, I wear a sword !—[*To* Lady
BRUTE.] And what do you wear now? ha! tell me.—
[*Sitting down in a great-chair.*] What! you are modest,
and can't.—Why then, I'll tell you, you slut you ! You

wear—an impudent lewd face—a damned designing heart
—and a tail—and a tail full of—   114

[He falls fast asleep snoring.

Lady Brute.   So ; thanks to kind Heaven, he's fast for
some hours.

Bel.   'Tis well he is so, that we may have time to lay our
story handsomely; for we must lie like the devil to bring
ourselves off.

Lady Brute.   What shall we say, Belinda ?

Bel. [*Musing.*]   I'll tell you : it must all light upon
Heartfree and I.   We'll say he has courted me some time,
but for reasons unknown to us, has ever been very earnest
the thing might be kept from sir John.   That therefore
hearing him upon the stairs, he run into the closet, though
against our will, and Constant with him, to prevent
jealousy.   And to give this a good impudent face of truth,
(that I may deliver you from the trouble you are in) I'll e'en
(if he pleases) marry him.   129

Lady Brute.   I'm beholding to you, cousin ; but that
would be carrying the jest a little too far for your own sake.
You know he's a younger brother, and has nothing.

Bel.   'Tis true : but I like him, and have fortune enough
to keep above extremity.   I can't say I would live with him
in a cell, upon love and bread and butter : but I had rather
have the man I love, and a middle state of life, than that
gentleman in the chair there, and twice your ladyship's
splendour.

Lady Brute.   In truth, niece, you are in the right on't :
for I am very uneasy with my ambition.   But perhaps, had
I married as you'll do, I might have been as ill used.   141

Bel.   Some risk, I do confess, there always is : but if a

man has the least spark, either of honour or good-nature, he
can never use a woman ill, that loves him, and makes his
fortune both.   Yet I must own to you, some little
struggling I still have with this teasing ambition of ours.
For pride, you know, is as natural to a woman, as 'tis to a
saint.   I can't help being fond of this rogue; and yet it goes
to my heart to think I must never whisk to Hyde-Park with
above a pair of horses; have no coronet upon my coach,
nor a page to carry up my train.   But above all—that
business of place.—Well; taking place is a noble prerogative.

Lady Brute.   Especially after a quarrel.   153

Bel.   Or of a rival.   But pray, say no more on't for fear
I change my mind.   For o' my conscience, were't not for
your affair in the balance, I should go near to pick up some
odious man of quality yet, and only take poor Heartfree for
a gallant.

Lady Brute.   Then him you must have, however things go?

Bel.   Yes.

Lady Brute.   Why, we may pretend what we will, but 'tis
a hard matter to live without the man we love.

Bel.   Especially when we are married to the man we hate.
Pray tell me : do the men of the town ever believe us
virtuous when they see us do so?   165

Lady Brute.   Oh, no : nor indeed hardly, let us do what
we will.   They most of 'em think, there is no such thing as
virtue, considered in the strictest notions of it: and
therefore when you hear 'em say, such a one is a woman of
reputation, they only mean she's a woman of discretion.
For they consider we have no more religion than they have,
nor so much morality; and between you and I, Belinda, I'm
afraid the want of inclination seldom protects any of us.

Bel. But what think you of the fear of being found out ? 175

Lady Brute. I think that never kept any woman virtuous long. We are not such cowards neither. No : let us once pass fifteen, and we have too good an opinion of our own cunning to believe the world can penetrate into what we would keep a secret. And so, in short, we cannot reasonably blame the men for judging of us by themselves.

Bel. But sure we are not so wicked as they are, after all?

Lady Brute. We are as wicked, child, but our vice lies another way. Men have more courage than we, so they commit more bold impudent sins. They quarrel, fight, swear, drink, blaspheme, and the like ; whereas we, being cowards, only backbite, tell lies, cheat at cards, and so forth. But 'tis late : let's end our discourse for to-night, and out of an excess of charity take a small care of that nasty drunken thing there.—Do but look at him, Belinda. 190

Bel. Ah—'tis a savoury dish !

Lady Brute. As savoury as 'tis, I'm cloyed with't. Prithee call the butler to take it away.

Bel. Call the butler !—call the scavenger !—[*To a* Servant *within.*] Who's there? Call Rasor! Let him take away his master, scour him clean with a little soap and sand, and so put him to bed.

Lady Brute. Come, Belinda, I'll e'en lie with you to-night ; and in the morning we'll send for our gentlemen to set this matter even. 200

Bel. With all my heart.

Lady Brute. Good night, my dear !

[*Making a low curtsey to* Sir JOHN.

Both. Ha ! ha ! ha ! [*Exeunt.*

Enter RASOR.

Ras. My lady there's a wag—my master there's a cuckold. Marriage is a slippery thing :—women have depraved appetites :—my lady's a wag. I have heard all ; I have seen all ; I understand all ; and I'll tell all ; for my little Frenchwoman loves news dearly. This story'll gain her heart, or nothing will.—[*To his Master.*] Come, sir, your head's too full of fumes at present to make room for your jealousy ; but I reckon we shall have rare work with you when your pate's empty. Come to your kennel, you cuckoldly drunken sot you ! [*Carries him out upon his back.*

———

SCENE III.—*A Room in* Lady FANCYFUL'S *House.*

Enter Lady FANCYFUL *and* MADEMOISELLE.

Lady Fan. But why did not you tell me before, Mademoiselle, that Rasor and you were fond?

Mad. De modesty hinder me, matam.

Lady Fan. Why truly, modesty does often hinder us from doing things we have an extravagant mind to. But does he love you well enough yet to do anything you bid him? Do you think to oblige you he would speak scandal?

Mad. Matam, to oblige your ladyship, he shall speak blasphemy. 9

Lady Fan. Why then, Mademoiselle, I'll tell you what you shall do. You shall engage him to tell his master all that passed at Spring-Garden : I have a mind he should know what a wife and a niece he has got.

Mad. Il le fera, matam.

Enter a Footman, *who speaks to* Mademoiselle *apart.*

Foot. Mademoiselle, yonder's Mr. Rasor desires to speak with you.

Mad. Tell him I come presently.—[*Exit* Footman.] Rasor be dare, matam.   18

Lady Fan. That's fortunate. Well, I'll leave you together. And if you find him stubborn, Mademoiselle— hark you—don't refuse him a few little reasonable liberties, to put him into humour.

Mad. Laissez-moi faire.   [*Exit* Lady Fancyful.

Rasor *peeps in ; and seeing* Lady Fancyful *gone, runs to* Mademoiselle, *takes her about the neck, and kisses her.*

Mad. How now, confidence !

Ras. How now, modesty !

Mad. Who make you so familiar, sirrah ?

Ras. My impudence, hussy.

Mad. Stand off, rogue-face.

Ras. Ah—Mademoiselle—great news at our house.

Mad. Why, what be de matter ?   30

Ras. The matter ?—why, uptails all's the matter.

Mad. Tu te moques de moi.

Ras. Now do you long to know the particulars—the time when—the place where—the manner how. But I won't tell you a word more.

Mad. Nay, den dou kill me, Rasor.

Ras. Come, kiss me, then.
                              [*Clapping his hands behind him.*
Mad. Nay, pridee tell me.

Ras. Good bye to ye !   [*Going.*

Mad. Hold, hold ! I will kiss dee.   [*Kissing him.*

Ras. So, that's civil. Why now, my pretty pall ; my goldfinch ; my little waterwagtail—you must know that— Come, kiss me again.   43

Mad. I won't kiss dee no more.

Ras. Good b'wy to ye !

Mad. Doucement. Dare : es tu content ? [*Kissing him.*

Ras. So : now I'll tell thee all. Why, the news is, that Cuckoldom in folio is newly printed ; and Matrimony in quarto is just going into the press. Will you buy any books, Mademoiselle ?

Mad. Tu parles comme un libraire, de devil no under- stand dee.   52

Ras. Why then, that I may make myself intelligible to a waiting-woman, I'll speak like a valet-de-chambre. My lady has cuckolded my master.

Mad. Bon !

Ras. Which we take very ill from her hands, I can tell her that. We can't yet prove matter of fact upon her.

Mad. N'importe.

Ras. But we can prove that matter of fact had like to have been upon her.

Mad. Oui dà !   62

Ras. For we have such bloody circumstances—

Mad. Sans doute.

Ras. That any man of parts may draw tickling conclu- sions from 'em.

Mad. Fort bien.

Ras. We have found a couple of tight well-built gentle- men stuffed into her ladyship's closet.

Mad. Le diable !   70

Ras. And I, in my particular person, have discovered a most damnable plot, how to persuade my poor master, that all this hide and seek, this will-in-the-wisp, has no other meaning than a Christian marriage for sweet Mrs. Belinda.

Mad. Un mariage !—Ah les drôlesses !

Ras. Don't you interrupt me, hussy. 'Tis agreed, I say; and my innocent lady, to wriggle herself out at the back-door of the business, turns marriage-bawd to her niece, and resolves to deliver up her fair body, to be tumbled and mumbled by that young liquorish whipster Heartfree. Now are you satisfied ?   81

Mad. No.

Ras. Right woman ; always gaping for more.

Mad. Dis be all den dat dou know ?

Ras. All ! ay, and a great deal too, I think.

Mad. Dou be fool, dou know noting. Ecoute, mon pauvre Rasor. Dou see des two eyes ?—Des two eyes have see de devil.

Ras. The woman's mad !

Mad. In Spring-Garden, dat rogue Constant meet dy lady.   91

Ras. Bon !

Mad. I'll tell dee no more.

Ras. Nay, prithee, my swan.

Mad. Come, kiss me den.

[*Clapping her hands behind her, as he had done before.*

Ras. I won't kiss you, not I.

Mad. Adieu !

Ras. Hold !—[*Gives her a hearty kiss.*] Now proceed.

Mad. Ah, ça !—I hide myself in one cunning place,

B B

where I hear all, and see all. First dy drunken master come mal à-propos; but de sot no know his own dear wife, so he leave her to her sport.—Den de game begin. De lover say soft ting: de lady look upon de ground.—[*As she speaks,* RASOR *still acts the man, and she the woman.*] He take her by de hand: she turn her head on oder way. Den he squeeze very hard: den she pull—very softly. Den he take her in his arm: den she give him leetel pat. Den he kiss her tétons: den she say—Pish! nay, fi! Den he tremble: den she—sigh. Den he pull her into de arbour: den she pinch him.   110

Ras.   Ay, but not so hard, you baggage you!

Mad.   Den he grow bold: she grow weak.   He tro her down, il tombe dessus, le diable assiste, il emporte tout.— [RASOR *struggles with her, as if he would throw her down.*] Stand off, sirrah.

Ras.   You have set me afire, you jade you!

Mad.   Den go to de river and quench dyself.

Ras.   What an unnatural harlot 'tis.

Mad.   Rasor!   [*Looking languishingly on him.*

Ras.   Mademoiselle!

Mad.   Dou no love me?   120

Ras.   Not love thee!—more than a Frenchman does soup.

Mad.   Den dou will refuse noting dat I bid dee?

Ras.   Don't bid me be damned then.

Mad.   No, only tell dy master all I have tell dee of dy laty.

Ras.   Why, you little malicious strumpet you; should you like to be served so?

Mad.   You dispute den?—Adieu!

Ras. Hold!—But why wilt thou make me be such a rogue, my dear? 131

Mad. Voilà un vrai Anglais! il est amoureux, et cependant il veut raisonner. Va-t'en au diable!

Ras. Hold once more! In hopes thou'lt give me up thy body, I resign thee up my soul.

Mad. Bon! écoute donc—If dou fail me—I never see de more.—If dou obey me—je m'abandonne à toi.

[*She takes him about the neck and gives him a smacking kiss, and exit.*

Ras. [*Licking his lips.*] Not be a rogue?—*Amor vincit omnia!* [*Exit.*

Enter Lady Fancyful *and* Mademoiselle.

Lady Fan. Marry, say ye? will the two things marry?

Mad. On le va faire, matam. 141

Lady Fan. Look you, Mademoiselle, in short, I can't bear it.—No; I find I can't.—If once I see 'em a-bed together, I shall have ten thousand thoughts in my head will make me run distracted. Therefore run and call Rasor back immediately, for something must be done to stop this impertinent wedding. If I can defer it but four-and-twenty hours, I'll make such work about town, with that little pert slut's reputation, he shall as soon marry a witch.

Mad. [*Aside.*] La voilà bien intentionnée. [*Exeunt.*

SCENE IV.—Constant's *Lodgings.*

Enter Constant *and* Heartfree.

Const. But what dost think will come of this business?

Heart. 'Tis easier to think what will not come on't.

Const. What's that?

Heart. A challenge. I know the knight too well for that : his dear body will always prevail upon his noble soul to be quiet.

Const. But though he dare not challenge me, perhaps he may venture to challenge his wife.

Heart. Not if you whisper him in the ear, you won't have him do't, and there's no other way left that I see. For as drunk as he was, he'll remember you and I were where we should not be; and I don't think him quite blockhead enough yet to be persuaded we were got into his wife's closet only to peep in her prayer-book.   14

Enter Servant *with a letter.*

Serv. Sir, here's a letter ; a porter brought it.   [*Exit*

Const. O ho! here's instructions for us. [*Reads.*] *The accident that has happened has touched our invention to the quick. We would fain come off without your help, but find that's impossible. In a word, the whole business must be thrown upon a matrimonial intrigue between your friend and mine. But if the parties are not fond enough to go quite through with the matter, 'tis sufficient for our turn they own the design. We'll find pretences enough to break the match. Adieu !*—Well, woman for invention! How long would

my blockhead have been a producing this !—Hey, Heartfree !   What, musing, man ! prithee be cheerful.   What
sayest thou, friend, to this matrimonial remedy?   27

Heart. Why, I say it's worse than the disease.

Const. Here's a fellow for you ! There's beauty and
money on her side, and love up to the ears on his ; and
yet—

Heart. And yet, I think, I may reasonably be allowed
to boggle at marrying the niece, in the very moment that
you are debauching the aunt.

Const. Why, truly there may be something in that.
But have not you a good opinion enough of your own parts
to believe you could keep a wife to yourself ?

Heart. I should have, if I had a good opinion enough
of hers, to believe she could do as much by me.   For to do
'em right, after all, the wife seldom rambles till the husband
shows her the way.   41

Const. 'Tis true ; a man of real worth scarce ever is a
cuckold but by his own fault. Women are not naturally
lewd, there must be something to urge 'em to it.   They'll
cuckold a churl out of revenge ; a fool, because they despise
him ; a beast, because they loathe him.   But when they
make bold with a man they once had a well-grounded value
for, 'tis because they first see themselves neglected by him.

Heart. Nay, were I well assured that I should never
grow sir John, I ne'er should fear Belinda'd play my lady.
But our weakness, thou knowest, my friend, consists in that
very change we so impudently throw upon (indeed) a
steadier and more generous sex.   53

Const. Why, faith, we are a little impudent in that
matter, that's the truth on't.   But this is wonderful, to see

you grown so warm an advocate for those (but t'other day)
you took so much pains to abuse !

Heart. All revolutions run into extremes ; the bigot
makes the boldest atheist ; and the coyest saint, the most
extravagant strumpet. But prithee advise me in this good
and evil, this life and death, this blessing and cursing, that
is set before me. Shall I marry—or die a maid? 62

Const. Why, faith, Heartfree, matrimony is like an army
going to engage. Love's the forlorn hope, which is soon
cut off; the marriage-knot is the main body, which may
stand buff a long long time; and repentance is the rear
guard, which rarely gives ground as long as the main battle
has a being.

Heart. Conclusion then : you advise me to whore on, as
you do ? 70

Const. That's not concluded yet. For though marriage
be a lottery, in which there are a wondrous many blanks ;
yet there is one inestimable lot, in which the only heaven
on earth is written. Would your kind fate but guide your
hand to that, though I were wrapped in all that luxury itself
could clothe me with, I still should envy you.

Heart. And justly, too : for to be capable of loving one,
doubtless is better than to possess a thousand. But how far
that capacity's in me, alas ! I know not.

Const. But you would know ? 80

Heart. I would so.

Const. Matrimony will inform you. Come, one flight of
resolution carries you to the land of experience ; where, in a
very moderate time, you'll know the capacity of your soul
and your body both, or I'm mistaken. [*Exeunt.*

SCENE V.—*A Room in* Sir JOHN BRUTE's *House.*

Enter Lady BRUTE *and* BELINDA.

Bel. Well, madam, what answer have you from 'em ?

Lady Brute. That they'll be here this moment. I fancy 'twill end in a wedding : I'm sure he's a fool if it don't. Ten thousand pound, and such a lass as you are, is no contemptible offer to a younger brother. But are not you under strange agitations? Prithee how does your pulse beat ?

Bel. High and low, I have much ado to be valiant : sure it must feel very strange to go to bed to a man !

Lady Brute. Um—it does feel a little odd at first, but it will soon grow easy to you.   11

·Enter CONSTANT *and* HEARTFREE.

Lady Brute. Good-morrow, gentlemen ! How have you slept after your adventure ?

Heart. Some careful thoughts, ladies, on your accounts have keep us waking.

Bel. And some careful thoughts on your own, I believe, have hindered you from sleeping. Pray, how does this matrimonial project relish with you ?

Heart. Why, faith, e'en as storming towns does with soldiers, where the hopes of delicious plunder banishes the fear of being knocked on the head.

Bel. Is it then possible after all that you dare think of downright lawful wedlock ?   23

Heart. Madam, you have made me so foolhardy I dare do anything.

Bel. Then, sir, I challenge you ; and matrimony's the spot where I expect you.

Heart. 'Tis enough ; I'll not fail.—[*Aside.*] So, now I am in for Hobbes's voyage ; a great leap in the dark.

Lady Brute. Well, gentlemen, this matter being concluded then, have you got your lessons ready? For sir John is grown such an atheist of late he'll believe nothing upon easy terms.   33

Const. We'll find ways to extend his faith, madam. But pray, how do you find him this morning?

Lady Brute. Most lamentably morose, chewing the cud after last night's discovery ; of which, however, he had but a confused notion e'en now. But I'm afraid his valet-de-chambre has told him all, for they are very busy together at this moment. When I told him of Belinda's marriage, I had no other answer but a grunt : from which you may draw what conclusions you think fit.—But to your notes, gentlemen, he's here.   43

Enter Sir John Brute *and* Rasor.

Const. Good-morrow, sir.

Heart. Good-morrow, sir John. I'm very sorry my indiscretion should cause so much disorder in your family.

Sir John. Disorders generally come from indiscretions, sir ; 'tis no strange thing at all.

Lady Brute. I hope, my dear, you are satisfied there was no wrong intended you.

Sir John. None, my dove.

Bel. If not, I hope my consent to marry Mr. Heartfree will convince you. For as little as I know of amours, sir, I

can assure you, one intrigue is enough to bring four people
together, without further mischief.   55

Sir John.   And I know, too, that intrigues tend to pro-
creation of more kinds than one.   One intrigue will beget
another as soon as beget a son or a daughter.

Const.   I am very sorry, sir, to see you still seem un-
satisfied with a lady whose more than common virtue, I am
sure, were she my wife, should meet a better usage.

Sir John.   Sir, if her conduct has put a trick upon her
virtue, her virtue's the bubble, but her husband's the
loser.   .   64

Const.   Sir, you have received a sufficient answer already
to justify both her conduct and mine.   You'll pardon me for
meddling in your family affairs; but I perceive I am the
man you are jealous of, and therefore it concerns me.

Sir John.   Would it did not concern me, and then I
should not care who it concerned.

Const.   Well, sir, if truth and reason won't content you,
I know but one way more, which, if you think fit, you may
take.   73

Sir John.   Lord, sir, you are very hasty.   If I had been
found at prayers in your wife's closet, I should have allowed
you twice as much time to come to yourself in.

Const.   Nay, sir, if time be all you want, we have no
quarrel.

Heart.   [*Aside to* CONSTANT.]   I told you how the sword
would work upon him.   [Sir JOHN *muses.*

Const.   [*Aside to* HEARTFREE.]   Let him muse; however, I'll lay fifty pound our foreman brings us in, Not
Guilty.   83

Sir John.   [*Aside.*]   'Tis well—'tis very well.—In spite

of that young jade's matrimonial intrigue, I am a downright
stinking cuckold.—Here they are—Boo !—[*Putting his hand
to his forehead.*]   Methinks I could butt with a bull.   What
the plague did I marry her for? I knew she did not like
me ; if she had, she would have lain with me ; for I would
have done so because I liked her : but that's past, and I
have her.   And now, what shall I do with her ?—If I put my
horns in my pocket, she'll grow insolent.—If I don't, that
goat there, that stallion, is ready to whip me through the
guts.—The debate, then, is reduced to this : shall I die
a hero ? or live a rascal ?—Why, wiser men than I have
long since concluded, that a living dog is better than a dead
lion.—[*Aloud.*]   Gentlemen, now my wine and my passion
are governable, I must own, I have never observed anything
in my wife's course of life to back me in my jealousy of
her : but jealousy's a mark of love ; so she need not trouble
her head about it, as long as I make no more words on't.

Enter Lady FANCYFUL *disguised ; she addresses* BELINDA
apart.

Const.   I'm glad to see your reason rule at last.   Give
me your hand : I hope you'll look upon me as you are
wont.   104

Sir John.   Your humble servant.—[*Aside.*]   A wheedling
son of a whore !

Heart.   And that I may be sure you are friends with
me too, pray give me your consent to wed your niece.

Sir John.   Sir, you have it with all my heart : damn me
if you han't !—[*Aside.*]   'Tis time to get rid of her :—a
young pert pimp ! she'll make an incomparable bawd in a
little time.   112

Enter a Servant, *who gives* HEARTFREE *a letter.*

Bel. Heartfree your husband, say you? 'tis impossible.

Lady Fan. Would to kind Heaven it were: but 'tis too true ; and in the world there lives not such a wretch. I'm young ; and either I have been flattered by my friends, as well as glass, or nature has been kind and generous to me. I had a fortune too was greater far than he could ever hope for ; but with my heart I am robbed of all the rest. I'm slighted and I'm beggared both at once ; I have scarce a bare subsistence from the villain, yet dare complain to none ; for he has sworn, if e'er 'tis known I am his wife, he'll murder me.   [*Pretends to weep.*

Bel. The traitor !   124

Lady Fan. I accidentally was told he courted you ; charity soon prevailed upon me to prevent your misery ; and as you see, I'm still so generous even to him, as not to suffer he should do a thing for which the law might take away his life.   [*Pretends to weep.*

Bel. Poor creature ! how I pity her !

[*They continue talking aside.*

Heart.   [*Aside.*]   Death and damnation !—Let me read it again !—[*Reads.*]   *Though I have a particular reason not to let you know who I am till I see you ; yet you'll easily believe 'tis a faithful friend that gives you this advice—I have lain with Belinda.*—Good !—*I have a child by her*—Better and better !—*which is now at nurse ;*—Heaven be praised ! —*and I think the foundation laid for another.*—Ha !—Old Truepenny !—*No rack could have tortured this story from me, but friendship has done it. I heard of your design to*

marry her, and could not see you abused. Make use of my
advice, but keep my secret till I ask you for't again. Adieu.

[*Exit* Lady FANCYFUL.

Const. [*To* BELINDA.] Come, madam, shall we send for
the parson? I doubt here's no business for the lawyer.
Younger brothers have nothing to settle but their hearts, and
that I believe my friend here has already done very faithfully.   146

Bel. [*Scornfully.*] Are you sure, sir, there are no old
mortgages upon it?

Heart. [*Coldly.*] If you think there are, madam, it
mayn't be amiss to defer the marriage till you are sure they
are paid off.

Bel. [*Aside.*] How the galled horse kicks!—[*To*
HEARTFREE.] We'll defer it as long as you please, sir.

Heart. The more time we take to consider on't, madam,
the less apt we shall be to commit oversights; therefore, if
you please, we'll put it off for just nine months.

Bel. Guilty consciences make men cowards; I don't
wonder you want time to resolve.   158

Heart. And they make women desperate; I don't
wonder you were so quickly determined.

Bel. What does the fellow mean?

Heart. What does the lady mean?

Sir John. Zoons! what do you both mean?

[HEARTFREE *and* BELINDA *walk chafing about.*

Ras. [*Aside.*] Here's so much sport going to be
spoiled, it makes me ready to weep again. A pox o' this
impertinent Lady Fancyful and her plots, and her French-
woman, too! she's a whimsical, ill-natured bitch; and when
I have got my bones broke in her service, 'tis ten to one

but my recompense is a clap; I hear 'em tittering without still. Ecod, I'll e'en go lug 'em both in by the ears, and discover the plot, to secure my pardon. [*Exit.*

Const. Prithee explain, Heartfree. 172

Heart. A fair deliverance, thank my stars and my friend.

Bel. 'Tis well it went no farther; a base fellow!

Lady Brute. What can be the meaning of all this?

Bel. What's his meaning I don't know; but mine is, that if I had married him—I had had no husband.

Heart. And what's her meaning I don't know; but mine is, that if I had married her—I had had wife enough.

Sir John. Your people of wit have got such cramp ways of expressing themselves, they seldom comprehend one another. Pox take you both! will you speak that you may be understood? 184

Re-enter RASOR, *in sackcloth, pulling in* Lady FANCYFUL *and* MADEMOISELLE, *both masked.*

Ras. If they won't, here comes an interpreter.

Lady Brute. Heavens! what have we here?

Ras. A villain—but a repenting villain. Stuff which saints in all ages have been made of.

All. Rasor!

Lady Brute. What means this sudden metamorphose?

Ras. Nothing, without my pardon.

Lady Brute. What pardon do you want? 192

Ras. *Imprimis*, your ladyship's; for a damnable lie made upon your spotless virtue, and set to the tune of Spring-Garden.—[*To* Sir JOHN.] Next, at my generous

master's feet I bend, for interrupting his more noble
thoughts with phantoms of disgraceful cuckoldom.—[*To*
CONSTANT.]   Thirdly, I to this gentleman apply for making
him the hero of my romance.—[*To* HEARTFREE.]   Fourthly,
your pardon, noble sir, I ask, for clandestinely marrying you,
without either bidding of banns, bishop's licence, friends'
consent—or your own knowledge.—[*To* BELINDA.]   And
lastly, to my good young lady's clemency I come, for
pretending the corn was sowed in the ground, before ever
the plough had been in the field.   205

Sir John. [*Aside.*]   So that, after all, 'tis a moot point
whether I am a cuckold or not.

Bel.   Well, sir, upon condition you confess all, I'll
pardon you myself, and try to obtain as much from the rest
of the company.   But I must know then who 'tis has put
you upon all this mischief?

Ras.   Satan and his equipage; woman tempted me, lust
weakened me—and so the devil overcame me; as fell Adam,
so fell I.

Bel.   Then pray, Mr. Adam, will you make us acquainted
with your Eve?   216

Ras.   [*To* MADEMOISELLE.]   Unmask, for the honour
of France.

All.   Mademoiselle!

Mad.   Me ask ten tousand pardon of all de good
company.

Sir John.   Why, this mystery thickens, instead of clearing up.—[*To* RASOR.]   You son of a whore you, put us out
of our pain.

Ras.   One moment brings sunshine.—[*Pointing to* MA-
DEMOISELLE.]   'Tis true this is the woman that tempted me;

but this is the serpent that tempted the woman ; and if my prayers might be heard, her punishment for so doing should be like the serpent's of old.—[*Pulls off* Lady Fancyful's *mask.*] She should lie upon her face all the days of her life.

All. Lady Fancyful !   231

Bel. Impertinent!

Lady Brute. Ridiculous !

All. Ha ! ha ! ha ! ha ! ha !

Bel. I hope your ladyship will give me leave to wish you joy, since you have owned your marriage yourself.—[*To* Heartfree.] I vow 'twas strangely wicked in you to think of another wife, when you had one already so charming as her ladyship.

All. Ha ! ha ! ha ! ha ! ha !   240

Lady Fan. [*Aside.*] Confusion seize 'em, as it seizes me !

Mad. [*Aside.*] Que le diable étouffe ce maraud de Rasor !

Bel. Your ladyship seems disordered : a breeding qualm, perhaps, Mr. Heartfree : your bottle of Hungary water* to your lady.—Why, madam, he stands as unconcerned as if he were your husband in earnest.

Lady Fan. Your mirth's as nauseous as yourself, Belinda. You think you triumph over a rival now : hélas ! ma pauvre fille. Where'er I'm rival there's no cause for mirth. No, my poor wretch, 'tis from another principle I have acted. I knew that thing there would make so perverse a husband, and you so impertinent a wife, that lest your mutual plagues should make you both run mad, I charitably would have broke the match. He ! he ! he ! he ! he !   254

[*Exit laughing affectedly,* Mademoiselle *following her.*

---

* A medicinal water distilled from rosemary.

Mad.   He! he! he! he! he!

All.   Ha! ha! ha! ha! ha!

Sir John.   [*Aside.*]   Why, now this woman will be married to somebody too.

Bel.   Poor creature! what a passion she's in! but I forgive her.

Heart.   Since you have so much goodness for her. I hope you will pardon my offence too, madam.

Bel.   There will be no great difficulty in that, since I am guilty of an equal fault.   264

Heart.   Then pardons being passed on all sides, pray let's to church to conclude the day's work.

Const.   But before you go, let me treat you, pray, with a song a new-married lady made within this week; it may be of use to you both.

SONG.

I.

When yielding first to Damon's flame,
    I sunk into his arms;
He swore he'd ever be the same,
    Then rifled all my charms.
But fond of what he'd long desir'd,
    Too greedy of his prey,
My shepherd's flame, alas! expir'd
    Before the verge of day.

II.

My innocence in lovers' wars   278
    Reproach'd his quick defeat;
Confus'd, asham'd, and bath'd in tears,
    I mourn'd his cold retreat.
At length, Ah, shepherdess! cried he,
    Would you my fire renew,
Alas! you must retreat like me,
    I'm lost if you pursue!

Heart. So, madam ; now had the parson but done his business—

Bel. You'd be half weary of your bargain.

Heart. No, sure, I might dispense with one night's lodging. 290

Bel. I'm ready to try, sir.

Heart. Then let's to church :
And if it be our chance to disagree—

Bel. Take heed—the surly husband's fate you see.

[*Exeunt omnes.*

EPILOGUE

(BY ANOTHER HAND)

SPOKEN BY LADY BRUTE AND BELINDA.

Lady Brute.   No Epilogue !

Bel.   I swear I know of none.   •

Lady Brute.   Lord ! How shall we excuse it to the
    town ?

Bel.   Why, we must e'en say something of our own.

Lady Brute.   Our own !   Ay, that must needs be
    precious stuff.

Bel.   I'll lay my life, they'll like it well enough.
Come, faith, begin—

Lady Brute.   Excuse me : after you.

Bel.   Nay, pardon me for that, I know my cue.

Lady Brute.   Oh, for the world, I would not have
    precedence.

Bel.   O Lord !

Lady Brute.   I swear—

Bel.   O fie !

Lady Brute.   I'm all obedience.
First, then, know all, before our doom is fix'd,   10
The third day is for us—

Bel.   Nay, and the sixth.

Lady Brute.   We speak not from the poet now, nor is it
His cause—(I want a rhyme)

Bel.   That we solicit.

Lady Brute. Then sure you cannot have the hearts to
    be severe,
And damn us—
Bel. Damn us ! Let 'em if they dare.
Lady Brute. Why, if they should, what punishment
    remains ?
Bel. Eternal exile from behind our scenes.
Lady Brute. But if they're kind, that sentence we'll
    recall,
We can be grateful—
Bel.   And have wherewithal.
Lady Brute. But at grand treaties hope not to be
    trusted,   20
Before preliminaries are adjusted.
Bel. You know the time, and we appoint this place ;
Where, if you please, we'll meet and sign the peace.

Additional Scenes, written by Vanbrugh, and substituted at a later date for the first and third Scenes of Act IV.*

ACT IV.

SCENE I.—*Covent-Garden.*

Enter Lord RAKE, Sir JOHN BRUTE, Colonel BULLY, *and others, with swords drawn.*

Rake. Is the dog dead?

Bully. No, damn him! I heard him wheeze.

Rake. How the witch his wife howled!

Bully. Ay, she'll alarm the watch presently.

Rake. Appear, knight, then. Come, you have a good cause to fight for, there's a man murdered.

Sir John. Is there? Then let his ghost be satisfied; for I'll sacrifice a constable to it presently, and burn his body upon his wooden chair.   9

Enter a Tailor, *with a bundle under his arm.*

Bully. How now! what have we got here? a thief?

Tailor. No, an't please you, I'm no thief.

---

* Genest is certainly in the right, and Cibber was mistaken, as to the year in which the following scenes were first put upon the stage. The *Daily Courant* announces performances of *The Provok'd Wife*, "with alterations," at the Haymarket Theatre, on the 19th, 21st, and 22nd of January, 1706. The 20th was Sunday.

Rake. That we'll see presently. Here—let the general examine him.

Sir John. Ay, ay, let me examine him, and I'll lay a hundred pound I find him guilty, in spite of his teeth—for he looks—like a—sneaking rascal. Come, sirrah, without equivocation or mental reservation, tell me of what opinion you are, and what calling; for by them—I shall guess at your morals.   19

Tail. An't please you, I'm a dissenting journeyman tailor.

Sir John. Then, sirrah, you love lying by your religion, and theft by your trade; and so that your punishment may be suitable to your crimes—I'll have you first gagged—and then hanged.

Tail. Pray, good worthy gentlemen, don't abuse me; indeed I'm an honest man, and a good workman, though I say it that should not say it.

Sir John. No words, sirrah, but attend your fate.

Rake. Let me see what's in that bundle.   30

Tail. An't please you, it's my lady's short cloak and wrapping gown.

Sir John. What lady, you reptile you?

Tail. My lady Brute, your honour.

Sir John. My lady Brute! my wife! the robe of my wife! with reverence let me approach it. The dear angel is always taking care of me in danger, and has sent me this suit of armour to protect me in this day of battle. On they go!

All. O brave knight!

Rake. Live Don Quixote the second!   40

Sir John. Sancho, my squire, help me on with my armour.

Tail. O dear gentlemen! I shall be quiteundone if you take the gown.

Sir John. Retire, sirrah! and since you carry off your skin, go home and be happy.

Tail. [*Aside.*] I think I'd e'en as good follow the gentleman's advice; for if I dispute any longer, who knows but the whim may take 'em to case me.—These courtiers are fuller of tricks than they are of money; they'll sooner break a man's bones than pay his bill.   [*Exit.*

Sir John. So! how do you like my shapes now?   52

Rake. To a miracle! he looks like a queen of the Amazons.—But to your arms, gentlemen! The enemy's upon their march—here's the watch.

Sir John. 'Oons! if it were Alexander the Great, at the head of his army, I would drive him into a horse-pond.

All. Huzza! O brave knight!

Enter Watch.

Sir John. See! here he comes, with all his Greeks about him.—Follow me, boys.

Watchman. Heyday! who have we got here? Stand!

Sir John. Mayhap not.   62

Watch. What are you all doing here in the street at this time of night? And who are you, madam, that seem to be at the head of this noble crew?

Sir John. Sirrah, I am Bonduca, queen of the Welshmen, and with a leek as long as my pedigree, I will destroy your Roman legion in an instant.—Britons, strike home!

[*Fights.*

Watch. So, we have got the queen, however! We'll make her pay well for her ransom.—Come, madam, will your majesty please to walk before the constable?   71

Sir John. The constable's a rascal ! and you are a son of a whore !

Watch. A most princely reply, truly ! If this be her royal style, I'll warrant her maids of honour prattle prettily. But we'll teach you a little of our court dialect before we part with you, princess.—Away with her to the Round-house.

Sir John. Hands off, you ruffians ! My honour's dearer to me than my life ; I hope you won't be uncivil.   80

Watch. Away with her !

Sir John. O my honour ! my honour !   [*Exeunt.*

SCENE III.—*The Street before the* Justice's *House.*

Enter Constable *and* Watch, *with* Sir John Brute.

Constable. Come, forsooth, come along, if you please. I once in compassion thought to have seen you safe home this morning ; but you have been so rampant and abusive all night, I shall see what the justice of peace will say to you.

Sir John. And you shall see what I'll say to the justice of peace.   [Watchman *knocks at the door.*

Enter Servant.

Con. Is Mr. Justice at home ?

Serv. Yes.

Con. Pray acquaint his worship we have got an unruly woman here, and desire to know what he'll please to have done with her.   12

Serv.   I'll acquaint my master.   [*Exit.*

Sir John.   Hark you, constable, what cuckoldly justice is this?

Con.   One that knows how to deal with such romps as you are, I'll warrant you.

Enter Justice.

Just.   Well, Mr. Constable, what's the matter here?

Con.   An't please your worship, this here comical sort of a gentlewoman has committed great outrages to-night.   She has been frolicking with my lord Rake and his gang: they attacked the watch, and I hear there has been a gentleman killed: I believe 'tis they have done it.   23

Sir John.   There may have been murder for aught I know; and 'tis a great mercy there has not been a rape too —for this fellow would have ravished me.

Watch.   Ravish! I ravish! O lud! O lud! O lud! I ravish her! why, please your honour, I heard Mr. Constable say he believed she was little better than a mophrodite.

Just.   Why, truly, she does seem to be a little masculine about the mouth.   32

Watch.   Yes, and about the hands too, an't please your worship.   I did but offer in mere civility to help her up the steps into our apartment, and with her gripen fist —ay, just so, sir.   [Sir JOHN *knocks him down.*

Sir John.   I felled him to the ground like an ox.

Just.   Out upon this boisterous woman!   Out upon her!

Sir John.   Mr. Justice, he would have been uncivil! It was in defence of my honour, and I demand satisfaction.

Watch. I hope your worship will satisfy her honour in Bridewell ; that fist of hers will make an admirable hemp-beater.   44

Sir John. Sir, I hope you will protect me against that libidinous rascal ; I am a woman of quality, and virtue too, for all I am in a sort of an undress this morning.

Just. Why, she really has the air of a sort of a woman a little somethingish out of the common.—Madam, if you expect I should be favourable to you, I desire I may know who you are.

Sir John. Sir, I am anybody, at your service.

Just. Lady, I desire to know your name.

Sir John. Sir, my name's Mary.

Just. Ay, but your surname, madam ?   55

Sir John. Sir, my surname's the very same with my husband's.

Just. A strange woman this !—Who is your husband, pray ?

Sir John. Why, sir John.

Just. Sir John who ?

Sir John. Why, sir John Brute.

Just. Is it possible, madam, you can be my lady Brute ?

Sir John. That happy woman, sir, am I ; only a little in my merriment to-night.   65

Just. I'm concerned for sir John.

Sir John. Truly so am I.

Just. I have heard he's an honest gentleman.

Sir John. As ever drank.

Just. Good lack ! Indeed, lady, I am sorry he should have such a wife.

Sir John. Sir, I am sorry he has any wife at all.

Just. And so, perhaps, may he.—I doubt you have not given him a very good taste of matrimony.

Sir John. Taste, sir! Sir, I have scorned to stint him to a taste, I have given him a full meal of it.   76

Just. Indeed I believe so! But pray, fair lady, may he have given you any occasion for this extraordinary conduct? —does he not use you well?

Sir John. A little upon the rough sometimes.

Just. Ay, any man may be out of humour now and then.

Sir John. Sir, I love peace and quiet, and when a woman don't find that at home, she's apt sometimes to comfort herself with a few innocent diversions abroad.

Just. I doubt he uses you but too well. Pray, how does he as to that weighty thing, money? Does he allow you what's proper of that?   88

Sir John. Sir, I have generally enough to pay the reckoning, if this son of a whore the drawer would bring his bill.

Just. A strange woman this!—Does he spend a reasonable portion of his time at home, to the comfort of his wife and children?

Sir John. Never gave his wife cause to repine at his being abroad in his life.

Just. Pray, madam, how may he be in the grand matrimonial point?—is he true to your bed?   98

Sir John. [*Aside.*] Chaste! oons! This fellow asks so many impertinent questions, egad, I believe it is the justice's wife, in the justice's clothes.

Just. 'Tis a great pity he should have been thus disposed

of.—Pray, madam, (and then I have done,) what may be
your ladyship's common method of life? If I may presume
so far.

Sir John. Why, sir, much like that of a woman of
quality.

Just. Pray, how may you generally pass your time,
madam? your morning, for example.   109

Sir John. Sir, like a woman of quality.—I wake about
two o'clock in the afternoon—I stretch—and then make a
sign for my chocolate.—When I have drunk three cups—
I slide down again upon my back, with my arms over my
head, while two maids put on my stockings.—Then, hanging
upon their shoulders, I am trailed to my great chair, where
I sit—and yawn for my breakfast.—If it don't come
presently, I lie down upon my couch to say my prayers,
while my maid reads me the play-bills.

Just. Very well, madam.   119

Sir John. When the tea is brought in, I drink twelve
regular dishes, with eight slices of bread and butter.—And
half an hour after, I send to the cook to know if the dinner
is almost ready.

Just. So, madam!

Sir John. By that time my head's half dressed, I hear
my husband swearing himself into a state of perdition, that
the meat's all cold upon the table, to mend which, I come
down in an hour more, and have it sent back to the kitchen,
to be all dressed over again.

Just. Poor man! .   130

Sir John. When I have dined, and my idle servants are
presumptuously set down at their ease, to do so too, I call

for my coach, go to visit fifty dear friends, of whom I hope
I never shall find one at home while I shall live.

Just. So; there's the morning and afternoon pretty
well disposed of!—Pray, madam, how do you pass your
evenings?

Sir John. Like a woman of spirit, sir, a great spirit.
Give me a box and dice.—Seven's the main! Oons, sir, I
set you a hundred pounds!—Why, do you think women are
married now-a-days, to sit at home and mend napkins?
Sir, we have nobler ways of passing time.   142

Just. Mercy upon us, Mr. Constable, what will this age
come to?

Con. What will it come to, indeed, if such women as
these are not set in the stocks?

Sir John. I have a little urgent business calls upon me;
and therefore I desire the favour of you to bring matters to
a conclusion.

Just. Madam, if I were sure that business were not to
commit more disorders, I would release you.

Sir John. None—by my virtue.   152

Just. Then, Mr. Constable, you may discharge her.

Sir John. Sir, your very humble servant. If you please
to accept of a bottle—

Just. I thank you kindly, madam; but I never drink in
a morning. Good-bye, madam, good-by-t'ye.

Sir John. Good-by-t'ye, good sir.—[*Exit* Justice.] So!
—Now, Mr. Constable, shall you and I go pick up a whore
together?

Con. No, thank you, madam; my wife's enough to
satisfy any reasonable man.   162

Sir John. [*Aside.*] He! he! he! he! he!—the fool is married then.—[*Aloud.*] Well, you won't go?

Con. Not I, truly.

Sir John. Then I'll go by myself; and you and your wife may be damned.   [*Exit.*

Con. [*Gazing after him.*] Why, God-a-mercy, lady!
                                                [*Exeunt.*

END OF VOL. I.